By Stephanie Laurens

The Cynster Novels
Devil's Bride • A Rake's Vow • Scandal's Bride
A Rogue's Proposal • A Secret Love
All About Love • All About Passion
The Promise in a Kiss • On a Wild Night
On a Wicked Dawn • The Perfect Lover
The Ideal Bride • The Truth About Love
What Price Love? • The Taste of Innocence
Where the Heart Leads • Temptation and Surrender

The Cynster Sisters Trilogy
Viscount Breckenridge to the Rescue
In Pursuit of Eliza Cynster
The Capture of the Earl of Glencrae

The Cynster Sisters Duo
And Then She Fell

The Bastion Club Novels
Captain Jack's Woman (prequel)
The Lady Chosen • A Gentleman's Honor
A Lady of His Own • A Fine Passion
To Distraction • Beyond Seduction
The Edge of Desire • Mastered By Love

The Black Cobra Quartet
The Untamed Bride • The Elusive Bride
The Brazen Bride • The Reckless Bride

Other Novels
The Lady Risks All

STEPHANIE LAURENS

A Lady of His Own

A BASTION CLUB NOVEL

AVON BOOKS
An Imprint of HarperCollinsPublishers

AVON BOOKS
An Imprint of HarperCollins*Publishers*
195 Broadway
New York, NY 10007

First Avon Books mass market printing: October 2004

A Lady of His Own

The Bastion Club

"a last bastion against the matchmakers of the ton"

MEMBERS

Christian Allardyce,
Marquess of Dearne

#2 ~~Anthony Blake,~~
~~Viscount Torrington~~

Alicia
"Carrington"
Pevensey

Jocelyn Deverell,
Viscount Paignton

*Please see page ii for a list of previous

Charles St. Austell,
Earl of Lostwithiel

Gervase Tregarth,
Earl of Crowhurst

Jack Warnefleet,
Baron Warnefleet of Minchinbury

#1 ~~Tristan Wemyss,~~ Leonora
~~Earl of Trentham~~ Carling

titles in the Bastion Club series.

CHAPTER

1

Restormel Abbey
Lostwithiel, Cornwall
April 1816

CRACK!

A log shattered in the grate; sparks sizzled and flew. Flames leapt, sending fingers of light playing over the leather spines lining the library walls.

Charles St. Austell, Earl of Lostwithiel, lifted his head from the padded depths of his armchair and checked that no embers had reached the shaggy pelts of his wolfhounds, Cassius and Brutus. Slumped in hairy mounds at his booted feet, neither hound twitched; neither was smoldering. Lips easing, Charles let his head loll back on the well-worn leather; raising the glass in his hand, he sipped, and returned to his cogitations.

On life and its vicissitudes, and its sometimes unexpected evolution.

Outside the wind whistled, faint and shrill about the high stone walls; the night tonight was relatively calm, alive but not turbulent, not always the case along Cornwall's southern coast. Within the Abbey, all was slumberingly still; it was after midnight—other than he, no human remained awake.

It was a good time to take stock.

He was there on a mission, but that was largely incidental; learning whether there was any truth in tales of Foreign Office secrets being run through the local smuggling channels wasn't likely to tax him, certainly not on a personal level. His principal objective in seizing the excuse his erstwhile commander Dalziel had created, and thus returning to the Abbey, his ancestral home, now his, was to gain sufficient perspective to examine and, he prayed, resolve the increasingly fraught clash between his desperate need for a wife and his deepening pessimism over finding a lady suitable to fill the position.

In London, he'd found himself hip deep in candidates, not one of whom was anything like the lady he needed. Being mobbed by giddy young misses with more hair than wit who viewed him only as a handsome and wealthy nobleman, with the added cachet of being a mysterious war hero, had proved something of a personal purgatory. He wasn't going back into society until he had a firm and definite vision of the lady he wanted for his own.

Truth to tell, the depth of his need of a wife—the right wife—unnerved him. When he'd first returned after Waterloo, he'd been able to assure himself that that need was only natural; his association with six others so very like himself, all equally in need of wives, and the camaraderie that had flowed through their formation of the Bastion Club—their last bastion against the matchmaking mamas of the ton—had reassured and soothed his impatience and blunted the spur for some months.

But now Tristan Wemyss and Tony Blake had both found and secured their wives, while he, with his more edgy, restless, desperate need, was still waiting for his lady to appear.

It had taken the last few weeks in London, being sucked into the whirl as society prepared for the intense months of the Season, to comprehend fully what fed that increasingly edgy need. For thirteen years, he'd been dislocated, cut off from the society to which he'd been born and to which he'd now returned. He'd spent thirteen tense years buried in enemy territory, never relaxing, never less than alert and aware.

Now, even though he knew he was home and the war was over, he still found himself, at parties, balls, any large gathering, mentally apart. Still the disguised outsider watching, observing, never able to let down his guard and freely merge.

He needed a wife to connect him again, to be a bridge between him and all around him, especially in the social sense. He was an earl with numerous sisters, relatives, connections, and obligations; he couldn't hide himself away. He didn't *want* to hide himself away—he was constitutionally unsuited to being a recluse. He liked parties, balls, dancing—liked people and jokes and having fun—yet at present, even though he might be standing in the middle of a ballroom surrounded by laughing hordes, he still felt he was outside, looking in. Not a part of it.

Connection. That was the one vital ability he needed in a wife, that she should be able to connect him to his life again. But to do so, she needed to connect with *him*, and that was where all the bright young things failed.

They couldn't even *see* him clearly, let alone understand him—and he wasn't at all sure they had any real interest in that latter. Their notion of marriage, of the relationship underlying that state, seemed determinedly and unalterably fixed in the superficial. Which, to his mind, came perilously close to deception, to pretense. After thirteen years of lying, both living a lie and constantly dealing in fabrication, the last thing he would permit to touch his life—his real life, the one he was determined to reclaim—was any element of deceit.

Fixing his gaze on the flames leaping in the hearth, he focused his mind on his objective—on finding the right lady. He'd had no difficulty rejecting all those he'd met thus far; accustomed to gauging character swiftly, it usually took him no more than a minute. Yet identifying what characteristics his *right* lady possessed, let alone her whereabouts, had thus far defeated him. If she wasn't in London, where else should he look?

The sound of footsteps, faint but definite, reached him.

He blinked, listened. He'd dismissed his staff for the night; they'd gone to their beds long ago.

Boots, not shoes; the boot steps marched nearer, and nearer, from the rear of the house. By the time the steps reached the back of the hall, not far from the library, he knew that whoever was strolling through his house after midnight wasn't any servant; no servant walked with that relaxed, assured tread.

He glanced at the hounds. As aware as he, they remained slumped, stationary but alert, their amber eyes fixed on the door. He knew that stance. If the person came in, the hounds would rise and greet them, but otherwise were content to let that person pass.

Cassius and Brutus knew more than he; they knew who the person was.

Straightening in his chair, he set his glass aside, almost disbelievingly listened as the intruder rounded the end of the stairs and calmly, steadily, climbed them.

"What the *hell?*" Rising, he frowned at the wolfhounds, wishing they could communicate. He pointed at them. "Stay."

The next instant he was at the library door, easing it open. Unlike the person marching through his house, he made less sound than a ghost.

Lady Penelope Jane Marissa Selborne reached the head of the stairs. Without conscious thought, she turned her riding boots to the left along the gallery, making for the corridor at its end. She hadn't bothered with a candle—she didn't need one; she'd walked this way countless times over the years. Tonight the shadows of the gallery and the peaceful silence of the abbey itself were balm to her restless, uncertain mind.

What the devil was she to do? More to the point, what was going on?

She felt an urge to run her hand through her hair, to loosen the long strands sleeked back in a tight knot, but she was still wearing her wide-brimmed hat. Dressed in breeches and an old hacking jacket, she'd spent the day and all of the evening surreptitiously following and watching the activities of her distant cousin Nicholas Selborne, Viscount Arbry.

Nicholas was the only son of the Marquess of Amberly, who, after her half brother Granville's death, had inherited her home, Wallingham Hall, a few miles away. While she felt respect and mild affection for Amberly, who she'd met on a number of occasions, she was less sure of Nicholas; when, in February, he'd appeared unheralded to stay at Wallingham and had started asking questions about Granville's habits and associates, she'd become suspicious. She had sound reasons for believing that anyone asking such questions bore careful watching, but Nicholas had left after five days, and she'd hoped that that would be the end of it.

Yesterday, Nicholas had returned, and spent all day visiting the various smugglers' dens dotted along the coast. Tonight, he'd visited Polruan, and spent two hours at the tavern there. She'd spent the same two hours watching from a nearby stand of trees, taverns at night being one of the few places hereabouts she accepted were off-limits to her, at least when on her own.

Irritated and increasingly alarmed, she'd waited until Nicholas came out, alone, then followed him back through the night. Once she was sure he was heading back to Wallingham, she'd turned her mare north and ridden here, to her sanctuary.

During her long wait in the trees, she'd thought of a way to learn what Nicholas had been doing in the taverns he'd visited, but putting her plan into action would have to wait for tomorrow. As would racking her brains, yet again, to try and make sense of what she'd thus far learned, of her suspicions and what she feared they might mean, might reveal, might lead to.

Despite the urgency she felt over that last, the long day had drained her; she was so tired she could barely think. She'd get a good night's sleep, then consider her best way forward tomorrow.

At the end of the gallery, she headed down the corridor; the bedchamber two from the end of the wing had been hers for the past decade, whenever she took it into her head to visit her godmother's home. The room was always kept ready, the Abbey staff long used to her occasional, unheralded appearances; the fire would be laid, but not lit.

Glancing to her right, through the long, uncurtained windows that gave onto the rear courtyard with its fountain and well-tended beds, she decided she wouldn't bother striking a flame. She was bone-weary. All she wanted was to peel off her breeches and boots, jacket and shirt, and tumble under the covers and sleep.

Exhaling, she turned to her bedchamber door and reached for the latch.

A large dense shadow swooped in on her left.

Panic leapt. She looked—

"*Ahhee!!*—"

Recognition hit; she clapped a hand over her mouth to cut off her shriek, but he was faster. Her hand landed over his, pressing *his* hard palm to her lips.

For an instant, she stared into his eyes, dark and unreadable mere inches away. Acutely conscious of the heat of his skin against her lips.

Of him *there*, tall and broad-shouldered in the darkness beside her.

If time could stand still, in that instant, it did.

Then reality came crashing back.

Stiffening, she dropped her hand and stepped back.

Lowering his hand, he let her go, eyes narrowing as he searched her face.

She dragged in a breath, kept her eyes on his. Her heart was still hammering in her throat. "Damn you, Charles, what the *devil* do you mean by trying to scare me *witless?*" The only way to deal with him was to seize the reins and keep them. "You could at least have spoken, or made some sound."

One dark brow arched; his eyes lifted to her hat, then lazily traced downward, all the way to her boots. "I didn't realize it was you."

Beneath the layers of her drab disguise, a lick of heat touched her cold skin. His voice was as deep, as languidly dark as she remembered it, the seductive power simply there whether he intended it or not. Something inside her clenched; she ignored the sensation, tried to think.

The realization that he was the very last person she wished to be there—within ten miles or even more of there—slammed through her and shook her to her toes.

"Well, it is. And now, if you don't mind, I'm going to get some sleep." Lifting the latch, she pushed open the door, went in, and shut it.

Tried to. The door stopped four inches short of the jamb.

She pushed, then sighed. Deeply. She dropped her forehead against the door. Compared to him, she was still a squib; her senses informed her he had only one palm against the door's other side.

"All right!" Stepping away, she flung her hands in the air. "*Be* difficult then." She uttered the words through clenched teeth. Tired as she was, her hold on her temper was tenuous— that, she knew, was the very worst state to be in when forced to deal with Charles Maximillian Geoffre St. Austell.

Stalking across the room, she pulled off her hat, then sat on the side of the bed. From under lowered brows, she watched as he entered. Leaving the door ajar, he located her, then scanned the room.

He saw her brushes on the dresser, glanced at the armoire, noting the pair of half boots she'd left under it, then he looked at the bed, confirming it was made up. All in the time it took him to prowl, long-legged, arrogantly assured, to the armchair before the window. His gaze returning to her, he sat. Not that that word adequately described the motion; he was all fluid grace somehow arranging long, muscled limbs into an inherently masculine, innately elegant sprawl.

His black hair grew in heavy loose curls; presently neatly cropped, the thick locks framed his face. A harsh-featured, aristocratic face with dramatically arched black brows over large, deep-set eyes, strong, sculpted nose and jaw, and lips she didn't need to dwell on.

For the space of ten heartbeats, his gaze rested on her; even through the dimness she could feel it. He'd always had better night vision than she; if she was to survive this interview with her secrets intact, she'd need every last ounce of her control.

Taking charge seemed wise.

"What *are* you doing home?" All her reasons for believing the Abbey empty, a safe haven, colored the words, transforming question into accusation.

"I live here, remember?" After an instant, he added, "Indeed, I now own the Abbey and all its lands."

"Yes, *but*—" She wasn't going to let him develop the theme of being her host, of being in any way responsible for her. "Marissa, Jacqueline, and Lydia, and Annabelle and Helen, went to London to help you find a wife. My stepmother—your godmother—and my sisters are there, too. They left here enthused, in full flight. There's been talk of little else in the drawing rooms here and at Wallingham Hall since Waterloo. You're supposed to be there, not here." She paused, blinked, then asked, "Do they know you're here?"

Knowing him, that was a pertinent question.

He didn't frown, but she sensed his irritation, sensed, as he answered, that it wasn't directed at her.

"They know I had to come down."

Had to? She fought to cover her dismay. "Why?"

Surely, *surely* it couldn't be . . . ?

Charles wished the light were better or the chair closer to the bed; he couldn't see Penny's eyes and her expressions—the real ones—were too fleeting to read in the dimness. He'd chosen the safe distance of the chair to avoid aggravating their mutually twitching nerves. That moment in the corridor had been bad enough; the urge to seize her, to have his hands on her again, had been so strong, so unexpectedly intense, it had taken every ounce of his will to resist.

He still felt off-balance, just a touch insane. He'd stay put and make do.

She appeared as he remembered her, tall, lithe, and slender, a fair sylph who despite her outward delicacy had always had his measure. Little about her seemed to have changed, but he mistrusted that conclusion. As a gently bred nobleman's daughter, the thirteen years between sixteen and twenty-nine had to have left their mark, but in what ways he had no clue, except in one respect. He would take his oath her quick wits hadn't got any slower.

"I'm here on business." True enough.

"What business?"

"This and that."

"Estate business?"

"I'll be attending to whatever's on my study desk while I'm here."

"But you're here for some other reason?"

He could sense agitation building beneath her words; his instincts were awake, alert, and suspicious. His mission here was to be open, overt not covert. For once there was no reason he couldn't cheerfully tell all, yet the very last person he'd expected to tell first—if at all—was her.

But if she was asking, then his most direct way forward was to tell her, and see how she reacted. Yet he wanted *quid pro quo*—what the devil was she doing traipsing about the countryside at midnight, let alone dressed as a male? And why the hell was she there and not at her home, Wallingham Hall, a mere four miles away? Come to that, why wasn't she in London, or safely married and living with a husband? Oh, yes, he definitely wanted answers to all those questions, which meant the distance between them wasn't going to work. If she lied . . . if he couldn't see her face, her eyes, he might not pick it up.

Unhurriedly, he stood; his gaze on her, he walked, as unthreateningly as he could, to the bed and propped one shoulder against the post at its end. Her gaze hadn't left him; he looked down into her eyes. "I'll tell you why, *exactly* why I'm here, if in return you'll explain to me why, *exactly* why you've arrived here at this hour, dressed like that."

Her grip on the edge of the bed had tightened, but otherwise she hadn't tensed. She stared up at him for a finite moment, then looked at the door. "I'm hungry."

She rose, walked to the door, and without a backward glance went through it.

Lips lifting, he pushed away from the bedpost and followed, closing the door behind him.

He caught up with her on the stairs and followed her to the

kitchen. She marched in and went straight to the kettle, left sitting to one side of the hob; taking it to the pump over the sink, she started filling it. Crossing to the stove, he hunkered down, opened the furnace door, and riddled the grate until the coals glowed red. He piled in kindling, then a few split logs, conscious of the sharp, assessing glances she threw him as she moved about the room.

Once the fire was blazing, he shut the furnace door and rose. Reaching across, she set the kettle to heat and placed a teapot into which she'd ladled leaves on the bench alongside. Glancing at the table, he noted the cups and saucers she'd set out, the plate of Mrs. Slattery's almond biscuits she'd fetched from the pantry. Not once had she hesitated in assembling those things. She knew where everything in his kitchen was stored better than he did.

He studied her as she sank into the chair at one end of the table. Mrs. Slattery, the Abbey's head cook and housekeeper, would never allow her to help herself, which meant she'd learned all she knew on forays like this, long after his staff were abed.

She'd set his cup and saucer halfway along the table, the plate of biscuits between them, beside a single candlestick. The plate was as far from her as she could reach, and equally far from his designated place. He drew up a chair to that spot without comment. The candle flame was steady in the well-sealed kitchen; he'd achieved what he'd wanted—he could see her face.

Picking up a biscuit, she nibbled, over it met his eyes. "So why are you here?"

Leaning back, resisting the lure of the biscuits for the moment, he studied her. If he answered simply, succinctly, what were his chances of getting anything out of her? "My erstwhile commander asked me to take a look around here."

Where to go from there? He could see the question in her gray-blue eyes, could only wonder why she was being so very careful.

"Your commander . . ." She hesitated, then asked, "What arm of the services were you in, Charles?"

Very few people knew. "Neither the army nor the navy."

"Which regiment?"

"Theoretically one of the Guards."

"In reality?"

If he didn't tell her, she wouldn't understand the rest.

She frowned. "Where were you for all those years?"

"Toulouse."

She blinked; her frown deepened. "With your mother's relatives?"

He shook his head. "They're from Landes. A similar distance south, so my coloring and accent were acceptable, but far enough away for me to be relatively safe from being recognized."

She saw, bit by bit realized. Her gaze grew distant, her expression slowly blanked, then she snapped her gaze, now appalled, back on him. "You were a *spy?*"

He'd steeled himself, so didn't flinch. "An unoffocial agent of His British Majesty's government."

The kettle chose that moment to shriek. His words had sounded sophisticated, dismissively cynical, but he suddenly wanted that tea.

She rose, still staring, lips slightly parted. Her eyes were round, but he couldn't read the expression in them. Then she turned away, snagged the kettle, and poured the boiling water over the leaves. Setting the kettle down, she swirled the pot, then left it to steep.

She turned back to him. Her gaze searched his face; she rubbed her hands down her breeches and slowly sat again. This time she leaned forward; the candlelight reached her eyes.

"All those *years?*"

He hadn't, until that moment, known how she'd react, whether she'd be horrified by the dishonor many considered spying to be, or whether she'd understand.

She understood. Her horror was for him, not over what he'd been doing. A massive weight lifted from his shoulders; he breathed in, lightly shrugged. "Someone had to do it."

"But from *when?*"

"I was recruited as soon as I joined the Guards."

"You were only *twenty!*" She sounded, and was, aghast.

"I was also half-French, looked completely French, spoke like a southern native—I could so easily pass for French." He met her gaze. "And I was ripe for any madness."

He would never tell her that part of that wildness had been because of her.

"But . . ." She was trying to work it out.

He sighed. "Back then, it was easy to slip into France. Within a few months I was established, just another French businessman in Toulouse."

She viewed him critically. "You look—and act—too aristocratic. Your arrogance would always mark you."

He smiled, all teeth. "I gave it out that I was a bastard of a by-then-extinct family on whose grave I would happily dance."

She studied him, then nodded. "All right. And then you did what?"

"I wormed my way into the good graces of every military and civilian dignitary there, gathering whatever information I could."

Exactly how he'd done that was one question he wasn't prepared to answer, but she didn't ask.

"So you sent the information back, but you stayed there—all that time?"

"Yes."

She rose to fetch the tea, returning to the table to pour; he watched, soothed in some odd way by the simple domestic act. So distracted was she that when she came close to fill his cup, she didn't seem to notice. As she leaned forward, his eyes traced the curve of her hip, plainly visible courtesy of her breeches. His palm tingled, but he ruthlessly kept both hands still until she straightened and moved away.

He nodded his thanks, picked up the cup, cradled it between his hands. He sipped, then went on, "Once it became clear how successfully I could penetrate the highest civil and military ranks, there was more at stake. Leaving became too risky. The French had to believe I was always there, always accounted for—not the slightest question over what I was doing at any time."

Leaving the pot on the sink, she returned to her chair. "So that's why you didn't come back for James's funeral."

"I managed to get out for Papa's and Frederick's, but when James was lost, Wellington's forces were closing on Toulouse. It was more vital than ever that I stay in place." Frederick, his eldest brother, had broken his neck on the hunting field; James, the second eldest, had succeeded Frederick, only to drown in a freak boating accident. He, Charles, was the third son of the sixth earl, yet here he now was, proclaimed and established as the ninth earl. One of the vicissitudes of fortune that had overtaken him.

She nodded, her gaze far away; lifting her cup, she sipped.

Eventually, she refocused on him. "Where were you at Waterloo?"

He hesitated, but he wanted the truth—all of the truth— from her. "Behind French lines. I led a few others, half-French like me, to join a detachment from Toulouse. They were guarding artillery on a hill overlooking the field."

"You stopped the cannons?"

"That's why we were there."

Her gaze remained steady on his face. "To reduce the slaughter of our troops."

By slaughtering others. He left the words unsaid.

"But after Waterloo, you sold out."

"There was no further need of us—agents like me. And I had other duties waiting."

Her lips curved. "Duties you and everyone else had never imagined you'd have to take up."

Indeed. The mantle of the earldom had fallen to him, the wildest, outwardly least suited, least trained to the challenge of his father's three sons.

She continued to study him, after a moment asked, "How does it feel—being the earl?"

She'd always had an uncanny ability to probe where he

was most sensitive. "Odd." He shifted in his chair, stared into his half-empty cup.

Impossible to explain the feeling that had enveloped him when he'd walked up the front steps and through the massive front door earlier that day. The earldom and the Abbey were *his*. Not just them, but the lands and the responsibilities that came with both, and more—the Abbey was not just his childhood home but the home of his ancestors, the place in which his family had its deepest roots. This was *home*, and its protection and fostering had fallen to him; to him fell the challenge of seeing it and the estates pass to the next generation not just intact but improved.

The feeling was as compelling as any bugle call had ever been, yet the impulses it stirred were not as yet so clear. Nevertheless, more than anything else, his need to respond by finding his countess, by properly linking himself back into this world, had brought him home; Dalziel had just provided a fortuitous excuse.

"I still find it hard remembering Filchett and Crewther are trying to get my attention when they say 'my lord.' " Filchett and Crewther were his butlers, here and in town respectively.

He'd told her enough. He drained his cup, intending to start his side of the interrogation.

She stopped him with the words, "I heard you and some others had formed a special club to help each other in your search for brides."

He stared at her, simply stared. "Have you been to London recently?"

"Not for seven years."

He'd accepted Dalziel knew all about the Bastion Club, but . . . "How the hell did *you* know?"

She set down her cup. "Marissa had it from Lady Amery."

He sighed through his teeth. He should have remembered Tony Blake's mother and godmother were French, part of the network of aristocratic emigrées who'd come to England years before the Terror. As was his mother. He frowned. "She didn't tell me she knew."

Penny snorted and stood to retrieve their cups. "She and the rest only went up to town four weeks ago. How much time have you spent with her?"

"I've been busy." He was grateful he didn't blush easily. He'd been actively avoiding, not so much his mother—she understood him so well it was frightening, but consequently she rarely attempted to tell him his business—but his younger sisters, Jacqueline and Lydia, and even more his sisters-in-law, Frederick's wife Annabelle and James's wife Helen.

Their husbands had died without heirs; for some mystical reason that had converted them into the most passionate advocates of marriage for him. They'd infected his sisters with the same zeal. Every time any of the four saw him, they'd drop names. He didn't dare go riding or strolling in the park for fear of being set on and dragged to do the pretty by some witless, spineless miss they thought perfect to fill his countess's shoes.

Initially, he'd welcomed their help, no matter his oft-voiced aversion to such feminine aid, but then he'd realized the young ladies they were steering his way were all wrong—that there apparently wasn't a right one in all of London—but he hadn't known how to explain, how to stop them, couldn't bring himself to utter a straight *No*; he could imagine their faces falling, the hurt look in their eyes . . . just the thought made him squirm.

"Have they driven you from town?" Penny watched his head come up, watched his eyes narrow. She held his gaze, amused. "I did warn them—and Elaine and my sisters, too—but they were all quite convinced they knew just who would suit you and that you'd welcome their assistance."

His snort was a great deal more derisive than hers had been. "Much they know . . ." He stopped.

She probed. "It's the start of the Season—the very first week—and you've already fled."

"Indeed." His voice hardened. "But enough of me." His eyes—she knew they were midnight blue, but in the weak light they looked black—fixed on her face. "What were you doing riding about the countryside dressed like that?" A flick of his eyes indicated her unconventional attire.

She shrugged. "It was easier than riding in skirts, especially at night."

"No doubt. But why were you riding at night, and sufficiently hard to appreciate the difference between sidesaddle and astride?"

She hesitated, then gave him one inch—dangerous, but . . . "I was following someone."

"Someone doing what?"

"I don't know—that's why I was following him."

"Who is he and where did he go?"

She held his gaze. Telling him was too great a risk, not without knowing why he was there. Especially now she knew the truth of his past.

That hadn't been that great a shock; she'd always suspected something of the sort—she'd known him quite well, the youth he'd once been. But thirteen years had passed; she didn't know the man he now was. Until she did, until she could be sure . . . she knew enough to be careful. "You said you were asked to look around here by your ex-commander. What sort of ex-commander does an ex-spy have?"

"A very determined one." When she simply waited, he grudgingly elaborated, "Dalziel is a something in Whitehall—exactly what, I've never known. He commanded all British agents on foreign soil for the last thirteen years at least."

"What has he asked you to look into down here?"

He hesitated. She could see him weighing the risk of telling her, of giving her the last piece of information she wanted without any guarantee she'd reciprocate.

She continued to wait, gaze steady.

A muscle shifted in his jaw. His gaze grew colder. "Information has surfaced that suggests there was a spy in the Foreign Office leaking secrets to the French during the war. The information suggests the route of communication lay somewhere near Fowey, presumably via one of the smuggling gangs operating hereabouts."

She'd thought she was up to hiding it, had put all her control into managing her expression. A tremor in her hands gave her away; she saw his eyes flick down before she suppressed it.

Then, slowly, his gaze rose to her face. His eyes locked on hers. "What do you know about it?"

His tone had grown harder, more forceful. She thought of playing the innocent for all of a heartbeat. Futile with him. He *knew*, and there was nothing she could do to erase that knowledge. Nothing she could do to deflect him, either.

But she could deny him. Refuse to tell him until she'd had time to think, to examine all the facts she'd gathered—as she'd been planning to do after a sound night's sleep.

She glanced at the old clock on the shelf above the stove, ticking stoically on. It was well after one o'clock. "I have to get some sleep."

"Penny."

She pushed back her chair, but then made the mistake of looking up and meeting his eyes. The candle flame glowed in them, giving his face a devilish cast, one the lean, harsh planes, wide brow and bladelike nose, and the tumbling locks of his thick black hair only emphasized. His eyes were heavy-lidded; his jaw was chiseled, but its hard lines were offset by the subtle beauty of lips sculpted by some demon to lure mortal women into sin.

As for his body, with broad, squared shoulders, lean torso, and well-muscled, rangy limbs, he exuded strength tempered by a grace only few men possessed. His hands were narrow, long-fingered, by themselves quite beautiful. The entire package was quite sufficient to make an angel weep.

Yet his sensual allure wasn't his greatest threat, not to her. He knew her, far better than anyone else in the world. With her, he had a card he could play—one she sensed he more than any man alive would know how to play—a weapon guaranteed to make her comply.

As he sat and looked at her—did nothing more than let the weight of his gaze rest on her—she had no difficulty imagining and believing what his life had been like for the past decade and more. He didn't need to tell her that he'd been alone for all those years, that he'd let no one close, or that he'd killed, and could kill again, even with his bare hands. She knew he had the strength for it; she now knew beyond doubt that he had the courage and conviction for it.

He never called her Penelope except on formal occasions; he used Penny when they were with family. When they'd been alone, he'd often teased her with a different moniker, Squib, a nickname that said it all; when it came to anything physical, he would always be the victor.

Yet this wasn't physical, and when it wasn't, he didn't always win. She'd dealt with him in the past; she could do so again.

Holding his gaze, she stood. "I can't tell you—not yet. I need to think." Stepping around the table, she walked neither hurriedly nor slowly toward the door. It lay beyond him; she had to pass him to leave.

As she did, he shifted. She sensed his muscles bunch, tense, but he didn't rise.

She reached the doorway, and silently exhaled.

"*Mon ange . . .*"

She froze. He'd called her that on only one occasion. His threat was there in his tone, unspoken yet unmistakable.

She waited a heartbeat; when he said nothing more, she looked back. He hadn't moved; he was looking at the candle. He didn't turn to face her.

He couldn't face her . . .

A knot inside unraveled; tension flowed away. She smiled, softly, knowing he couldn't see. "Don't bother—there's no point. I know you, remember? You're not the sort of man who would."

She hesitated for another second, then quietly said, "Good night."

He didn't reply, didn't move. She turned and walked away down the corridor.

Charles listened to her footsteps retreating, and wondered what malevolent fate had decreed he'd face this. Not the sort of man to blackmail a lady? Much she knew. He'd been exactly such a man for more than a decade.

He heard her reach the front hall, and exhaled, long and deep. She knew not just some minor piece of the puzzle but something major; he trusted her intelligence too well to imagine she was overreacting to some inconsequential detail she'd inadvertently stumbled on. But . . .

"*Damn!*" Shoving away from the table, he stood and stalked back to the library. Opening the door, he called Cassius and Brutus, then headed out to the ramparts to walk. To let the sea breeze blow the cobwebs and the memories from his brain. He didn't need them clouding his judgment, especially now.

The ramparts were raised earthworks ringing the Abbey's gardens to the south. The view from their broad, grassed top took in much of the Fowey estuary; on a clear day, one could see the sea, winking and glimmering beyond the heads.

He walked, at first steering his thoughts to mundane things, like the wolfhounds lolloping around him, diverting to investigate scents, but always returning to his side. He'd got his first pair when he'd been eight years old; they'd died of old age just months before he'd joined the Guards. When he'd returned home two years ago with Napoleon exiled to Elba, he'd got these two. But then Napoleon had escaped and he'd gone back into the field, leaving Cassius and Brutus to Lydia's care.

Despite Lydia's affection, much to her disgust, the instant he'd reappeared the hounds had reattached themselves to him. Like to like, he'd told her. She'd sniffed and taken herself off, but still sneaked treats to the pair.

What was he going to do about Penny?

The question was suddenly there in his mind, driving out all else. Halting, he threw back his head, filled his lungs with the cool, tangy air. Closed his eyes and let all he knew of the Penny who now was flood his mind.

When he'd first returned home, his mother, unprompted, had informed him, presumably by way of educating his ignorance of their neighbors, that Penny hadn't married. She'd had four perfectly successful London Seasons; she was an earl's daughter, well dowered and, if not a diamond of the first water, then more than passably pretty with her delicate features, fair, unblemished skin, long flaxen hair, and stormy gray eyes. Her height, admittedly, was to some a serious drawback—she was about half a head shorter than he, putting her eye to eye with many men. And she was . . . he'd have said willowy rather than skinny, with long limbs and svelte, subtle curves; she was the antithesis of buxom, again not to every man's taste.

Then, too, there were the not-inconsequential elements of her intelligence and her often waspish tongue. Neither bothered him—indeed, he greatly preferred them over the alternatives—but there were, admittedly, not many gentlemen who would feel comfortable with such attributes in their wives. Many would feel challenged in a threatening way, not an attitude he understood but one he'd witnessed often enough to acknowledge as real.

Penny had always challenged him, but in a way that delighted him; he appreciated and enjoyed their near-constant battles of wits and wills. Witness the one they were presently engaged in; despite the seriousness of the situation, he was conscious of the past stirring, elements of their long-ago association resurfacing—and part of that was the challenge of dealing with her, of interacting with her again.

According to his mother, she'd received dozens of perfectly good offers, but had refused every one. When asked, she'd said none had filled her with any enthusiasm. She was, apparently, happy living as she had for the past seven years, at home in Cornwall watching over her family's estate.

She was the only offspring of the late Earl of Wallingham's first marriage; her mother had died when she was very young. Her father had remarried and sired one son and three daughters by his second wife Elaine, a kindly, good-hearted lady—his godmother as a matter of fact. She'd taken Penny under her wing; they'd grown to be not so much mother and daughter as close friends.

The earl had died five years ago; Penny's half brother Granville had succeeded to the title. A sole male with a doting mother and four sisters, Granville had always been spoiled, tumbling from one scrape into the next with nary a thought for anyone or anything beyond immediate gratification.

He'd last met Granville when he'd returned home in '14; Granville had still been reckless and wild. Then had come Waterloo. Fired by the prevailing patriotic frenzy, Granville had shut his ears to his mother's and sisters' pleas and joined one of the regiments. He'd fallen somewhere on that bloody plain.

The title and estate had passed to a distant cousin, the Marquess of Amberly, an older gentleman who had assured Elaine and her daughters that they could continue to live as they always had at Wallingham Hall. Amberly had been close to the previous earl, Penny's father, and had been Granville's guardian prior to Granville attaining his majority.

And thus the freedom to get himself killed, leaving his mother and sisters, if far from destitute, then without immediate protectors.

That, Charles decided, opening his eyes and starting to pace again, was what bothered him most. Here was Penny already involved in God knew what, and there wasn't any male in any position to watch over her. Except him.

How she'd feel about that he didn't know.

At the back of his mind hovered a lowering suspicion over why she hadn't been eager to marry, why no gentleman had managed to persuade her to the altar, but how she now thought of him, how she now viewed him, he didn't know and couldn't guess.

She'd be prickly almost certainly, but prickly-yet-willing-to-join-forces, or prickly-and-wanting-nothing-whatever-to-do-with-him? With ladies like her, it wasn't easy, or safe, to guess.

He did know how *he* felt about *her*—*that* had been an unwelcome surprise. He'd thought thirteen years would have dulled his bewitchment, but it hadn't. Not in the least.

Since he'd left to join the army, he'd seen her a few times in '14, and then again over the past six months, but always at a distance with family, both his and hers, all around. Nothing remotely private. Tonight, he'd come upon her unexpectedly alone in his house, and desire had come raging back. Had caught him, snared him, sunk its talons deep.

And shaken him.

Regardless, it was unlikely there was anything he could do to ease the ache. She'd finished with him thirteen years ago—cut him off; he knew better than to hold his breath hoping she'd change her mind. She was, always had been, unbelievably stubborn.

They would have to set that part of their past aside. They couldn't entirely ignore it—it still affected both of them too intensely—but they could, if they had to, work around it.

They'd need to. Whatever was going on, that matter he'd been sent to investigate and that she, it seemed, had already discovered, was potentially too dangerous, too threatening to people as yet unknown, to treat as anything other than a battlefield. Once he knew more, he'd try to separate her from it. He didn't waste a second considering if she, herself, was in any way involved on the wrong side of the ledger; she wouldn't be, not Penny.

She was on the same side he was, but didn't yet trust him. She had to be protecting someone, but who?

He no longer knew enough about her or her friends to guess.

How long before she decided to tell him? Who knew? But they didn't have a lot of time. Now he was there, things would start happening; that was his mission, to stir things up and deal with what rose out of the mire.

If she wouldn't tell him, he'd have to learn her secret some other way.

He strode along the ramparts for half an hour more, then returned to his room, fell into bed, and, surprisingly, slept.

CHAPTER

❧ 2 ❧

HE AWOKE THE NEXT MORNING TO THE SOUND OF HOOF-beats. Not on the gravel drive circling the house, but farther away, not nearing but retreating.

He'd left the French doors to his balcony open, a very un-English act, but in Toulouse he'd grown accustomed to open windows at night.

Fortuitous. Rolling from the bed, he stretched and strolled across the room. Naked, he stood in the balcony doorway watching Penny, garbed in a gold riding habit, steadily canter away. If the doors hadn't been open, he'd never have heard her; she'd left from the stables, a good distance from the house. Sidesaddle on a roan, she was unhurriedly heading south.

To Fowey? Or her home? Or somewhere else?

Five minutes later, he strode into the kitchen.

"My lord!" Mrs. Slattery was shocked to see him. "We're just starting your breakfast—I had no idea—"

"My fault entirely." He smiled charmingly. "I forgot I wanted to ride early this morning. If there's any coffee? And perhaps a pastry or two?"

In between muttering dire warnings over what was sure to befall gentlemen who didn't start their day by sitting down to a proper breakfast, contemptuously dismissing his prof-fered excuse that he'd grown accustomed to French ways—

"Well, you're a proper English earl now, so you'll need to forget such heathenish habits"—Mrs. Slattery provided him with a mug of strong coffee and three pastries.

He demolished one pastry, gulped down the coffee, scooped up the remaining pastries, planted a quick kiss on Mrs. Slattery's cheek, eliciting a squawk and a "Get along with you, young master—m'lord, I mean," and was out of the back door striding toward the stables ten minutes behind Penny.

Fifteen minutes by the time he swung Domino, his gray hunter, out of the stable yard and set out in her wake.

He hadn't had the big gray out since early March; Domino was ready to run, fighting to stretch out even before he loosened the reins. The instant they left the drive for the lush green of the paddock rising to the low escarpment, he let the gelding have his head. They thundered up, then flew.

Leaning low, he let Domino run, riding hands and knees, scanning ahead as they sped southwest. Penny, sidesaddle and believing herself unobserved, would stay on the lanes, a longer and slower route. He went across country, trusting he'd read her direction correctly, then he saw her, still some way ahead, crossing the bridge over the Fowey outside the village of Lostwithiel, a mile above where the river opened into the estuary. Smiling, he eased Domino back; he clattered across the bridge five minutes later.

Returning to the high ground, from a distance he continued to track her. Fowey, her home, or somewhere else, all were still possible. But then she passed the mouth of the lane leading west to Wallingham Hall, remaining on the wider lane that veered south, following the estuary's west bank all the way to the town of Fowey at the estuary mouth.

But the town was still some way on; there were other places she might go. The morning was sunny and fine, perfect for riding. She kept to her steady pace; on the ridge above and behind, he matched her.

Then she slowed her roan and turned east into a narrow lane. Descending from the ridge, he followed; the lane led to Essington Manor. She rode, unconcerned and unaware, to the front steps. He drew away and circled the manor, finding a vantage point within the surrounding woods from where he could see both the forecourt and the stable yard. A groom led Penny's horse to the stables. Charles dismounted, tethered Domino in a nearby clearing, then returned to keep watch.

Half an hour later, a groom drove a light gig from the stables to the front steps. Another groom followed, leading Penny's horse.

Charles shifted until he could see the front steps. Penny appeared, followed by two other ladies of similar age, vaguely familiar. The Essington brothers' wives? They climbed into the gig. Penny was assisted back into her saddle. He went to fetch Domino.

He reached the junction of the Essington lane and the Fowey road in time to confirm that the ladies were, indeed, on their way south. Presumably to Fowey, presumably shopping.

Charles sat atop Domino and debated. At this point, Penny was his surest and most immediate link to the situation he'd been sent to investigate.

She was concerned enough to follow men about the countryside at night, concerned enough to refuse to tell him what she'd discovered, not without thinking and considering carefully first. Yet there she was, blithely going off to indulge in a morning's shopping with such concerns unresolved, circling her head.

She might be female, but he'd grown up with four sisters; he wasn't that gullible.

Penny stayed with Millie and Julia Essington for the first hour and a half of their prearranged foray through Fowey's shops—two milliners, the haberdasherer's, the old glovemaker's, and two drapers. As they left the second draper's establishment, she halted on the pavement. "I must pay my duty call—why don't you two go on to the apothecary's, then I'll meet you at the Pelican for lunch?"

She'd warned them before they set out that morning that

one of the retired servants from Wallingham had fallen gravely ill and she felt honor-bound to call.

"Right-oh!" Julia, rosy-cheeked and forever sunny-tempered, linked her arm in Millie's.

Quieter and more sensitive, Millie fixed Penny with an inquiring gaze. "If you're sure you don't need support? We wouldn't mind coming with you, truly."

"No—there's no need, I assure you." She smiled. "There's no question of them dying, not yet." She'd managed not to mention any name; both Millie and Julia were local landowners' daughters, had married and continued to live locally—it was perfectly possible anyone she might mention would have relatives working at Essington Manor.

"I won't be long." She stepped back. "I'll join you at the Pelican."

"Very well."

"We'll order for you, shall we?"

"Yes, do, if I'm not there before you."

With an easy smile, she left the sisters and crossed the cobbled street. She followed it slowly uphill, then, hearing the distant tinkle she'd been listening for, she paused and glanced back. Millie and Julia were just stepping into the apothecary's tiny shop.

Penny walked on, then turned right down the next lane.

She knew the streets of Fowey well. Tacking down this lane, then that, she descended to the harbor, then angled up into the tiny lanes leading to the oldest cottages perched above one arm of the wharves. Although protected from the prevailing winds, the small cottages were packed cheek by jowl as if by huddling they could better maintain their precarious grip on the cliff side. The poorest section of the town, the cottages housed the fishermen and their families, forming the principal nest of the local smuggling fraternity.

Penny entered a passageway little wider than the runnel that ran down its center. Halfway up the steep climb, she halted. Settling her habit's train more securely on her arm, she knocked imperiously on a thick wooden door.

She waited, then knocked again. At this hour, in this

neighborhood, there were few people about. She'd checked the harbor; the fleet was out. It was the perfect time to call on Mother Gibbs.

The door finally cracked open an inch or two. A bloodshot eye peered through the gap. Then Penny heard a snort, and the door was opened wide.

"Well, Miss Finery, and what can I do for you?"

Penny left Mother Gibbs's residence half an hour later, no wiser yet, but, she hoped, one step nearer to uncovering the truth. The door closed behind her with a soft thud. She walked quickly down the steep passageway; she would have to hurry to get back to the Pelican Inn, up on the High Street in the better part of town, in reasonable time.

Reaching the end of the passage, she swung around the corner.

Straight into a wall of muscle and bone.

He caught her in one arm, steadied her against him. Not trapping her, yet . . . she couldn't move.

Couldn't even blink as she stared into his eyes, mere inches away. In daylight, they were an intense dark blue, but it was the intelligence she knew resided behind them that had her mentally reeling.

That, and the fact she'd stopped breathing. She couldn't get her lungs to work. Not with the hard length of him against the front of her.

Had he seen? Did he know?

"Yes, I saw which house you left. Yes, I know whose house it is. Yes, I remember what goes on in there." His gaze had grown so sharp it was a wonder she wasn't bleeding. "Are you going to tell me what you were doing in the most notorious fishermen's brothel in Fowey?"

Damn! She realized her hands were lying boneless against his chest. She pushed back, dragged in a breath as he let her go and she stepped back.

Having air between them was a very good thing. Her lungs expanded; her head steadied. Grabbing up her skirt, she stepped past him. "No."

He exhaled through his teeth. "Penny." He reached out and manacled her wrist.

She halted and looked down at his long tanned fingers wrapped about her slender bones. "Don't."

He sighed again and let her go. She started walking, then recalled the Essingtons and walked faster. He kept pace easily.

"What could you possibly want from Mother Gibbs?"

She glanced briefly at him. "Information."

A good enough answer to appease him, for all of six strides. "What did you learn?"

"Nothing yet."

Another few steps. "How on earth did you—Lady Penelope Selborne of Wallingham Hall—make Mother Gibbs's acquaintance?"

She debated asking him how he—now Earl of Lostwithiel—knew of Mother Gibbs, but his response might be more than she wanted to know. "I met her through Granville."

He stopped. "*What?*"

"No—I don't mean he introduced me." She kept walking; in two strides he was again by her side.

"You're not, I sincerely hope, going to tell me that Granville was so mullet-brained he frequented her establishment?"

Mullet-brained? Perhaps he hadn't met Mother Gibbs by way of her trade. "Not precisely."

Silence for another three steps. "Educate me—how does one *imprecisely* frequent a brothel?"

She sighed. "He didn't actually enter the place—he grew enamored of one of her girls and took to mooning about, following the poor girl and buying her trinkets, that sort of thing. When he started propping up the wall in the passageway, languishing—for all I know serenading—Mother Gibbs said enough. She sent word to me through our workers and the servants. We met in a field and she explained how Granville's behavior was severely disrupting her business. The local fisherlads didn't fancy slipping through her door with the local earl's son looking on."

He muttered a derogatory appellation, then more clearly said, "I can see her point. So what did you do?"

"I talked to Granville, of course."

She felt his glance. "And he listened?"

"Regardless of what else he was, Granville wasn't stupid."

"You mean he understood what would happen if you mentioned his habits to his mother."

Looking ahead, she smiled tightly. "As I said, he wasn't stupid. He saw that point quite quickly."

"So Mother Gibbs owes you a favor, and you've asked her for information in return."

That, in a nutshell, was it—her morning's endeavor.

"You are not, I repeat *not*, going back there alone."

His voice had changed. She knew those tones. She didn't bother arguing.

He knew her too well to imagine that meant she'd agreed.

A frustrated hiss from him confirmed that, but he let the matter slide, which made her wonder what *he* was planning.

Regardless, they'd reached the High Street. She turned onto the wider pavement with Charles beside her.

And came face to face with Nicholas, Viscount Arbry.

She halted.

Charles stopped beside her. He glanced at her face, noted the momentary blankness in her expression while she decided what tack to take.

He looked at the man facing them. He'd also halted. One glance was enough to identify him as a gentleman of their class. No real emotion showed in his face, yet the impression Charles received was that he hadn't expected to meet Penny, and if given the choice, would have preferred he hadn't.

"Good morning, cousin." Penny nodded in cool, distinctly mild greeting; smoothly, she turned to him. "I don't believe you've met. Allow me to introduce you." She glanced at the other man. "Nicholas Selborne, Viscount Arbry—Charles St. Austell, Earl of Lostwithiel."

Arbry bowed; Charles nodded and offered his hand. While they shook hands, Penny said, "Nicholas is a distant cousin. His father is the Marquess of Amberly, who inherited Papa's title and estates."

Which might explain her coolness, but not Arbry's hesitation. How distant was the connection, Charles wondered. More than the stipulated seven degrees? There was definitely more in the "cousins'" interaction that required explanation.

"Lostwithiel." Arbry was studying him. "So you're back at . . . the Abbey, isn't it? A fleeting visit, I expect."

Charles grinned, letting his practiced facade of bonhomie bubble to his surface. "Restormel Abbey, yes, but as to the fleetingness of my visit, that remains to be seen."

"Oh? Business?"

"In a manner of speaking. But what brings you here with the Season just commenced?" It was the question Arbry had wanted to ask him. Charles capped his inquisition with a studiously innocent, "Is your wife with you?"

"Nicholas isn't married," Penny said.

Charles glanced at her, then directed a look of mild inquiry at Arbry. He was a peer in line for a major title, appeared hale and whole, and looked to be about Charles's age; if Charles should be in London getting himself a bride, so, too, should Arbry.

Arbry hesitated, then said, "I act as my father's agent—there were aspects of the estate here that needed attention."

"Ah, yes, there's always something." Charles darted a look at Penny. She'd managed the Wallingham Hall estate for years; if there was anything requiring attention, she would know, yet not a hint of anything resembling comprehension showed in her face.

Arbry was frowning. "I vaguely recall . . . I met your mother and sisters last time I was here. They gave me to understand you would be marrying shortly, that you intended to offer for some lady this Season."

Charles let his smile broaden. "Very possibly, but unfortunately for all those interested in my private life, duty once again called."

"Duty?"

The question was too sharp. Arbry definitely wanted to

know why he was there. Charles glanced again at Penny, but she was watching Arbry; she wasn't giving him any clues.

She was protecting someone. Could it be Arbry?

"Indeed." He met Arbry's eyes, dropped all pretense. "I've been asked to look into the possible traffic of military and diplomatic secrets through smuggling channels hereabouts during the late wars."

Arbry didn't blink. Not a single expression showed on his pale face.

Which gave him away just as surely; only someone exercising supreme control would be so unresponsive in the face of such a statement.

Still blank-faced, he said, "I hadn't realized the . . . government had any real interest in pursuing the past."

"As certain arms of the government are controlled by those who fought, or sent others to fight and die over the last decade and more, you may be assured the interest is very real."

"And they've asked you to look into it? I thought you were a major in the Guards?"

"I was." Charles smiled, deliberately cold, deliberately ruthless. "But I have other strings to my bow."

Penny glanced around, desperate to break up the exchange of pleasantries. Nicholas might be good, but Charles could be diabolical. She didn't want him to learn more, guess more, not yet. God only knew what he'd make of it, or how he might react.

Her gaze found Millie and Julia, both with faces alight, hurrying as fast as they decorously could to join her. And the two handsome gentlemen she'd somehow acquired. For quite the first time in her life she thoroughly approved of their blatant curiosity.

"Penelope! We were just coming to join you." Julia beamed as the three of them turned. "We got held up in the apothecary's." She directed her gaze to the gentlemen; Millie did the same. "Lord Arbry, isn't it?"

Nicholas had met them before; he bowed. "Mrs. Essington. Mrs. Essington."

Charles turned fully to face them. He was taller than

Nicholas; Millie's and Julia's gazes rose to his face. They both blinked, then delighted smiles lit their countenances.

"Charles!" Julia all but shrieked. "You're back!"

"How delightful," Millie cooed. "I had thought, from what your dear mama let fall, that you were quite fixed in London for the Season."

Charles smiled, shook their hands, and deflected their questions. Penny heaved a sigh of relief. Now if only Nicholas would grab his chance and escape.

She was turning to nudge him along, when Julia gaily said, "You both *must* join us for luncheon—it's gone one o'clock. If I know anything of gentlemen, you must be ravenous, and the Pelican has the best food in Fowey."

"Oh, yes!" Millie's eyes shone. "We've booked a private parlor—do join us."

Charles glanced at Penny, then at Nicholas. "Indeed, why not?" His smile as he gazed at Nicholas was distinctly predatory. "What say you, Arbry? I can't see any reason not to take advantage of such an invitation from such delightful company."

Millie and Julia preened. They turned shining eyes on Nicholas.

Penny inwardly swore. Nicholas couldn't do anything but agree.

With Julia, Millie, and Charles providing most of the conversation, the five of them walked the short distance to the Pelican Inn. As the landlord, all delighted gratification, bowed them into his best parlor, Penny hoped Nicholas understood that he was walking into a lion's den, with a lion with very sharp teeth and even sharper wits beside him.

She was nursing an incipient headache by the time lunch ended. Predictably, Millie and Julia had filled the hour with bright conversation, retelling all the repeatable local gossip for Charles's edification. He'd encouraged them, leaving him able to direct the occasional unexpected and unpredictable query at Nicholas, not that he'd learned anything from the exercise.

Nicholas was clearly on his guard, his attention focused on Charles, his attitude to everyone as it usually was, reserved and rather standoffish. She'd clung to the cool demeanor she always adopted around him; most put it down to understandable distance over his father's assumption of her father's estates.

Little did they know.

As they all rose and together quit the parlor, it occurred to her that, with Charles now present to draw his attention, Nicholas might lower his guard with her. She'd never given him reason to think she suspected him of anything; he had no idea she knew of the questions he'd asked the Wallingham grooms and gardeners, or of his visits to the local smugglers. He certainly didn't know she'd been following him.

She raised her head as they emerged into the bright sunshine. Charles appeared beside her as she went down the steps into the inn yard. An ostler was holding her mare; she was about to wave him to the mounting block when Charles touched her back.

"I'll lift you up."

She would have frozen, stopped dead, simply refused, but he was walking half-behind her; if she stopped, he'd walk into her.

They reached the mare's side. Charles's hands were already sliding around her waist as she halted and turned.

Lungs locked, she glanced into his face as he gripped and effortlessly hoisted her up. But he wasn't even looking at her, much less noticing her embarrassing reaction; his gaze was locked on Nicholas, helping Millie and Julia into their gig.

"How long has he been here?"

Slipping her boot into the stirrup he'd caught and positioned for her, she managed to breathe enough to murmur, "He arrived yesterday."

That brought Charles's dark gaze to her face, but an ostler appeared with his horse, and he turned away.

Nicholas had also asked for his horse—one of Granville's hacks—to be brought out. He, too, mounted. Without actually discussing the matter, the five of them clopped out of the inn yard together, Nicholas riding attentively beside the gig, she and Charles bringing up the rear.

She watched Nicholas's attempts to be sociable. Millie and Julia were thrilled, their day crowned by being able to claim they'd spent time conversing with *both* the two most eligible, and most elusive, gentlemen of the district.

"Has he been spending much time down here?"

Charles's tone was low, noncommittal.

If she didn't tell him, he'd ask around and find out anyway. "It's his fourth visit since July, when he and his father came for Granville's funeral. The longest he's stayed is a week in December, but that was their first formal visit as owner, so to speak. He came down alone in February for five days, then turned up yesterday."

Charles said nothing more, but was aware she was watching her "cousin" with an assessing and cynical eye. He wasn't surprised Nicholas had joined them on their way home; all through luncheon, he'd shot swift glances at Penny, concerned, yes, but not just in the usual way. There was definitely something between them.

They reached the Essington lane and farewelled Millie and Julia. By unspoken consent, he, Penny, and Nicholas cantered on together.

Until they came to the lane to Wallingham. Nicholas drew up, his chestnut stamping as he half wheeled to face them. Penny slowed and halted. Charles drew rein beside her.

Nicholas looked at him, then at Penny. "I, er . . ." His features hardened. "I had thought, or rather understood, that you believed the countess was still at the Abbey."

Penny had an instant to decide which way to jump. Charles, being Charles, would already have guessed she'd left Wallingham for the Abbey because of Nicholas. A nobleman with four sisters, two of them married, Charles would also know there was no social reason behind her decamping; she hadn't gone to the Abbey to avoid possible scandal. Nicholas, of course, thought she had, because she'd led him to think so.

But now here she was, staying at the Abbey apparently alone with Charles, to whom she was in no way related.

She had three options. One, take advantage of Nicholas's misconstruction and seek refuge at Essington Manor, free of both Charles and Nicholas. Unfortunately, Lady Essington, Millie and Julia's mama-in-law, was a dragon and would expect her to remain with Millie and Julia during the days, and even more during the evenings and nights. She'd never find out what was going on, and what she needed to do to protect Elaine and her half sisters.

Alternatively, she could return to Wallingham Hall on the grounds that residing under the same roof as Nicholas was scandalwise preferable to sharing a roof with Charles; no one could argue that. However, she'd then be using the same stables as Nicholas, the same house, and she'd much rather he remained ignorant of her comings and goings while following him.

Living at Wallingham *might* be useful if Nicholas lowered his guard while distracted by Charles, but she'd seen enough of Nicholas to be sure that if Charles wasn't physically present, being distracting, then Nicholas would have defenses aplenty deployed against her.

All in all, her last option seemed preferable.

She smiled reassuringly. "The countess's elderly cousin Emily is at the Abbey, so there's no reason I can't remain there, at least while you're at Wallingham."

She glanced at Charles; his expression deceptively open, he was watching Nicholas. His horse didn't shift. Not by a flicker of a lash did he betray her.

"Ah . . . I see." It was Nicholas's horse that shifted. After a fractional pause, during which she sensed he searched for some other reason to have her return to Wallingham, he conceded. "I'll bid you farewell, then." He nodded to Charles. "Lostwithiel. No doubt we'll meet again."

"No doubt." Charles returned the nod, but his tone made the comment anything but comforting.

Enough. With a gracious nod of her own, she set her mare trotting, then urged her into a canter.

Charles's gray ranged alongside. He waited until they'd rounded the next bend to murmur, "Where did Cousin Emily come from?"

"If she's your mother's elderly cousin, then presumably she came from France."

"Presumably. And what happens when dear Nicholas asks around, innocently or otherwise?"

She kept her gaze forward. "Until recently, Cousin Emily has been staying with other relatives—she only arrived two days ago to spend some time here, in warmer climes—"

"Warmer climes being recommended for her stiff joints, I suppose?"

"Precisely. However, Cousin Emily still prefers to converse in French, and considers herself too old to socialize, so she's something of a curmudgeonly recluse, and not at home to callers."

"How convenient."

"Indeed. Your Cousin Emily is the perfect chaperone."

She felt his gaze, scimitar-sharp on her face.

"What is it about Arbry that sent you to the Abbey?"

She exhaled, but knew he'd simply wait her out. "I don't trust him."

"On a personal level?"

His tone was uninflected, perfectly even; latent menace shimmered beneath. "No," she hurried to say, "it's not personal. Not at all."

They rode on; sure of what his next question would be, she strove to find words to explain her suspicions without revealing their cause.

"Is Arbry the person you're protecting, or the person you were following, or both?"

She glanced at him, eyes widening. How had he seen, deduced, known all that?

He met her gaze, his own steady. And waited.

Lips setting, she looked ahead as they slowed for the bridge over the river. She knew him; correspondingly, he knew her. The noise as they clattered over the wooden bridge gave her a minute to think. As they set out again along the well-beaten lane, she replied, "He's not who I'm protecting. He is who I was following."

That said, she urged Gilly, her mare, into a gallop. Charles's gray surged alongside, but Charles took the hint; as they rode on through the fine afternoon, he asked no further questions.

She escaped him in the stables, leaving him holding both their horses. He cast her a dark look, but let her go. She reached the house, glanced back, but he hadn't made haste to follow her.

Just as well. Last night, after leaving him in the kitchen, she'd gone to bed, but memories had swamped her, claimed her; she hadn't slept well, but neither had she analyzed. She desperately needed to think, to put together the information she'd gathered and decide what it might reveal, especially to someone used to dealing with such matters, like Charles. Telling him . . . she accepted she would ultimately have to, but if there was a way to present the facts in a more favorable light, she needed to find it first.

Entering the house through the garden hall, she halted, wondering where to hide to gain the greatest time alone. She might wish to have the rest of the evening to assemble the facts and cudgel her brains, but of that she held little hope. Charles had never been renowned for patience.

Persistence, yes; patience, no.

"The orchard." Grabbing up her habit's train, she whirled, reopened the door, and peered out. Charles hadn't left the stables; he was probably brushing down her mount. Slipping outside, she ran for the shrubbery, then used the cover of the high hedges to make her way to the orchard, currently a mass of pink and white blossom effectively screening her from the house.

An old swing hung from the gnarled branch of an ancient apple tree. She sank onto the seat with a sigh and turned her mind to her troubles. To all she'd learned over the last months, to all she now suspected.

And to all that in turn suggested.

Charles found her half an hour later. The house was huge, but it hadn't taken him long to check in her room and discover neither she nor her riding habit was there. So he'd returned to the gardens; there were only so many places she could hide.

She was facing away from the house, apparently looking out over his fields. She was slowly swinging, absentmindedly pushing away from the ground with one booted toe; she was thinking, and didn't yet know he was there.

He considered going near enough to push the swing higher, but he didn't think he could get so close without her knowing. Not that she'd hear or see him, but she'd sense him the instant he got nearer than two yards.

That had been the case for as long as he could remember. He could effectively silence enemy pickets, but sneaking up on Penny had never worked. He'd only succeeded the previous night because, unsure of her identity, he'd kept his distance until the last.

Now, however, there were things she had to tell him. He needed to make clear that, no matter what she thought, she had no choice; telling him, and soon, was her only option. After meeting Arbry, he wasn't prepared to allow her to keep her secrets to herself for even one more day; he needed her to tell him so he could effectively step between her and all he'd been sent to investigate, including, it now seemed, her "cousin" Arbry.

If he could separate her from the investigation, he would, but he couldn't see any way of managing that yet.

One step at a time. He needed to learn all she knew about this business. Had she been any other woman, he'd already have started plucking nerves of various sorts, but with Penny such tactics weren't an option, at least not for him. His plucking her nerves was too painful for them both. Just lifting her to her saddle that afternoon had been bad enough, and he hadn't even been trying. He'd distracted her by asking after Arbry, and she'd recovered quickly, but . . . not that way. All he could do was be water dripping on stone.

He strolled toward her, deliberately making noise. "Tell me—why did you choose to come to the Abbey?"

Penny glanced at him. Slowly swinging, she watched as he leaned against a nearby tree trunk; hands in his breeches' pockets, he fixed his dark gaze on her.

They'd been lovers once. Just once.

Once had been enough for her to realize that continuing to be lovers would not be wise, not for her. He'd been twenty, she sixteen; for him, the encounter had been purely physical, for her . . . something so much more. Yet their physical connection continued; even now, after thirteen years and her best efforts to subdue her susceptibility, it still sprang to quivering life the instant he got close. Close enough for her to sense, to be able to touch—to want. Even now, looking at him leaning with casual grace against the tree, the breeze stirring his black hair, his eyes dark and brooding fixed on her, her heart simply stopped. Ached.

Her susceptibility irritated, annoyed, sometimes even disgusted her, yet she'd been forced to accept that regardless of him having no reciprocal feelings for her, she would always love him; she didn't seem able to stop. That, however, was something he didn't know, and she had no intention of letting him guess.

Forcing her eyes from him, she looked ahead and continued to swing. "Nicholas is no fool. If I was following him out of the Wallingham Hall stables, he'd notice."

"How often have you followed him?"

She swung a little more, considering how much, if anything, to reveal. "I first realized he was visiting places no nonlocal gentleman such as he should know of in February. I don't think he'd started before then—none of the grooms were aware of it if he had—but in February he spent all five days he was down here riding out. I'd done the same then as I did this time, coming here to the Abbey when he arrived, so I didn't realize he was also riding out by night until it was too late."

His silence made it clear there was a lot in that he didn't

like. Eyes on the corn rising green in his fields, she said nothing more, just waited.

"Where did he go? Smugglers' haunts, I assume, but which?"

She hid a resigned smile; he hadn't missed the point of her seeing Mother Gibbs. "All the major gathering places in Polruan, Bodinnick, Lostwithiel, and Fowey."

"No farther afield?"

"Not as far as I know, but I missed his nighttime excursions."

"Did you ask Mother Gibbs what he'd been doing in those places?"

"Yes."

When she didn't elaborate, he prompted, his voice carrying a wealth of compulsion—no, intimidation. "And?"

She set her jaw. "I can't tell you—not yet."

A moment passed, then he said, "You have to tell me. I need to know—this isn't a game."

She looked at him, met his eyes. "Believe me, I know it's not a game."

She paused, holding his gaze, then went on, "I need to think things through, to work out how much I actually know and what it might mean *before* I tell you. As you've already realized, what I know concerns someone else, someone whose name I can't lightly give to the authorities. And regardless of all else, you, in this, are 'the authorities.' "

His gaze sharpened. For a long moment, he studied her, then quietly said, "I may represent the authorities in this, but I'm still . . . much the same man I was before, one you know very well."

She inclined her head. "My point exactly. Much the same, perhaps, but you're not the same man you were thirteen years ago."

That was the matter in a teacup. Until she knew how and in what ways he'd changed, he remained, not a stranger but something even more confusing, an amalgam of the familiar and the unknown. Until she understood the here-and-now him better, she wouldn't feel comfortable trusting him with what she knew.

What she thought she knew.

Recalling her intention in coming to the orchard, she rubbed a finger across her forehead, then looked at him. "I haven't yet had a chance to work out what the snippets I've learned amount to—I need time to think." She stopped the swing and stood.

He straightened away from the tree.

"No." She frowned at him. "I do not need your help to think."

That made him smile, which helped her thought processes even less.

She narrowed her eyes. "If you want me to tell you all, soon, then you'll allow me a little peace so I can get my thoughts in order. I'm going to my room—I'll tell you when I'm prepared to divulge what I've learned."

Head rising, she stepped out, intending to sweep past him. The trailing skirt of her habit trapped her ankle.

"Oh!" She tripped, fell.

He swooped, caught her to him, drew her upright. Steadied her within his arms.

Her lungs seized. She looked up, met his eyes.

Felt, as she had years ago, as she always did when in his arms, fragile, vulnerable . . . intensely feminine.

Felt again, after so many years, the unmistakable flare of attraction, of heat, of flagrant desire.

Her gaze dropped to his lips; her own throbbed, then ached. Whatever else the years had changed, this—their private madness—remained.

Her heart raced, pounded. She hadn't anticipated that he would still want her. Lifting her eyes to his, she confirmed he did. She'd seen desire burn in his eyes before; she knew how it affected him.

He wasn't trying to hide what he felt. She watched the shades shift in those glorious dark eyes, watched him fight the urge to kiss her. Breath bated, helpless to assist, she waited, tense and tensing, eyes locked with his, for one crazed instant not sure what she wanted . . .

He won the battle. Sanity returned, and she breathed shallowly again as his hold on her gradually, very gradually, eased.

Setting her on her feet, he stepped back. His eyes, dark and still burning, locked with hers. "Don't leave it too long."

A breeze ruffled the trees, sent a shower of petals swirling down around them. She searched his eyes. His tone had been harsh. She wished she had the courage to ask what he was referring to—divulging her secrets, or . . .

Deciding that in this case discretion was indeed the better part of valor, she gathered her skirts and walked back to the house.

SWEEPING INTO THE ABBEY'S DRAWING ROOM AT SEVEN o'clock, just ahead of Filchett, she fixed Charles, watching her from before the massive fireplace, with a narrow-eyed glare, then stepped aside to allow Filchett to announce that dinner was served.

Unperturbed, Charles nodded to Filchett and came to take her hand.

Steeling herself, she surrendered it, but didn't bother to curtsy. As he laid her fingers on his sleeve and turned her to the door, she stated with what she felt was commendable restraint, "I would have been quite happy with a tray in my room."

"I, however, would not."

She bit her tongue, elevated her nose. She knew better than to waste breath arguing with him.

Half an hour after she'd regained her room, a maid had tapped on her door and inquired whether she would like a bath. She'd agreed; a long, relaxing soak was just what she'd needed. The steam had risen, wreathing about her; her thoughts had circled, constantly returning to the crucial question. Could she trust Charles, the Charles who now was?

She still wasn't sure, but now understood she couldn't—wasn't going to be allowed to—put him off for much longer. Witness this dinner he'd jockeyed her into.

When the maid, Dorrie, had returned to inquire which gown she wanted laid out, she'd replied she intended to have dinner in her chamber. Dorrie's eyes had grown round. "Oh, no, miss! The master's told Mrs. Slattery you'll dine with him."

An exchange of notes had followed, culminating in one from Charles informing her she would indeed be dining with him—where was up to her.

She'd opted for the safety of the dining parlor, the smaller salon the family used when not entertaining. He sat her at one end of the table, then walked to the carved chair at its head. The table was shorter than usual—every last leaf had been removed—yet there was still eight feet of gleaming mahogany separating them. Nothing to overly exercise her.

Reaching for the wineglass Filchett had just filled, she smiled her thanks as the butler stepped back, and reminded herself that dinner alone with Charles didn't mean they'd actually be alone.

A gust of wind splattered rain across the window. It had been pouring for the last twenty minutes. At least Nicholas wouldn't be scouting about tonight; she wasn't missing anything.

As soon as the first course was served, Charles signaled Filchett, who, along with the footmen, withdrew.

Charles turned his gaze on her. "I checked in *Debrett's*. Amberley, Nicholas's father, was with the Foreign Office."

She nodded and continued eating her soup. She waited as long as she dared before replying, "He retired years ago—'09, or thereabouts."

What else had he pieced together? There was only one major fact she knew that he still didn't. Would he guess . . . or might he connect Nicholas directly with the smugglers and not realize there was—had been—an intervening link?

Setting down her spoon, she reached for her napkin, glanced at him as she patted her lips. He was finishing his soup, his expression uninformative, but then he glanced down the table and caught her eye.

He'd seen the alternatives.

She looked away as Filchett and his minions returned.

Leaning back in his chair, Charles waited until the main course had been served and Filchett had once more retreated. "Did Nicholas visit Wallingham often over the years before Granville's death?"

She kept her gaze on her plate. "He's visited off and on since he was a child—Amberly and Papa were close friends."

"Indeed?"

The word sounded mild; she wasn't deceived.

"But Nicholas hasn't been a regular visitor here over the last decade?"

She wished she could lie, but he'd check and find her out. "No."

To her surprise, he left it at that and gave his attention to the roast lamb.

From beneath his lashes, Charles watched her, and let her nerves stretch. She was waiting, keyed up to meet his next tack, his next inquisitorial direction. In lieu of intimidating her in any other fashion, he'd opted for demonstrating that he wouldn't retreat, but instead, question by question, would press harder until she capitulated and told him all she knew.

The time he was willing to give her to think had become severely limited the instant he'd realized Arbry was involved; it had shortened even further when he'd learned Amberly had been with the Foreign Office, the very office the putative traitor was supposed to have graced.

He held his peace until Mrs. Slattery's lemon curd pudding was set before them and Filchett departed. Lemon curd pudding was his favorite; delicious, it was gone in too few bites. Lifting his wineglass, he sat back and sipped, and looked down the table at Penny.

"You're protecting someone, but it isn't Arbry."

She looked up; he trapped her gaze.

"So who else? Your family is all female, as is mine these days. None of them are involved."

She swallowed her last mouthful of pudding. "Of course not."

"So who else could be involved in running secrets out of the Fowey estuary—who that you would feel compelled to protect?" That was what was fueling her refusal to tell him; that was the point he needed to attack.

When she set down her spoon and looked back at him, unmoved, he arched a brow. "The staff at Wallingham, perhaps?"

Her gaze turned contemptuous. "Don't be silly."

"Mother Gibbs herself?"

"No."

"Her sons, then—are the Gibbses still running the Fowey Gallants?"

She frowned in mock confusion. "I'm not sure how to answer—yes, or no. But yes, they're still in charge of the Gallants. I daresay they always will be—Gibbses have been Gallants for over four hundred years."

"Do they still meet at the Cock and Bull?"

"Yes."

So she'd been there—followed someone there—recently. "Do you have any idea if they've been involved in running secrets?"

"I don't know."

"So which other gangs are still operating?"

He took her on a seemingly peripatetic ramble around the district; often it wasn't her answer that enlightened, but the fact she gave any answer at all that told him who she'd recently had contact with, or thought to ask about.

It was the speed at which his questions came that finally opened Penny's eyes. They were immersed in a rapid-fire discussion of the Essington brothers, Millie's and Julia's husbands, when the scales fell. She stopped midsentence, stared at him for a moment, then shut her lips. Firmly.

He accorded her glare no more than an arched brow, a what-did-you-expect look.

Indeed. Tossing her napkin on the table, she rose. He, more languidly, rose, too.

"If you'll excuse me, I believe I'll retire for the night."

She turned, but by then he'd reached her. He walked beside her to the door. Closing his hand about the knob, he paused and looked down at her. Waited . . . until she steeled herself, looked up, and met his eyes.

"No game, Penny. I need to know. Soon."

They were no more than a foot apart; regardless of her senses' giddy preoccupation, the look in his midnight eyes was unmistakable. He was deadly serious. But he was dealing with her straightly, no histrionics, no attempt to dazzle her, to pressure her as only he could.

He had to know he could; that moment in the orchard had demonstrated beyond question how much sensual power he still wielded over her.

If he wished to use it.

Tilting her head, she swiftly studied his eyes, realized, understood that he'd made a deliberate choice not to invoke their personal past, not to use the physical connection that still sparked between them against her, to overcome, overwhelm, and override her will.

He was dealing with her honestly. Just him and her as long ago they'd used to be.

Moved, feeling oddly torn—tempted to grasp the chance of dealing openly with him again—she raised a hand, briefly clasped his arm. "I will tell you. You know that." She drew in a tight breath. "But not yet. I do need to think—just a bit more."

He searched her eyes, her face, then inclined his head. "But only a little bit more." He opened the door, followed her through. "I'll see you in the morning."

She nodded a good night, then climbed the stairs.

Charles watched her go, then headed for the library.

In one respect his prediction went awry; he saw her next very late that night.

After spending three hours leafing through *Burke's Peerage* and *Debrett's*, studying Amberly's connections, then looking for locals with connections to the Foreign Office or other government offices, trying to identify who Penny might feel she should protect, all to no avail, he turned down the lamps and climbed the stairs as the clocks throughout the house struck half past eleven.

Halting on the landing, he looked up at the huge arched window, at the stained glass depicting the St. Austell family crest. Rain beat a staccato rhythm against the panes; the wind moaned softly. The elements called, tugged at that wilder, more innocent side of him the years had buried, teased, tempted . . .

Lips curving in cynical self-deprecation, he took the left branch of the stairs and climbed upward, heading not for his apartments as he'd originally intended but to the widow's walk.

High on the Abbey's south side immediately below the roof, the widow's walk ran for thirty feet, a stone-faced, stone-paved gallery open on one side, the wide view of the Fowey estuary framed by ornate railings. Even in deepest night with the moon obscured by cloud and the outlook veiled by rain, the view would be magnificent, eerily compelling. A reminder of how insignificant in Nature's scheme of things humans really were.

His feet knew the way. Courtesy of the years, he moved silently.

He halted just short of the open archway giving onto the walk; Penny was already there.

Seated on a stone bench along the far wall, one elbow on the railing, chin propped on that hand, she was staring out at the rain.

There was very little light. He could just make out the pale oval of her face, the faint gleam of her fair hair, the long elegant lines of her pale blue gown, the darker ripple of her shawl's knotted fringe. The rain didn't quite reach her.

She hadn't heard him.

He hesitated, remembering other days and nights they'd been up here, not always but often alone, just the two of them drawn to the view. He remembered she'd asked for time alone to think.

She turned her head and looked straight at him.

He didn't move, but Penny knew he was there. To her eyes he was no more than a denser shadow in the darkness; if he hadn't been looking at her, she'd never have realized.

When he didn't move, when she sensed his hesitation, she looked back at the wet night. "I haven't yet made up my mind, so don't ask."

She sensed rather than heard his sigh.

"I didn't realize you were here."

He'd thought her in her chamber; he couldn't have known otherwise. She returned no comment, unperturbed by his presence; he was too far away for her senses to be affected— she didn't, otherwise, find him bothersome to be near. And she knew why he'd come there—for much the same reason she had.

But now he was present, and she was, too . . . she tried to predict his next tack, but he surprised her.

"You weren't *that* amazed to learn I'd been a spy. Why?"

She couldn't help but smile. "I remember when you returned for your father's funeral. Your mother was . . . not just happy to see you, but grateful. I suppose I started to wonder then. And she was forever slipping into French when she spoke to you, far more than she usually does, and you were so secretive about which regiment you were in, where you were quartered, which towns you'd been through, which battles . . . normally, you would have been full of tales. Instead, you avoided talking about yourself. Others put it down to grief." She paused, then added, "I didn't. If you'd wanted to hide grief, you would have talked and laughed all the harder."

Silence stretched, then he prompted, "So on the basis of that one episode . . ."

She laughed. "No, but it did mean I had my eyes open the next time you appeared."

"Frederick's funeral."

"Yes." She let her memories of that time color her tone; Frederick's death had been a shock to the entire county. "You were late—you arrived just as the vicar was about to start the service. The church door had been left open, there were so many people there, but the center aisle had been left clear so people could see down the nave.

"The first I or anyone knew of your presence was your

shadow. The sun threw it all the way into the church, almost to the coffin. We all turned and there you were, outlined with the sun behind you, a tall, dramatic figure in a long, dark coat."

He humphed. "Very romantic."

"No, strangely enough you didn't appear romantic at all." She glanced at him. He was concealed within the shadows of the archway, leaning back against the arch's side, looking out; she could discern his profile, but not his expression. She looked back at the rain-washed fields. "You were . . . intense. Almost frighteningly so. You had eyes for no one but your family. You walked to them, straight down the nave, your boots ringing on the stone."

She paused, remembering. "It wasn't you but them, their reactions that made me . . . almost certain of my suspicions. Your mother and James hadn't expected to see you; they were so *grateful* you were there. They knew. Your sisters *had* been expecting you, and were simply reassured when you arrived. They didn't know.

"Later, you explained you'd been held up, and that you had to rejoin your regiment immediately. You didn't exactly say, but everyone assumed you meant in London or the southeast; you intended to leave that night. But it had rained on and off for days—it rained heavily that night. The roads were impassable, yet in the morning you were gone."

She smiled faintly. "I don't think many others, other than I presume the Fowey Gallants, realized your appearance and your leaving coincided with the tides."

Minutes ticked past in silence, the same restful, undisturbing silence they'd often shared up there, as if they were perched high in a tree on different branches, looking out on their world.

"You were surprised I didn't return for James's funeral."

She thought back, realized she'd felt more concern and worry than surprise. "I knew you'd come if it was possible, especially then, with James's death leaving your mother and sisters alone. Your mother especially—she'd buried her husband and two eldest sons in the space of a few years, something no one could have foreseen. Yet that time even more than the previous one, she didn't expect you; she wasn't surprised when you didn't appear—she was worried, deeply worried, but everyone saw it as distraction due to grief."

"Except you."

"I know your mother rather well." After a moment, she dryly added, "And you, too."

"Indeed." She heard him shift, heard the change in his tone. "You do know me well, so why this hesitation over telling me what you know you should?"

"Because I don't know you that well, not anymore."

"You've known me all your life."

"No. I knew you until you were twenty. You're now thirty-three, and you've changed."

A pause ensued, then he said, "Not in any major way."

She glanced at where he stood. After a moment she said, "That's probably true. Which only proves my point."

Silence, then, "I'm only a poor male. Don't confuse me."

Poor male her left eye. Yet revisiting her knowledge of him, talking matters through with him, was helping; she was starting to grapple with the new him. The irony hadn't escaped her; she'd deliberately avoided thinking of him for the past thirteen years, but now fate and circumstance were forcing her to it. To understand him again, to look and see him clearly.

She drew breath. "All right—think of this. I saw you with Millie and Julia today. The charm, the smile, the laughter, the teasing, the hedonistic hubris. I recognized all that, but now it's subtly and significantly different. At twenty, that was you—*all* of you. You were the epitome of 'devil-may-care'—there wasn't anything deeper. Now, however, the larger-than-life hellion is a mask, and there's someone behind it." She glanced at him. "The man behind the mask is the one I don't know."

Silence.

Charles didn't correct her; he couldn't. He knew in his bones she was right, but he wasn't sure how the change had come about, or what to say to reassure her.

"I think," she continued, surprising him, "that perhaps the

man behind the mask was always there, or at least the potential was always there, and the past thirteen years, what you've been doing during that time, made him, you, stronger. More definite. The real you is a rock the years have chiseled and formed, but what smooths your surface is lichen and moss, a social disguise."

He shifted. "An interesting thesis." He couldn't see how her too-perceptive view would improve his chances of gaining her trust.

"A useful one, at any rate." She glanced at him. "I note you're not arguing."

He held his tongue, too wise to respond. She continued to gaze at him, then her lips lightly curved, and she looked out once more. "Actually, it will help. If you must know, I'm not sure I would have trusted the hellion you used to be. I wouldn't have felt certain of your reaction. Now . . ."

He let minutes tick by, hoping . . . eventually, he sighed and leaned his head back against the arch. "What do you want to know?"

"More, but I don't know exactly what I'm searching for, so I don't know what questions to ask. But . . ."

"But what?"

"Why did you leave London to come here? I know your ex-commander asked you to look around, but you're no longer his to command—you didn't have to agree. You've never willingly run in anyone's harness—that I'm sure hasn't changed—but more importantly you *knew* what hopes and, well, dreams your sisters and sisters-in-law were nurturing when they went to London. You—helping you find a wife, planning your wedding—gave them purpose, invigorated them; they were so excited, so flown with anticipation."

She stared out at the rain-drenched vista. "If you'd stayed there, indulged them, teased, laughed, and joked, and then gone your own way regardless, I wouldn't have been surprised. But you did something I never would have predicted—you left them."

Her struggle to comprehend colored her tone. "It's as I said before—I had it right. You *fled*."

He closed his eyes. She paused, then asked the one question he'd hoped she wouldn't, "Why?"

He stifled a sigh. How had he allowed things to develop to this pass? Given the bafflement in her voice, he couldn't very well not explain.

"I . . ." Where to start? "The work I was engaged in, in Toulouse, involved . . . a great deal of deception. On my part, primarily, although sometimes, through my manipulation, others deceived others, too."

"I imagine spywork rather depends on deceit—if you hadn't lied well, you would have died."

His wry smile was spontaneous; he opened his eyes, but didn't look her way. Talking to her—someone who'd once known him so well—in darkness sufficiently complete that he couldn't see her expression and knew she couldn't see his, was strangely comforting, as if the dark gave them a degree of privacy in which they could say almost anything to each other in safety.

"That's true, but . . ." He paused, conscious that telling her the rest would be the first time he'd put his feelings into words. Decided it didn't matter; it was the truth, his reality. "After spending thirteen years living a deception with lies as my daily bread, to return to the ton, to the artful smiles and glib comments, the sly falsity and insincerity, the glamour, the patent superficiality . . ." His face and tone hardened. "I couldn't do it.

"Those chits they want me to consider as my bride— they're not so much witless as intentionally blind. They want to marry a hero, a wild and reckless handsome earl who everyone knows cares not a snap for anything."

Her laugh was short, incredulous. "*You?* A care-for-naught?"

"So they believe."

She snorted. "Your brothers may have been the ones trained to the estates, but it was always you who knew this place—loved this place—best. You're the one who knows every field, every tree, every yard."

He hesitated, then said, "Others don't know that."

His deep rapport with the Abbey was why he'd retreated there, irrevocably sure that despite his desperate need for a wife, he couldn't stomach a marriage of, if not outright deceit, then one built on politely feigned affection. Feigning anything of that ilk was now beyond him, while the thought of his wife being only superficially fond of him, smiling sweetly but in reality thinking of her next new gown . . .

He drew in a deep breath. He knew she was watching him, but continued to stare out at the black night. "I can't pretend anymore."

That was the crux of it, the source of the revulsion that had sent him flying from London to the one place he knew he belonged. The one place where he didn't need to fabricate his emotions, where all was true, clear, and simple. He felt so much cleaner, so much freer, there.

When he said nothing more, Penny looked away, into the darkness broken by the constant curtain of the rain. She knew without doubt that he'd spoken the truth; he might be able to lie to others, but he'd rarely succeeded with her. Tone, inflection, and a dozen tiny hints of stance and gesture were still there in her mind, still familiar—still real. Looking back, between them there never had been deceit or lies; misunderstanding or lack of perception yes, but those had been unintentional on both sides.

What he'd revealed in the past minutes, over the past day, had reassured her, made her believe she could trust him. More, his words, his attitudes, had convinced her the man he now was was stronger, more hardheaded and clear-sighted, more committed to the values she valued, more rigid in adherence to the codes she believed important than the hellion of his youth had been.

But she couldn't yet speak; she still needed to think about what she knew to tell. That was still not clear in her mind. So she let the silence stretch. They were comfortable in the quiet dark; neither felt any need to speak.

A light winked, far out in the night.

"Did you see it?" she asked.

"Yes. The Gallants are out."

She thought of Granville, thought of the nights he must have spent out on the waves. She could imagine him clinging to the side of a boat, a wild and reckless light in his eyes. If ever there had been a care-for-naught, it was he. "At Waterloo, did you hear anything of Granville?"

"No." After a moment, he asked, "Why?"

"We never really heard, just that he'd died. Not how, or in what way."

She could almost hear him wondering why she'd asked; on the face of things, she and Granville hadn't been all that close. She kept her counsel. He eventually asked, "Were you told in which region he was lost?"

"Around Hougoumont."

"Ah."

"What do you know of it?" It was clear from his tone he knew something.

"I wasn't close, but it was the most fiercely contested sector in the whole battle. The French under Reille thought the farmstead an easy gain. They were wrong. The defenders of Hougoumont might well have turned the tide that day. Their defiance pricked the French commanders' collective pride; they threw wave after wave of troops against it, totally out of proportion to the position's strategic importance." He paused, then more quietly added, "If Granville was lost near there, you can be certain he died a hero."

She wished—oh, *how* she wished—she could believe that.

She asked no more, and he volunteered no more. They remained on the walk, watching the rain, listening to the steady downpour, the constant drum on the lead above, the merry gurgling in the gutters, the splatter as spouts of water hit the flagstones far below. Three more times they spotted flashes out at sea, out beyond the mouth of the estuary.

At last, she stood; shaking out her skirts, she regarded him across the shadowed space. "Good night. I'll see you in the morning."

He considered her for an instant—an instant in which she had no idea what he was thinking. Then he swept her a bow, all fluid masculine grace.

"In the morning. Sleep tight."

She turned and left him, going through the archway into the west wing.

At eight o'clock the next morning, she walked into the breakfast parlor, sat in the chair Filchett held for her, smiled her thanks, then looked up the table at Charles. He'd looked up when she'd entered, was watching her still.

"Granville was involved."

Charles's gaze flicked to Filchett.

He stepped forward and lifted the coffeepot. "I'll fetch some fresh coffee, my lord."

"Thank you." The instant Filchett had left the room, closing the door behind him, Charles transferred his gaze to her. "What precisely do you mean?"

She reached for the toast rack. "It's Granville I'm protecting."

"He's been dead for nearly a year."

"Not him himself, but Elaine and Emma and Holly. And even Constance, for all that she's married. Myself, too, although the connection is less direct." Elaine was Granville's mother, Emma and Holly his younger, still-unmarried sisters. "If it becomes known Granville was a traitor . . ." Charles had unmarried sisters, too; she was sure she didn't need to spell it out.

"So Granville was the link to the smugglers." He looked at her, not uncomprehending yet clearly not convinced. "Start at the beginning—why do you think Granville was a traitor?"

Between bites of toast and jam, and sips of tea, she told him. Filchett didn't return with the coffeepot, probably just as well.

The frown remained in Charles's eyes. "So you never had a chance to tax Granville with this?"

"I *had* taxed him over what he was doing with the smuggling gangs—I'd known of his association with them for years, at least since he was fifteen. But of course I never got any answer other than that he was just larking about." She paused, then added, "I never suspected there might be more to it until last November."

"Tell me again—your housekeeper knew of this priest hole?"

"Yes. I gather Figgs has always known it was there, but that Papa and later Granville had insisted it be left alone, that they kept important things in there they didn't want the maids disturbing. So Figgs never told the maids, but when it came time to prepare the master bedchamber for Amberly's first visit—he came in early December—Figgs thought it must be time to clean and dust in there, so she asked me if she should."

"When you went to check, did anyone go with you?"

"No. Figgs told me how to open it—it's easy enough if you know what to twist."

"And you found a large number of pillboxes."

She sighed. " 'A large number' doesn't adequately describe it, Charles. Trust me—Papa was a collector, but I never knew he had boxes like these. They're . . . wonderful. Gorgeous. Some jewel-encrusted, others with beautiful miniatures, grisailles, and more. And I've never seen any of them before—not the ones on the shelves in the priest hole."

Setting down her teacup, she looked at him. "So where did he get them?"

"Through the trade, collecting. Simply buying."

"I kept the estate accounts for all the years Granville was earl, and I checked the ledgers for the years before that. Yes, Papa did occasionally buy pillboxes, but those purchases were relatively few and far between, and, tellingly, those are the boxes in the library display cases. The boxes he bought, he kept openly. Why did he hide these others—so much more beautiful—so completely away? I didn't know of them, and I'd swear no one else in the household other than Granville has seen them."

"A clandestine pillbox collection."

"Yes!" She narrowed her eyes at him. "There's no viable conclusion other than that those hidden pillboxes were payment for something. And it's something Granville knew about. But initially I couldn't think of anything either Papa or Granville might have to 'sell,' as it were."

"Indeed. Neither Granville nor your father ever had access to sensitive information, the sort the French would pay for. So it can't—"

"Wait!" She held up a hand. "I said initially—there's more. After finding the boxes, I shut up the priest hole and put Figgs off. Amberly and Nicholas arrived; the visit went smoothly. Then, on the last day they were there, I heard from the grooms that Nicholas had been asking after Granville's friends, those he spent time with in the neighborhood, where he went in the evenings when on his own, what taverns he frequented."

"Maybe Nicholas wanted to find a place to drink?"

"Are you playing devil's advocate, or are you just being difficult?"

He smiled. "The former, so go on."

She cast him a repressive glance, then reassembled her train of thought. "When they left, I checked the priest hole. Someone had been examining the boxes. Many were out of line, turned around, that sort of thing." She sighed. "I went down to dinner, trying to puzzle it out. Elaine was telling the girls how distinguished Amberly and his branch of the family were. She mentioned that Nicholas was following in his father's footsteps—at the Foreign Office."

"Ah." Charles sat up, all expression leaching from his face.

"Indeed." Feeling vindicated, she nodded. "So now you see why I started to seriously worry. And the further I looked, things only got blacker."

"What did you find?"

"Not so much found as recalled. Papa and Amberly grew up together—they shared a schoolroom, went up to Oxford together, did the Grand Tour together. They were only distantly related, but very close friends, and the connection continued all their lives. Papa started collecting pillboxes when he was staying in Paris with Amberly, who at that time had a minor role in our embassy there."

Charles said nothing; his eyes locked on her face, he nodded for her to continue.

"The other pertinent facts are that Amberly was Granville's godfather, and his guardian after Papa died. And Nicholas and Granville knew each other, how well I don't know, but Granville often visited Amberly's house, so presumably Nicholas and Granville were frequently in each other's company.

"And as I told you earlier, when Nicholas arrived unheralded in February, the week after Elaine and the girls had left for town, he spent five days contacting all the local smuggling gangs. According to Mother Gibbs, he was putting it about that in the matter of Granville's activities with them, he was Granville's replacement. Anything to do with Granville, they should see him—send word via the grooms at Wallingham Hall, and he'd come down and speak with them."

"What did the local lads think of that? Were there any takers?"

"No." She hid a ghost of a smile. "They see Nicholas as an outsider, almost a foreigner, but more than that, I don't think they actually understand what fish he's trawling for."

"Very likely."

Charles heard his voice, deep, resonant, cut across her lighter tones. She shouldn't be involved in any of this, but she was. Leaning back in his chair, he caught her eye. "So you believe that Granville, possibly with your father's connivance, was running secrets to the French via the smuggling gangs. He got said secrets from either Amberly or Nicholas, but regardless, Nicholas at least is involved."

She nodded. "Yes. And—"

"You don't think Granville enlisting to fight the French at Waterloo argues against his involvement? Or that perhaps he wasn't aware of the nature of what he was doing?"

She met his gaze. "No. Granville . . . he was ten when you

left to join the Guards. You didn't really know him. He was a reckless, feckless boy, and he never grew up. Yes, he was spoiled, indulged in every degree, but as he didn't possess a malicious bone in his body, everyone simply smiled, shook their heads, and let him be.

"Ferrying information to the French? He'd have considered that a great lark—the thrill, the danger, would have seduced him. He wouldn't have really thought about what he was ferrying, that wouldn't have been important. Pursuing excitement and thrills—*that* was Granville's sole purpose in life. That was why he joined the army for Waterloo. Any contradiction honestly wouldn't have occurred to him."

He studied her eyes and thought she was wrong, but she'd pushed herself to accept what was for her a hugely painful interpretation. No hypothetical argument was likely to sway her.

And what she thought—the question of whether Granville and, the point she was trying to think of even less, her father before him had been knowingly involved in treason—was not of immediate importance. Not with her "cousin" Nicholas about, ferreting around, stirring up things even more effectively than he himself was.

She was watching him measuringly, lips and jaw set. Before he could speak, she did.

"If Granville is labeled a traitor, even posthumously, Elaine will be ostracized, to a lesser extent Constance— she's now Lady Witherling—will be, too, and neither Emma nor Holly could hope to make a decent match. No gentleman of the ton will want to marry a traitor's sister."

She paused, then added, her gaze steady on his, "I would prefer not to be known as a traitor's half sister, either, but at twenty-nine with my fortune my own, at least my future doesn't rest so completely on society's opinion."

He waited, but she didn't ask for any promises or assurances that he would keep her family safe, that he would find some way to protect them from the consequences should the truth prove as dire as she thought.

All of which made him even more determined to do so.

She'd trusted him with all she knew; he was tempted to ask what in their conversation last night had tipped the scales, but he wasn't sure he truly wanted to know. She saw through him, to the real him, more easily than anyone save only his too-perceptive mother.

"I should mention that my commander, Dalziel, has investigated thoroughly but could find no evidence of any sensitive information from the Foreign Office actually reaching the French." He grimaced. "Indeed, until I realized you'd already stumbled on something illicit, I was half-inclined to think the affair might prove to be all smoke and no fire."

He caught her gaze. "However, even if we prove that what you suspect is true, and Nicholas is apprehended, the details will not be made public. Nicholas won't stand trial, nor, indeed, will most of England even know of his apprehension or his crime, and even less of any others he might name as coconspirators."

She frowned. "You mean it's simply buried? Not"—she gestured—"paid for?"

"Oh, no—if he's been involved in treason, he'll pay." He smiled one of his coldly dangerous smiles. "It's just that no one will hear of it."

She blinked. "Oh."

While she digested that, he rapidly reviewed all she'd told him, all he now accepted, all he now suspected. "The first thing to do"—he looked up as her eyes snapped up to meet his—"is to take a look at this pillbox collection."

CHAPTER

❧ 4 ❧

"MY APOLOGIES. I'D THOUGHT YOU WERE EXAGGERATING."

The look Penny threw him wasn't difficult to interpret. She turned back to her self-appointed task of counting the dozens of pillboxes ranged on shelves in the ancient priest hole concealed behind a wall panel in the master bedchamber of Wallingham Hall.

She'd been right; this wasn't a collection it was easy to explain away. Row after row of superb examples of the jeweler's art glowed and winked and tempted. Charles wondered if she'd realized there were too many boxes to have been amassed over only a decade of spying. Too many boxes for the collection to have been Granville's work alone.

He glanced around, mentally orienting the six-foot-by-twelve-foot chamber within the walls of the old manor. They'd ridden over, arriving midmorning, prepared to engage Nicholas in a discussion of the estate if he was there and they couldn't avoid him. He was there, but in the library. As the house was Penny's home, there was no reason to announce her arrival, or, therefore, his; regardless of his years away, the staff knew him as well as the Abbey staff knew Penny. She and he had walked upstairs, straight to the master bedchamber, to this hidden room.

One tiny window high on one wall let in a shaft of light. The walls themselves were solid stone. As in many priest holes, there was a second door, a narrow wooden one set low in the wall opposite the main entrance, by the corner with the outer wall. An old key sat in the lock. The escape route of last resort for any priest trapped there.

They'd closed the door to the master bedchamber, but left the hinged panel wide open. Charles caught the sound of footsteps plodding up the stairs. Penny continued counting, unaware. More out of instinct than real concern he moved to the priest hole's threshold; Nicholas was not yet master there—he wasn't using the master bedchamber.

He was, however, heading for it.

Charles cursed beneath his breath, caught the edge of the panel, and hauled it shut. Penny looked around, straightened, but blessedly made no sound as the panel dully clicked into place.

He looked at her; she stared at him. Beyond the panel they heard the sound of a boot step on the floorboards.

If Nicholas wasn't using the room, then why had he come there?

Charles grabbed Penny's arm and drew her to the small door. Grasping the key, he turned it, trying to be careful, but eventually had to force it; the lock hadn't been used in years. It grated, then the bolt clunked over.

Just as the faint whirring of the panel's mechanism reached them.

The panel popped open. The catch to release it was concealed in the ornate mantelpiece surrounding the fireplace farther down the bedchamber.

Charles wrenched the narrow door open, unceremoniously thrust Penny through, and followed on her heels. He pulled the door shut, fast and silent, rammed the key into the keyhole, turned, and heard the lock fall home.

Just as the panel hinges squeaked.

They held their breaths. Nicholas took a few steps into the priest hole, then stopped.

Penny closed her eyes, then opened them. There was no real difference in what she could see. Blackness.

The . . . corridor?—wherever they were was narrow, musty,

and dusty; the wall against which Charles had crammed her was cold, hard stone. The space hadn't been designed for two people; they were jammed together, his shoulder wedged against hers, her back to the wall opposite the wooden door.

She could hear her own breathing, shallow and rapid. Her senses were in knots, reacting to the black prison on the one hand, Charles's nearness on the other. Her skin started to chill, then flushed, prickled.

Through the darkness, Charles found her hand and gripped reassuringly. She gulped and fought down a mortifying urge to grab him, to cling and burrow against his solid warmth.

He shifted; releasing her hand with a gentle pat, he slowly crouched, his shoulder and back sliding down her.

Her legs weakened; mentally cursing, she stiffened them.

A pinprick of light glowed faintly. She blinked, blinked again, realized Charles had extracted the key from the keyhole.

He moved. The light vanished; absolute darkness once again reigned. He was peeking through the keyhole.

She bit her lip, trying not to form any mental image of their surroundings. Cobwebs, bits of stone, lots of dust, insects, and small creatures . . . not helpful.

Charles moved, then smoothly, carefully rose. His hand found hers, squeezed, then followed her arm up to grip her shoulder. He leaned nearer. She felt his breath brush her ear, felt the reactive shiver to her marrow.

"He didn't see us. He's studying the boxes. Doesn't look like he'll leave soon."

He paused, then added, his voice the faintest thread of sound, "Let's see where this goes." He stepped away.

She clutched at him, caught the back of his hacking jacket.

Halting, he reached around and caught her hand. He pried it free, but didn't release it; he drew her arm around him, then flattened her hand on his chest, over his ribs. He reached back and caught her other hand, and did the same, bringing her close—very close—behind him.

Leaning his head back and to the side, he breathed, "We're going to move very slowly. Hold on to me—I think there are stairs a little farther along."

How could he tell? Could he actually see anything? To her it was as dark as a sepulchre.

Regardless of the abrading of her senses, she wasn't about to let him go.

He was right about the stairs. They'd only shuffled a few feet when she felt him step down. He stepped down again, then waited. Feeling with her toes, she found the edge and stepped down behind him.

In tandem, one step from him, one from her, they slowly descended. With every step, the hard strength of his back shifting before her, the steely muscles of his chest flexing beneath her palms, blatantly impinged on her senses. Although the air was growing cooler, she felt increasingly warm.

It was a long, steep, straight but narrow stairway; rough stone walls caught at her arms, her skirts. Charles reached up, moved his arms. An instant later, ghostly fingers trailed caressingly over her cheeks.

She jumped, valiantly swallowed a shriek.

"Just cobwebs," he whispered.

Just cobwebs? "If there are cobwebs, there must be spiders."

"They'll leave you alone if you leave them alone."

"But . . ." They were destroying the spiders' webs. By the feel of it, dozens of them.

She shivered, then heard a faint sound. A scratching . . . her fingers spasmed on his chest. "Rats! I can hear them."

"Nonsense." He descended another step, drawing her on. "There's no food here."

She stared at where she knew his head must be. Were rats that logical?

"We're nearly there," he murmured.

"There where?"

"I'm not sure, but keep your voice down."

They reached the bottom of the stairs. He took a longer

step. Reluctantly, she let her hands slide from him. It was unquestionably safer to have greater space between them, yet . . .

Dragging in a breath, she reached out, and found more stone walls. They were in a tiny chamber, barely wider than the stairway. She couldn't tell how much farther it went, but she sensed the answer was not far. The atmosphere was different, the air cool, damp rather than dusty; although she still stood on stone, the smell of earth and leaf mold was strong.

"There's another door here."

She could sense Charles reaching about, examining the walls.

"The lock's an old one, but our luck's held—the key's in it."

She heard him working it. After a moment, he muttered, "This isn't going to be easy."

A good many minutes and a number of muffled curses later, the lock finally groaned and surrendered.

Charles lifted the latch, set his shoulder to the door's edge, and eased it open. In the end, he had to exert considerable force to push it open enough to see out. He looked, tried to place the spot.

Penny stepped nearer. He gave ground so she could look out. "It's the side courtyard, isn't it?"

"Yes." Her voice was full of wonder. She reached through the narrow gap, caught and turned a leaf dangling beside the door. "This is the ivy covering the west wall."

She tried to push the door farther open. It didn't budge. She looked down as did he; the door was blocked across its base by earth and leaves piled outside. He sighed. "Step back."

Ten minutes and considerable effort later, she slipped past him and escaped into the bright sunshine. "Stay close," he hissed as she pushed past.

Eventually, he widened the gap enough to follow her.

Gratefully inhaling fresh air, he walked the few paces to where she waited and turned; side by side, they studied the wall and the door. Even ajar and with the accumulated detritus of decades banked before it, the door was difficult to see, screened by the thick curtain of broad-leafed ivy.

"It's built into the outer wall, isn't it? I never knew it was there."

"If we smooth out the leaves and earth, then rearrange the ivy, there's no reason anyone would guess."

Returning to the door, he retrieved the key, pushed the door closed, locked it, and pocketed the key, then kicked back the disturbed earth and leaves enough to disguise their passage. Stepping back, he studied the ivy; a touch here, a trailing branch untangled there, and the door had disappeared.

He walked back to where Penny stood, still staring.

"Amazing. I wonder if Granville ever knew of it."

He glanced back at the now innocent wall. "I doubt it. Those locks hadn't been used in years."

She looked up at the corner of the building. The master bedchamber didn't have a window facing the courtyard; only lesser bedchambers overlooked it. "I wonder if Nicholas is still up there?"

He'd followed her gaze. "Regardless, I believe we should pay him a visit."

"Hmm . . . I've been thinking."

Always dangerous. He swallowed the words.

"You've told him the outline of your mission. He didn't want me staying at the Abbey, where I'd be talking to you, even though until then he'd been perfectly happy for me to leave him alone here. So perhaps we ought to prod him a bit."

"How?"

"If you want to investigate the smugglers along this coast, a set of excellent maps would be particularly helpful, don't you think?"

"As you know perfectly well, I know this stretch of coast rather better than the back of my hand—I don't need any maps."

She smiled. "Nicholas doesn't know that."

He considered. "Not a bad idea. What exactly did you have in mind?"

"Well, obviously, staying with you, we've been chatting over the breakfast cups and, keen to help with your mission, I've volunteered a set of detailed maps Papa had in his library. We've come to fetch them."

"Excellent." He meant it; he could see just how to make the scene play out to put, not just the wind but a definitely chilly gale, up Nicholas.

Penny nodded. "Let's go." She spun on her heel.

"Wait." When she turned back, he simply said, "Cobwebs."

She blinked, then her gaze trailed over him. "Oh—I didn't notice."

Stepping nearer, she reached up and plucked cobwebby lace from his shoulder, then, scanning up and down, she circled him. He felt her fingers plucking here and there. He waited patiently until she'd worked her way back to stand before him, close, face-to-face, but not focusing on his eyes.

She picked cobwebby bits from the hair framing his face, then rapidly scanned his features. "There. You're done."

"Now for you."

Her eyes flashed up to his. Widened. "If you find a spider anywhere on me, I'll never follow you anywhere again."

He laughed. Plucked a long tendril of soft gray from above her left ear. Briefly met her eyes. "If I find one, I won't tell you." He started to circle her, fingers lightly touching, brushing to free the fine wisps from the velvet of her riding habit. "What is it about spiders and females anyway? They're only tiny insects much smaller than you."

"They have eight legs."

An unarguable fact. He debated asking the obvious, but doubted he'd learn anything. Removing the clinging webs from her skirts took time; she stood silent and still while he bent to the task.

Penny concentrated on breathing, on trying to ignore the way heat seemed to flare wherever he touched. It was nonsense; she couldn't truly feel his fingers through the layers of velvet and linen, just the fleeting pressure, yet . . . every time his fingertips brushed, she felt it to her bones.

Witless, wanton nonsense. Even if he did still desire her,

that was one road she definitely wasn't following him down. The price would be high, far too high for her to contemplate. Her misguided senses would just have to grow inured. Deadened.

His fingers brushed her shoulder, once, twice. Sensation streaked down her arm, across her chest. Tightened her already tight lungs.

Clearly her senses weren't deadened yet.

She glanced at him, watched him peel a long trailing web down off her shoulder. And farther, off the velvet covering the side of her breast.

The thought of him touching, brushing there, flashed into her mind. She quivered, felt her flesh react—closed her eyes and prayed he'd put it down to her fear of spiders.

When she lifted her lids again, he'd circled to face her; she could read nothing beyond concentration in his face as he picked fine wisps from lower on her jacket, then crouched, scanning her skirts.

At last, he rose. She exhaled in relief—then sucked in a breath as his gaze fixed on her face.

"Hold still."

She did, frozen as he raised one hand to the side of her face, fingers lightly tracing as he teased a thread of cobweb from the fine hair at her temple. Then his eyes tracked across her face. With his other hand, he delicately untangled a last fine strand from beside her ear.

His eyes locked with hers. Midnight blue, his gaze was sharp, sure. His hands were still raised; if he moved both an inch inward, he'd be cradling her face.

After a moment, he murmured, "That's it, for now."

Lowering his hands, he stepped back.

She breathed in, quickly turning away to conceal how desperate she was for air. "If we go around to the garden door, it'll look like we've just arrived." She started off as she spoke, embarrassed that after all these years, she still couldn't control her reaction to him, her wayward senses.

He prowled beside her, blessedly silent.

Her stage setting proved inspired; as they walked into the

front hall from the direction of the stables, Nicholas came down the stairs.

She looked up. "Good morning, Nicholas."

"Penelope." Gaining the hall, he nodded in greeting, his gaze shifting immediately to Charles.

Who smiled. "Good morning, Arbry."

"Lostwithiel."

A pregnant pause.

"I've offered Charles the use of Papa's maps," she cheerily announced—anything to bring their masculine eyeing contest to an end. "We've just come to fetch them. They're in the library—we won't disturb you."

Charles hid a grin at her phrasing; she'd already disturbed Nicholas greatly, no matter he concealed it well.

"Maps?" Nicholas hesitated, then asked, "What sort of maps?"

"Of the area." Turning, Penny led the way to the library.

As Charles had hoped, Nicholas followed.

Flinging the double doors of the library wide, Penny sailed through. "Papa had a wonderfully detailed set showing every little stream and inlet all along this stretch of coast. Invaluable if one wishes to scout the area thoroughly."

She made for a bookcase at the end of the long room. "They were somewhere around here, I believe."

Nicholas watched as she crouched, studying the large folios housed on the bottommost shelf. Hanging back, Charles studied his face; Nicholas was reasonably skilled in hiding his thoughts, but rather less adept at hiding his reactions. His pale features, clean-cut and patrician, remained studiously expressionless, yet his eyes, and his hands, were more revealing.

His fingers plucked restlessly at his watch chain as, a frown in his eyes, he tried to decide what to do.

In the end, he glanced at Charles. "I take it there's evidence the smugglers in this area were involved in passing secrets?"

Charles smiled one of his predatory smiles. "Finding the

evidence is what I've been sent here to do, so we can follow it back to the traitor involved."

Was it his imagination, or did Nicholas's pale face grow a touch paler?

Looking down, Nicholas frowned. "If there's no real evidence . . . well, isn't it likely you're simply chasing hares?"

His grin grew intent. "Whitehall expects its minions to be thorough." He glanced at one of the two six-foot-long display cases flanking the library's central carpet. "If after I've shaken every tree and turned every stone, no substantiating evidence is forthcoming, then doubtless it'll be concluded that there was no truth in the information received."

"Here they are." Penny pulled a thick folio from the shelf; cradling it in her arms, she rose and went to the desk.

Laying the heavy tome down, she opened it. Nicholas went to look; Charles followed.

"See?" With one finger, Penny traced the fine lines of the highly detailed hand-drawn maps. "These show every little inlet along the estuary and the nearby coast." She looked up at him, transparently delighted at having found such a valuable tool to aid him. "With these, you can be certain you're not missing any of the landing places."

"Excellent." Reaching out, he turned the book his way, then shut it and picked it up. "Thank you—these will indeed help enormously."

Nicholas's lips had set in a thin line; Charles could easily imagine his chagrin. For a nonlocal seeking to learn about the local smugglers, the maps would be a godsend. Nicholas had had access to them, but hadn't known. He now had to watch as Charles, of all people, tucked the tome under his arm.

Looking at Penny, with his head he indicated the display case he'd glanced at earlier. "Your father's collection seems just the same as I remember it as a child. I'm surprised he never added to it."

Penny met his eyes briefly, played to his lead. "I'm not sure why he stopped collecting." Rounding the desk, she glanced at both cases. "But you're right—it's been, well, decades since he last bought a new one."

Sweeping up to one case, she trailed her fingers across the glass, studying the pillboxes laid neatly on white satin with small cards engraved in her father's precise hand describing each one.

Charles came up beside her. "Perhaps he grew bored with pillboxes."

Nicholas was watching, listening to every word, every inflection, his intensely focused attention the equivalent of a red flag waving in Charles's face. Any notion Nicholas wasn't deeply involved in whatever scheme had been operating was untenable. He had been involved, and was now intent on ensuring Charles did not find the evidence he was seeking.

"Perhaps." Penny shrugged, then turned to Nicholas. "Now we've found the maps, we won't disturb you further, Nicholas."

Nicholas blinked, then seemed to shake himself. "Why— ah, surely you'll stay for tea. Take some refreshment?"

"No, no!" Penny waved aside the invitation. "Thank you, but no. By the time we ride back to the Abbey it'll be time for luncheon."

She glanced at Charles, a question in her eyes. He smiled approvingly, adding just a hint of wicked anticipation— enough, he hoped, to prick Nicholas.

From the way Nicholas's jaw set, he succeeded.

Nicholas rather stiffly took his leave of them. Together, they left the house.

It was indeed time for luncheon when they clattered back into the Abbey stable yard. Charles's grooms came running. Penny slid from her saddle without waiting to be lifted down; handing the reins to a groom, she joined Charles, and they started across the gently rising lawn toward the house.

"That went well!" Head up, she savored the exhilaration still singing through her veins. They hadn't talked on their journey home, just exchanged triumphant smiles, and ridden, laughing, before the wind.

"We've certainly given Nicholas a few things to think about." The book of maps under his arm, Charles paced beside her.

"He was put out about the maps—and your questions about the pillboxes were inspired. He was hanging on every word."

"With luck, he'll accept that you—and thus I—have no knowledge of the pillboxes hidden in the priest hole."

She frowned. "Why didn't you want him knowing we knew?"

"Because they're the proof—the irrefutable evidence—that some presently inexplicable but clandestine relationship has existed between the French and your family's menfolk for decades. I'd rather they remained where they are, accessible should we need them."

She glanced at him. "Decades?"

He met her eyes, baldly reiterated, "Decades. You counted the boxes—how many were there?"

"Sixty-four."

"If we assume every piece of information was paid for with a pillbox, and I checked—most are the work of French jewelers—then given the rate at which sufficiently valuable information would crop up to be passed, it would take something like thirty years to amass sixty-four boxes."

"Oh." The knowledge cast a pall on the day, leaving her feeling as if clouds had covered the sun.

"Do you still want to help me?"

She looked up to see Charles regarding her, understanding very clear in his midnight eyes. She stared into them for a moment, then looked ahead. "Yes. I have to."

She didn't need to explain. He nodded, and they walked on, passing beneath the spreading branches of the huge oaks bordering the south lawn, the side door their goal.

Despite the confirmation that it wasn't only Granville but her father, too, who'd been involved in the traitorous scheme, she still felt curiously buoyed by their success, minor though it had been.

That morning, for the first time in she couldn't remember when, she'd shared fears and concerns with someone she trusted, someone who understood. Just being able to air such thoughts had been a catharsis in itself.

As for her specific concern, while the problem hadn't gone away, its weight had lessened, lifted in part from her shoulders—truly shared. She now felt immeasurably more confident that whatever the truth was, Elaine, her half sisters, and she would be safe. Shielded as far as it was possible to be.

Whatever was going on would be properly and appropriately dealt with; actively contributing to that end would help soothe her lacerated family pride.

Forty hours before, she'd been lost and uncertain; now she felt confident, all because she'd joined forces with Charles.

She glanced at him.

He caught her gaze. Arched a brow. "What?"

She was tempted to look away; instead, she held his gaze as she said, "It seems I made the right choice in confiding in you."

Three heartbeats passed; he didn't release her gaze.

Then he caught her hand, halted, waited until she did the same, then smoothly drew her to him.

All the way to him. He bent his head and kissed her.

She hadn't been expecting it—her lungs locked, her senses froze, her very heart seemed to stop . . . but he'd kissed her before. Even starved of breath and with her senses reeling, she recognized the feel of his lips against hers.

Clung to the sensation. Found memories pouring in. Found reassurance in the familiar, no matter that it had been years.

She found herself drifting on a familiar tide, one of subtle warmth, simple pleasure, gentle waves of delight.

Then . . . something changed.

He shifted closer, angled his head, and what had started as a simple exchange became more—much more. More complex, more complicated, infinitely more absorbing. His lips moved on hers, compelling, hungry but not ravenous, not frightening in any way. He supped, sipped, as if needing to explore her lips again, needing to taste them. He'd always excelled at kissing, but now . . . it seemed as if he felt the leaping of her heart, felt and understood the sudden up-welling of yearning that, entirely unbidden, totally against her will, filled her soul.

She kissed him back—raised her free hand to his shoulder and pressed her lips to his. She hadn't meant to, yet was in-capable of denying not him but herself. It had been a long time since she'd kissed any man, but it wasn't only that that impelled her to want and take what he offered.

Just a kiss, or so it seemed. No reason not to part her lips and invite him in, as she had so long ago . . .

He accepted, not as if he took her offer for granted, yet not as if he'd forgotten their past either. The languid surge of his tongue against hers made her bones melt. What followed demonstrated beyond all doubt that he'd learned volumes in the years since they'd last indulged, acquired skills and tal-ents far beyond those he'd had.

Lips, tongues, and hot, wet pleasure; her starved senses whirled, giddily luxuriating as she savored the long-forgotten delight. Let him and the moment be reason enough.

When he lifted his head with a reluctance she knew wasn't feigned—a reluctance echoed in her veins—she was breathless, her heart thudding in her throat, one hand still locked in his, the other fisted in his lapel as she leaned close to boneless against him.

Just a kiss, and he could still reduce her to that nearly swooning state where nothing in the world seemed to matter—just them, and what they made each other feel.

She drew a shaky breath, blinked up at him. "Why did you do that?"

His midnight gaze roamed her face, then settled on her eyes. He studied them before replying, "Because I wanted to. Because I've been wanting to since the first moment I saw you again."

She searched his eyes; he wasn't lying, prevaricating, or evading. His simple words were the simple truth.

Clearing her throat, she eased back. Conscious of the whirlpool of potent sensuality that lurked beneath his surface, and hers, too. That had always been her problem with him; the desire that burned so readily between them had never been his alone. She drew in another breath, felt her wits steady. "That wasn't very wise."

His shoulders lifted in a Gallic shrug. He let her step away, but retained his hold on her hand; he caught her gaze. "When were we ever wise?"

A valid point, one she wasn't about to attempt to answer.

When she said nothing more, he turned her, and they walked on to the house, her father's book of maps under his arm, her hand still locked in his.

IMMEDIATELY AFTER LUNCH WAS OVER, CHARLES INVOKED the specter of estate business and took refuge in his study. *He* was the one who now needed time to think.

His steward, Matthews, had left various documents prominently displayed on his desk; he forced himself to attend to the most urgent, but left all the rest. Leaning back in his chair, he stared at the volume of maps he'd carried in. Abruptly, he swiveled the chair so its back was to the desk, and he was facing the window and the undemanding view.

He had to find his mental footing, determine where he was and where he wanted to be—and then work out how to get there. Not, as he'd supposed, solely in terms of his investigation, but, it now seemed, with his personal quest, too.

He'd arrived at the Abbey three days ago with two goals before him, both needing to be urgently addressed—one professional goal, his investigation, and his personal goal, his search for a wife. It had been unsettling to discover that his way forward with *both* involved Penny.

Of all the potential ladies in the ton, he hadn't considered her, because he hadn't believed *she* would consider *him.* He'd always known that she *could* be his wife, that she could fill all aspects of the position without effort—*if* she would. He hadn't imagined after the way they'd parted thirteen years ago that she might, but after kissing her an hour ago, he now knew beyond question that the possibility was there, and he wasn't about to pass up the chance of turning that possibility into reality.

Possibility. He wouldn't, yet, rate it as more. From the moment he'd stepped close to her in the upstairs corridor at midnight, he'd been aware of her response to him, that it was as it had been all those years ago—intense, immediate, always there. Over the past days, he'd known every time her senses had flared; he wasn't sure she knew how acutely his senses spiked at her reaction, how sensually attuned to her he was.

Yet none knew better than he and she that that connection wasn't, of itself, enough. It hadn't been years ago; he doubted it would be now.

He needed to build on it, to pursue it and her, explore what lay between them, what might evolve from that, and where it might lead them.

In between pursuing his investigation.

That wasn't very wise. Indeed. She remained his most direct link to the Selbornes' scheme; he now had to deal with her on two different levels simultaneously, juggling the investigation and his personal pursuit of her.

Yet he couldn't regret kissing her; he'd had to learn whether the possibility was there. He'd been tempted to kiss her in the courtyard at Wallingham, but it hadn't been the right time or place. He'd pulled back, but when on their way from the stables she'd smiled at him and acknowledged she'd been right to trust him with her family's secret, he'd been buoyed and encouraged enough to seize the moment, to learn if she would trust him in that other sphere, too. Whether there was a chance he could mend their fences even if he wasn't sure what had flattened them in the first place.

Such uncertainty, unfortunately, was his norm with her. He was an expert with women; he'd studied them for years, understood their minds, and was adept at managing them—all except Penny. She . . . he was never sure how to deal with her, had never succeeded in managing her, and had long ago given up attempting to manipulate her—the result had never been worth the price. For one of his ilk, such complete and utter failure with a woman was hard to stomach, and somewhat unnerving; he was always alert and watchful with her.

But that kiss had answered his question. Not only had she allowed him to kiss her, she'd enjoyed it and kissed him back, deliberately and considerably prolonging the interlude.

Well and good. He'd cleared the first hurdle, but he knew her too well to presume too much. All he'd gained was a chance to progress to the next stage, to determine how real the possibility that she might consent to be his wife was, how real his chance to convert wish into fact.

He sat staring unseeing out of the window while the clock on the mantelpiece ticked on; eventually, its chiming drew him back, reminding him of the other challenge requiring his attention.

Swinging back to his desk, he turned his mind to his mission. There, at least, the way forward was clear. The information Caudel, an exposed villain, had divulged before he'd died seemed in essence correct; it was now up to him, Charles, to ferret out the details and hand them over to Dalziel. He was very good at ferreting; one way or another, he'd get to the bottom of the Selbornes' scheme.

First things first. Reaching for the book of maps, he set it on his blotter and opened it.

Penny wandered the gardens, thinking, to her considerable distraction reliving those minutes on the lawn under the trees. Those minutes she'd spent in Charles's arms. She could still feel his lips on hers, still feel the effects of the kiss; it had definitely not been a wise indulgence.

On the other hand, it had been fated to happen; that elemental attraction she recognized from long ago had been steadily building over the past days and would inevitably have led to the same culmination, somewhere, sometime. He'd been right to choose an unthreatening setting. Now he'd kissed her and his curiosity—if she was truthful *both* their curiosities—had been appeased and satisfied, presumably that would be the end of it.

She paused, frowning at a rosebush. It wouldn't, of course, be the end of her susceptibility—that, she'd realized, was an affliction for life—but presumably they could now put their mutual attraction behind them, ignore it, or at least accord it no importance. That undoubtedly was the best way forward; that was what she would do.

His investigation had only just commenced; as she intended to be beside him throughout, getting that kiss out of the way had been a good thing.

She returned to the parlor. When Charles didn't reappear, she muttered an oath, then rang for tea; when Filchett entered with the tray, she told him to follow her and headed for the study. She knocked once, barely waited for Charles's "Come" before opening the door and walking in. "It's time for tea."

He looked up, met her gaze, paused as if considering his response.

Blithely waving Filchett to the desk, she sat in one of the chairs before it. She heard Charles's half-stifled sigh as he set down his pen and shut her father's book to make room for the tray.

He'd been composing some list; that much she'd seen. She waited until Filchett withdrew. Sitting forward, she picked up the pot and poured. "What have you decided?"

If he thought she was going to let him deal her out of this game, he was mistaken. Lifting her cup from the tray, she sat back.

He looked at her, then picked up his cup and saucer. "My ex-commander's focus is on identifying who in the ministry handed your father and Granville the information we're assuming they traded for the pillboxes. Making a case against your father or Granville won't interest him; not only are they dead, but they're also clearly not the prime instigators of the scheme. Your father never had access to government secrets; he remained in the country most of his life—no self-respecting French agent would have even considered approaching him."

"You think Amberly was the instigator."

He sipped his tea, nodded. "Originally, yes. You said your father started collecting pillboxes while staying with Amberly in Paris. However, Amberly retired seven years ago, and the passage of information continued until recently."

"So the baton, as it were, was passed from father to son, both in Amberly's case as well as Papa's?"

"It fits. Especially with dear Nicholas hot-footing it down here just as I appear on the scene."

She frowned. "Could he have heard you were coming to investigate?"

"It's possible." He set down his cup. "While Dalziel takes these matters seriously, not everyone in the ministries is so inclined. Many think that now the war is over, secrecy isn't an issue anymore."

"Hmm . . ." After a moment, she refocused on his face. "So what now?"

"Now . . . even though the pillboxes' existence confirms that some traffic, presumably in secrets, occurred with the French, they don't implicate Nicholas or Amberly, no matter that Nicholas clearly knows of them. I need evidence that specifically ties Amberly or Nicholas to the traffic of Foreign Office secrets—how I'm to get that is what I'm presently wrestling with."

She glanced pointedly at his list. "You've decided on something."

He hesitated, then reluctantly said, "I've contacts of my own with the local smuggling gangs—as you so perspicaciously noticed, I've used them on and off over the years." Picking up his pen, he toyed with it. "I can see two reasons for Nicholas behaving as he is—either he's trying to ensure that Granville's and therefore his tracks remain covered, or, just possibly, he believes there might be some new contact made, or at least some reason he might again need to use the smugglers as a conduit to the French. Either way, he's out there asking questions." His lips curved, not in a smile. "I'm considering whether I should arrange for him to receive some answers."

"Such as what?"

"I won't know until I get a better idea of what he's been asking. Is he really setting himself up as Granville's active replacement, or is he merely trawling to learn which group Granville used for running the secrets so he'll know who has to be kept quiet?"

She shook her head. "I haven't heard enough to say." Leaning forward, setting her elbow on the desk, she propped her chin in her hand.

Charles watched her face as she thought, watched her thoughts flow through her expressive eyes.

"Given we're certain Granville and Nicholas were in this hand in glove, wouldn't Granville have told Nicholas which group he used?"

He shook his head. "Secrecy is a byword among the fraternity. Granville played at being a smuggler for a good many years; he would have absorbed that lesson well. Unless there was some exceptionally strong reason—and I can't see what it might be—I seriously doubt telling Amberly or Nicholas who his smuggling friends were would have entered Granville's head."

She grimaced. "That sounds right. He was as close as a clam over anything to do with smuggling." Her gaze dropped to his list. "So what have you written there?"

He had to smile, even though the message she was sending his way—that she wasn't going to let him pat her on the head and tell her to go and embroider—wasn't one he was happy about. "It's a list of the gangs that might have been involved. I'll need to contact them myself. They'll hear soon enough why I'm here—I need to make clear that neither I nor the government has any interest in them but only in what they can tell me."

"What if you run into Nicholas?"

"I won't. You said he visited Polruan two nights ago—I'll start there."

"When? Tonight?"

No point trying to prevaricate. "I'll ride down after dinner. If they ran goods last night, they should be in the Duck and Drake this evening."

She nodded; he couldn't tell what she was thinking.

"Tell me about Amberly—how frequently did your father and he meet?"

She thought, then answered, telling him little he hadn't already surmised. But his questions served to distract her. After ten minutes of steady inquisition, she stirred. "I'll take the tray—I want to speak to Mrs. Slattery."

He rose and held the door for her. She departed with the air of a lady with her mind on domestic concerns. Closing the door, he paused, then returned to his desk and his plans.

They met again over dinner; he came prepared with a stock of friendly familial inquiries designed to keep her mind far away from his evening appointment in Polruan. In that, he thought he succeeded; when they rose from the table, she retired for the evening, electing to go straight to her chamber. She didn't even mention his planned excursion; he wondered if it had slipped her mind.

He returned to his study to read through the report he'd penned for Dalziel. He'd thought long and hard, but in the end he'd named names, accurately setting down all he'd learned thus far. Even more than his six collegues from the Bastion Club, he'd entrusted his life to Dalziel's discretion for thirteen years; Dalziel had never let him down.

Even though they'd yet to solve the riddle of who exactly Dalziel was, whoever he was he was one of them—a nobleman with the same sense of honor, the same attitude toward protecting the weak and innocent. Penny and Elaine and her daughters stood in no danger from Dalziel.

Sealing the letter, he addressed it, then rose. The clock on the mantelpiece chimed ten o'clock. Opening the study door, he called Cassius and Brutus from their sprawl before the fire; stretching, grumbling, they clambered up and obeyed.

Shutting the door, he strolled to the front hall, dropped his letter on Filchett's salver on the sideboard, then went upstairs, the hounds at his heels.

* * *

Ten minutes later, dressed to ride, he opened the garden door, stepped outside, softly closed the door, and turned for the stables.

He'd taken three strides before the shadow glimpsed at the edge of his vision registered. He halted, swore softly, then, hands rising to his hips, swung around to face Penny. Clad once more in breeches, boots, and riding jacket, with a soft-brimmed hat cocked over her brow, she'd been leaning against the wall a yard from the door—waiting.

So much for his successful distraction.

He set his jaw. "You can't come."

The moon sailed free tonight; she met his eyes. "Why not?"

"You're a lady. Ladies don't frequent the Duck and Drake."

She straightened from the wall, shrugged. "You'll be there—I'll be perfectly safe."

He watched her tug on her gloves. "I'm not taking you with me."

Lifting her head, she looked at him. "I'll follow you, then."

With an exasperated hiss, he dropped his head back and looked up into a nearly cloudless sky. She knew the area almost as well as he did; with the moon shining down, she could follow him easily, and in any case she knew his destination—because he'd been idiot enough to tell her!

"All right!" He looked at her again, scanned her attire, shook his head. "You're never going to pass for a male."

"It's not a disguise." She smiled—a light, relaxed smile as if she'd never doubted his capitulation—and fell in beside him as he turned and strode for the stables. "Everyone in Polruan knows who I am. They know it's easier to ride astride than sidesaddle around here, and they're not the sort to be scandalized by my wearing breeches. They'll barely notice."

He glanced down at her long legs, booted to the knee, sleek thighs occasionally visible when the material of her breeches drew taut, and managed not to snort. The smugglers of Polruan were no more blind than he.

Exercising rigid control, he managed to keep his mind from contemplating her anatomy—any part of it—while he saddled their horses, then tossed her up to her saddle. On her mare, she trotted out of the stable beside him. Inwardly shaking his head—how *had* he let this happen?—he set course south, over the moonlit fields to Polruan.

A small fishing village situated on the easterly head of the Fowey estuary, Polruan consisted of little more than a cluster of tiny cottages and the obligatory tavern in which the men of the village, virtually all fishermen, usually spent their evenings, at least when they weren't out running some illicit cargo through the breakers just east of the estuary mouth.

Although the area was riddled with smuggling gangs, each had its own patch, its own favored inlets and coves. While the Fowey Gallants, who had taken their name from the local pirate raiders who'd been the bane of the French coastal towns throughout the Hundred Years War, were the largest and best organized gang in the area, Charles suspected Granville might have used one of the smaller gangs for making contact with the French.

As Penny had said, Granville hadn't been a fool. The fewer people who knew anything of his business, the better.

They reached the Duck and Drake and dismounted. Charles gave their horses to a towheaded lad from the crude stable beside the tavern. Returning to where Penny waited near the door, he yanked her hat low. A floppy, wide-brimmed affair sporting a pheasant's feather, it would pass for a man's hunting hat at first glance. "Keep your head down and do exactly as I say."

She muttered something unintelligible; he didn't think it was a compliment. Grasping her elbow, he opened the door, swiftly glanced around as he propelled her over the threshold. Giving thanks for the poor light, he steered her to an unoccupied table and benches in one corner.

He released her. "Slide in."

She did. As he followed, forcing her along the bench into the corner, she murmured, "Am I allowed to speak?"

"No." He looked around, noting familiar faces, nodding to two. He glanced at her. "Wait here—keep your head down. I'll be back in a moment."

Rising, he went to the bar, a simple wooden counter balanced atop two old kegs. He nodded to the barkeep, who recognized him; taciturn but friendly, the man murmured a "m'lord" and drew the two pints he requested.

Charles didn't bother chatting—that wasn't how things were done, how business was conducted with the gentlemen.

The barkeep thumped two frothing tankards on the counter. Charles tossed him some coins and a nod, picked up the tankards, and walked back to the corner table. Setting down the tankards, he slid in beside Penny, pushing one tankard her way. Raising the other, he sipped, then let his gaze wander the room. And settled to wait.

Penny, gaze still dutifully cast down, peered into the tankard before her. She assumed it was the local ale; it had a foamy froth on top. Mentally shrugging, using both hands she lifted the tankard and sipped.

Choked. Spluttered. Coughing, she put the tankard down the instant before Charles thumped her back.

Blinking rapidly, clearing her watering eyes, she met his. "That's . . . *disgusting*."

He rolled his eyes. "It was only supposed to be for show."

"Oh." She wondered if there was any other drink one could order in a tavern, but decided against asking. They were sitting shoulder to shoulder; she could feel a faint tension in him, even though outwardly he appeared relaxed.

He said nothing, simply drank the vile brew, and in between stared into his tankard, or into space.

She pretended to sip, and wished something would happen.

More than ten minutes dragged by, then two burly fishermen at the table before the fire nodded to their friends and rose. Straightening, the pair studied Charles and her, then slowly came their way.

Watching from beneath the brim of her hat, Penny kicked Charles's ankle.

He kicked her back. Since he'd been staring into his ale for the past several minutes, she cast him a narrow-eyed glare.

The fishermen paused by the bench on the other side of the table.

"Evening, Master Charles—ah, no, that'd be m'lord now, I reckon."

Charles looked up, his expression easy, and returned the men's nods. "Shep. Seth. How's buisness?"

Both men grinned, showing gaps in yellowed teeth.

"Fair to middling. Can't complain." Shep raised his brows. "We was wondering if you was after anything special-like?"

Charles waved them to sit, simultaneously shifting sideways, squashing Penny farther into the shadows of the corner. She moved as far as she could, but he crowded her, his hip and thigh against hers, trapping her, his shoulder partially screening her even from the men settling on the bench opposite.

Both had thus far rather pointedly kept their gazes from her.

Charles signaled the barkeep, who came, wiping his hands on his apron. Charles ordered three more pints; Seth and Shep were clearly pleased.

He waited until the tankards were delivered and Seth and Shep had taken a long draft before saying, "You'll hear soon enough for it's no secret. I'm down here looking for information on meetings Granville Selborne had with the French. Before I go on, I should explain that *I* was sent to ask the questions because the government has no interest in anyone who might have helped Granville meet the French. All the bods in Whitehall want is to know how he did it, anything I can learn about who he met, and about any English gentleman who might have been Granville's associate in such matters."

Both Seth and Shep held Charles's gaze, then both lifted their tankards again. As they lowered them, they exchanged a sidelong glance. Then Seth, older and sitting more or less opposite Penny, said in his slow, ponderous way, "That'd be Master Granville as was killed at Waterloo."

The implication was clear; neither Shep nor Seth wanted to speak ill of the dead, especially one who had died on that bloody field.

Especially with her sitting there; she was perfectly sure they knew who she was.

She drew in a breath, held it, and looked up. "Yes, that's right. Granville, my brother."

Her voice, so much lighter and clearer than the men's deep rumbles, startled them. Both Seth and Shep blinked at her.

Beside her, she felt Charles's muscles turn to steel.

She could almost hear his teeth grinding, but both Shep and Seth deferentially bobbed their heads to her.

"Lady Penelope. Thought as it was you."

"We're right sorry about Granville—he was a good 'un. A real lad."

She found a smile, lowered her voice. "Indeed. But we—Lord Charles and I—need to know what Granville was up to. It's quite important, you see."

Shep and Seth studied her, looked at each other, then Seth nodded. "As it's you asking, m'lady, I guess it'd be all right." He nodded to Charles. "Beggin' your pardon, m'lord, but it wouldn't seem right otherways."

Charles waved aside the comment. "I quite understand."

Only she noticed how clipped his accents had become. "So what can you tell us?" she prompted.

"Well, let's see." With considerable qualification, the two described how on several occasions over a period of years, Granville had asked them to take him out to meet with a lugger.

"Never would come close, but it always seemed the same ship." Shep's gaze had grown distant. "We assumed she was French, but we thought as how she must sail for those on the same side as us—Frenchies who didn't like Old Boney. Howsoever, we never did see who Master Granville met with—he'd take the dinghy out, and the man he met would do the same. They'd meet on the waves like, alone, each in his own boat."

"How often?" Charles asked.

"Not so often—maybe once a year."

"Nah—not so often as that. P'raps once in two."

"Aye." Shep nodded. "Reckon you're right."

"Did he ever carry anything to give to the person he met?"

"Naught but once. I did see him hand over a packet, one time."

"Letters?"

"Something like that. Most often, though, he just talked."

"Speaking of talking . . ." Shep and Seth exchanged glances, then Shep continued, "That other one—the new lordling up to the Hall. He's been asking after much the same, wanting to know who Master Granville used to deal with hereabouts. Who took him to sea."

"Did you tell him what you've just told us?" Charles asked.

Seth blinked. " 'Course not. He's not one of us, is he? We couldn't rightly figure why he needed to know." Seth ducked his head at Penny. "Didn't feel it was our place, what with the young master being dead and all."

Penny smiled. "That was well-done of you. There's no reason for the gentleman to know anything about Granville's business."

"Aye." Shep nodded. "So we thought."

Charles asked the last question he could think of. "Do you know if Granville ever went out with any of the other gangs?"

"Oh, aye!" Shep and Seth both grinned widely. "A real lad for the life, was Master Granville. Don't reckon there was a gang anywhere about the estuary he didn't run with at least a time or two."

Penny smiled, albeit weakly. Charles treated Seth and Shep to another round of ale; with good wishes all around, he rose, tugged Penny to her feet, and steered her outside.

"I can't believe it!" She and Charles, once more mounted, were trotting out of Polruan. "It sounds like we're going to have to speak with every single smuggling gang." After a moment, she observed, "That might not be a bad thing—surely someone must know more than the Polruan crew."

"I wouldn't wager on it." Charles glanced at her. "The operation seems to have been well organized, and don't forget, the procedures must have been set up by your father long before Granville got involved."

He purposely hadn't asked if the previous earl had been known to join the smuggling gangs; none knew better than he that those of the local aristocracy who ran with the gentlemen as lads had only to ask to be accommodated. On both occasions he'd had to rush home, the Fowey Gallants had answered his call with an alacrity he'd found disarming. They'd risked the might of the French navy to pick him up, and then later return him to Brittany, purely because they considered him one of their own and he'd asked. None of which he needed to explain to Penny; she nodded and trotted on.

Once they were past the last cottages, he urged Domino into a canter. On her mare, Penny kept pace.

They'd covered just over a mile when he slowed. Penny followed suit, glancing at him inquiringly; he signaled her to silence, and to follow as he turned off the lane onto a narrow track. A little way along, he veered into a clearing, halted, and dismounted. Stopping her mare, Penny kicked free of her stirrups, swung her leg over the pommel, and slid to the ground. She led the mare over to the tree to which he was tying Domino's reins.

"Where are we?" she whispered, glancing around as she secured the mare alongside.

He looked at her. Instinct insisted he leave her with the horses, but he wasn't sure that was safe—at least not any safer than taking her with him. On top of that, it was likely the reservations of the Polruan crew over speaking of the dead would surface there, too.

It hadn't occurred to him, but her presence had loosened tongues far faster than his own persuasions would have.

He mentally sighed and reached for her hand. "We're near the Bodinnick smugglers' meeting place." Bodinnick was a hamlet and didn't boast a tavern; the fishermen made do with an establishement of their own. "I hadn't intended stopping here, but as we apparently have to interview all the gangs, then as we're down this way . . ."

Turning, he strode back to the track, slowing when she hissed at him.

She came up close, just behind his shoulder; her proximity made him feel a fraction easier on one hand, rather more tense on the other. Gritting his teeth, he grasped her hand more firmly and led her on to the crude hut almost hidden by bushes that the Bodinnick smugglers had built.

He marched directly to the plank door and rapped, a complicated succession of taps and pauses. The instant he'd finished, the door was opened; a ruddy-looking seaman stared out at them.

"My lord! Why, we're honored! And who . . ." Johnny's eyes widened.

"Never mind, Johnny—just let us in, and you'll learn all soon enough."

Johnny stepped back, waving them in with a flourish, his gaze riveted on Penny as she followed Charles across the threshold.

He scanned the faces that turned to stare at them. Many were familiar; the Bodinnick gang was one of the smaller crews in the area, but he'd sailed with them often enough in his reckless youth.

The procedure was the same as in Polruan; he donated generously to their drinking fund, accepted a mug, then told them of his mission. They, too, recognized Penny; bobbing their heads deferentially, they answered his questions in much the same way.

Yes, Granville had on occasion asked them to take him out to meet with a specific lugger that had stood well out in the Channel. The tale was the same; he'd always rowed out to meet a man who had rowed out from the lugger. In their case, no one could recall Granville handing any item over.

They also confirmed that Nicholas had contacted them in much the same way he had the Polruan crew.

"Setting hisself up as Master Granville's replacement, insistent about it, too. Not that we've any contacts to give him, o'course, nor likely to have. 'Twas Master Granville himself always had things set up."

They left having ensured Nicholas would learn nothing, but also having learned that there was nothing more to know.

Once they'd remounted, Penny using a fallen log to clamber up into her saddle, Charles headed for the Abbey. He was barely conscious of the fields they passed, his mind revolving about one simple fact.

They clattered into his stable yard in the dead of night. His stableman looked out; Charles called a greeting and waved him back to bed. Pausing to light a lamp left hanging beside the stable door, he led Domino into the stable; Penny followed, leading her mare.

The horses were housed in neighboring stalls; Charles set the lamp on a hook dangling from a roof beam, and they set to work. Penny unsaddled, as adept as he, but when she hefted her saddle onto the dividing wall between the stalls, she paused and caught his eye.

"How was it organized? Granville went out with the smuggling gangs, and the lugger was waiting. How did it know to be there?"

He held her gaze, then nodded. It was precisely the question he'd been wrestling with. "There has to be someone—someone who carried a message, or some way, some manner, some route through which Granville communicated with the French. We haven't found it yet."

Grabbing a handful of fresh straw, Penny turned away to brush down the mare. "So we'll have to keep looking."

He hesitated, but then said, "Yes." He wasn't going to stomach her "we," but he'd fight that battle when he came to it.

They finished with their mounts. He went to help her shut the stall door. She headed out of the stall; the mare shifted, catching Penny with her rump, propelling her forward—into his arms. Into him.

He caught her against him, body to body, saw in the lamplight her eyes flare wide. Heard the hitch as her breathing suspended. Sensed surprise drown beneath a wave of sensual awareness so acute she quivered.

Her shoulder was angled to his chest, his left hand spread over her back, fingers curving around her side, his right splayed over her waist. He only had to juggle her and she would be in his arms, knew that if he did, she'd look up—and their lips would be only inches apart.

He hauled in a breath and found it almost painful. Gritting his teeth, jaw clenched, he steadied her on her feet and forced his hands from her, forced himself to set her aside and give his attention to securing the stall door.

He didn't—couldn't—risk meeting her eyes. With any other woman, he'd have made some rakish comment, turned the whole off with a wicked smile. With her, he was too busy subduing his own reaction, quelling his own impulses, to worry about soothing hers.

Not in the stable. That would be far too reminiscent, too foolhardily dangerous. If he wanted to persuade her to look his way again, that was precisely the sort of misstep he didn't need.

With the door safely shut, he reached up and unhooked the lamp; she'd already turned and was ahead of him, walking out of the stable. He followed, dousing the lamp and replacing it. Crossing to the well in the middle of the yard, he took the pump handle she yielded without a word and wielded it so she could wash her hands.

He did the same, then they set off once more to walk side by side up the grassed slope to the house.

Except it was after midnight.

Except he'd kissed her the last time they'd walked this way under the spreading branches of the oaks.

She strode briskly along, sparing not a glance for him.

He walked alongside and said nothing; he didn't even try to take her hand.

Penny noted that last and told herself she was glad. Indeed, now she thought of it, she couldn't imagine why she'd allowed him to claim her hand over the past days, although of course he never asked. Far better they preserve a reasonable distance—witness that heart-stopping moment in the stable. She really didn't need to dwell on how it felt to be in his arms, or her apparently ineradicable desire to experience such moments.

When it came to Charles, her senses were beyond her control. They had been for over a decade, and demonstrably still were, no matter how much she'd convinced herself otherwise. The best she could hope for was to starve them into submission, or if not that, then at least into a weakened state.

The oaks neared, the shadows beneath them dense.

It wasn't the darkness that tightened her nerves.

She walked steadily on, no suggestive hitch in her stride, her senses at full stretch . . . but he made not the slightest move to reach for her, to halt her.

He didn't even speak.

As they emerged from the shadows and approached the garden door, she quietly exhaled. Relaxed at least as far as she was able with him by her side. Just because he'd kissed her, almost certainly impelled by some typical male notion over seeing what it would be like after all these years, that didn't mean he'd want to kiss her again. Her senses might be alive, her nerves taut with expectation, but he, thankfully, couldn't know that.

He opened the door, held it for her, then followed her in.

The house had many long windows; most were left uncurtained, spilling swaths of moonlight across corridors and into halls. Even the wide staircase was awash in shimmering light, tinted here and there by the stained glass of the central window.

Peace and solidity enfolded her, unraveling her knotted nerves, soothing away her tension. Reaching the top of the stairs, she stepped into the long gallery. She walked a few paces, then halted in a patch of moonlight fractured into shifting splashes of shadow and light by a tree beyond the window. The master suite lay in the central wing; Charles and she should part company. She turned to face him.

He'd prowled in her wake; he halted with a bare foot between them.

She raised her eyes to his face, intending to issue a cool, calm, controlled "good night." Instead, her eyes locked with his, dark, impossible to read in the shadows, yet not impossible to know. To feel.

To realize that as she often did, often had, she'd misread him.

He did want to kiss her again—fully intended to kiss her again.

She knew it beyond doubt when his gaze lowered to her lips.

Knew when hers lowered to his that she should protest.

She knew when his hands rose, slowly, unhurriedly—giving her plenty of time to react if she wished—just what he was going to do.

Knew it wasn't wise. Knew she shouldn't allow it.

Yet she did nothing beyond catch her breath when his hands touched, so achingly gentle for such powerful hands, then cradled her face. Slowly raising it, tipping it up so he could lower his head and close his lips over hers.

From the first touch, she was lost. She didn't want, yet she did. She told herself it was confusion that made her hesitate, held her back from calling a halt to this madness.

All lies.

It was fascination, plain and simple, a fascination she'd never grown out of, and perhaps, God help her, never would.

His lips moved on hers, bold, wickedly sure; her lips parted, by her command or his she didn't know. Didn't care. His tongue surged over hers, and she shivered. Her hand touched the back of one of his; she wasn't even aware she'd raised it.

Was barely aware when he angled his head, deepening the kiss, and one hand drifted from her face to slide around her waist and draw her—slowly, deliberately—to him.

She went, hungry and wanting, while some distant remnant of sanity cursed and swore. Yet it was she who was cursed, condemned always to feel this madness, this welling tide of unquenchable desire that he and only he evoked, and that he and only he, it seemed, had any ability to slake.

Only with him did she feel this way, did her senses whirl, her wits melt away. Only with him did her bones turn to water while heat rose and beat under her skin.

And he knew.

She would have given a great deal to keep the knowledge from him, but even as the remaining vestige of her consciousness noted that his skills had developed considerably over the years, she was aware that behind his controlled hunger, behind the skillfully woven net of desire he cast over her, he was watchful and intent.

He'd known thirteen years ago that she had been his; as his hands slid beneath her coat and fastened about her waist, and he drew her flush against him, it was abundantly clear he knew she still was.

Her breath was long gone; arms twined about his neck, she clung to their kiss as her breasts pressed against the hard planes of his chest, as his long fingers curved about her hips and brought them flush against his thighs.

He moved against her, suggestive, seductive. The feel of his body against hers, all masculine strength, reined passion, and wickedly flagrant desire, flung open a door she'd closed, bolted, and thought rusted shut years ago.

A living ache flooded her, deeper than she recalled, more powerful, more compelling.

She'd been so young then, just sixteeen; what she'd then deemed frighteningly urgent was, she now realized, a mere cipher compared to the compulsion she was capable of feeling, of the sheer wanting that rose and raged through her now.

Oh, God! She tried to pull back, to at least catch her breath—to think.

Only to discover he'd backed her against the wall. With lips and tongue he'd captured her mouth; he pressed deeper and feasted, lured her further, swept her into deeper waters until she had to cling to him to survive. Until her very life seemed to depend on it.

Until nothing else mattered. Until there was no life beyond the circle of their arms.

She felt unbearably grateful, unbearably eager when she felt his hand between them slipping free the buttons that closed her shirt. Then he pushed the halves apart, with practiced flicks of his long fingers stripped away her chemise and set his palm to her naked breast.

Her senses swooned. Her knees buckled.

His other hand slid lower, cupping her bottom, supporting her. Absently fondling as with knowing fingers he caressed her breast, captured her nipple, gently rolled, tweaked, then soothed.

Within seconds, her senses had totally fractured, unable to fix, to focus on anything, overwhelmed by the sensations of his mouth steadily plundering hers, heated and commanding, of his hand and fingers artfully pleasuring her breasts, already swollen and aching, of his other hand subtly exploring, molding her to him, of the heady, even more potent reality of his hard, heavy, aroused body against hers, surrounding hers.

Making her feel fragile, defenseless—so achingly vulnerable.

No—not again.

She dropped her hands to his shoulders, sank her fingers in, pushed back, and pushed him away.

He acquiesced, letting her break from the kiss. Letting her put a few inches between their lips, enough for her to drag in a breath and gasp, "Charles—no."

For five heartbeats, he said nothing, his eyes midnight pools behind his long lashes. She realized they were both breathing quickly, her breasts rising and falling; his chest swelled against them.

"Why?"

Charles watched her struggle to summon her wits, felt considerable satisfaction in watching how much effort it cost her. Almost as much as it was costing him to rein in his raging need.

She licked her lips. "We . . . can't. Not again."

"Why not?"

She blinked, and couldn't muster a single reason. That much he could read in her wide eyes, in her blank expression.

He bent his head, not to kiss her, but to the side of hers. Extended his tongue and with the tip delicately caressed the whorl of her ear.

Felt the shiver that racked her from her head to her toes. "Penny . . ." He breathed all his persuasiveness into the word.

Yet he wasn't surprised when her fingers tensed again on his shoulders, and she shook her head. "No, Charles. No."

He hesitated, but he'd told her the truth—he could no longer pretend. He wasn't even able to attempt it with her; blatant honesty was the only currency he could offer her.

"I want you." He let the words slide, glide over the delicate hollow of her temple.

"I know."

She sounded shaky, slightly desperate.

"You want me, too."

"I *know* that, too." She dragged in a huge breath, and pushed at his shoulders. "But we can't. *I* can't."

With a sigh, he eased back, accepting that tonight he'd have to let her go. That he'd be sleeping alone yet again.

Not, he vowed, for long. He'd learned what he most needed to know, about her and him and where they now stood. Learned enough to know that he'd been right; she could be his salvation, if she would—with the right persuasion, she might consent to marry him.

She still wanted him as much as he wanted her. It was enough to start with; they could build from there.

Not, however, tonight. Making no attempt to conceal his reluctance, he set her on her feet and released her.

She stepped to the side, tugging her shirt closed, through the dimness met his eyes. She briefly scanned his face, then murmured, "Good night."

He clamped his lips shut, thrust his hands into his pockets and watched her walk away, turning down the corridor and disappearing from view. Still he remained, listening, until he heard the distant clunk of her bedchamber latch falling. Only then did he let out his disgusted snort.

Turning, he headed for his apartments and his bed.

He stood very little chance of its being a good night.

❧ 6 ❧

THEY NEXT MET OVER THE BREAKFAST TABLE. HE WAS already there, waiting. Penny walked in, nodded his way, smiled at Filchett, sat in the chair he held for her, then poured herself a cup of tea and helped herself to toast.

Charles watched her. He'd got precious little sleep last night. Consequently, he'd had plenty of time to think, enough for the inconsistency in her response to him to rise out of his memories and stare him in the face.

Thirteen years ago he'd thought she'd had enough of him, that after their first and only bout of lovemaking she'd finished with him, never wanted to see him, speak with him, or do anything else with him ever again. That message had reached him loud and clear, but from a distance. A distance she'd insisted on preserving and that, with their families all about, she'd had no difficulty arranging.

Because of that distance, he hadn't realized the truth. She hadn't stopped wanting him; she still did. She hadn't so much been giving him his marching orders as holding him at bay until his real marching orders had taken him away.

Thirteen years ago, she'd been running. Something about their lovemaking had frightened her, but he still didn't know what. He'd originally, reluctantly, put her adverse reaction down to the physical pain, but he'd never been sure; it hadn't seemed much like the Penny he knew, but how could he tell when she'd refused to talk about it?

Considering the question now, there were other aspects—her independence, her pride, some unexpected sensibility—that might have contributed to make her take against him, but he knew better than to think he could follow the tortuous processes of her mind. That was the mistake he'd made thirteen years ago; he wasn't about to make it again.

If she had any difficulty, he'd make her tell him in words incapable of misconstruction. He wouldn't allow her to deflect him; he had no intention of taking a pert *No* for an answer, or accepting a dismissal, no matter how distant and haughty. This time the situation favored him; their families, the gaggle of females who, with the best of intentions, perennially managed to get in his way, weren't there for her to use as a screen. This time, there was just him and her and what lay between them. He wasn't going to let her—the one and only lady for him—slip through his fingers again.

With that resolution firmly made, he'd spent the small hours deciding how to proceed. How to seduce her. The first step was obvious, an absolute requirement; he couldn't seduce her under his own roof.

Courtesy of his investigation, which investigation she was determined to immerse herself in, that requirement wouldn't be difficult to meet.

He waited, patient, unperturbed, his gaze on her. Filchett, reading the undercurrents accurately, left in search of more coffee.

Penny buttered her toast, then reached for the jam. After last night, she'd made a firm resolution to restrict her interaction with Charles to the field of his investigation. And to keep at least a yard between them if at all humanly possible.

He'd accepted her refusal last night, but she had no wish to repeat the exercise, even less to tempt him or herself. She might not have the strength to utter the word next time; the likely consequences didn't bear contemplating. She had absolutely no ambition to be his sometime lover, warming his bed for however long he was there, only to be alone again when he returned to London. To be forever alone once he found his bride.

Eventually, unable to continue to pretend to be unaware of his gaze, she looked up and met it. "How are we going to learn how Granville communicated with the French?"

Down the length of the table, his dark eyes held hers. "Other than by continuing to ask, perhaps being rather more specific in our questions, I'm not sure we have that many avenues to follow."

He looked down, long fingers idly stroking his coffee cup.

Suddenly realizing she was staring at those mesmerizing fingers, she looked up as he did.

"One thing—I think we need to pay more attention to Nicholas."

She swallowed. "In case he knows how Granville arranged things?"

"I doubt he knows—if he did, he wouldn't be asking so many questions, and so widely. But it's possible, even likely, that he knows a piece of the puzzle—he at least knows enough to realize that there has to be someone else, or something else, involved."

"Hmm . . . so how can we learn more from him?"

Charles resisted the temptation to jump in with his solution. Not yet—let her ponder, weigh up the options, think things through. If she came up with the answer he wanted by herself, so much the better. "There's still the other gangs to speak to. The more we learn of Granville's activities, the better chance we stand of stumbling onto some clue. But Nicholas is the one person we're sure was involved—keeping apprised of his movements would be wise."

He set down his cup, pushed back his chair. "I've estate matters to attend to. If you can think of any way to improve our intelligence of Nicholas's activities, I'll be in the study."

Rising, he walked out of the room, knowing he'd surprised her. Finding Filchett hovering in the hall with a fresh pot of coffee, he directed him to the study, and followed.

Penny remained at the breakfast table, sipping her tea, nibbling her toast, and trying to fathom Charles's direction. Eventually reflecting it was never wise to question the benevolence of the gods, she rose and headed for the parlor. A sun-warmed, feminine sitting room his mother, sisters, and sisters-in-law used when relaxing *en famille*, the parlor was empty.

She sat on a window seat, looked out over the manicured lawns, and considered what to do. What she could do.

For years she'd been accustomed to keeping a close eye on all estate matters, yet once Amberly and his stewards had taken over at Wallingham, she'd been restricted to distantly overseeing hers, Elaine's, and her half sisters' inheritances; she'd filled in her time helping Elaine run the house. Now . . . she had nothing to do, and idleness fretted her. She felt restless and worse, useless. Good for nothing because she had nothing to do. Some part of her mind was examining and studying the problem of how to keep a more comprehensive watch on Nicholas, but she thought better while doing.

Ten minutes passed before the quietness about her finally fully registered. There were no ladies in this house, only her.

In lieu of managing her home, there was no reason she couldn't manage Charles's. In the absence of his mother— her godmother—there was no reason she couldn't keep herself occupied by performing the myriad overseeing tasks involved in ensuring the smooth running of the Abbey.

Mrs. Slattery certainly wouldn't mind.

Rising, she headed for the housekeeper's quarters.

In the study, Charles noted their findings from the previous night and his consequent direction for inclusion in his next report to Dalziel. That done, he sat back and reviewed his plans for Penny. Despite his personal goal, if it had been possible to isolate her from the investigation he would already have done so, his preferred option being to send her to his mother in London with strict instructions she be kept under lock and key until he came to fetch her.

A lovely conceit, but not an achievable one. And given his personal goal, not a wise one, either.

He would have to work with the options fate had dealt him.

At least he now knew what his personal goal was; he just had to ensure she didn't get too tangled in the web of his investigation while he was steering her to it.

The thought of steering, of influencing her female mind, left him considering the piece of the puzzle she'd given him that he was finding difficult to ease into the picture; to his mind, it didn't fit.

She seemed to have accepted it, but his instincts were prodding him, experience insisting that pieces that didn't fit meant he was seeing some part of the solution wrongly.

He couldn't question Granville. There was, however, one thing he could check, and despite her apparent acceptance, it might go some way to easing Penny's mind. After fifteen minutes of mulling over his contacts and how best to approach them, he drew out fresh sheets of paper and settled to write two letters. One to his mother, who suitably adjured would deliver the other to her old friend Helena, Duchess of St. Ives.

If anyone had a hope of establishing the details of how Granville Selborne had died, Devil Cynster, now Duke of St. Ives, was that man. He'd led a cavalry troop in the relief of Hougoumont; he would know, or know how to learn of, the survivors, and how to elicit the pertinent facts.

Charles hadn't known Granville well; for all he knew, Penny might be right. Yet the contradiction between running military and government secrets to the French, and then enlisting to fight them at Waterloo, was too big for him to swallow easily.

If they could discover exactly how Granville had died, it might shed some light, and perhaps relieve him of the premonition that in all he'd learned of the Selbornes' scheme, he was misreading something. His memories of Penny's father, too, didn't fit well with coldly calculated long-term treason.

The heat of battle burned away all falsity; if Granville had gone to his end unswervingly pitted against the French, then no matter Penny's stance, he would find it very hard to believe Granville, at least, had knowingly assisted the enemy.

He'd just set his seal to the packet of letters when Filchett tapped and entered.

"Lady Trescowthick's carriage is coming up the drive, my lord. Are you at home?"

Charles raised his brows. "I suspect I better be."

Rising, he went out to meet her ladyship, one of his mother's bosom-bows, also his sister-in-law Annabelle's mother—no surprise Lady T knew he was in residence. If she didn't catch him now, she was perfectly capable of laying seige to his house, and with Penny about . . .

He paused in the front hall, then turned to issue an order to the footman who'd come hurrying from the kitchen. The footman bowed and retreated. Overhearing the exchange, Filchett cast him a surprised look. Ignoring it, Charles donned an easy smile and went forth to greet her ladyship.

A small, rotund, matronly lady, Amarantha Trescowthick was delighted to have him hand her down from her carriage and escort her up the steps.

"But I really can't stay, my boy—oh!" She lifted a hand to her bosom. "It's *so* hard to think of you as the earl. Such a tragedy—first Frederick, then poor dear James. I've no idea how your mother kept her sanity—so brave, she was. But at least you survived and are here to take up the reins. I never did think to be 'my lording' you, bent on every dangerous venture as you were."

"Such are the vagaries of fate," Charles murmured, well aware that as part of those vagaries, her ladyship's daughter, while still styled countess, would not be the mother of the next earl.

"To what do I owe this honor?" he asked as he guided Lady T into the hall.

"I'm holding a small party tomorrow night—just the usual crowd, those of us who haven't gone up to town—and I expressly wished to invite *you*. It'll be an excellent opportunity for you to get to know us better. Why"—she fixed him with a stern look—"what with one thing and another, we've hardly set eyes on you since you returned from Waterloo."

His most charming smile to the fore, he bowed. "Tomorrow night will suit admirably."

Her ladyship blinked, then beamed, having, it seemed, been girded for battle. "Excellent! Well, then—"

She broke off, following the direction of his gaze as he glanced to the rear of the hall.

The baize-covered door swung open, and Penny came through. She saw him—he'd positioned Lady T so the stairs blocked Penny's view of her.

Penny smiled. "There you are." She came forward.

Lady T leaned across and peered around the stairs. "Penelope?"

For one fraught instant, the two ladies stared at each other, speculation clearly rife in both their minds. Then Penny's smile, which hadn't faltered in the least, widened; she continued smoothly toward them.

"Lady Trescowthick! How lovely to see you. I hope you haven't looked for me at Wallingham—I've been here all morning consulting with Mrs. Slattery over a recipe for quince jelly *Tante* Marissa gave me—it just *won't* come right."

Charles inwardly grinned; she was really very good at necessary lies.

Lady T offered her cheek to be kissed; Penny had known her since childhood. "I know just how difficult that recipe is—my chef Anton swore it was impossible, and he's French, after all! But indeed, it's fortuitous I caught you here, my dear—I'd intended to call at Wallingham on my way home. I'm giving a party tomorrow evening, and I've just inveigled Charles here into attending, and you must come, too, of course."

Penny kept her smile in place. "I'll be delighted. It's been rather quiet since Elaine and the girls went up to town."

"Indeed! I'm sure I don't know why—" Lady Trescowthick broke off, raising a hand in surrender. "But we won't retread that argument. For whatever reasons you dislike the ballrooms, you're here, and must come tomorrow night." She turned to the door. "Now I must be on my way. Oh—and George bumped into your relative, Arbry, yesterday, and invited him, but of course George forgot to mention you, assuming goodness knows what."

With Charles on her ladyship's other side, Penny saw her out of the house and into her carriage.

Lady Trescowthick leaned out of the window. "Eight sharp—none of your London ways here, Charles—Lostwithiel!" She sighed. "Will I ever get used to calling you that?"

The question was clearly rhetorical; the carriage lurched into motion. Her ladyship waved and sat back. Charles stood beside Penny on the steps, hands raised in farewell.

"Quince jelly?" he murmured.

"Your mama's recipe is justifiably famous. Why the devil did you send for me?"

"I sent the message before Lady T arrived." Just before.

The carriage was gone; turning, he waved Penny into the house. "I wanted to discuss how best to achieve an adequate watch on Nicholas."

She was mollified. "Have you thought of something?"

"Several somethings." He walked beside her to his study door and held it open. "Indeed, Lady T confirmed some of my thoughts."

"Oh?"

He followed her into the room, leaving her to settle in the chair before his desk while he rounded it and sank into the chair behind. Leaning back, he met her gaze. "You need to return to Wallingham."

She narrowed her eyes. Her lips started to form the word *No*, then she changed her mind. "Why?"

"Because you can't stay here for at least two powerful reasons. And also because you should be there, for a few more excellent reasons."

Her eyes were like flints. "What are the two reasons I can't stay here?"

"One, because visitors like Lady T are going to start turning up on the doorstep with distressing regularity. Far from dissuading them, the fact Mama is not in residence will only make them more determined to ensure I'm . . . doing whatever it is they think I should be doing. Like Lady T, they have difficulty viewing wild and reckless me as the earl."

She made a dismissive sound. "That's their problem."

"But it's also likely to be *our* problem because, of course, while dear Nicholas could be fobbed off with Cousin Emily, I wouldn't like to mention her supposed existence to Amarantha Trescowthick, or indeed any of Mama's other friends. They've all known each other far too long, and, witness Lady T's descent—she knew I was here—are clearly in communication."

Her eyes remained narrowed; her lips thinned. "I'm twenty-nine, and your mother's goddaughter. There's an entire regiment of staff in this house, all who know me nearly as well as they know you."

Unperturbed, he responded, "Your age is immaterial—in the same way they still think of me as a wild and reckless youth, they see you as no more than twenty-three if that. And while you might be Mama's goddaughter, Mama is not here—that being the pertinent point. Lastly, everyone knows this house is huge and come nighttime, all the servants are in the attics, and it's over nighttime that imaginations run amok."

He held her gaze. "Regardless of any excuses, should the ladies of the district learn of you sharing my roof with no chaperone in sight, there'll be hell and the devil to pay. Despite—or perhaps because of—my legendary wildness, that is not a scenario I wish to court."

The look she threw him was disdainful. "I don't regard

that as a reason of any great weight. But you said there were two powerful reasons—what's the second?"

He held her gaze for three heartbeats, then evenly stated, "Because, should you remain under this roof, I seriously doubt I'll be able to keep my hands off you."

She stared at him, and stared, her features expressionless while she decided how to respond. Eventually, she said, "You're joking."

More an uncertain question than a statement. He shook his head.

Her lips thinned again; exasperation filled her eyes, still searching his. "You're just trying to . . . bully me into doing as you wish."

He didn't shift his eyes from hers. "If you think I'm bluffing, by all means call me on it." He paused, then added, "If you remain here, I can assure you that you'll end beneath me in my bed or yours, whichever is closer at the time, within three nights."

Penny managed not to gape. What she could read in his eyes, what she could feel reaching for her across the polished expanse of his desk . . . she could barely breathe. "You're serious." The faint words were more for her than him, a point he seemed to realize; he didn't respond. She drew a tight breath. "I don't think that's at all fair."

He smiled. Intently. "At least I've given you fair warning."

Warning enough to prod her into running home to Wallingham—indeed. She'd have given a great deal to laugh lightly and assure him he was indulging in fantasies, yet after last night . . .

She refused to look away, to simply give in. "What are the reasons I should be at Wallingham?"

His menacing sensuality receded; she breathed a little easier.

"So we can mount a watch on Nicholas. In case it's escaped your notice, he and I are the definition of antipathetic—I can't turn up there looking for a drinking companion, or invite him out for a night of carousing, or even to put up our feet with a glass of brandy and swap stories of London and the ladies. Nicholas and I are never going to be that close. If you, however, are at Wallingham, then I'll have a perfect excuse to haunt the house. Simple."

She would have loved to blow a hole in his plan—for instance, by refusing in light of his declaration of moments before to have him paying her visits—but they were in this together. "Hmm. And I'll be there even at night . . . I don't suppose, now we're certain he's involved, that it matters if he suspects we're watching him—it can only make him more nervous."

"True. With you at home, we can effectively watch him most of the time, which will certainly make him feel crowded and cramped. If we can make him desperate enough, he'll make some slip, somewhere."

The more she thought, the more she favored the idea; if she was at Wallingham with Nicholas under her nose, Charles would find it impossible to edge her out of the investigation—she was well aware he would if he could.

And there was the not insignificant consideration that if she was at Wallingham, there would be far less scope for Charles to fan the still-smoldering embers—they should have been long dead but demonstrably weren't—of their long-ago association into a flaming affair, an entanglement she definitely didn't want or need.

Retreating to Wallingham could well be her best move all around.

She'd been staring into space. "Very well." She refocused on his face, and caught a subtle shift in the dark blue of his eyes that had her rapidly reviewing all they'd done, learned, still needed to do . . . "You're going to visit the Fowey Gallants tonight, aren't you?"

Exasperation flashed through his eyes. "Yes."

She nodded. "I'll come with you and return to Wallingham tomorrow morning."

"No."

She opened her eyes wide. "You've changed your mind about me going home?"

His eyes darkened; she met his frustration with complete assurance, enough for him to growl, "I should pack you off to London."

"But you can't, so you'll just have to make the best of it."

After a moment, he sighed through his teeth. "Very well. We'll call on the Gallants tonight, then tomorrow morning after breakfast you'll be on your way home. Agreed?"

She nodded. "Agreed."

"Now that we have that settled"—he rose—"I'm going for a ride."

She came to her feet, swiftly rounding her chair to come between him and the door. "Where are you going?"

"You don't need to know." He walked toward her, toward the door.

She met his eyes and held her ground.

He kept walking.

She backed until her shoulders met the panels; reaching behind her she clamped her fingers about the doorknob.

He halted with less than a foot between them. Looked down at her, and sighed.

Then he ducked his head and kissed her.

Witless.

She hadn't expected such a direct attack, hadn't been braced mentally or physically for it. With consummate mastery he swept her wits away, sent them tumbling, spinning; he captured her senses and held them in his palm.

While he reached around her and with both hands tried to pry her fingers from the doorknob.

That she'd expected; she'd locked them tight.

Charles inwardly cursed. He couldn't break her grip, not without exerting force and very likely hurting her. Not something he could contemplate.

And the kiss . . . it was so tempting to simply fall headfirst into it.

He moved into her, ratcheting the intensity up several notches, pinning her to the door . . . her grip on the knob only seemed to tighten, as if she were clinging to it like an anchor.

His mind started to shift focus from what he was supposed to be doing, to what he wanted to do. . . .

It took considerable effort to lift his head and break the kiss. Yet he couldn't seem to get his lips more than an inch from hers.

"Penny . . ." He nipped her lower lip, trying to focus her attention. "This is seriously unwise."

Eyes still closed, she dragged in a breath. "I know."

Her breasts swelled against his chest; his breathing hitched. He caught enough breath to acerbically comment, "You might have reservations over performing certain acts in daylight, but I don't, if you recall."

She recalled very well; a sensual shiver ran through her, sending desire spiraling through him all over again.

But at least she opened her eyes. She searched his, then sighed. "I know I can't go visiting smugglers' dens by daylight—I know I can't go with you. But where are you going?"

If she accepted she couldn't go with him . . . he mentally cursed. He was losing his touch; she was winning too many concessions. "Lostwithiel first, just to ask around. Then down to Tywardreath. I doubt Granville would have gone that far afield, but I'll see if they know him down there."

He released her hands, still locked on the doorknob, his fingers trailing the length of her bare forearms as he stepped back.

She held his gaze, then arched a brow. "See? It wasn't that hard."

Before he could respond, she whirled, opened the door, and walked out into the hall.

He followed, shutting the door. He caught her gaze as she faced him. "Behave yourself while I'm gone—go ask Mrs. Slattery for more of Mama's recipes."

That earned him a glittering, tight-lipped smile.

He grinned, reached out with one finger and traced her cheek. "I'll be back for dinner."

Penny watched him walk off, arrogantly assured, heading for the stables. Her lips eased into a genuine smile. Now she knew where he was going, she could make sure their paths didn't cross.

After an early luncheon, she rode into Fowey, left her mare at the Pelican Inn, and once again descended to the harbor. After checking that the fishing fleet was indeed out, she climbed the narrow lanes to Mother Gibbs's door.

Mother Gibbs welcomed her with a cackle, and a shrewd eye for the sovereign she'd promised, but the old biddy was as good as her word; when Penny left some twenty minutes later, all they'd heard thus far and surmised of Nicholas's interests had been confirmed.

She turned out of the narrow passageway onto the quay.

And walked into Charles. Again.

One look into his eyes was enough to confirm that he now understood why she'd wanted to know wither he'd been bound.

She raised her brows at him. "You must have ridden like the wind."

"I did, as it happens." His accents were clipped, his jaw tight; he clearly recalled telling her he didn't want her visiting Mother Gibbs alone. His fingers locked about her elbow, he turned and walked beside her along the harbor wall.

Refusing even to acknowledge his very male irritation at her intransigence, she looked ahead. "What did you learn?"

After a tense moment, he conceded. "There wasn't much to learn in Lostwithiel—no one around who could name any local lads Granville may have called friend. As for Tywardreath, the fraternity there knew of him only by repute—he'd never run with them."

"If he hadn't gone as far west as Tywardreath, it's unlikely he'd have gone farther."

"So I think. With all the gangs about the estuary to choose from, and the Fowey crews are some of the best, why venture to more distant territory?"

They turned away from the harbor to climb back to the High Street.

"Incidentally, I'm not amused."

"How did you know I was there?"

"I stopped to chat to the head ostler at the Pelican and saw your mare. The rest was easy." His gaze lifted to her face. "So what did *you* learn?"

She told him.

Charles listened, inwardly conceding that Mother Gibbs was an excellent source—an inspired choice on Penny's part, much as he disapproved of the connection. "So Nicholas is definitely setting himself up as Granville's replacement, specifically putting it about that any contact looking for Granville should now be referred to him."

"That must mean he's expecting someone to make contact." Penny looked at him. "But why would that be? The war's over. There's nothing, surely, that the French would pay to learn—is there?"

"Nothing military. But Nicholas is Foreign Office, and they're involved in trade pacts and so on." After a moment, he added, "I'll ask Dalziel."

Twisting her elbow from his grip, Penny closed her hand over his wrist and halted. She lifted her eyes to his. "Is there any way you can ask without mentioning names?"

He held her gaze for a moment, then turned his hand and caught hers. Confessed. "I've already told Dalziel about Nicholas, but believe me, Dalziel's no threat to you. I trusted him with my life for thirteen years—no danger to you or your family will come through him."

When she just looked at him, her gray eyes momentarily blank, inward-looking, he squeezed her hand. He wished he could read her mind as well as he could most women's, then made a plea he wasn't sure it was wise to make. "Trust me."

She refocused, stared at him for a moment longer, then nodded. "All right." Turning, she slid her hand back on his arm.

They continued on, while he grappled with his reaction.

All right. Just like that, without further questions, she trusted his decision, one involving her family's honor, no less. He steered her back to the Pelican, buoyed and touched by her accepting his word on a matter so profoundly important to her with so little reservation.

Reaching the Pelican, they retrieved their horses; once more side by side, they rode back to the Abbey.

Cassius and Brutus came lolloping up as they walked out of the stables. The hounds gamboled about them, pushing shaggy heads under their hands for pats. Penny laughed and complied. Charles looked across at her.

"Come for a walk—it's too early for dinner, and these two need a run."

The hounds had understood enough; they circled, barked encouragingly.

She smiled. "All right."

They followed the dogs east to the long sweep of the ramparts. Steps led up to the broad grassed walk atop the sloping mound; they climbed them side by side. In companionable silence, they walked along, drinking in the wide views over the lush green fields to the silvery blue estuary and farther, to where the waves of the Channel glittered on the horizon, gilded by the sun.

The breeze was brisk, tugging wisps of her hair from her chignon, rakishly ruffling Charles's black curls. The hounds bounded up and down the slopes, ranging out, noses to the ground, then circling back to check on them before ambling off once more.

Charles scanned the fields as they walked along. "What was it like around here during the war?" He gestured with one hand, encompassing all before them. "Did anything change?"

She understood what he was asking; she shook her head. "Not fundamentally. There was more activity in the estuary— naval ships and the like putting in, and our local privateers were especially active. There was always talk of the recent engagements whenever one went into village or town, and no dinner party was complete without a full listing of all the latest exploits.

"But underneath, no, there was no real change. The same day-to-day activities still consumed us—the fields, the crops, the fishing. Which family's son was walking out with which family's daughter." She paused, remembering. "Life rolled on."

It was on the tip of her tongue to ask why he'd asked; instead, she observed, "But if there were any real changes wrought by those years, you, coming back to it so rarely, would notice more than anyone." She glanced at him. "Has it changed?"

He halted, looked at her, then looked out over the fields, now his fields, to the sea. His chest swelled as he drew in a deep breath, then he shook his head. "No."

Turning, he walked on; she kept pace beside him.

"If I had to identify the most important motivation driving those who fought in the war, then it would be that we fought to keep this"—he gestured to the fields—"and all the other little pieces of England unchanged. So the things that define us weren't washed away, debris cleared to allow a victor's rule, but would endure and still be here for the next generation."

A moment passed, then he added, "It's comforting to find things the same."

She caught the waving wisps of her hair. "You spent years over there, years at a time. Did you think of us often?"

He looked over her head at the Channel, beyond which he'd spent all those years; there was, to her educated eyes, something bleak in his gaze. "Every day."

Her throat tightened; she knew how he felt about this place—the fields, the sky, the sea. There were no easy words she could offer him—would offer him—in the face of what she more than anyone understood had been his sacrifice. Small wonder those years had chipped and chiseled and separated the man from the superficial mask.

She was watching when he glanced down. His blue eyes met hers. For an instant, recognition and acceptance were simply there, as they so often had been in years past.

"Why didn't you marry?"

The question took her aback, then she nearly laughed; it was typical of him to cut to the heart of things, blatantly ignoring all social convention. Her lips curved; she continued strolling. "As I'm sure your mother told you, I had four perfectly successful Seasons, but none of the gentlemen caught my eye."

"As I heard it, you amply caught theirs. Several of theirs—a small platoon, it sounded like. So what didn't you like about them—they can't all have had warts."

She laughed. "As far as I know none of them did."

"So why were you so fussy?"

Why did he want to know? "You're not going to give up, are you?"

He hesitated. She wondered, but then he said, "Not this time."

She glanced at him, surprised at the undercurrent of steel in his tone, at a loss to account for it.

He caught her glance, lightly shrugged. "You were one of the things I was sure *wouldn't* be here when I got back."

She owed him no explanation, yet it was hardly a state secret. Looking ahead, she walked on. He walked beside her and *didn't* press.

Eventually, she said, "I didn't accept any of the offers for my hand because none of the gentlemen who made them could give me what I wanted."

She'd known what she wanted from marriage from an early age. When it came to the point, she hadn't been prepared to accept second best.

He didn't pressure her for more. The riddle of what she'd wanted had stumped all her suitors; she doubted he'd understand any more than they had. Not that it mattered.

They reached the far end of the ramparts; they both stopped to look back one last time at the view.

Her senses flared a second before she felt his hand touch her waist, felt it slide around, strong and assured, turning her, effortlessly drawing her to him.

She placed her hands on his chest, but they weren't any use with no strength behind them. But she remembered a few tricks; she kept her head down so he couldn't kiss her—he was tall enough that that would work.

His arms closed around her, not trapping but simply holding her; she heard, and felt, his low laugh.

He bent his head to the side; his breath wafted over her ear. "Penny . . ."

She tensed against the temptation to glance his way, to give him the opening, the opportunity he was angling for. Her fingers locked in his coat as his lips, then the tip of his tongue languidly caressed her ear.

Then he did the one thing she'd prayed he wouldn't. He switched to French, the language of his heritage, the language of love, the language he'd used in such interludes years ago—God help her, it was a language she understood very well.

He'd taught her.

"Mon ange . . ."

He'd called her that once, his angel. She hadn't heard the words that followed for thirteen years, yet they still had the same effect; uttered in his deep, purring voice, they slid over her like a tangible caress, then sank deeper, warming her to her bones. Unraveling her resistance.

His hands moved on her back, easing her closer, settling her against him. She caught her breath, sharp and shallow, realizing just how close they were, how truly he'd spoken when he'd warned her how little stood between them physically; when it came to him, she had no defenses to speak of.

Lifting her head only a little, she glanced sideways and met his eyes. A clear dark blue in the daylight, they held no hint of wicked triumph, but an intentness she didn't understand.

The altered angle was enough; he leaned closer, slowly. When she didn't duck away, he touched his lips to hers. Brushed them gently, temptingly, persuasively.

Oh, he was good, so very good at this; she gave up the battle, pushed her arms up around his neck, and lifted her lips to his.

The invitation was all he'd been waiting for; he accepted, took charge. For several long minutes, she simply let go, let herself flow on his tide, let him steer the kiss where he would, and greedily gathered to her lonely heart all the pleasures he willingly shared.

There was danger here, yes, but it was a danger she would dare. They were standing on the ramparts in full view of any who might chance to look that way; no matter how wild and reckless he was, no matter he had not a sexual inhibition to his name, in this setting, a kiss was as far as he would go.

She stood in no danger of him taking things too far; the danger did not lie there.

Just where it lay, and in what form, she wasn't entirely sure. When he finally lifted his head and, looking down at her from under his long lashes, drew in a deep breath, and she felt his hands at her sides, thumbs artfully cruising the sensitive sides of her breasts, and felt her inevitable reaction, felt how swollen and tight her breasts were, she suddenly wasn't sure of anything.

He was studying her *far* too intently. He'd warned her and was packing her off home so he wouldn't seduce her, yet . . .

She drew a tight breath, captured his eyes. "Charles, listen to me—we are not, *ever*, traveling that road again."

Planting her hands on his chest, she pushed back. He let her go, but the intensity of purpose behind his dark eyes didn't fade.

He held her gaze, caught her hand, raised it to his lips. Kissed. "Yes, we are. Just not as we did last time."

His tone screamed arrogant self-assurance; she would have argued, but he turned and whistled for the dogs. They came bounding up. Her hand locked in his, he gestured to the house. "Come—we should go in."

Lips setting, she consented, leaving her hand in his as they walked back to the house through the slanting rays of the slowly setting sun. No matter what he thought, what he believed, he and she together as they once had been was never going to happen again; he'd learn his error soon enough.

LATER, OVER DINNER, SHE WONDERED IF HE'D KISSED HER to distract her from his evening's appointment, or perhaps make her sufficiently wary about returning alone with him late at night to change her mind about accompanying him in the first place. Either way, he'd misjudged.

When they rose from the table, she went with him to the library. Selecting a book of poetry, she settled in one of the chairs before the fire.

He eyed her darkly, then picked up a book left on a side table, sprawled with typical loose-limbed grace in the chair that was the mate of hers, and settled to read, too. The hounds collapsed in twin heaps at his feet.

She noticed he began some way into the book; the way he was holding it, she couldn't read the title. After ten minutes of reading the same ode and not taking it in, she asked, "What is that?"

He glanced at her, then murmured, "*A Recent History of France.*"

"How recent?"

"From the beginning of Louis XIV's reign to the Terror."

That span included many of the years during which her father had been "collecting" pillboxes.

Charles continued without prompting, "It's by a French historian, one who belonged to the *Academie* and was quite pleased to see the end of the aristocracy. There's a lot of detail here from the French point of view."

"Do you think you'll find any reference to Amberly, or to secrets he and Papa sold?"

"No. I'm not sure I'd recognize what might have been a secret all those years ago." He returned his gaze to the book. "I'm looking for mention of some covert source—that's probably the most we can hope for."

She watched him read for a minute, then returned to her ode; this time, it drew her in.

He didn't stir when the clock struck nine, but when it started to chime the hour again, he shut his book, looked up, and caught her eye. "Time to go."

They went upstairs to change; she hurried, not wanting to risk his losing patience and riding off without her, but he was waiting at the head of the stairs when she rushed into the gallery. She slowed. His gaze raked her from her crown, over her jacket and breeches, to her boots; his lips tightened as she joined him, but he said nothing, merely waved her down the stairs.

Ten minutes later, they were mounted and cantering along the road to Fowey. The Fowey Gallants were the oldest, largest, and best-organized smuggling gang in the area, not least because the group included all those who sailed as privateers whenever matters of state permitted it. In many ways they were a more professional crew, yet equally only one remove from pirates.

Charles fitted right in. Penny saw that the instant they set foot in the Cock and Bull, the dimly lit tavern on Fowey's dockside that the senior members of the Gallants frequented when not on the waves. Three of Mother Gibbs's sons were there, in company with five others. None were gentle simple souls like Shep and Seth; these were seafarers of a quite different ilk.

They'd all turned, suspicious and wary, to eye the new arrivals; at sight of Charles, their closed faces split into wide grins. They stood to welcome him, clapping him on the shoulder, asking all manner of questions. She hung back in

Charles's shadow, wary of being clapped on the shoulder, too. Such a blow from one of these ham-fisted men would probably floor her.

It was Dennis Gibbs who, looking past Charles, noticed her. Nearly as tall as Charles and broader, his hard eyes narrowed. "What've we here, then?"

The other men shifted to look at her, eyes widening as they took in her garb. Before she could step back, as she was tempted to, Charles reached behind him and manacled her wrist. "Lady Penelope," he said, "who you haven't seen."

All eight Gallants looked at him, then Dennis asked, "Why's that?"

Charles gestured to their table and the deserted benches. "Let's order another round, and I'll tell you."

She was again squashed into a corner; this time she could barely expand her lungs enough to breathe. But the Gallants weren't anywhere near as friendly as Shep and Seth, nor even the Bodinnick crew, even though they knew her rather better. She recognized the son of the head gardener at Wallingham; he worked on the estate, yet there he sat, scowling blackly whenever he glanced her way.

This time it was Charles who carried the day. The Gallants listened to his explanation of his mission, then answered the questions he put to them freely; they knew and, it was patently obvious, respected him. She was relegated to a mere cipher; Charles explained her presence in terms of reassuring them over any reticence they might feel over speaking ill of her dead brother. They looked at her; all she was required to do was nod.

Their attention deflected immediately to Charles.

The tale the Gallants told was similar to what they'd heard at Polruan and Bodinnick, except that the Gallants were more specific about the lugger—a French vessel running no colors and always holding well back from their faster, lighter ships, ready to turn tail if they'd made any move to draw near.

"Always hovered nervous, and hoisted sail the instant their man was back aboard."

"Did you ever get any indication of what Granville was doing?"

Dennis looked around the group, then shook his head. "Truth be told, I always assumed they—the Selbornes—were taking in information. I never imagined it was going the other way."

Jammed against Charles, she felt him still. Then he murmured, "Actually, we don't know which way it was going, not for certain. That's why I'm here, trying to work out what was going on."

"What about this new bugger, Arbry, then?" Dennis described the overtures Nicholas had made to the group, somewhat more definite than with the other crews, not least because, as Dennis put it, the Gallants had strung him along. "A good source of ale, he is, when he comes in."

Charles made a less-than-civilized comment, then, laughing, called for another round. As earlier, he didn't order anything for her. Although she was thirsty, she wasn't game to mention it.

"You can rest assured, though"—for the first time, Dennis met her eyes—"we ain't told Arbry anything. Nor likely to."

Penny nodded, not even sure she was supposed to do that.

Charles asked, "Have any of you ever been involved in, or ever heard tell, of how Granville set up these meets? We've learned he went out with one or other of the Fowey gangs, and therefore at different points along the coast, twice or three times a year, yet each time the lugger was there, waiting."

The eight Gallants exchanged glances, then shook their heads.

Charles persisted. "Could the lugger have been on more or less permanent station?"

"Nah." Dennis lifted his head. "If that had been the way of it, we'd've come across it often enough, and we never did—not once except it was a run for Master Granville or the old earl."

"It was the same arrangement even back then?"

"As long as I've been leading the Gallants, and even in my da's day, back before then."

Charles nodded. "So there had to be some way Granville sent word to the lugger to meet him."

"Aye." There were nods all around.

"It'd be through the Isles, most like."

Charles grimaced. Attempting to trace any connection through the Channel Isles would be almost certainly wasted effort. Besides . . . "There still has to be some connection here—someone who took the message to the Isles, if that was how it was done."

The Gallants agreed; they offered to ask around. "Quiet-like," Dennis said. "Just a friendly natter here and there. We'll see what we can learn. Meanwhiles, do you want to know if Arbry asks to do a run?"

"Yes. I doubt he will, but if he does, send word to the Abbey."

With assurances all around, the men stood. She slid out of her corner; absorbed with farewelling Charles, none of the Gallants so much as registered her presence, then she remembered they weren't supposed to see her.

She slipped through the shadows to the door and waited there. Two old sailors, long past the age of going to sea, had been hunched over a table a few feet from the Gallants; they watched her—when she noticed, one bobbed his head her way. Uncertain, she nodded briefly in reply.

With one last slap on the back for Dennis, Charles joined her.

"Come on." He gripped her arm and hustled her outside, releasing her only when they were in the stable yard.

She headed to where her mare was tethered, then spotted a rain barrel; it even had a dipper. She detoured. Lifting the heavy lid, she ducked her shoulder under it so she could pour water into her hand. Charles appeared beside her; with exceedingly thin lips but not a word he held the lid for her.

When she'd drunk her fill, she glanced at him as he replaced the lid. "Why the devil are you all glowering? Brendan Mattock scowled at me the entire time we were in there."

Charles looked at her, she sensed in exasperation. "*I'd*

scowl at you the entire time if I thought there was anything to be gained by it. The only difference between Brendan and me is that I know you and he doesn't."

With what sounded like a suppressed growl, he swung away, striding toward their horses. She was about to follow when the old sailor who'd nodded to her hobbled out of the shadows. He raised a hand; when she hesitated, he beckoned.

"Charles . . ."

He was back by her side in an instant. "Let's see what he wants."

Together they retraced their steps to where the old man waited, leaning heavily on his cane.

He ducked his head to them both. "Couldn't help but overhear ye in there. You was asking after how young Master Granville might have got messages to a French lugger."

Charles merely nodded.

Penny asked, "Do you know something?"

"May do, not that I'm sure, mind, but I doubt there's many left would think of 'em to tell ye." The old man regarded her through eyes still sharp and shrewd. "'Twas your father, m'lady, what brought them over—or rather, it were just the one man, a Frenchie he was, but from somewhere on the coast—Breton, maybe. Came here with your pa when he came home from abroad years ago. Smollet was the name he went by. François, or something frenchified like that."

"Is this Smollet still alive?" Charles asked.

The old man shook his head. "Nah. Married a local lass he did, but then she up and left him—left their lad, too, but the lad—Gimby he's called—he's still here. He ain't all that bright. A bit slow, you might say. Not dangerous, but not one for company."

The man paused to draw in a wheezy breath. "Anyways, the reason you put me in mind of 'em was that they, father and son, were both weedy-like, not much brawn to 'em— none of the gangs would'a looked twice at 'em. But I tell you, they could sail. Soon a'ter he came back here with your pa, Smollet the elder left the Hall and went to live in a cottage by the river, near that marshy bit by the river mouth."

He looked at Charles. "You'd know it, like as not."

Charles nodded. "Go on."

"Don't know where he got 'em from, but Smollet had two boats. One was just a rowboat, a dinghy he used to fish from, nothing special. The other—well, that was the mystery. A sleek little craft that just flew under sail. Didn't often see it out, but when I did, Smollet would have it running before the wind."

"Where did he run it to?" Charles asked.

The old man nodded encouragingly. "Aye, you've twigged it. I caught a glimpse of it a time or two, well out and headed for the Isles. Not many hereabouts would risk it in such a small craft, but those Smollets, they was born to the waves. No fear in 'em at all. And I do know your pa"—he nodded at Penny—"kept in touch. He was there when they buried Smollet the elder some fifteen years ago. Not many others at the graveside, but I'd gone to remember a good sailor."

"Did you ever see my brother with the Smollets?" Penny asked.

The man's nod was portentious. "Aye. Gimby was a year or so older than Master Granville—it was he taught your brother to sail. Gimby was as close to your brother, mayhap even closer, than his pa had been to your pa—well, they more or less grew up together on and about the water. Howsoever, not many others would know. My cottage is on the water's edge, just around on the estuary, so I see the Smollets more than most. Otherwise, they was always next to hermits. Don't know as many of the younger ones"—with his head he indicated the tavern and presumably the Gallants inside—"would even know they existed."

Penny realized she'd been holding her breath; she exhaled. "Thank you."

"Here." Charles handed over two sovereigns. "You and your friend have a few drinks on the Prince Regent."

The old man looked down at the coins, then cackled. "Aye—better us than him, from all I hear."

He raised a hand in salute. "Hope ye find what you're

looking for." With that, he turned and shuffled back into the tavern.

Penny stared after him.

Charles caught her hand and pulled her away. "Come on."

The marshy stretch by the river mouth lay just off their route home.

"No!" Charles said. "I'll come back tomorrow."

Tomorrow, when she was safely stowed at Wallingham. "No. We should go there tonight."

From the corner of her eye, Penny glimpsed the opening of the track to the river mouth coming up on their right. She didn't look that way, but kept her gaze on Charles's face.

He was frowning at her. "It's nearly midnight—hardly a useful hour to go knocking on some poor fisherman's door."

Riding on her right, he and his mount were between her mare and the track. She had to time her move carefully. "If he's a fisherman, it's the perfect time to call—he'll almost certainly be in, which is more than you can say during the day."

Exasperated, Charles looked ahead. "Penny—"

He whipped his head around as she checked the mare, swore as she cut across Domino's heels and plunged down the narrow track. It took him a moment to wheel the big gray. By the time he thundered onto the track she was a decent distance ahead.

Too far for him to easily overhaul her, too dangerous as well.

He knew the track; it remained narrow for all its length, wending this way and that as it tacked between trees and the occasional thick bush. It led to the river mouth, then an even narrower spur angled north, following the river bank. The Smollet cottage had to be along there. He could vaguely remember a rough stone cottage, rather grim, glimpsed from the river through the trees.

Muttering resigned curses, he urged Domino forward, closing the gap, then settled to follow in Penny's wake. She glanced back; realizing he wasn't pressing to overtake her, she eased the mare to a safer pace.

Ahead, through a screen of trees, the river glimmered. Penny slowed even more as the track became steeper. It ended in a small clearing above the river; beyond lay low-lying, reed-infested marsh.

Penny swung left onto the even narrower path that followed the bank upriver. Lined on the landward side by a stand of thick trees, it was reasonably well surfaced but barely wide enough for a cart. She cantered along through the shadows, searching for a clearing.

She was almost past the cottage before she realized. Alerted by a glimmer of moonlight on stone, she abruptly drew rein, wrestling the mare to a halt, peering through the trees at a single-roomed cottage—more a hovel—gray and unwelcoming; any paint that might once have brightened the door and shutters had flaked away long ago.

Not a flicker of light shone through the shuttered windows, but it was after midnight.

Charles, coming up hard on the mare's heels, swore, rearing and wheeling his big gray.

She glanced at him; for an instant, in the silvery moonlight with his curling black hair, he appeared a black pirate on a moon-kissed steed, performing a dramatic maneuver that should have demanded his full attention—yet his attention was fixed on the cottage.

His horse's front hooves touched ground; Charles urged him under the trees screening the front of the cottage. She turned her mare and followed.

Charles halted under the trees between Penny and the cottage. His senses, honed by years of danger, had tensed, condensed; something was wrong.

He took a moment to work out what. Even at night, even if there was no human about, there were always insects, small animals, always a faint, discernible hum of life. He couldn't detect any such hum in or around the cottage. Even the insects had deserted it.

He'd seen death too often not to recognize its pall.

He dismounted. "Stay here with the horses." He tossed his reins to Penny, briefly met her eyes. "*Don't* follow me. Wait until I call."

He turned to the cottage, went forward silently even though he felt sure there was no one there. The door was ajar; his sense of foreboding increased.

Glancing back, he saw Penny, dismounted, tying the reins of both horses to a tree. Looking back at the cottage, he put out a hand, pushed the door wide, simultaneously stepping to the side. The door swung inward, almost fully open before it banged on something wooden.

No other sound came from within.

Charles glanced inside. It took a moment for his eyes to adjust to the deeper darkness, then he saw a form slumped unmoving on the floor.

He swore, scanned with his senses one last time, but there was no one else there, then stepped to the doorway. The smell told him what lay in the cottage wasn't going to be a pretty sight. He sensed Penny drawing nearer. "Don't come any closer—you don't need to see this."

"What?" Then, more weakly, "Is he *dead*?"

No point pretending. "Yes."

He saw tinder and a candle on a rough wooden table. Hauling in a breath, he held it, then stepped over the threshold. The wick caught, flared; he shielded the flame until it was steady, then he lifted the candle and looked.

His senses hadn't lied.

He heard Penny's sharp, shocked gasp, heard her quit the doorway, slumping back against the cottage wall. His gaze locked on the body strewn like a broken puppet on the rough plank floor, he moved closer, holding the candle up so he could better see.

After a moment, he hunkered down, through narrowed eyes studied the young man's face.

"What happened?"

He glanced at the doorway, saw Penny clutching the jamb, looking in.

"Is it Gimby?" she asked.

He looked again at the face. "I assume so—from what the old man told us, he's the right age and build."

Putting out a hand, he unfurled one of the youth's slack, crumpled hands, and found the calluses and ridges marking him as one who earned his living from the sea. "Yes," he said. "It's Gimby Smollet."

Again his gaze went to the youth's face, noting the ugly weals and bruises. He recognized the pattern, could predict where on the youth's body other bruises would be found—over his kidneys, covering his lower ribs, most of which would be broken. His hands and fingers had been methodically smashed, repeatedly, over some time, hours at least.

Someone had wanted information from Gimby, information Gimby either had refused to give or hadn't known to give. He'd been beaten until his interrogator had been sure there was no more to learn, then Gimby had been dispatched, his throat cut with, it seemed, a single stroke.

Charles rose, his gaze going to Penny. "There's nothing we can do, other than inform the authorities."

Waving her back, he joined her, pulling the door closed on the dead youth, careful to keep buried all signs of the deep unease flooding him.

"He was murdered, wasn't he?" Penny said. "How long ago?"

A good question. "At least yesterday, possibly the day before."

She swallowed; her voice was thready. "After we started asking questions."

He reached for her hand, gripped hard. "That may have nothing to do with it."

She glanced at him; he saw in her eyes that she believed that no more than he. At least she didn't look to be heading for hysterics.

"What now? Who should we tell?"

He paused, considering. "Culver's the local magistrate—I'll ride over and inform him first thing in the morning. There's no sense in rousing him and his staff at this hour—there's nothing anyone can do now that won't be better done in daylight." He looked at Penny, caught her eye. "Incidentally, you aren't here."

Her lips tightened, but she nodded. She glanced back at the cottage. "So we just leave him?"

He squeezed her hand again. "He's not really there." He drew in a breath, filling his lungs with cleaner air, noting the faint breeze rising off the estuary. "Before we go, I want to look at his boats."

Leaving that to the morning was a risk he was no longer prepared to take. Someone else was there, someone with training similar to his own.

Someone with a background similar to his own.

He didn't let go of Penny's hand. Towing her with him, he checked she'd tied the horses securely, then crossed the track to the river. They were both local-born; they knew what they were searching for—a tiny inlet, a miniature cove, a narrow gorge cut by a minor stream—some such would be the Smolletts' mooring place.

They found it a hundred yards upriver, an inlet carved by a minor stream just wide enough for a boat and heavily overhung by the arching branches of the trees that at that spot marched down almost to the river's edge.

The rowboat, moored to a heavy ring set in a tree trunk, bobbed on the rising tide. A quick glance inside revealed nothing more than the usual fisherman's clutter—ropes, tackle, two rods, assorted nets, and two lobster pots.

Charles turned his attention to the second boat, hauled up out of the water and lashed to trees fore and aft. One glance and his eyes widened; the old sailor hadn't been embellishing—the craft was a superb piece of work, sleek and trim. Under sail, it would fly.

Penny had already gone to it. When he came up, she was sitting on a log beside the prow; with one hand she was tracing, it seemed wonderingly, the name painted there.

Charles hunkered down beside her. *Julie Lea.* The name meant nothing to him.

"It's my mother's name."

He glanced at Penny; he couldn't see well enough to read her eyes. He reached for her hand, simply held it.

"Her name was Julie—everyone knew her as that, just Julie. Only my father ever called her by *both* her names— Julie Lea."

He stayed beside her, let a few minutes tick by, then rose. "Stay there. I need to search inside."

Not as easy as with the rowboat; the yacht, for it was that, just a very small one, had a canvas cover lashed over it. The knots were sailors' knots; he unraveled those at the stern, then peeled the cover back.

Mast, rigging, sails, oars—all the necessary paraphernalia. But he suspected there would be more. Eventually, he found what he was looking for; leaning into the yacht, reaching beneath the forward bench, he pulled out a crumpled bundle of line and material, a set of signals.

Penny saw; she stood, dusting off her breeches as he strung out the line. She came around the boat to peer at the flags, colored squares carrying various designs. "What are they? I don't recognize them."

He hesitated, then said, "French naval signals." He recognized enough to be sure. "Flying these, the yacht wouldn't need to make actual contact with any French ship, just come within spyglass sight of them."

Penny reached out and tapped one flag. "And this?"

Charles paused, then said, "You know what that is."

She nodded. "The Selborne crest." Drawing breath was suddenly difficult. "How *could* they?"

He regathered the flags, bundling them up. Evenly said, "We don't yet know exactly what they did."

She felt her face harden. "Yes, we do. Whenever Amberly gave Papa a secret worth selling, he sent Smollet out to sail close to the Isles, running these signals in sight of some French ship. The flags told the French when and where to send the lugger, and then Papa went out with one of the smuggling gangs and spoke with some Frenchman and gave our enemies English government secrets in exchange for pillboxes. Later, when it was Granville, he sent Gimby to fetch the French—and now Gimby's been murdered."

Disgust and revulsion colored her words, the emotions so strong she could almost taste them.

"Actually"—Charles's voice, in contrast, was cool, his tones incisive—"while your mechanism is almost certainly correct, we don't yet know what they were passing."

"Something the French were willing to pay for with jeweled antiquities—you've seen the pillboxes." She looked away.

"True, but—" He thrust the bundled flags into her hands, then caught her arms, forcing her to look at him. "Penny, I know this type of game—I've been playing it for the last thirteen years. Things are often not what they seem."

She couldn't read his eyes, but could feel his gaze on her face.

His grip gentled. "I need to send a messenger to London— there's a possibility Dalziel might not have checked. You heard Dennis Gibbs. Your father might have been involved in something deeper than the obvious."

He was trying to find excuses so she wouldn't feel so devastated, so totally betrayed by her father and brother. It was an actual pain in her chest, quite acute. Charles was trying his best to ease it, but . . . numbly, she nodded.

She watched while he covered the yacht and lashed the canvas down. Grateful for the dark; grateful for the quiet. She felt dreadful. She'd had her suspicions, not just recently but for years; over the last months, it seemed every few weeks she'd discover something more, uncover something worse that painted her father and brother in ever-more-dastardly shades.

In some distant recess of her mind, she was aware that her deep-seated reaction to the whole notion of treason was tied up with what she'd felt—if she was truthful still felt—for Charles. The idea that her father and brother could, purely for their own gain, have done things that would have put Charles and those like him in danger—even more danger than they'd already faced—rocked her to her core, filled her with something far more violent than mere fury, something far more powerful and corrosive than disdain.

Charles straightened, checked his knots, then tested the ropes holding the yacht. She wondered vaguely at the fate that had landed her there, a hundred yards from her brother's fishing friend who'd almost certainly been murdered for his part in their scheme, with the evidence of their perfidy in her hands—and it was Charles beside her in the night.

"Come on." He lifted the signals from her, took her arm. "Let's go home."

He meant the Abbey, and she was glad of it. Wallingham Hall was her home, yet her thoughts of her father and Granville were presently so disturbing she doubted she'd find any peace there.

Reaching the horses, Charles tied the signals to his saddle, tossed her up to hers, then mounted and led the way, not back but on. A little farther along, the river path connected with another wider track leading back to the Lostwithiel road.

They clattered into the Abbey stable yard in the small hours. Again Charles waved his stableman back to his bed. Catching the mare's reins, he led both horses in and turned them into their stalls.

Penny went to unsaddle, only then realized she was shaking. It was, apparently, one thing to speculate and wonder, even to acknowledge and investigate, but quite another to find a recently murdered henchman along with indisputable proof of her father and brother's complicity in treason.

Her mind felt battered, oddly detached. Dragging in a breath, she held it, and forced her hands to work, to unsaddle the mare and rub her down.

Charles glanced her way, but said nothing.

When he finished with his horse, he came to help her, without a word taking over rubbing the mare down. She relinquished the task, checked the feed and water, then leaned against the side of the stall and waited.

He'd left the tangle of signal flags on top of the stall wall.

From amid the jumble, the Selborne crest mocked her. She turned away.

Charles came out of the stall, shut the door, picked up the flags, with his other hand took hers. They walked up to the house and entered through the garden door; in the front hall, he tugged her away from the stairs. "Come into the library."

She went, too exhausted even to wonder why. He towed her across the room, paused beside his desk to thrust the signal flags into a drawer, then towed her farther—to the tantalus.

Releasing her, he poured two glasses of brandy. Catching one of her hands, he lifted it and pressed one glass into it. "Drink."

She stared at the glass. "I don't drink brandy."

He sipped his own drink, met her gaze. "Would you prefer I tip it down your throat?"

She stared at him through the shadows, wondered if he was bluffing . . . realized, rather dizzyingly, that he wasn't. She sipped. Pulled a face. "It's ghastly."

Nose wrinkling, she held the glass away.

He shifted nearer.

Eyes flaring, she whipped the glass back to her lips, and sipped.

He stood there, a foot away, sipping his own drink, watching her until she'd drained the glass.

"Good." He took it from her, put both glasses down, then took her hand again.

She was getting rather tired of being towed, but on the other hand, it meant she didn't have to think.

Her acquiescence worried Charles. He knew what she believed, knew it was eating at her. He didn't like seeing her in this state; she seemed so internally fragile, as if something inside might shatter at any moment. He'd always seen her as someone he should protect; for that very reason, he couldn't utter the platitudes he might have used to calm another. He couldn't offer her false hope.

He would send a rider to London tomorrow; although there shouldn't have been any contact with the French that

Dalziel hadn't known about, hadn't, indeed, been in charge of, it was possible there had been something going on that Dalziel hadn't got wind of.

A long shot, but a possibility, one he needed checked.

Meanwhile, Penny's state of mind was only one of his worries, and potentially the easiest to address.

His state of mind was even more uncertain.

He pulled her to a halt in the gallery, in front of a window so the moonlight, now fading, spilled in and lit her face. He studied it as, surprised, she blinked up at him.

Foreseeing the battle looming, he hissed out a frustrated breath. Releasing her, he raked a hand through his hair. "I'm no longer sure it's a wise idea for you to go back to Wallingham Hall."

Her attention abruptly refocused; she frowned as she followed his train of thought. "You mean because Gimby was murdered?" Her frown grew more definite. "You think Nicholas did it."

"Other than you and me, who else has been asking after Granville's associates?"

"Why?"

"To stop us learning whatever Gimby knew—whatever he presumably learned from Gimby before he killed him."

Slowly, she nodded; her gaze went past him—he couldn't see her eyes, couldn't imagine what she was thinking.

Reaching out, he caught her chin and turned her face back to him. "You should remain here. We can set up a closer watch on Nicholas—"

"No." She lifted her chin from his hand, but kept her eyes on his. "We agreed. If I'm there, I can keep a much more comprehensive eye on him, and you can visit freely as well. The more we're about, the more likely he'll grow rattled—"

"And what happens if, growing rattled, he decides perhaps *you* know too much?"

He thought she paled, but her gaze didn't waver. If anything, her chin set more mulishly.

"Charles, there are two very good, very powerful and

compelling reasons why I should return to Wallingham. The first is because keeping a close eye on Nicholas, *especially* if he was the one who killed Gimby, is vital. We need to know what Nicholas is doing, and I'm the person best able to learn that from inside the Hall, which also gives you a reason for visiting often and generally being around. *Moreover*, there's the fact it was *my* father and brother who were running secrets to the French. It's *my* family's honor that's been besmirched—"

"It's not up to *you* to make restitution." Hands on his hips, he loomed over her. "*You* don't have to do that. No one would expect—"

"I don't *care* what anyone else expects!" She didn't budge an inch. "It's what *I* expect, and it's what I'll do."

"Penny—"

"No!" She fixed her eyes, glittering belligrently, on his. "Just tell me one thing—if you were in my shoes, wouldn't you feel, and do, the same?"

His jaw set so hard he thought it would crack. Lips tightly compressed, he made no answer.

She nodded. "Exactly. So I'll go to Wallingham in the morning as arranged."

"What was your second oh-so-compelling reason?" If he could find any weakness, he'd exploit it.

She thought, then thought some more. He simply waited.

Eventually, her eyes steady on his, she said, "Because you were right. It's not at all wise for me to stay under the same roof as you. You are a far greater threat to me than Nicholas is likely to be."

He looked down into her stormy gray eyes, drank in the directness, the blatant honesty in her gaze, and felt the inevitable reaction to her words—to her admission—rise through him. He clenched his hands tight on his hips. Slowly said, "I would much rather you were at risk from me than from any other man. I, at least, am not interested in murdering you."

But what you could do to my heart would hurt even more.

Penny held back the words, forced herself to take a long slow breath before saying, "Nevertheless, I'll leave for Wallingham in the morning."

She went to step back.

He swore, and reached for her.

She'd been watching, but was far too slow; he grabbed her, jerked her to him, then his lips came down on hers.

CHAPTER

8

CHARLES TRAPPED HER AGAINST HIM, CRUSHED HIS LIPS TO hers, surged into her mouth and laid claim.

It was the stupidest thing he could have done, an approach doomed to fail before he'd begun. He knew it, and couldn't stop. Couldn't rein in the primal instinct that had slipped its leash, that insisted he should simply claim her and be done with it. That if he did he'd be able to command her, to impose his will on her and keep her safe.

The compulsive, driving need to keep her safe, given teeth and claws by the discoveries of the past days, was more than powerful enough to make him lose his head.

Penny's defenses vaporized beneath his onslaught, beneath that hard, fast, scorching kiss—hard enough to knock her wits from her head, fast enough to send them whirling. Scorching enough to cinder any resistance.

It was totally unfair. That he could so simply stop her thoughts, capture her awareness so utterly . . .

His arms locked around her and he pulled her flush against him. Heat to burning heat, breasts to chest, hips to hard thighs.

She gasped through the kiss, burned, ached. Any second, the last shred of her will would catch alight, and she'd be swept away. She gave up the fight to think, and just reacted. Raising both hands, she grabbed his head, speared her fingers through the silky tumble of his black locks, and gripped.

And kissed him back.

Poured every ounce of her frustrated emotions into the act. Pressed her lips to his, mouth to mouth, sent her tongue to tangle with his in a wild, pagan, wholly uninhibited dance.

And for the first time in their lives, in this arena, she knew she'd shocked him. Rocked him enough to have him hesitate, then scramble to follow her lead, to regain the reins, to wrest control back again.

She didn't want to give it up.

In seconds, the exchange became a heated duel; initially, she held the upper hand. They were more evenly matched than they had been years ago, yet he was still a master and she a mere apprentice. Step by step, inch by inch, he reclaimed the ascendancy, reclaimed her senses. Dragged each down into a languorous sea of wanting. Of needing. Of having to have more.

She felt his arms ease, and his hands slide down, over her back, down over her hips to grip her bottom; he drew her closer still, molding her to him, suggestively provoking, evoking again that never-forgotten heat.

He rocked against her, and the heat spread. Wildfire down her veins, blossoming beneath her skin. Melting her bones, sapping her will . . .

Deliberately, she dropped her guard, let everything she'd held back, all that had grown, all that had been pent-up for thirteen years with nowhere to go, well and pour through her. Held him to the kiss and let it pour into him.

And felt him pause, then shudder. Felt the change in him, muscles tensing, locking, steeling against the tide.

She gloried, exulted—and sent the tide raging. She wanted so much more than he'd ever offered to give, and for once he was, if not helpless, then uncertain.

Charles couldn't find solid ground. She'd cut it from under him; the only thing his senses could find that was real was her, and the desire that flamed between them, hotter, more powerful, more intense, frighteningly more potent than it had been before—so much more than he'd ever felt before. It—she—was passion and desire, heat and longing incarnate in a dimension he'd never before explored. She'd rocketed them into it, then set them both adrift . . . he had no idea how to return to the real world.

And no real wish to do so.

She was fuel to his fire; he needed her under his hands, under him. At that moment, he needed to be inside her more than he needed to breathe.

But not here.

The warning came in a fleeting instant of lucidity; this was madness and he knew it. But he couldn't stop; he was helpless to draw back from her.

She pressed closer, arms twining about his neck; he couldn't resist her lure, couldn't resist slanting his mouth over hers and taking the kiss deeper. Whirling them both into deeper waters yet, to where the currents ran strong, to where the tug of desire became a tangible force, pulling them under.

She wasn't safe, and neither was he.

He raised his hands to her breasts, closed them and kneaded, then sent them racing, covetously tracing the sleek planes of her back, the globes of her bottom, the long sweeps of her thighs. He felt her breath hitch; he wanted her naked under his hands, under his mouth, now.

But not HERE!

Some remnant of his mind screamed the words, battling to remind him . . . they had to stop. *Now. Before—*

She framed his face again, pressed an incendiary kiss on his ravening lips—then abruptly pulled back and broke the kiss.

Thank God! Eyes closed, he hauled in a ragged breath, then opened his eyes.

Gasping, panting, holding his face between her hands, she stared at him; eyes wide, through the moon-washed dimness she searched his. They were both reeling. Both fighting to breathe, both struggling desperately to regain their wits, and some measure of control.

To hold against the fiery tide that surged around them.

Never in his life had he felt so swept away, been so helpless in the face of something stronger than he. Something beyond his will to contain or restrain.

He was acutely conscious of her slender body wrapped in his arms, plastered against the much harder length of his.

She was, too.

He saw her eyes widen, simultaneously saw her grasp on her wits firm.

She hauled in a huge breath, then pushed back in his arms.

"*That*"—her voice shook, but, eyes locked with his, she went on—"is why I'm leaving for Wallingham in the morning."

He couldn't argue. The last ten minutes had amply demonstrated how desperately urgent and necessary it was that she quit his roof.

She wrenched away—had to—he couldn't, yet, get his arms to willingly let her go. He had to battle just to let her step away, to force himself to lose the feel of her body against his and not react—not grab her and pull her back.

Watching him, still struggling to breathe, she seemed to sense his fraught state; she swung on her heel and walked, albeit unsteadily, away.

He watched her go, watched her turn into the corridor; unmoving in the shadows, he listened to her footsteps fade, then heard the distant thud of her bedchamber door. Only then did he manage to drag in a full breath, to fill his chest, to feel some semblance of sanity return.

Never before had he felt like that, not with any other woman, not even with her long ago.

Eventually, when the thunder in his veins had subsided enough for him to hear himself think, he stirred, his body once more his own. Nevertheless, his strongest impulse was to follow her to her room. To her bed, or anywhere else she wished.

With one soft, succinct curse, he turned and headed for his apartments.

Tomorrow she'd be at Wallingham.

Tomorrow, *thank God*, would be another day.

Despite her earnest expectations, Penny wasn't ready to leave the Abbey until late the next morning.

She'd had difficulty falling asleep, then had slept in. She had breakfast on a tray in her room the better to avoid Charles.

Her behavior the previous night had been a revelation. Until she'd lost her temper and stopped holding everything back, she hadn't appreciated just how much she'd been concealing, bottled up inside her. Until that moment, she hadn't fully understood how much she still felt for him, or more specifically the nature of what she felt for him.

That last had been a revelation indeed.

It was more, far more in every way, than before, and now he was home, spending more time close to her than he ever had, her feelings only seemed to be growing, burgeoning and extending in ways she hadn't foreseen.

On the one hand she was appalled, on the other . . . fascinated.

Just as well she was going back to Wallingham.

Crunching on her toast, she replayed that last interlude; she couldn't tell whether he'd seen what she had. In the past, he hadn't been at all perceptive where she was concerned; she hoped and suspected that would still be the case. For all she knew, women habitually threw themselves at him; if he hadn't realized that with her, such an act meant a great deal more, well and good. Bringing her unexpected feelings to his attention was the last thing she needed. That his attention in a sexual sense had fixed on her anyway was no surprise. It always had; it seemed it always would.

Her thoughts circled to her principal reason for returning to Wallingham—Nicholas, the investigation, and now Gimby's murder. Her determination to do her part was set in stone; sober, committed, she drained her teacup and rose to dress.

It was only as she left her room properly gowned in her riding habit that she recalled Charles had planned to go that morning to report Gimby's death to Lord Culver, the nearest magistrate. If she hurried, she might get away before he returned.

She whisked through the gallery and was pattering down the stairs before she looked ahead.

Charles stood in the center of the hall watching her rapid descent. She slowed. He was dressed in riding jacket, breeches, and boots; his hair was windblown, as if he'd just come in. So much for an easy escape.

He dismissed Filchett, with whom he'd been talking, and came to meet her as she stepped off the stairs. "Come into the library."

Together they walked the few steps to the library door. He held it for her, and she went in, walking to one of the chairs before the fire. She turned and coolly faced him. She doubted he'd mention their interlude last night. If he didn't, she certainly wouldn't; the less he dwelled on it, the better.

When he waved her to sit, she did. He took the chair opposite.

"I've seen Culver. He'll do all that's necessary, but the crux of the matter—the reason behind Gimby's death—is the subject of my investigation, so beyond managing the formalities, Culver won't be further involved."

Charles locked gazes with Penny. "I've sent a messenger to London with a report of Gimby's death and a request that the possibility of the traffic through here being incoming rather than outgoing be thoroughly checked."

Something flickered behind her eyes. "You don't believe it was."

"I don't at this stage know what to believe. I've been in this business too long to jump to conclusions that may not prove warranted."

One fine brow arched, but she made no reply. Her face was a calm mask; he could read nothing in it, certainly nothing about how she felt about last night. "Have you reconsidered your decision to return to Wallingham?"

She shook her head; her lips set in a determined line. "It's my family that's involved. Even Nicholas is a relative, albeit distant. It's only right I do all I can . . ." She gestured and let her words trail away.

"Uncovering the truth is my mission, my job, not yours." He kept his tone even, all aggressive instinct harnessed.

"Indeed, but I consider it obligatory that I do all I can to assist, and that means returning to Wallingham and watching Nicholas."

He wasn't going to sway her; he hadn't thought he would, but had felt compelled to try. If anything, the night seemed to have hardened her resolve.

So be it.

"Very well. I'll ride over with you. But before we go, tell me more of Nicholas. Does he have servants with him? Anyone who might be an accomplice?"

"No, he brought no one. He drove himself down."

"Do you know anything about his life over the last decade? How long has he been at the Foreign Office?"

"I got the impression he'd started there quite young—he's thirty-one now. Elaine spoke of him as following in his father's footsteps—she made it sound like that had always been the case."

He nodded. He'd asked Dalziel for a complete report on Nicholas, but hadn't yet received it. After seeing the marks on Gimby's body, he was looking for some indication that Nicholas had the necessary qualifications to inflict such finely honed damage. It wasn't a skill acquired at Oxford, nor yet at the Foreign Office. So where, and when, had Nicholas, if it was he, learned the finer points of brutal interrogation?

With an inward sigh, he rose and waved her to the door. As he followed her, he murmured, "I'm not happy about your going back."

Without glancing around at him, she answered, "I know."

He walked with her to the stables. His meetings with Nicholas thus far had been equivocal; while he could view him as cold-blooded, he hadn't seen him as a killer, as the sort of man who could execute another. None knew better than he that such men didn't conform to any particular style, yet if he'd had to guess . . . but he couldn't afford to guess, not with Penny going back to Wallingham, back under the same roof as Nicholas.

He'd thought long and hard about summoning his mother or Elaine back from London, but he knew all too well what would happen. The whole gaggle—his sisters, her half sisters, his sisters-in-law—would come jauntering home to see what was going on, ready to help. The prospect was horrifying.

Gimby's death had confirmed beyond doubt that there was some treasonous scheme to be uncovered, one involving persons still alive. Indeed, the killer's appearance only emphasized the necessity of bringing the whole to a rapid end, of exposing the scheme and cleaning the slate.

Penny returning to Wallingham was, unfortunately, the fastest way to that rapid end. He didn't have to approve or like it, but there was plenty he could and intended to do to ease his mind.

Their horses were waiting; he lifted her to her saddle, noting as he subsequently swung up to Domino's back that she no longer reacted so skittishly to his nearness—her senses still leapt, but she was once more growing accustomed to his touch. Well and good. Step by small step.

They rode across his fields, eschewing conversation and the lanes to jump the low hedges, then thunder over the turf. The wind off the Channel was fresh, faintly warm; it blew in their faces, ruffled their horses' manes. After crossing the river, they followed the low escarpment, descending to the fields only when in sight of Wallingham Hall.

Riding into the stables, he dismounted and lifted Penny down, then watched as she told the stablemen and grooms that she was home to stay. They were patently glad she was back. He surmised Nicholas hadn't won them over, something he did with a few well-placed queries and a joke. They grinned, bobbed their heads deferentially, but they remembered him well; he strolled to the house beside Penny, confident they would be his to command should the need arise.

"Was Nicholas's mount in the stables?"

"His pair were there. He's been riding Granville's hacks—all of them were there, too."

"So he's at home. I wonder what he's up to?"

Ransacking the library was the answer. After sweeping into the house and informing the housekeeper, Mrs. Figgs, and the butler, Norris, that she was home to stay, Penny, on being informed Lord Arbry was in the library, waved Norris away, crossed the hall to the library's double doors, set them wide, and walked in.

"Ah! There you are, Nicholas." She smiled at Nicholas, scrambling, faintly flushed, to his feet. He'd been sitting on the floor, clearly working his way through the large tomes on the shelf from which Penny had removed the book of maps. Various books on the locality lay open around him.

Recovering, Nicholas stepped forward, away from the books, which he ignored. "Penelope." His gaze went past her to Charles, watching from the doorway; his expression drained. "Lostwithiel."

"Arbry." Charles returned Nicholas's nod. Shutting the doors, he followed Penny into the room.

Nicholas looked from him to Penny, uncertain whom to address. He settled on Penny. "To what do I owe this visit?" He attempted to make the question jocularly light, but failed; it was patently clear he wished them elsewhere.

With a brilliant smile, Penny swung her heavy skirts about and sank gracefully into a chair before the fireplace. "I just came to tell you this isn't a visit. Charles's Cousin Emily's sister has taken poorly, so Emily has gone north to be with her. She left this morning, so here I am"—she spread her arms—"returning to my ancestral home."

Nicholas studied her, then frowned. "I thought . . ."

"That my residing here while you, too, are in residence is inappropriate?" Penny's smile turned understanding. "Indeed, and with the Abbey so close, my second home, and with Cousin Emily there, it seemed wise not to give even the highest stickler cause to whisper. *However.*"

She looked at Charles; a faint smile curving her lips, she returned her gaze to Nicholas. "As Charles pointed out, residing under my ancestral roof with a distant relative is far more acceptable than residing under *his* roof with only him for company. That, even the least censorious would find difficult to countenance."

They hadn't discussed how to explain her return to Nicholas; Charles watched, more wryly amused than she could know as she airily, with quite spurious ingenuousness, informed Nicholas that sharing a roof with him was indisputably the lesser of two evils.

All he had to do to lend her story credence was to meet Nicholas's eyes, and smile.

Nicholas considered his smile for only a second, then swallowed Penny's story whole. Facing her, he manufactured a smile. "I see. Of course, in the circumstances, I'm happy to have you home again. Perhaps you could speak with Mrs. Figgs. She had a number of questions that I'm afraid I had no notion of. I'm sure she'll be glad to have your hand on the tiller again."

Penny rose. "Yes, of course. I'll go and see her now, and I must change before luncheon."

She looked at Charles. He'd turned to view the jumble of books Nicholas had been studying. "Learning the local lore, or were you looking for something specific?" He glanced at Nicholas. "Perhaps I could help?"

His gaze on the books, Nicholas hesitated, then said, "It was more by way of learning the local history." He looked at Charles. "I understand there's a tradition in these parts of preying on the French from the sea."

Charles grinned, relaxed, unthreatening. "There's the Fowey Gallants, of course—historical and contemporary. Have you come across them yet?"

"Only in the books." Nicholas took the bait. "Are they still in existence?"

"I'll leave you two to your discussions." Penny picked up her trailing habit; already intent on furthering their quite different aims, the pair accorded her no more than vague nods as she turned away. Leaving the library, she inwardly shook her head. If Nicholas wasn't careful, he'd soon be thinking the big bad wolf with the very sharp teeth was his very best friend.

She returned to the library an hour later, with luncheon shortly to be served. Garbed in a round gown of soft gray—perfect for the excursion she planned for later that afternoon—she walked in on a scene that had subtly altered.

It wasn't just that Charles was now seated, elegantly relaxed in the chair before the fireplace, holding forth, or that Nicholas was leaning against the front edge of the library desk, hanging on Charles's every word. No. Something had happened while she'd been out of the room. She knew it the instant they both looked at her.

Charles smiled, and a tingle ran from her crown to her heels, leaving all places between alert, on edge. Tensing. Slowly, employing to the full that ridiculous extreme of languid grace he possessed, he uncrossed his long legs and stood.

Nicholas looked from her to Charles and back again, a hint of concern in his eyes. "Ah . . . Charles explained your . . . understanding."

She blinked. Managed not to parrot, *Understanding?*

"Mmm," Charles purred, strolling toward her. His sensuality, not this time menacing so much as enveloping, was unrestrained, a tangible force, a current carried on thin air, reaching for her, wrapping about her. "Given you're now fixed here, and he'll therefore no doubt see us together, I didn't want Arbry getting the wrong idea."

His eyes had locked on hers; reading all that glittered in the deep dark blue, she saw not just satisfaction at the consummate mastery with which he'd exploited the situation, making Nicholas feel that he had no real interest in him, but also a devilish glint she'd seen often enough in the eyes of a wild and reckless youth. "I see."

His long lips lifted; he smiled into her eyes. "I felt sure you would."

Halting beside her, he reached for her hand, lifted it to his lips.

Eyes locked on hers, he kissed.

Damn, he was good. She was distantly aware that Nicholas was watching, yet was far more aware of the compulsion drawing her to Charles, weakening her resistance, making her wish to lean into him, to lift her face and offer her lips . . . the clearing of a throat behind her broke the spell.

"Luncheon is served, my lady, my lords."

Thank heaven! She managed to half turn and acknowledge Norris. Charles lightly squeezed her fingers, then set her hand on his sleeve.

He turned her to the door, glancing back at Nicholas. "Shall we?"

Luncheon had been set out in the small dining parlor overlooking the back garden. Charles seated her at the round table, then took the chair on her left; Nicholas claimed the one on her right.

Under cover of the conversation—about horses, local industries, the local crops—the casual conversation any two landowners might exchange, she tried to imagine what "understanding" Charles had revealed to Nicholas.

The basic element was easy to guess, but just how far had he gone? Having glimpsed that glint in his eye, she was longing to get him alone and wring the truth from him. And most likely, knowing him, berate him after that. She spent most of the meal planning for that last.

In between, she watched Nicholas. Even though he was distracted by Charles's glib facade, still wary yet not sure how wary he needed to be, there remained an essential reserve, a nervous watchfulness that didn't bode well for a guilt-free conscience.

Was she sitting beside a murderer?

She lowered her gaze to Nicholas's hands. Quite decent hands as men's hands went, passably well manicured, yet they didn't seem menacing.

Glancing to her left, she reflected that if she had to judge the murderer purely on the basis of hands, Charles would be her guess.

She'd seen Gimby's body, still felt a chill as the vision swam into her mind. Yet she couldn't seem to fix the revulsion she felt certain she would feel for whoever had slain Gimby on Nicholas.

Then again, as Charles had pointed out, an accomplice might have committed the actual deed, someone they didn't yet know about.

She was making a mental note to check with Cook and Figgs to make sure there were no food or supplies mysteriously vanishing—she knew how easy it was to move about any big house at night—when the men finally laid down their napkins and stood.

Rising, too, she fixed a smile on her lips and extended her hand to Charles. "Thank you for seeing me home."

Taking her hand, faintly smiling, he met her eyes. "I thought you wanted to go into Fowey?"

She stared into his dark blue eyes. How the devil had he known?

Smile deepening—she was quite sure he could read her mind at that moment—he went on, "I'll drive you in." His tone altered fractionally, enough for her to catch his warning. "You shouldn't go wandering the town alone."

Not only had he guessed where she was going, but why.

Nicholas cleared his throat. "Thank you, Lostwithiel—now Penelope is living here, I confess I'd feel happier if she had your escort."

She turned to stare at Nicholas. Had he run mad? She was no pensioner of his that he need be concerned. She drew breath.

Charles pinched her fingers—hard.

She swung back to him, incensed, but he was nodding, urbanely, to Nicholas. "Indeed. We'll be back long before dinner."

"Good. Good. I must get back to the accounts. If you'll excuse me?"

With a brief bow, Nicholas escaped.

Penny watched him depart; the instant he cleared the doorway she swung to face Charles—

"Not yet." He turned her to the hall. "Get your cloak, and let's get out of here."

In the past, she'd been quite successful at bottling up the feelings he provoked; now . . . it was as if letting loose one set of feelings had weakened her ability to hold back any others. By the time she'd gone upstairs, fetched her cloak, descended to where he waited in the hall, nose in the air allowed him to swing the cloak over her shoulders, then take her arm and escort her outside, she was steaming.

"What in all Hades did you tell him?"

The question came out as a muted shriek.

Charles looked at her, his expression mild, unperturbed; he knew perfectly well why she was exercised but clearly believed himself on firm ground. "Just enough to smooth our way."

"What?"

He looked ahead. "I told him we had an understanding of sorts. Recently developed and still developing, but with its roots buried in the dim distant past."

She stopped dead. Stared, aghast and flabbergasted, at him. "You didn't tell him?"

"Tell him what?"

His clipped accents, the look in his eyes, warned her not to pursue that tack; he'd never breathed a word of their past to anyone, any more than she had.

She found her voice. "We have Lady Trescowthick's party tonight. He's invited. What happens when he mentions our 'understanding'?"

He shook his head, caught her hand and drew her on. "I told him it's a secret. So secret even our families have yet to hear of it."

"And he believed you?"

He glanced briefly at her. "What's so strange about that?" Looking ahead, he went on, "I've recently returned from the wars to assume an inheritance and responsibilities I never thought would be mine. I accept I need to marry, but have little time for the marriage mart nor liking for chits with hay for wits, and here you are—a lady of my own class I've known for forever, and you're still unmarried. Perfect."

She didn't like it, not one bit. Taking three quick strides, she got ahead of him and swung to face him, forcing him to halt.

So she could look him in the eye. Study those midnight blue eyes she couldn't always read . . . they were unreadable now, but watching her. "Charles . . ."

She couldn't think how to phrase it—how to warn him not to imagine . . .

He arched a brow. They were almost breast to chest. Without warning, he bent his head and brushed his lips, infinitely lightly, across hers.

"Fowey," he breathed. "Remember?"

She closed her eyes, mentally cursed as familiar heat streaked down her spine, then jerked her eyes open as, her hand locked in his, he towed her around and on.

"Come on."

She let out an exasperated hiss. If he was going to be difficult, he would be, and there was nothing she could do to change that.

Granville's curricle was waiting when they reached the stable yard, a pair of young blacks between the shafts. Charles lifted her up to the seat, then followed. She grabbed the rail as the curricle tipped with his weight, then he sat; she fussed with her skirts, helpless to prevent their thighs, hips, and shoulders from touching almost constantly.

It was not destined to be a comfortable drive.

Charles flicked the whip and expertly steered the pair down the drive. She paid no attention to the familiar scenery; instead, she revisited the scene in the library before luncheon, and luncheon, too, incorporating Nicholas's belief in their "understanding" . . . Nicholas's reactions still didn't quite fit.

She drew in a tight breath. "You told him we were lovers."

Eventually, Charles replied, "I didn't actually say so."

"But you led him to think it. Why?"

She glanced at him, but he kept his gaze on the horses.

"Because it was the most efficient way of convincing him that if he so much as reaches out a hand toward you, I'll chop it off."

Any other man and it would have sounded melodramatic. But she knew him, knew his voice—recognized the statement as cold hard fact. She'd seen the currents lurking beneath his surface, the menace, knew it was real; he was perfectly capable of being that violent.

Never to her, or indeed any woman. On her behalf, however . . .

She let out a long breath. "It's one thing to protect me, but just remember—you don't own me."

"If I owned you, you would at this moment be locked in my apartments at the Abbey."

"Well, you don't, I'm not—you'll just have to get used to it."

Or do something to change the status quo. Charles kept his tongue still and steered the curricle down the road to Fowey.

They left the curricle at the Pelican and strolled down to the quay.

Penny scanned the harbor. "The fleet is out."

"Not for long." He nodded to the horizon. A flotilla of sails were drawing nearer. "They're on their way in. We'll have to hurry."

He took her arm, and they turned up into the meaner lanes, eventually reaching Mother Gibbs's door. He knocked. A minute later, the door cracked open, and Mother Gibbs peered out.

She was flabbergasted to see him, a point he saw Penny note.

"M'lord—Lady Penelope." Mother Gibbs bobbed. "How can I help ye?"

Somewhat grimly he said, "I think we'd better talk inside."

He didn't want to cross the threshold himself, much less take Penny with him, but she'd already been there, alone; they didn't have time to accommodate his sensibilities.

Mother Gibbs would speak much more freely in her own house.

"*Dead*, you say?" Mother Gibbs plopped down on the rough stool by her kitchen table. "Mercy be!"

It was transparently the first she'd heard of Gimby's death.

"Tell your sons," he said. "There's someone around who's willing to kill if he believes anyone knows anything."

"Here—it's not that new lordling up at the Hall, is it?" Mother Gibbs looked from him to Penny. "The one you was asking after." She looked back at Charles. "Dennis did mention this new bloke had been asking questions and they'd strung him along like . . ." She paled. "Mercy me— I'll tell 'em to stop that. He might think they really do know something."

"Yes, tell them to stop hinting they know anything, but we don't know that it was Lord Arbry. Tell Dennis from me that it's not safe to think it was him, in case it's someone else altogether."

He would have to speak to Dennis again, but not tonight. He refocused on Mother Gibbs. "Now, tell me everything you know about Gimby."

She blinked at him. "I didn't even know he was dead."

"I don't mean about his death, but when he was alive. What do you know of him?"

It was little enough, but tallied with what the old sailor had told them.

Penny asked after Nicholas; Mother Gibbs had little to add to her earlier report. "Been down Bodinnick way, he has, talking to the men there again, saying the same thing— that he's in Granville's place now and anyone asking for Granville should be sent to him."

"All right." He took a sovereign from his pocket and placed it on the table. "I want you to keep your ears open for anything anyone lets fall about Gimby or his father, and especially about anyone seen near his cottage recently, or anyone asking for him recently."

Mother Gibbs nodded and reached for the sovereign. "I'll

tell me boys to do the same. Those Smollets might not have been sociable-like, but there was no 'arm in them that I ever saw. That Gimby didn't deserve to have his throat cut, that's fer certain."

He wasn't entirely sure that was true, but said nothing to dampen Mother Gibbs's rising zeal. "If you hear anything, no matter how insignificant it may seem, get Dennis to send word to me—he knows how."

Mother Gibbs nodded, face set, chins wobbling. "Aye, I'll do that."

They left and walked quickly back to the harbor. They reached the quay to see the first of the boats nudging up to the stone wharf. Charles hesitated. If he'd been alone, he would have gone down to the wharf and lent a hand unloading the catch, and asked his questions under cover of the usual jokes and gibes, and later in the tavern. But he had Penny with him, and . . .

"Lady Trescowthick's party, remember? She's unlikely to approve of the odor of fresh mackerel."

She'd leaned close, speaking over the raucous cries of the gulls. He glanced at her, met her eyes, then nodded toward the High Street. "Come on, then. Let's head back."

They did, driving along in the late afternoon with the sun slowly sinking in the west and the breeze flirting with wisps of Penny's hair.

She sat in her corner of the curricle's seat, and tried unsuccessfully to think of ways to further their investigation. Impossible; if she'd kept on her habit and ridden into Fowey, she might have been able to focus her mind. As it was, she'd very willingly *unfocus* it, suspend all thought, all awareness.

Being close to Charles for any length of time had always suborned her senses. She tried, kept trying, to tell herself she found his nearness uncomfortable . . . lies, all lies. She was good at them when it came to him.

The truth, one she'd known for years and still didn't understand, couldn't unquestioningly accept, was that, quite aside from the titillation of her senses, he made her feel *comfortable* in a way no other ever had. It was a feeling that reached deeper, that was more fundamental, that meant more than the merely sensual.

One word leapt to mind whenever she thought of him—*strength*. It was what she was most aware of in him, that when he was beside her, his strength was hers to command, or if she wished, she could simply lean on him, and he would be her strength and her shield. He'd protect her from anything, lift any and all burdens from her shoulders, perhaps laugh at her while he did and call her Squib, but yet he would do it—she could rely on him in that.

No other had been so constant, so unchanging and unwavering in his readiness to support and protect her. Not her father, not Granville. No one else.

Charles was the only man in her life she'd ever turned to, the only man, even now, she could imagine leaning on.

She sat back in the curricle, felt the breeze caress her cheeks. It seemed odd to be sitting next to him after all their years apart, and only now comprehend just how much she'd missed him.

CHAPTER

❧ 9 ❧

THEY RATTLED INTO THE STABLE YARD, AND THE GROOMS came running; Charles tossed them the reins and came to hand her down.

For a moment, he seemed distracted, then he focused on her. "I'll come over and we can go to Branscombe Hall in your carriage. You might suggest to Nicholas that he drive himself there."

She arched a brow, but he merely said, "I'll be here at seven-thirty."

He took her arm and walked her to the edge of the lawn. "I'll see you then. I want to check that pair before I leave."

Releasing her, he stepped back, saluted her, and turned away. Remaining where she was, she watched him walk back toward the stables.

Waited. Caught his eye when he glanced back.

Saw the exasperated twist of his lips as he stopped and, hands rising to his hips, looked back at her.

She laughed, shook her head at him, then turned and headed for the house. He wanted to go and play horses with the grooms and ask God only knew what questions, and he didn't want her cramping his style. All well and good—he should simply have said so.

A cynical smile curved her lips. Surely he didn't imagine she wouldn't guess and remember to interrogate him later?

* * *

Later was seven-thirty, when true to his word he strode up from the stables. She heard his footsteps in the hall and left the drawing room to join him.

He'd entered from the garden; he walked out of the shadows at the back of the hall into the light cast by the chandelier.

Her breath caught; she felt her chest tighten, felt her heart contract. All he needed was an earring dangling from one lobe to be the walking embodiment of any lady's private dream.

Halting, he arched a brow at her.

Smiling at her own fantasy, she went forward. He was perfectly turned out in an evening coat the same color as his eyes, a dark, intense blue one shade removed from black. His shirt and cravat were pristine white, his waistcoat a subdued affair of dark blue and black swirls, his long legs draped in black trousers that emphasized rather than concealed their muscled strength.

The cut of coat, waistcoat, the style of his trousers, was austere. On any other man, the effect would be too severe, yet he exuded an impression of high drama, of larger-than-life abilities—a strong hint of the piratical remained.

She raised her gaze to his face, only to discover his had reached her toes, clad in gilded Grecian sandals and fleetingly, flirtingly visible beneath her skirt's hem. She halted before him.

He looked up—slowly—his gaze tracing the lines of her gray-blue silk gown. The hue was several shades darker than her eyes, chosen to complement them and her fair hair. She'd had her maid dress her hair in a stylish knot, leaving tendrils trailing to bob about her ears and caress her bare shoulders.

Just as his gaze did before lifting to her throat, her chin, her lips, finally meeting her eyes. He looked into them and smiled. As if he was some fantastical beast and his only thought was to devour her.

Ruthlessly, she suppressed a shiver. Casting him what she hoped was a worldly, cynical, and warning look, she gave him her hand.

His smile only deepened; his eyes flashed as he raised her fingers to his lips and lightly kissed. "Come. Let's go." He turned her to the front door as the sound of wheels on the gravel reached them. "Did Nicholas go ahead?"

"Yes." She smiled. "He was rather unsure what to make of our arrangements. He left in his curricle about ten minutes ago."

"Good."

The footman was holding the carriage door; Charles handed her in, then followed, sitting beside her on the mercifully wide seat.

As the footman shut the door, she asked, "Why good?"

"So that by the time we arrive, he'll be involved with other guests. I want to watch him, but from a distance, not as one of the same circle."

Relaxing against the seat as the carriage rolled down the drive, she digested that, then remembered. "What did you learn from the grooms?"

He was looking out of the window. She waited, confident he would reply, yet she would have given a great deal to know what he was thinking.

Eventually he said, "Nicholas has been riding out during the day and at night. Sometimes to Fowey, sometimes to Lostwithiel and beyond. Not as constantly as he did in February, but often enough. As far as I can make out, he could have killed Gimby, but there's no evidence he actually did."

After a moment, she asked, "Do you think he did?"

Another long pause ensued, then he looked at her. "Gimby wasn't simply killed—he was interrogated, then executed. I'm having a difficult time seeing Nicholas as interrogator-cum-executioner. I can imagine him ordering it done, but not getting his hands soiled with the actual doing. He may well be guilty of Gimby's death, but might never have set foot in that cottage.

"And no, before you ask, I haven't any idea who he might have got to do the deed. I doubt they're local, which means they shouldn't be that difficult to trace. I've put the word

around that I'm looking for news of any passing stranger—
we'll see what turns up."

The gates of Branscombe Hall loomed ahead. In short order, the carriage rocked to a halt; Charles descended and
handed her down.

Lady Trescowthick, waiting to greet them inside her front
hall, all but cooed at the sight of them—not, Penny reminded herself, because her ladyship thought there was anything between them, but purely because she'd succeeded in
getting them both, as individuals, to her event.

Parting from her ladyship, they walked to the archway
leading into the ballroom; Penny glanced sidelong at Charles.

He saw, raised a brow.

Lips twitching, she looked ahead. "Just as well most of
the unmarried young ladies are in London, or you'd be in serious trouble."

"Ah, but I'm entering the arena well armed."

"Oh?"

His hand covered hers on his sleeve. "With you."

She nearly choked on a laugh. "That's a *dreadful* pun."

"But apt." Pausing on the threshold, he scanned the room,
then glanced down at her. "It would be helpful if you could
resist temptation and remain by my side. If I have to guard
my own back against feminine attack, I won't be able to concentrate on Nicholas."

She threw him a look designed to depress pretension, not
that she expected it to succeed, then swept forward to greet
Lady Carmody. Yet as she and he commenced a slow circle
of the room, she bore his words in mind; he hadn't been joking. In this situation, staying by his side undoubtedly qualified as doing all she could to further his investigation.

Ladies had always chased him; at twenty, he'd been a
magnet for feminine attention, far more than his brothers
had ever been. And he hadn't been the earl then, not even
next in line for the title.

She'd been one of the few who had never pursued him—
there'd never been any need. She'd simply let him chase her.

And look where that had landed them.

Ruthlessly, she quashed the thought. Thinking of such things while he was anywhere near wasn't wise. Let alone when he was standing beside her.

True to form, he glanced sharply at her.

She pretended not to notice and gave her attention to Lady Harbottle. "I had no idea Melissa was feeling so low."

"Oh, it's just a passing thing. I daresay now she's been a week in Bath she'll be right as rain again and back any day." Lady Harbottle smiled delightedly at Charles. "I know she'll want to hold a party as soon as she gets back—to renew old acquaintances, if nothing else."

Charles smiled, and pretended he couldn't see the speculation running through her ladyship's head. The instant an opening offered, he steered Penny away. "Refresh my memory—didn't Melissa Harbottle marry?"

"Yes. She's now Melissa Barrett. She married a mill owner much older than she. He died over a year ago."

"Ah." After a moment, he asked, "Am I to infer that her trip to Bath wasn't to try the waters?"

"Melissa?" Penny's incredulous tone was answer enough.

"So she might now be described as a widow with aspirations?"

"Quite definite aspirations. She's now wealthy enough to look rather higher than a mill owner."

"If by any chance she asks you, do be sure to tell her to look somewhere other than the Abbey."

She chuckled. "I will if she asks, but I doubt she will. Ask me, that is."

He swore beneath his breath and steered her to the next group of guests.

It was a relaxed affair. Most of the local gentry who'd resisted the lure of the capital were present; it was indeed a useful venue to renew acquaintances and realign his memory. Whenever any lady with a daughter yet unwed eyed him too intently, he glibly steered the conversation in Penny's direction—most took the hint. Some, indeed, suspected rather more.

Their speculation didn't bother him, but he took care to

avoid jogging Penny's awareness to life. Juggling her while dealing with a serious investigation was difficult enough without fashioning rods for his own back.

A waltz, however, was too much of a temptation to resist.

"Come and dance." He caught her hand and drew her through the still-chattering guests.

"What . . . ? Charles—"

Reaching the dance floor, he swung her into his arms, and into the swirling, twirling throng.

Penny frowned at him. "I was going to say I don't want to waltz."

"Why not? You're passably good at it."

"I spent four Seasons in London—of course, I can waltz."

"So can I."

"I'd noticed." She could hardly help it; she felt as if her senses were whirling, twirling, around him.

He smiled, and drew her a fraction closer as they went through the turn, predictably didn't ease his hold as they came out of it. "We've danced before."

"But never a waltz—if you recall, before, it was considered too fast." For good reason, it seemed. She'd never felt anything but elegantly graceful when waltzing with other men. Now she felt breathless, close to witless.

The waltz might have been designed as a display for Charles's brand of masculine strength. With effortless grace, he whirled her down the room. Heads turned as they passed; others looked on in patent envy.

She had to relax in his arms, let her feet follow his lead without conscious thought, or she'd stumble—and he'd catch her, laugh, and set her right again. She was determined she wouldn't let that happen, that for once, she'd match him on a physical plane.

And she did. Calmly, serenely.

Not, however, without paying a price.

It was impossible not to note how well they suited, he so tall, so large, she a slender reed in his arms, but tall enough, with legs long enough to match him. Impossible not to be aware of how easily he held her, how much in his physical control she was, albeit he wasn't truly exercising that control; this time, in this exchange, she was a willing partner.

That exchange itself tightened her nerves, left her senses in a state of abraded alert. In the cocoon the revolutions of the waltz wove about them, it was impossible not to know, to feel, just how powerful was the attraction that, contrary to her expectations, still existed between them.

Impossible not to know that she still evoked the same sexual interest and intentness in him. Impossible not to acknowledge that she reacted to that, responded far more deeply, in a more fundamental way than was wise.

His hand spread low on her back, burning through her thin gown, his other hand engulfing hers, were not simple contacts but statements, his hard thigh pressing between hers as they whirled through the tight turns both a memory and a declaration.

Her senses quivered; the moment shook her, yet focused on him, on staying with him and not letting him sweep her wits away, she realized that however much she felt and knew and experienced, he did, too.

That last was apparent when the music ended, and he reluctantly slowed, halted, and released her. She heard the breath he drew in—as tight, as constricted, as her own. The knowledge buoyed her; if there was weakness here, it wasn't hers alone.

"Nicholas," Charles murmured. Nicholas was standing a short distance away, talking with Lord Trescowthick; he looked rather pale, his stance was stiff, and he shifted frequently. "He seems rather tense. Is he always like that?"

Penny studied him, eventually replied, "He wasn't when he first came down last year, but over the past few months, yes. He doesn't look like he's sleeping all that well."

"Indeed." Charles took her arm. "There are at least five gentlemen present I can't place." She'd already filled him in on the marriages he'd missed over the years, and the deaths, and the changes they'd wrought in the local community. "Five is more than I would have expected at this time of year. Let's see what we can learn about them."

The guests had spread out, making it easy to drift from group to group. They approached Lady Essington, Millie and Julia's formidable mother-in-law; a large, heavyset gentleman had remained by her side throughout.

He proved to be a Mr. Yarrow, a relative of Lady Essington, come to the milder Cornish coast to convalesce after a bout of pneumonia. A taciturn man in his late thirties, he had hard hazel eyes and seemed hale enough.

Lady Essington, an old gorgon, was not of a mind to let Penny leave on Charles's arm; indeed, Charles wondered if she had designs on Penny with a view to Mr. Yarrow. The impasse was resolved without him having to resort to earlish arrogance by Mr. Robinson, a local gentleman who requested Penny's hand for a country dance.

Charles let her go. Extracting himself from Lady Essington's clutches, he retreated to the side of the room to wait, not patiently, for Penny to return.

Propping against the wall, he swiftly reviewed his dispositions. With respect to Penny's safety, his pickets were in place, all the elements of his plan to protect her now she'd returned to the Hall successfully deployed. As for his investigation, that was proceeding as fast as was wise; there was nothing he could do beyond what he already had in train until he heard back from Dalziel.

In his personal pursuit of Penny, he was still reconnoitering the terrain. He was too wise to ride blithely in and end in a quagmire, as he somehow had all those years ago; this time, he was going in extrawarily. He'd learned her reason for *not* marrying all the gentlemen who'd wooed her; quite what that told him of what would convince her to say *yes* he hadn't yet worked out.

That was one point he needed to pursue. Another was why she didn't agree that she was the perfect wife for him. She'd been bothered by his recitation of the obvious; that didn't bode well. He was going to have to learn what her reservation was and work to address it.

And, knowing her, work it would be; influencing Penelope Jane Marissa Selborne had never been easy.

He straightened from the wall as she returned to his side—of her own volition, so he didn't have to go and openly reclaim her hand, for which he gave due thanks; he needed to avoid being obvious, but there was a limit to his forbearance.

Retaking the arm he offered, she dismissed Robinson with an easy smile, then glanced up at him. "Who next?"

It was the investigation that had brought her back. Nevertheless, he was grateful for small mercies.

He looked across the room. A well–set up gentleman in his late twenties stood talking to Mr. Kilpatrick. "Any idea who he is?"

"None. Shall we find out?"

Together, they crossed the room.

Mr. Julian Fothergill was an ardent bird-watcher come to the district intent on spotting all the species peculiar to the area.

"Quite a challenge to do it in a month, but I'm determined." Brown-eyed, brown-haired, with pale patrician features and an easy smile, Fothergill, a few inches shorter than Charles, was a distant relative of the socially reclusive Lord Culver. "I remembered the area from when I visited as a boy."

They discussed the local geography, then moved on to join Lord Trescowthick and a Mr. Swaley. A gentleman of middle years, middle height, and wiry build, Mr. Swaley was staying with the Trescowthicks. He became rather reserved when Charles politely inquired what had brought him to the district. "Just looking around—a pleasant spot."

With an amiable expression, but tight lips, Swaley added nothing more.

Charles didn't press, but, smiling easily, extolled the virtues of the district. Realizing his tack, Penny did her part; it soon became clear that Mr. Swaley's interest was focused more on the land than the sea.

"Though what that tells us," she murmured as they moved on, "I can't imagine."

Charles said nothing but steered her to where Mr. and

Mrs. Cranfield of nearby Cranfield Grange were entertaining the fourth mystery man.

He'd alerted his grooms and sent word to the smuggling gangs to let him know of any itinerant visitor. Gimby's murderer, however, might move in higher circles; none knew better than Charles that executioners could be as aristocratic as he. He'd warned Dennis Gibbs not to assume Nicholas was the murderer, specifically not to let that assumption blind him to other potential candidates. That was excellent advice.

Mr. Albert Carmichael, a gentleman Charles guessed to be much his own age, was indeed a houseguest of the Cranfields. Before he could ask what had brought Carmichael to the area, the man asked about the local hunting, then progressed to what shooting might be expected and when, and what type of fishing was to be had, both in the rivers and the sea.

"Is it easy to get the local fishermen to take one out?"

Inwardly bemused, Charles answered, encouraged by a nodding Mrs. Cranfield. Then Imogen Cranfield, who'd been dancing with Mr. Farley, returned to her mother's side, and all became clear.

Imogen had been a plain, rather dumpy girl; she'd grown into a plainer, still somewhat dumpy woman, but she greeted him quite happily, then turned to Carmichael. In seconds it was apparent just what hopes the Cranfields had of Carmichael.

Mrs. Cranfield turned to Penny. "Now, dear, you will remember to send me that recipe, won't you?"

Penny smiled and pressed her hand. "I'll send a groom over with it tomorrow." Sliding her hand onto Charles's arm, she nodded in farewell.

Mrs. Cranfield beamed and let them go.

Another waltz had just commenced. Charles glanced over the heads, noting the dancers, then, taking her arm, he steered her to the French doors left open to the terrace. They stepped out into the cooler air. The terrace was presently deserted; they strolled a little, away from the open doors.

"That's four," she said, halting by the balustrade. "None of them seem at all likely, do they?"

Stopping beside her, Charles glanced back at the ballroom. "None, however, is out of contention. Gimby was slight. All four are physically capable of having murdered him and, most annoyingly, all four have been in the area for at least four days—over the time Gimby died."

"You were hoping only one would have been?"

"It would have made life simpler."

The music drifted out through the windows into the cool stillness of the night. When Charles reached for her she reacted too slowly to prevent him gathering her into his arms. He held her close, far closer than permissible in a ballroom, yet they'd been closer, even recently.

Their hips brushed, her gown shushed against his trousers as he revolved to every second beat, a slower, far more intimate dance than that being performed inside. As they turned, she glanced briefly about, but there was no one else on the terrace to see. Refocusing on his face, on the strong line of his jaw, the seductive curve of his lips, she stated the obvious. "Charles, this is not a good idea."

"Why not?" His voice was a dark caress. "You like it."

That was precisely why not. She didn't dare take a deep breath or her breasts would press against his chest. She looked into his eyes, aware of the compulsion rising in her veins, that had always afflicted her when in his arms. Her senses might leap, alert and tense, but only in expectation; the more time she spent with him, the more often she was in his arms, the more she enjoyed, the more she was tempted, the less resistance she could muster. That had been the case long ago; she hadn't thought that it still would be, yet it was.

What she saw in his eyes nearly made her heart stop, sent a lick of something like fear down her spine.

"Charles, listen to me. We are not, definitely not, revisiting the past."

He didn't smile, didn't flash his pirate's grin and return some teasing answer. Instead, he read her eyes, yet she sensed he assessed himself as well before replying, his voice deep and low, "It's not the past I want to visit."

In the ballroom the music ended with a flourish; somewhat to her surprise, he halted and released her, his palm sliding caressingly over her silk-clad hip, a last, illicit, heat-laden caress. Taking her hand, he set it on his sleeve. "Come. We've one more stranger to meet."

Back inside, he led her to a group of younger gentlemen who'd been partnering the few young ladies present. Most of marriageable age were in London, but for various reasons a few remained.

The Trescowthicks' youngest son Mark, an effete, foppish young man not long down from Oxford, was holding court surrounded by his local contemporaries and one other—a tall, thin, dark-complexioned man Penny had never seen before.

All the local youth accorded Charles a near-godlike status; they instantly came to attention. With his usual bonhomie, he nodded to each, acknowledging them by name, leaving most with their tongues tied.

Mark Trescowthick, stuttering, hurried to introduce his friend. "Phillipe, the Chevalier Gerond."

The Chevalier bowed. Penny bobbed a curtsy. The Chevalier was, she judged, a few years older than Mark, somewhere in his midtwenties. He was as tall as Charles, but blade-thin, appearing rather elongated.

Charles nodded urbanely. "Chevalier—are you visiting our country, or . . . ?"

"I have lived here most of my life—my family arrived among the earliest emigrés, fleeing the Terror." His tone defensive, the Chevalier's gaze traveled Charles's face, taking in his un-English features.

Charles smiled faintly. "My mother, too, was an emigrée."

"Ah." The Chevalier nodded, and looked back to the other members of the group, but they were all waiting on Charles's direction.

"What brings you to our neck of the woods, Chevalier? I would have thought London more . . . rewarding."

The Chevalier flushed faintly, but met Charles's eyes. "I have decisions to make—whether this peace will hold, and if so, whether I should return to France. There is nothing left of my family's estate, but"—he shrugged—"the land is still there." He looked over the room. "It is, if not quiet here, then peaceful. Mark was kind enough to invite me to stay for a few weeks—it seemed the perfect spot to consider and let my thoughts come clear."

"I say!" Mark put in. "Charles was in France for years with the Guards. Perhaps he knows of your house and village?"

"I doubt it," the Chevalier said. "It is near to St. Cloud— far, far from the battlefields."

Charles confirmed he knew nothing of that area. He put a few questions to the local young men, asking after the shooting and fishing, enough to account for his approaching them, also enough to learn that the Chevalier had been at Branscombe Hall for the past five days. Having gained answers to their immediate questions, he steered her away.

The party was starting to break up, the first guests departing. They fell in with the general exodus. Chatting with others, they strolled side by side into the front hall; Penny noted that Nicholas was one of the first to make his bow to Lady Trescowthick and go quickly down the front steps and out into the night.

The Chevalier was in the ballroom behind them; she wondered if he and Nicholas had met . . . would meet, perhaps tonight. They could check in the stables when they reached Wallingham; Nicholas should be home well ahead of them.

After thanking Lady Trescowthick for an enjoyable evening—and despite their absorption it had been that— Charles handed her into the carriage and followed, shutting the door on the rest of the world.

She sat back in the shadows, waited only until the carriage was rolling to murmur, "What odds finding a French emigré, one who might shortly be returning to France, who just happens to have arrived in the neighborhood at much the same time as Nicholas, who we suspect is passing secrets to the French and might have some complicity in Gimby's murder?"

"Indeed, but it never helps to leap to conclusions. Nicholas made every effort to socialize tonight, despite his preoccupation with something that's causing him considerable concern, yet he didn't single out any of our five visitors—I don't think he spoke to the Chevalier at all."

"If they already know each other, they wouldn't go out of their way to make that known, would they?"

"Possibly not." Charles wanted, very definitely, to get her mind off his investigation; he would much rather she focus on him, on them. Reaching out, he cupped her nape, and drew her to him.

Smoothly drew her lips to his, saw her eyes flare briefly before her lids fell. He held her to the kiss until she softened against him, then let the pleasure well and spill through them both.

She resisted for an instant, then surrendered and sank against him, and he almost groaned. Why with her was it so very different? She was the only woman who had ever had the power to make him ache like this, with a weakness, a longing, a need so potent it made him feel helpless.

Helpless to resist.

He parted her lips and sank into her mouth, into the hot lushness. Released her nape, reached farther, turned her, and lifted her onto his lap.

She pressed her hands to his shoulders, fought to keep her spine rigid. When he lifted his head, her eyes flew wide. "What about the coachman?"

"He's on the box—he can't see." Closing his hands about her waist, he nipped her lower lip. "If you don't shriek, he won't hear."

"Shriek? Why—"

He slid his hands up.

"*Charles*—"

He covered her lips. Let his thumbs cruise the fine silk of her bodice, locating and slowly circling her pebbled nipples. He let his palms cup the soft weight of her breasts, felt them swell and firm. Gloried in the tremor that shook her, that tangled her breath until she breathed through him.

After a long, thorough, painfully arousing exchange, he released her lips and drew in a huge breath. He knew exactly how far it was between Branscombe and Wallingham—not far enough.

Eyes closed, Penny shuddered between his hands, feeling his fingers hard and steely holding her so easily, confident, so certain of her. She'd told herself it would be just a kiss, something she could simply take and enjoy. She'd forgotten that with him there was more, always more.

His head was bowed beside hers; he brushed his lips to her temple. "God, how much I've missed you."

There was a longing in his tone she couldn't mistake, that resonated through her.

I've missed you, too. She held the words back. Yet she *had* missed him, so deeply she was amazed. She hadn't realized . . . only now, now he was back, kissing her again, did she feel the yawning emptiness inside, recognize it, realize it had been with her for a very long time.

Thirteen years, more or less.

The carriage dipped as it passed through the gates of Wallingham. Charles sighed, lifted her and set her on the seat beside him once more.

When the carriage halted and the footman opened the door, she was wrapped in her cloak. Charles descended and handed her out.

She expected him to part from her, to go on to the stables and drive himself home. Instead, he led her up the steps. Catching her puzzled glance, he murmured, "I want to see if Nicholas is home."

According to Norris, he was, but had already retired to his chamber.

Charles pressed her hand, stepped back and saluted her. "I'll call on you later."

His eyes met hers, then he turned and strode off toward the back of the house and the garden door.

She stood watching him, wondering what she was supposed to infer from that last look, then, inwardly shaking her head, she climbed the stairs and headed for her room.

Her maid, Ellie, was waiting. She climbed out of her gown, into her nightgown, then sat on the stool before her dressing table and let down her hair, brushing it while Ellie fussed, shaking out the gown and hanging it, then brushing down her cloak, finally shutting away the pearl necklace and earrings she'd worn in her jewel box.

"Good night, miss. Sleep tight."

In the mirror, she smiled at Ellie. "Thank you, Ellie. Good night."

She continued to brush, laying the long strands of shining pale hair over her shoulders, then she sighed, stood, and snuffed the candles in the sconces on either side of her mirror. Crossing to her bed, she extinguished the candle left burning beside it.

The moonlight streamed in through her windows, a ghostly white light painting all in muted shades.

She was tired, she decided, that was why her mind wouldn't focus, wasn't interested in thinking about the five strangers or whether Nicholas knew Phillipe Gerond. Slipping her robe from her shoulders, she tossed it across the foot of her high bed; drawing back the covers, she hitched up her nightgown and set one knee on the white sheet.

A faint, muted click reached her.

She looked toward the door—and saw it opening.

Her mouth opened, but no sound came out. Frozen, she stared as Charles slipped around the door, shut it silently, then locked it.

He turned, saw her, nodded, then walked to the armchair before the fireplace. Dropping into it, he stretched out his long legs, crossing his booted ankles . . . with a start she noticed that he'd changed out of his evening clothes; he was now garbed in breeches and boots, a neckerchief loosely knotted about his throat, a soft hunting jacket hugging his shoulders.

Sitting up again, he pulled the cushion out from behind him and tossed it on the floor, then he shrugged out of his coat and flung it over the chair's back, then relaxed back once more.

Remembering her position, her raised and bare knee, and that he could see extremely well in poor light, she abruptly lowered her leg, twitched her nightgown down, fleetingly considered redonning her robe, but decided that smacked too much of accommodation. She wasn't feeling accommodating at all.

She marched around the end of the bed, but halted a safe five paces from him. "What the devil are you doing here?"

Her hissed whisper filled the room.

He turned his head and looked at her. "I told you I'd see you later."

"I thought you meant tomorrow. What on earth do you think you're about, settling down there like that?"

"I was thinking of going to sleep."

"You can't sleep *here*, in my room—you know that perfectly well!"

He regarded her for a long moment. "You don't seriously imagine I'll allow you to sleep under the same roof as Nicholas, a potential murderer, unguarded?"

CHAPTER

10

THE QUESTION HADN'T, UNTIL THAT MOMENT, OCCURRED to her, but now he'd uttered it, the answer, she realized, was in fact *No.*

However... she drew in a deep breath, focused on his face. "This is not possible. You can't just sleep here, in my room."

"I grant you this chair isn't the most comfortable bed"—he shifted his shoulders—"but I've slept in far worse. I'll manage." Putting his head back, he closed his eyes. "Where's Nicholas's room?"

"In the other wing. You can't stay here—if you insist on guarding me, I'll lock my door, and you can sleep in the next room."

"The lock on your door's too easy to pick—I looked. If I'm next door and Nicholas is good at this game, I'll never hear him. Get into bed and go to sleep."

The sheer command in his voice had her turning back to the bed before she caught herself; exasperated, she swung around and, seeing his eyes were closed, marched up to the chair. "Charles. *No.* Wake up." She put a hand to his shoulder. "This is simply—"

He moved.

She landed in his lap. Swallowed her shriek.

"I did tell you to get into bed."

His arms came around her.

Planting her hands on his shoulders, she tried to hold him off—tried to stop him from drawing her to him. "Don't you *dare* kiss me!"

From a distance of inches, his eyes met hers. A fraught second passed, then one black brow arched. "Or you'll what?" His voice had dropped an octave. "Scream?"

She blinked at him.

He closed the distance, closed his lips over hers.

He kissed her. Not as before but as he never had before. *Ravenously.* With a hunger, a need, that simply slayed her. That poured through her, vanquished any resistance she might have made, vaporized any wish to do anything other than gather to her that greedy, rapacious, devastatingly desperate need, and appease it.

Her hands rose; she wrapped them about his head, clung rather than pushed him away. Held on until she found her feet in the welling, surging tide. Until she could meet him and kiss him back—give all he so flagrantly wanted, take all he so blatantly offered in exchange.

Their mouths melded; their tongues dueled. Heat flared and raced under their skins.

Sexual awareness awoke; she had nothing on beneath her lawn nightgown. The realization only fired her more, anticipation flashing like lightning down her nerves—neither modesty nor caution rose to cool her ardor.

Nothing, she was sure, could cool his; he was like a living flame, burning for her. She spread her palms over his chest, through the fine linen of his shirt drank in the pulsing heat of him.

Like before, yet not. He'd been twenty then, not a boy yet a mere shadow of the man he now was. What he now was held more than fascination, was more than enthralling. To her, he was life, all she'd denied herself for so long, all she'd forced her lonely self to do without—and he was here, potent, powerful, and so clearly hers if she wished.

He was temptation incarnate, at least to her.

She wasn't even aware of undoing the buttons down the

front of his shirt, yet the instant it fell open, she wrenched the halves apart and spread voracious hands over his burning skin.

Traced the taut muscles, fingertips curling, sinking in.

She sighed with satisfaction, felt giddy delight surge as through their kiss she sensed his groan. Sensed his pleasure. She pandered to both—his and hers—and let the sensations pour through her.

She was unaware he was opening her nightgown until his hand closed over her bare breast, skin to naked skin. Something leapt within her; for one instant, she thought it was fear, then she recognized it as excitement.

He caressed, artfully stirred her senses, and excitement heightened to anticipation. Anticipation that grew with every sweep of his fingertips, every whorling caress, until her nerves were tight, and anticipation edged into desire, and desire became edged with need.

She gasped, pulled back from the kiss, had to; she needed to breathe. He let her lean back against his arm and catch her breath.

His lips traced her jaw, then dipped beneath to follow the long line of her throat. They skated into the hollow between her collarbones, pressed heat into her veins, then drifted lower.

Over the full curve of her breast, to just lightly, oh so lightly brush the aching peak. Then with his tongue, he traced the same path; when he reached the end, she heard a shocked gasp and realized it was hers.

Realized her fingers had speared through his black locks and she was holding him to her, arching in his arms.

He accepted her wanton invitation, caressing her with lips and tongue, following some slow, orchestrated score that ran in counterpoint to the fiery compulsion that seemed to hover about them, enfolding them yet not infusing, not driving them.

Not yet.

This was new, at least to her. She knew in her bones he'd traveled this road so often he knew every inch of the way.

Yet last time he hadn't known this, hadn't known to linger as he was, stirring her in ways she'd never experienced, never even imagined.

From beneath his lashes, Charles watched her, watched passion swirl through her stormy eyes and draw her lids down, watched desire fraction by fraction lay seige to her features, watched it color her delicate skin a soft rose.

If she'd returned to her bed, he would have stayed in the chair and pretended to sleep, but she hadn't. She'd argued, and the fastest way to resolve the looming battle in his favor had been to kiss her. It was also the perfect opportunity to take the next step in his personal pursuit of her, a pursuit that with every night that passed took on a keener, hungrier edge.

Pressing the halves of her nightgown wide, he languidly feasted, let his senses drink their fill, let his eyes see, his hands possess, his mouth and tongue claim. As he'd imagined doing for years; triumph lent a subtle edge to his exploration, a hint of possessiveness creeping in to tinge his ministrations.

He was not so much surprised as reassured by her responsiveness. On this plane, she'd always been his equal no matter how little she knew it. He'd always known, an instinctive knowledge, one that had fired his ardor all those years ago; it still smoldered, unquenched.

One thing the passage of the years had taught him was a greater, more educated appreciation. The heated silk of her skin was a wonder, the dusky rose peaks of her swollen breasts a temptation he couldn't resist. Dampening one, he rasped it with his tongue, then gently drew it into his mouth.

He suckled, lightly, then more powerfully. Her breathing fractured; with a strangled cry she arched in his arms, fingers tightening on his skull, tangling in his hair. He released her, caught a glimpse of her eyes, beaten silver beneath her lashes, took in her parted lips, her harried breathing, the rise and fall of those beautiful breasts—blew gently over the ruched peak and heard her sigh.

Lips curving, he transferred his attention to her other

breast. She made no attempt to distract or divert him. Her breathing fractured further; skillfully he tightened the tension that held her, notch by notch, until she was quivering.

He had her complete and focused attention. If Nicholas had chosen that moment to walk in, he doubted she would have noticed. He would have; he'd long ago mastered the knack of leaving a part of his mind on watch while otherwise devoting himself to the woman in his arms.

This time, with her, his absorption ran fathoms deep; more than with any other, he wanted, needed, to learn, to explore. To know not only in the biblical sense, but in every imaginable way. To understand and be sure. His concentration was enough to block the ache in his loins, strong enough for him to set his own needs aside, wholly to one side. This time with her he had to get everything right—fate had handed him a second chance; he had no faith he'd be granted a third.

Having her as his—seizing that second chance he'd always craved—was now too important to risk.

She'd grown restless, urgent under his experienced touch—to his mind flying too high too fast, but she'd always been impatient. And, perhaps, given where they presently stood, not yet where he wanted them to be, a quick, uncomplicated end would serve them best.

Relinquishing her breasts, he raised his head, found her lips, and covered them with his. Plunged into her mouth, intending to harness what little consciousness she still possessed and draw her back to earth—instead, he discovered she had her own demands to make, her own agenda.

Her tongue surged against his; her hands slid from his head to his chest, swept, lightly exploring, over the heavy muscles, then slid lower—and made him shudder.

Her unexpected boldness shook him, distracted him, and left him momentarily disoriented. *He* was the one in charge—in this arena, he always had been, always would be; he knew much more than she. Yet . . . for long, heated moments, he followed her script, just to see where it led.

Unwise, but he realized too late—realized that while his control had been forged over the years, hers hadn't. She was still his impulsive *ange*; her reckless play had only tightened the tension gripping her to an unbearable degree.

He heard the truth in her shaky gasp as she pulled back from a kiss that had plunged into desperation. Read confirmation in the tremors racking her, in the frantic pressure of her nails on his skin.

She'd journeyed too close to the edge.

Her nightgown opened to below her waist; pushing the halves wide, he bent his head to the furled peak of one breast, simultaneously slid his palm down, over her taut belly to the fine thatch of curls at the apex of her thighs. Brushing through them, he found and circled her slick, swollen flesh, with one fingertip caressed until she sobbed.

Drawing her tightly furled nipple deep, he suckled powerfully, at the same time stroked lightly, then increasingly firmly.

She shattered.

With a choked cry, she fell from the peak she'd so intently yet unexpectedly, he suspected unintentionally, climbed.

Cupping her mons, he felt completion sweep her, draining away the almost painful tension, blunting desire's spurs.

She sighed, and the last of passion's fury left her, and she relaxed, boneless, in his arms.

He blew lightly, soothingly, over her breast, then lifted his head, reluctantly withdrew his hand, leaning back in the chair the better to support her. He ached, yet all he wanted at that moment was to study her face, faintly limned by the moonlight; he'd never seen it as it now was, peaceful and serene in aftermath.

Long-buried memory intruded; he pushed it aside, only to have the thought that some other man must have seen her like this fill the void.

It was his thought, yet a faint frown tangled her brows; slowly, she lifted her lids and looked at him.

Puzzled. For an instant, he thought he couldn't have read

her look aright, but then she put up a hand to push back the fine curtain of her hair, and said, "That was . . . strange."

Her voice shivered, quivered. She looked at him. This time her look was clear—she expected him to explain.

He stared at her. Disorientation wasn't the half of what he felt; she was the one who'd climaxed—he was the one who felt giddy. But he had to know. "How many men have you been with since . . . before?" Since before when he'd botched things so thoroughly.

Outrage flowed into her face; she stared at him, then struggled to sit up, but she really was boneless. "None, of course! What a stupid question."

Not stupid at all. He bit his tongue. She was an attractive, twenty-nine-year-old nonvirgin who he knew had more than her fair share of sexual need—what was he supposed to think?

Suddenly, he wasn't sure at all.

Hands on his chest, lips setting, she tried again to sit up and push away. He held her easily. "Stop wriggling."

She knew enough to freeze at his growl.

She frowned at him warily, but he simply drew her closer, settled her more comfortably in his arms. "Just lie there and go to sleep."

Cradled in his arms, she stared up at him. Opened her lips.

"*Shut up*, lie there, and go to sleep."

Her eyes narrowed, but after a moment, she shifted carefully and settled her head against his chest. The last of her fight went out of her. She muttered, "I'll never be able to fall asleep like this."

She did, of course, leaving him painfully aroused, yet content enough. Content that she was sleeping sated in his arms. He hadn't planned the interlude, yet was more than satisfied that it had occurred.

Bringing her to her first climax was another role he'd never thought would fall to him, not after what had happened thirteen years ago. Yet it had.

Which left him wondering why it had.

As the moonlight faded and the shadows closed in, he changed his mind and did what he'd told her he didn't want to do. He revisited their past, and tried to fill in the gaps to her present.

Penny awoke the next morning, warm and relaxed, snuggled in her bed. She remained where she was, eyes closed, deeply, oddly blissfully comfortable. The brightness beyond her lids informed her the sun was shining. It was another lovely day . . .

She remembered. She sat bolt upright and stared across the room.

Charles wasn't in the chair.

She searched, but could see not a single sign that he ever had been.

But she hadn't dreamed it; he'd been there—he had, they had . . .

She glanced down. Her nightgown gaped to her waist.

Muttering a curse, she yanked the halves together. Doing up the buttons, she tried not to blush as memories crowded in. She would have liked to lay the entire incident at his door, but, unfortunately, remembered all too well that she had, somehow, succumbed, and been a more-than-willing partner.

It was because it had all been so different—in many ways novel, the sensations so very pleasant and prolonged. Long, slow, *sweet* caresses—and he'd let her touch him, explore and indulge her own desires, too. So unlike that long-ago grappling in the barn—rushed, heated, frantic, and rather painful.

Last night, she'd enjoyed and consequently encouraged him far beyond what was wise; she couldn't now blame him for how much further than a kiss the engagement had gone. She was loweringly aware that he could have taken matters much further, but hadn't. Instead . . .

Her breasts tingled; remembered delight glowed, then flowed through her veins.

She'd never in her life felt like that—so *desperate*, and then so blessed. So amazingly alive.

And then he'd asked . . .

With another muttered curse, she kicked the covers aside, got down from the bed, and stalked across the room to ring for Ellie.

By the time she'd washed and dressed, she'd compiled a long list of questions she ought to have asked last night. Such as where had Charles changed? He couldn't have gone home, so who else knew he'd remained at Wallingham overnight? Where were his curricle and pair—he had driven himself over, hadn't he? How had he got back into the house? How had he left again, and *when*?

Most important of all, just what was he thinking? He'd insisted she leave *his* house so he wouldn't succumb to his baser instincts and seduce her—and yet here he was, insisting on sharing her bedchamber.

She wasn't naive enough to suppose that his baser instincts ran any less strongly at Wallingham than they did at the Abbey.

Sweeping down the stairs, she turned toward the breakfast parlor—and heard their voices. Nicholas's and Charles's. She slowed, considering, then picked up her pace and glided into the room.

They saw her; both made to stand—she waved them back. Nicholas murmured a greeting, to which she replied. She nodded vaguely in Charles's direction; he responded with a polite "Good morning." Going to the sideboard, she helped herself to ham and toast, conscious of the silence behind her.

When she turned to the table, Charles rose and held the chair beside his. As she sat, he murmured, "Did you sleep well?"

She'd fallen asleep in his arms. "Indeed." She glanced at him as he resumed his seat; he must have carried her to her bed and tucked her in. "And you?"

He met her eyes. "Not, perhaps, as well as I might have."

With a light, ostensibly commiserating smile, she gave her attention to her plate; she wasn't going to comment.

Charles turned to Nicholas. "As I was saying, I haven't been out on the waves since I returned last September, but I'm sure the Gallants would be happy to take you out sometime."

Nicholas waved his fork. "It was just a thought—a passing fancy. Purely hypothetical. Why"—he paused, drew breath—"I'm not even sure for how much longer I'll be here."

Penny glanced up, startled not so much by the words as the undercurrent rippling beneath them. Nicholas sounded rattled, not his usual coolly distant self. Indeed, now she looked, he appeared even more tense than he had the previous evening, and distinctly more ashen. Of the three of them, he looked to be having the greatest trouble sleeping.

"Is your room quite comfortable?" The question was out before she'd thought.

Nicholas stared at her blankly. "Yes—that is . . ." He gathered himself. "Yes, thank you. Perfectly comfortable."

Grasping the opening she'd unwittingly created, she looked at him encouragingly. "It's just that you seem rather under the weather."

Nicholas's eyes flicked to Charles, apparently engrossed with ham and sausages, then returned to her face. "It's just . . . I have a lot to do, and there've been more details to attend to here than I'd foreseen."

"Oh? If I can help, please ask. I used to run the estate, so I'm acquainted with most of the arrangements."

He looked uncomfortable. "It's not so much any difficulty, as the pressure of what I need to attend to back in London."

She brightened. "Elaine mentioned you were with the Foreign Office. Have you been there long?"

He stilled. "Ten years." His tone was hollow, his expression grim and grave, his gaze fastened on some point beyond her.

She stared, then recollected herself and gave her attention to her toast.

Nicholas said no more; after a moment, he resumed eating.

Charles said nothing at all, but when he sat back and reached for his coffee cup, he caught her eye.

Interpreting that look with ease, she kept her tongue between her teeth. They finished the meal in silence. Rising together, they parted in the hall. She announced she would speak with Figgs about the menus. Nicholas inclined his head and declared his intention of returning to the library.

Charles halted beside her, waited until they heard the library door shut. "I'm going to the folly—come up when you're finished with Figgs." He caught her gaze. "Whatever you do, don't say anything more to Nicholas. I'll explain later."

He raised her hand to his lips, kissed it, and, with an arrogant nod, left her.

She let out an exasperated breath. Obviously, she'd missed something. What had he done?

The fastest way to find out was to finish her household duties; turning on her heel, she marched off to find Figgs.

An hour and a half later, she toiled up the grassed slope of the long sweep of man-made bank on which the folly stood.

She knew why Charles had chosen to lurk there; she'd often wondered what had prompted her great-great-grandfather to create the bank and the folly itself, screened by trees from the house—any part of the house—yet commanding unrestricted views over both the front drive and forecourt as well as the stable yard and the area between it and the house.

If one wanted to keep an unobtrusive watch on all arrivals and departures, the folly was the place from which to do it.

In true folly style, it was fanciful in appearance, designed to look like a carousel. The rear was actually set into the escarpment behind it, but viewed from the front it was all graceful, ornate arches and delicately worked pillars, the roof rising to a point like a conical hat with a gilded ball atop it. In white-painted wood on a stone foundation, the structure exuded a fairy-tale lightness but was in fact quite solid, with a scrollwork balustrade filling in the arches, forming a deep semicircular porch, open but protected from the elements. Beyond the porch was a room created by glass panes set between the slender columns that, had it been a carousel, would have supported seats for riders.

The inner room, big enough to accommodate a chaise and

two chairs with a low table between, was well lit, courtesy of a ring of windows set into the folly roof.

From their earliest years, she and Charles had taken refuge in the folly often. Memories circled as she climbed the wide steps and stepped onto the tiled floor.

As she'd expected, he was sitting in his usual masculine sprawl on one of the wicker chaises on the porch. It was where people most often sat; the inner room was used only in inclement weather.

The day was fine, the faint breeze off the Channel barely ruffling his black locks as she walked toward him. His gaze flicked to her, but then he returned to his contemplation of the house's approaches.

He was frowning, brooding. As she sat beside him, grateful that he shifted and gave her more space, she read enough in his face, his pose, to know he was brooding over something to do with his investigation.

Not to do with her.

That, she decided, was a very good thing. Instead of learning from experience and steeling themselves against him, against the effects of his nearness, her witless senses were doing the opposite. Now she'd fallen asleep in his arms and survived—more, had been unexpectedly entertained—her defenses against him seemed to be melting away, fading like ghosts into the woodwork as if convinced she had nothing to fear from him—and even more, everything to gain. To look forward to . . .

Jerking her wits from that dangerous track, one she remained determined to avoid, she forced her mind to focus. "What upset Nicholas?"

Charles's gaze remained fixed on the view. "I mentioned, by way of passing on local news, that a young fisherman, apparently a friend of Granville's, had been found foully murdered."

"How did Nicholas react?"

"He turned green."

She frowned. "He was shocked?"

Charles hesitated, then said, "Yes, and no. That's what's

bothering me. I'd take an oath he didn't know Gimby was dead. I still don't think he'd met Gimby—I don't think he knew his name. But he *wasn't* surprised to learn Granville had a fisherman as a close associate. Gimby's existence didn't surprise Nicholas, but the news of the lad's demise and the manner of it shook him badly." After a moment, he added, "If I had to define the primary emotion the news evoked in Nicholas, I'd say it was *fear*."

She stared unseeing at the landscape. "Where does that lead us?"

"That's what I've been trying to figure out. Nicholas came here asking after Granville's associate—he at least knew enough to guess there was one. There are two reasons he could have had for searching for Gimby—either to ensure his silence now the war is over, or to use him again to make contact with the French because something new has come up."

"If Nicholas had located or heard of Gimby, and sent some henchman to . . ." She frowned. "That doesn't make sense."

"Indeed. Neither of Nicholas's reasons would call for Gimby to be killed unless Gimby had been trying his hand at blackmail, and not only is there no evidence nor even much likelihood of that, if Nicholas had desired Gimby's death, he wouldn't have been shocked and shaken to hear of it."

"But he was . . . you don't think it was an act?"

"No act. Nicholas might have perfected a diplomatic straight face, but it's under severe strain and crumbling. You saw it yourself—he was visibly upset."

"So he's frightened . . . of someone else."

Grimly, Charles nodded. "Someone else, and that someone isn't under Nicholas's control. He's not a henchman. If Nicholas had learned of Gimby and sent someone to treat with him for his silence, and something had gone wrong ending in Gimby's death and Nicholas hadn't heard about it until I told him, he might have been shocked, perhaps a little shaken, but I can't see any reason for fear. He'd have been calculating where that left him, and feeling free of Gimby's threat. Yet I detected not a glimmer of satisfaction—he was appalled, and struggling to hold himself together, to not show that the news meant anything to him."

Penny humphed.

Leaning forward, Charles rested his elbows on his thighs. "There's someone else involved. Someone acting independently of Nicholas. Some other player in the game."

He'd suspected as much when he'd stood looking down at Gimby's broken body. He'd hoped it was Nicholas's work; he was now convinced it wasn't.

"Does Nicholas know who this other person is?"

The crucial question. "I don't know—at present there's nothing to say either way."

Penny glanced at him; from the corner of his eye he saw her gaze flit over his hunting jacket, note his cravat, then rise to his freshly shaved chin. He'd ridden home at dawn, bathed, changed, attended to business, then ridden back in time to shake Nicholas over breakfast.

"Have you heard anything from London?"

"No—it'll be tomorrow at the earliest." He straightened. "Filchett knows to send word to Norris if anything arrives unexpectedly, but I'll go back every morning to check. I've alerted both my stablemen and yours to ferry any messages that might arrive to me." He glanced at her, lips curving. "There are some benefits to being a mysterious war hero."

"Hmm." She held his gaze for a moment, then looked away, over the gardens. "That leaves us with this unknown someone lurking about—presumably he's Gimby's murderer. How do we flush him out?"

We don't. He kept his lips shut, said nothing at all.

She frowned. "Perhaps we can raise a hare? Create some situation that would lure him out—that would prompt him, if he knows Nicholas, to contact him. Or perhaps"—she warmed to her theme—"we could start a rumor that there's some secret something to be obtained at a certain time and place—"

"Before you get too carried away, we'll need to wait on the information from London before we play any more hands in this game."

His dry tones had her turning his way. "I thought you were the reckless one?"

"The years have taught me wisdom and restraint."

Her humph was derisive; he hid a smile.

She glanced at the stables. "Do you think Nicholas will go out today?"

"If he's feeling half as rattled as he looked, I doubt it—not unless he does in fact know who the murderer is."

After a moment, she said, "It has to be one of those five visitors, doesn't it?"

He hesitated, then agreed. "I don't know of any local who would have known to do what was done to Gimby." *Except me.* He stirred. "One of the five visitors would be my guess."

"Which one? The Chevalier?"

"There's no way to tell, not from the faces they show the world."

"How do you expose someone like that?" She looked at him, searched his eyes. "And don't bother suggesting that I just leave it to you."

He smiled faintly, took her hand, idly toyed with her fingers. "I think he—whoever he is—would have hoped Gimby's body wouldn't be found, at least not so soon. Now it has, he'll lie low for a time, a few days at least. Unfortunately, it won't take long for such news to fade, then he'll . . ."

She followed his line of thought easily. "What's he after? What's his purpose in this?"

He was silent for a moment as the possibility took shape. "Revenge. That would explain why Nicholas is afraid."

They tossed around the possibility that one of their five suspects had somehow stumbled onto Nicholas's scheme and was now bent on making all those involved pay. "Presumably because of lives lost—perhaps a specific life," Penny suggested. "Like a brother in the army killed because of some secret that was passed."

He grimaced. "That scenario calls for access to highly restricted information, but . . . it's not impossible." He was already formulating the queries he'd send to Dalziel. "It makes the Chevalier a more likely candidate."

"Because he might have heard something from France?"

"I'll get Dalziel to investigate his connections."

They fell silent, each pursuing their thoughts.

He still held her hand, his own closed over it. She seemed unperturbed by that, engrossed in thinking of how to trap a murderer. He was alive to the murderer's presence, sensitive to the villain's proximity to her, the potential danger, but his chances of distancing her from the investigation were too slight to be worth pursuing.

She, however, was another matter. Not much would occur for a day or so. In that time . . . somehow he had to exorcise their past and steer their present onto the track he wanted it on. He hadn't fully appreciated the potential between them, not consciously, years ago; he'd been young, naive, much less experienced then. But now he clearly saw what could be, not just for him, but for her, too—and he wanted that.

On finding her strolling through the Abbey at midnight, he'd unintentionally got close enough to reach over the chasm that had opened between them, and the opportunity to grasp what he'd always wanted—what he now desperately needed—had come his way again. He was determined to seize that second chance.

If he wasn't the sort of man he was, and she the sort of female he knew her to be, setting aside their personal interaction, leaving any attempt to redefine it until after the murderer was caught, the mystery solved, would be the wisest course. But they were who they were, and when it came to them together, wisdom had never featured greatly. Witness last night. He couldn't—wouldn't—risk not being with her every night and through as much of the day as possible, and that being so, nothing was more certain than that they'd end as he'd warned her sooner rather than later—far sooner than capturing the murderer or solving the riddle of Nicholas and Granville's scheme.

They were closer than they'd been for thirteen years, but he needed them to be closer still. He needed to know she was as safe as he could make her, that she would allow him to protect her and accept his protection, that if danger threatened, she would do as he asked—ultimately that she was under his hand, behind him, shielded to the best of his considerable abilities.

Between them, nothing else would suffice.

If he was to influence her in the direction he wanted—and influence was the best he could hope for—then he had to act soon; now was the time. This brief hiatus was the only pause the murderer was likely to grant them.

Tightening his hold on her hand, he turned his head and looked at her; when she met his eyes, he baldly asked, "Why haven't you been intimate with any other man?"

She gaped at him. Eyes wide, she stared into his, opened her mouth to speak, then shut it. He'd half expected her to blush; instead, she looked stunned.

"*What?*" Her tone had risen, shrill and tight. She tugged her hand free—then held it up, palm toward him. "No! Wait." She drew a deep breath, held it for a second, then calmly stated, "My personal life is none of your business, Charles."

Her dismissive tone had him tensing; his jaw tightened. "What happened between us thirteen years ago is very much my business, and if that incident has affected you over all these years, then that, too, is my business."

She stared at him as if he were a spider—a species beyond her comprehension. "If it's affected me . . ." Her voice trailed away as she stared, but then her chin firmed, her eyes narrowed, and she snapped, "What the *devil* are you talking about?"

Gritting his teeth, he spoke through them; he was determined to have it out, all open between them, so they could put it behind them and go on. "Thirteen years ago, *if* you recall, you and I were intimate in that damned barn down by the cliffs. It was your first time, and I hurt you. A lot." He narrowed his eyes on hers, ruthlessly forced himself to go on, "You were upset. Very upset. You refused to let me touch you again, then or later. You rushed off, and avoided me for the next several weeks, until I left to join the Guards. You wouldn't even talk to me or let me talk to you."

The naive hurt he'd felt welled up again, fresh and unexpectedly stinging; he thrust it back down. As evenly as he could, he continued, "I returned last year to learn that despite a string of highly eligible offers, you'd elected to remain a spinster. It was impossible not to wonder if what I'd done—what happened between us—was behind your reluctance to marry. And then last night I learned you'd never—"

"No. Stop." Abruptly, she stood. Eyes like flint, she looked down at him. "What happened last night, what I said—forget it. My life is my own. I made my decisions as I wished. It's none of your business—"

He swore and surged to his feet. "Of *course* it's my damned business!" The barely restrained roar rolled away across the lawns; he forced his voice lower, pinned her with his gaze. "If I hurt you that much, caused you so much pain that you were so upset you've never let any other man even *touch* you . . ."

He stepped closer; her eyes flared, but she stood her ground, raised both hands and waved them between them. "Wait—*wait*!" She frowned at him. "Slow down—just go back a minute . . ."

Her expression said she was replaying his words . . . then her eyes widened, darkened, grew even more stormy. After a moment, she raised them to his. "Are you telling me that for all these years you thought I was hurt—upset—because of the *pain*?"

He couldn't read her eyes. He frowned, sensing a catch in the question, but . . . drawing a tight breath, he nodded. "What else?"

It hadn't occurred to her, but it should have. Penny dragged in a huge breath and swung away. She started to pace. "Don't move. Just wait."

He stiffened at the order, but did as she'd asked; just as well—she had to think, and quickly.

She'd always known what he *hadn't* realized, that he hadn't seen that she'd loved him, but she'd assumed he'd realized that her intense upset hadn't been driven by something as minor as a little pain. When he'd spoken of hurt, she hadn't thought he'd meant *physical* hurt.

Thinking back, she wasn't sure what she'd thought he'd thought; at the time, she'd been so caught up in her own re-actions, her intense disappointment, the dashing of her naive expectations—the shattering of her heart as she'd then thought—that beyond knowing that he knew he'd upset her, she hadn't stopped to consider what he'd seen as the reason why.

He'd thought she'd been upset because of the pain!

She hauled in a huge breath, and swung to pace back to him.

Given he had, he was patently suffering from a burgeon-ing case of guilt, to which he was not entitled, and through that developing a sense of responsibility over her life, to which he was even less entitled.

Responsibility had always been a strong motivator for him, witness his devotion to his family and his country. If she didn't act quickly to correct his thinking and dissolve any responsibility he was nurturing toward her life, they would shortly find themselves in a hideous state. He would try to make amends, she would refuse, her conscience would prick while her independence would kick, and he'd become ever more subbornly determined to put right his perceived wrong . . . it would end in animosity if not outright war, and that she definitely didn't deserve or need. Neither did he.

She had to correct his understanding of the past, but *with-out* revealing the truth of why he'd hurt her.

Folding her arms, she lifted her head, and halted directly before him. "Very well." She met his eyes. "As you're so de-termined to revisit our past, let's do so, but let's get the facts correct. Thirteen years ago, *I* decided we should make love. Yes, you'd wanted me for years, but you wouldn't even have suggested such a thing—*I* plotted and planned to meet you out riding, to inveigle you into the barn. Everything that hap-pened that day happened because *I* wished it to."

"You didn't know how much it would hurt."

"True." She tightened her grip on her arms, and tried not to think about boxing his ears; he was so damned male. Holding his gaze, she went on, "However, I did know I was a virgin, and you"—she managed not to glance down—"were you. I wasn't so ignorant I didn't expect the experience to be attended by some degree of pain."

"A considerable degree of pain." His jaw was so clenched she was surprised it didn't crack.

She shrugged, deliberately dismissive. "However one measures pain." It *had* been more than she'd expected, but that hadn't been what had hurt. "Regardless, it didn't scar or scare me—I can assure you of that."

His eyes remained narrowed, boring into hers. "You were hurt, upset—you almost cried." He knew she rarely did. "If it wasn't the pain, then what the hell was it?"

When she didn't answer, he spread his arms wide. "For God's sake—*what did I do?*"

The torment in his eyes—something he wouldn't have felt let alone shown years ago—stopped her breath, stopped her from ripping back at him.

Lips compressing, she held his dark gaze. She couldn't tell him the truth. If he ever learned she'd loved him . . . given their present situations, he might well press for marriage. He'd see it as an honorable obligation on the one hand and a suitable alliance for them both. And it would be suitable on many levels, except one.

She loved him still, and having to marry him knowing he didn't love her would, for her, be hell on earth. She'd rejected her other suitors because they hadn't loved her, and she hadn't loved them. Now, after all her years of dogged independence, of refusing to marry without the love she craved, to be pressured to marry Charles of all men, and very possibly jockeyed into it . . .

Her eyes steady on his, she quietly said, "It wasn't anything you did."

Charles read her eyes, confirmed she was telling the truth. Confusion swamped him. After all these years, he was still at sea; he hadn't understood then, and nothing had changed.

Except, perhaps, his persistence; this time he wasn't going to play the gentleman and let her fob him off. Lowering his arms, he searched her eyes, casting about for some other approach, some other way to draw an explanation of what he didn't know, and now desperately wanted and needed to know, from her.

Eventually, he quietly, evenly, said, "You haven't answered my question."

Penny blinked, thought back, fleetingly gave thanks as her temper sparked. She refocused on his eyes, studied them, narrowed hers. "What are you thinking? That what happened in the barn that day blighted my life?"

"Can you swear to me that what happened that day hasn't stopped you from being with other men?"

"*Yes!*" As belligerent as he was relentless, she faced him down. "I swear on my mother's grave that the events of that day in no way influenced my decisions regarding my suitors. *Or* any of the others who offered to seduce me." Her temper soared. "You are so damned *arrogant*! It might interest you to know that sex and men don't rule my life—*I* do. *I* decide what I want and what I don't. Unlike you, I don't need sex on a regular basis to be happy!"

Charles couldn't remember when last he'd dined at that particular table; he clenched his jaw and held back a retort.

She glared at him, then gestured dismissively and swung away. "If you insist on feeling guilty for causing me pain that day, then do so, but don't you *dare* presume to assume responsibility for any other part of my life. My decisions were and are mine to make, my life is and always has been my own." She paced back, met his eyes, lifted her chin. "*I* decide who I'll let seduce me."

He held her gaze for a heartbeat, then reached for her, pulled her to him, and kissed her.

As always, desire leapt to instant life; between them, the flames *whooshed*, then roared. Penny knew what he was doing, what track his mind had taken; so be it. She relaxed into the kiss, gave him back fire for flame; pointless to attempt to do otherwise.

He broke the kiss. Lifted his head just enough to look into her eyes. "*Why*, then? You'll let me seduce you—"

She opened her lips.

Brusquely, he shook his head. "Don't bother pretending—

we both know you will. You'll let me, but not any other man. All those years ago, you wanted me to seduce you, you encouraged me—and yes, I remember every tantalizing, fraught, uncertain minute. And now . . ." His gaze was so hard, so sharp, she wondered he couldn't cut through and see her soul. "Now you'll be with me, but not any other man. *Why?*"

Because, God help her, she loved him still. It took a moment for her wits to formulate a useful answer; she didn't rush them. Drawing a breath restricted by their embrace, she didn't try to escape his gaze, but calmly held it. "I told you. *I* decide who I'll admit to my bed. Those others—none of them interested me sufficiently to warrant an invitation. Apparently I'm exceedingly fussy. You, I issued an invitation to years ago, and for some reason and certainly against my better judgment, the grounds on which I made that decision still appear to be valid."

Something leapt behind the dark blue screens of his eyes; her breath was suddenly even shorter.

"Be that as it may . . ." Eyes locked on his, increasingly watchful, she tried to ease back, out of his hold, but his arms gave not an inch. "You shouldn't presume on that previous invitation, not after all these years."

As always with her, Charles felt . . . not quite in control. "Forget your previous invitation." He bent his head, brushed her lips—just enough to refocus her attention on what was, still, burning between them. "Issue another."

His voice had lowered of its own accord. He watched, following the battle within her, between physical desire on the one hand and a desire to escape it on the other. She distrusted getting caught, enmeshed in physical desire—and he was the only man capable of weaving a web strong enough to hold her; in that instant, he saw that much clearly.

It only led to the next *Why?*

Her palms on his chest, she tried to push back. "Your mission. You're supposed to be keeping watch, remember?"

"I haven't forgotten." He had no intention of letting her escape, her desire, his, or the strands they wove together. "If anyone comes driving or riding up, I'll hear them. If Nicholas sends to the stables, I'll hear that, too."

"What if he goes out walking?"

"He can't leave the house without walking on gravel—I'll hear him."

"He might creep out."

"Why? He doesn't know we're here watching."

She looked at him, thought, frowned.

He smiled, blatantly intent. "That's check—"

"Wait!" She was starting to panic. "What about the reason you insisted I come home to Wallingham? It was so you wouldn't seduce me—remember?"

His smile deepened. "So I wouldn't seduce you *under my own roof*."

Her jaw fell. "Your own . . . ?"

"There are a few elements of honor not even I will compromise—that's one of them."

When she simply stared, dumbfounded, he lowered his head. "And mate."

CHAPTER

11

HE INTENDED TO DO PRECISELY THAT, WITH HER, AS SOON as possible. For now, however . . . he kissed her. For now it was enough that he had her in his arms, that regardless of all else he'd secured his second chance. He still had the twin mysteries of what had upset her years ago and why she'd turned her back on marriage to solve, but it was difficult to think when she was in his arms, her lips soft and pliant beneath his.

She held aloof at first, not resisting yet not actively participating, her attitude more in the nature of a sulk. He enjoyed teasing her from it, holding her lightly while tempting her with slow, sultry kisses, until she sighed, softened, and offered him her mouth.

Penny simply gave up—surrendered, resigned the battle to remain apart from him, impervious to the heat that licked around them, over them, through them—a battle she seemed forever doomed to lose. But she should have known, should have guessed that he wouldn't simply set aside his desire. Sexual passion was an integral part of him, entrenched in every fiber of his being; she couldn't imagine him without a sexual agenda. She shouldn't have forgotten he would have one, no matter what else was afoot.

Pushing her arms up, she twined them about his neck, leaned into him, met him boldly, and launched herself on his tide. Met his thrusting tongue, met his desire with her own, boldly engaged his expertise with her own brand of assurance. She'd be damned if she let him have things all his own way; she fanned the flames, let pleasure rekindle, rise and drag them both down, in, under.

It was pointless pretending she didn't enjoy this, that with him she demonstrably could have a sexual agenda of her own. If she wasn't going to be able to hold him off, then she'd take what she wanted, take all her starved senses wished from what he so readily offered. As he was determined to escort her to this particular banquet, then why not savor and enjoy? She had absolutely no doubt he would be a generous lover. He was an openly generous man. A good man . . .

She caught her thoughts, hauled them back from the brink. Not that way. She would enjoy all he brought her, but she wasn't going to—didn't need to—let her heart become involved. She might still love him, but she didn't need to offer her heart to him, didn't need to let him, however unwittingly, break it into pieces again.

What lay between them, what fired that compulsive, flaring heat, was physical attraction. Deep, intense, and abiding, tinged perhaps with shared memories, shared background, with long friendship and the ease that brought. But it *was* simply physical; she'd learned that thirteen years ago and wouldn't forget; but he was here again now, wanting her as he always had, and—she pulled back from the kiss, gasping, letting her head fall back as his hands claimed her breasts, as his lips traced a line of fire down her throat . . . she'd been cold, physically cold, for a very long time.

Now she burned, and it was hotter, sweeter, infinitely more real than her memories. He set her alight in so many ways, with such deliciously pleasurable flames. She wallowed, distantly aware that he lifted her and sat on the chaise with her on his lap. They were supposed to be keeping watch, yet although with her senses wholly focused on the magic his hands and mouth wrought she couldn't hear, she knew he could, and would, if there was anything beyond the cocoon of their world to react to.

She could safely leave the outside world to him and concentrate solely on theirs.

On the frankly amazing fact that she was lying once again in his arms, this time bared to her waist, that he'd managed to unlace her gown, open her bodice, ease her arms free, then untie her chemise and draw it down, all without raising a single qualm in her mind. Not a single impulse to protest.

From under lids grown heavy, she looked down, watched as with mouth, lips, and tongue he pandered to her senses, caressing her breasts in ways he hadn't all those years ago.

She'd never permitted it, wouldn't have even if he'd pressed; in those days, she'd had a very definite aversion to allowing him to see her naked. Doubtless a product of her conventional upbringing, that aversion had clearly withered with the years.

Now . . . there was little she could imagine might be so pleasurable as lying in his arms, in the shade, with the sun bright outside and birdsong drifting on a gentle breeze, feeling the brush of that breeze over her flushed and dampened skin, a counter to his heated caresses. She slid her fingers along his skull, arched lightly when he rasped her nipple, then relaxed as, with his mouth, he soothed the sudden ache.

She cupped his head and held him to her, very aware of the surrender and encouragement the action implied, quite sure he would recognize it, too. Quite sure. His fingers drew fiery patterns over her swollen breasts. The brush of his black hair against her white, now rosy and taut skin added another tactile sensation to the mix, one he orchestrated with a master's touch.

With a devotion she hadn't seen in him before. He wasn't rushing, wasn't rushed; he was content to spend long minutes pleasuring her, but it wasn't simply patience he'd learned. What she glimpsed in his face as he glanced briefly up, what she felt through every caress, was a different, novel reality. He took pleasure in pleasuring her, drew pleasure from all that she felt, that he made her feel.

That, too, was new, just as the joy welling inside her, the

joy she found in this new facet of their interaction, was new, different, enticing.

He raised his head to view the effects of his ministrations. Sliding her hands across his chest, over his shirt, she found the buttons closing it.

Without shifting his gaze from her breasts, he closed one hand over hers. "No. Not this time." He drew her hands away, lifted his gaze to her eyes. "This time is just for you."

It was too hard to frown. "Charles—"

He raised her, kissed her.

In seconds she'd forgotten how to think. Forgotten there was any existence outside the fire he whirled her into, a giddy waltz of desire, of flaring passion, of sudden greedy need.

That need was hers, not his. He drew it up, evoked and provoked it, yet his desire seemed dependent on hers, subservient to hers. She didn't understand, but couldn't think enough to do anything other than cling to him, fingers sinking into steely muscles that flexed as he shifted her, as he drew her around . . . her bare breasts rode, lightly abrading, against his jacket; she suddenly wanted, burned, ached with an intensity she'd never felt before.

On a gasp, she broke from the kiss, realized he was lifting her skirts, that the frolicking breeze was sending teasing fingers dancing along her legs.

She wasn't wearing stockings, just the slippers she wore in the house. His fingers touched, then his palm cruised along bare skin.

"*Charles!*" Protest or demand, she wasn't sure. Her fingertips sank deeper; she clung even more desperately as her nerves tensed and flickered, as physical longing reared like a wave and rushed through her.

"Ssshh." He touched even more boldly, his palm gliding in a long caress up one naked thigh. "*Mon ange*, let me show you heaven again."

The words were so deep she could barely hear them, so imbued with a longing that was the counterpart of hers they sounded like a supplicant's plea.

One she couldn't refuse, didn't have time to refuse, even had she had the strength. His lips returned to hers, but lightly, engaging yet not seizing her senses as he touched her curls, stroked, then nudged her thighs wider, slid his hand between, and cupped her.

She felt the intimate touch to her soul. He'd touched her there before, all those years ago, but only briefly. Not as he was touching her now.

Slowly. Exploring, caressing, stroking. Finding every pleasure point and coaxing it to life, then lavishing caresses upon it, and her.

She shuddered, and let him. Took all he gave and held to their kiss, her anchor in a world suddenly tilting. The road he now seemed so intent on taking, on showing her, was a great deal longer than before, more involving, with so much more to experience. So much more to feel. She gave herself over to it—to simply feeling, letting the delight well and wash through her, letting the pleasure rise and sweep her senses away.

At some level she missed his hunger, the driving need she was so used to in him. It hadn't gone, but was veiled, there but held back so her own need could flower more strongly, so she could sense it more clearly as hers without the competing demands and distractions of his.

She was almost floating on a tide of pleasure, no longer clinging to their kiss, barely able to breathe, aware of him murmuring endearments, aware of her body as she never had been before, of how it rose to his practiced caresses, of how it wanted. And what it wanted.

His finger slid into her; what little breath she had tangled in her throat. Her impulse was to tense, but her body didn't respond, then he stroked, and a languid wave of heat rose and washed through her.

Sheer unadulterated pleasure.

That built, and built, until she thought she would scream.

Charles watched her, watched passion claim her, watched her rise to each increasingly intimate caress. Knowingly he pushed her deeper, further into the fire, into the conflagration of molten desire and greedy, hungry need.

She was slick, hot, had been from the moment he'd touched her. She was also tight, so tight that working a second finger in alongside the first very nearly brought her, and him, undone.

He'd slammed a dungeon door on his lust, caged it so he could achieve what was needed—what he and she both needed so they could move quickly on—yet every gasping breath she took, every eager response her body made to his increasingly flagrant caresses, made it harder to concentrate, harder to remember that this moment, this time, had to be. That he had to, should, spin the moments out as far as he could, as far as her responsiveness allowed, the better to ready her, prepare her for the next stage, their next time.

She arched in his arms, a soft cry on her lips. His lungs seized, a vise cinching tight as he eased back, desperately tried to hold her back from the brink. Not yet. Just a little further . . .

He ached. The scalding heat of her sheath, the evidence of her desire, the incredibly soft swollen flesh he repeatedly caressed, her bare breasts, peaked and rosy, riding against his chest, all called to him, urged him, whispered darkly to him at some level that was deeper, more intimate, more fundamental than any other woman had ever touched.

Need was a spur embedded in his side, yet this was the way forward, the only way to successfully return to her bed, to join with her again, so he could rescript the past and set them on course for the future.

He'd been right in predicting she'd lie beneath him very soon.

There was a limit to all things, even his control, forged though it had been through thirteen long years. He was no longer naive enough to underestimate the effect she had on him, the sheer potent power of the need she and only she had always evoked in him.

It was awake now, very much alive, a beast prowling just beneath his skin, persuaded to reluctant patience only by the promise of a greater reward later. But not much later.

The wave within her rose again, higher still, and he couldn't hold her back any longer. He sensed her fighting it, trying to stand against the onrushing tide, a sudden lick of distrust of the unknown flaring.

"Let go." He breathed the words over her swollen lips. "There's nothing to fear—let it take you, *mon ange*. Go."

Her eyes, slivers of silver beneath her lashes, met his.

Between her thighs, he reached deeper, probed, pressed.

Her lids fell. And she flew.

To the stars. He watched as she arched in his arms, her nails sinking into his shoulders, her features blanking as completion claimed her. He felt the implosion of the tension he'd stoked in her, the final unraveling of her nerves, felt the powerful rippling contractions as release swept her.

He knew women's bodies better than his own; he'd studied them more intensely. He knew enough to track the more subtle changes, the quivers of bright tension streaking down her nerves, the heat coalescing, then washing through her, spreading under her skin.

Easing back, he let her slump in his arms, cradled, safe. Let his eyes drink in the smoothing of her features, the bewitching curve that came to haunt her lips.

Glorious.

It was a moment he'd experienced many times, but the content, the sheer pleasure he took in seeing her slide from that convulsive peak into sweet oblivion, was both deeper and more evocative than he'd expected.

Satisfaction laced with that very real content gave him the strength to hold against the pain of a need more intense, more violent than he'd ever known, and simply hold her.

Minutes ticked by. He looked out over the lawns, over the drive, the forecourt, the approach to the stables. All basked peaceful and undisturbed in the morning sunshine. Out there, nothing had changed.

Within the folly, something had.

The step he'd taken, the course he'd embarked upon, was ineradicable, at least for him. In no way did he regret it; he was more committed to this venture than to anything in life.

Eventually, she stirred.

To his surprise, she didn't try to cover herself, to screen her breasts from his gaze, or to remove his hand from beneath her rucked skirts where it lay proprietorially clasped over one bare hip. She didn't even move to flick her skirts down over her long legs, but simply lay there, relaxed and at peace—and more dangerous to him than she'd ever been.

Her gaze traveled his face, then returned to his eyes.

"I don't understand you—not anymore."

He studied her in return, studied her stormy gray eyes that had already seen far more than any other. "You do. You know all you'll ever need to—you just haven't realized it yet."

Truth again; blessedly, with her, it was their customary currency, the one in which they always dealt. She'd seen the change in him, experienced it, but hadn't yet consciously understood. He wasn't, however, in any hurry to explain; she would grasp the full picture soon enough, of that he had no doubt. Time enough, then, for her to know just how much power she wielded over him; there was no need for her to learn that now, while they were stuck in the middle of an investigation and a murderer lurked in the shadows.

He smiled at her. "It's nearly time for luncheon. I believe, if you consult your stomach, you'll discover you're ravenous."

The look she bent on him stated clearly that she would prefer he kept his so-accurate knowledge of what she was feeling to himself. He laughed, raised her, kissed her soundly, then helped her to straighten her clothes.

She, he was surprised but pleased to note, evinced no shyness; she accepted his help, not as she would from a maid but as she might from a lover, one who had the right to assist and sufficient knowledge of her body to make modesty redundant.

He might have changed, but she had, too. As they strolled down to the house hand in hand, he wondered how, and in what ways, the years had laid their hand on her. What other surprises might she have in store for him?

Luncheon was a quiet affair. Nicholas accepted his presence with nothing more than a nod; he seemed even more withdrawn, more distant—more worried but trying to hide it—than before.

Penny was still recovering; he doubted she knew how much it showed. If Nicholas had been capable of thinking of anything beyond his troubles, he would have noticed her uncharacteristic silence and the softly glowing, telltale smile that on and off flirted about her lips.

She didn't, of course, feel at all compelled to make polite conversation for him, so the meal passed in a quiet, rather pleasant daze.

At the end, she stirred and glanced at him. He watched her struggle to find acceptable words with which to ask *What next?*—meaning with the investigation.

He grinned; her eyes narrowed. "I thought we could go riding. It's a glorious day, and there are people I need to speak with in Lostwithiel."

Penny nodded, set her napkin down, and rose. "I'll get changed and meet you in the stables."

Nicholas mumbled something about returning to the library; he barely noticed their departure. Parting from Charles, she climbed the stairs, changed into her habit, then headed for the stables.

He was waiting under a tree outside the garden door.

"So where are we going?" she asked as she reached him.

He took her hand and started toward the stables. "Lostwithiel first, then I want to check at the Abbey. There wasn't anything from London this morning, but there might be something by late afternoon."

She tugged him to a stop. "What about watching Nicholas?" She'd thought his suggestion of riding a ruse; she hadn't expected to leave the estate.

He met her gaze, grimaced. "I've suborned Norris and Canter. I told them I'm working on a final mission and Nicholas is in some way under threat—exactly how I don't yet know. I've asked them to keep a close eye on him. Given the way he's reacting, I don't expect him to go out, but he can't, and no one can reach him, without alerting either Norris or Canter. If he receives any message, Norris will know of it; if he leaves, Canter will set one of the grooms to follow him."

He glanced at the house, then back at her. "Regardless of Nicholas's involvement, he didn't kill Gimby. I need to learn more about our potential murderers."

"The five visitors?"

He nodded. They started walking again. "The best way to learn revealing snippets is to be out and about where we can meet and talk to others, especially the people hosting those five. And it's market day in Lostwithiel."

She smiled. "That should be perfect."

So it proved. They mounted and rode across country until they met the road from St. Blazey and followed it into Lostwithiel. While Fowey with its port and quays bustled with fishing and shipping, Lostwithiel was the district's commercial hub and had been for centuries. The Guildhall looked the part, the market square before it filled with a bustling, good-natured throng, the gentry rubbing shoulders with farmers and their wives, laborers and field workers, all eyeing the wide variety of wares displayed on the stalls and trestles.

Leaving their mounts at the King's Arms at one corner of the square, they ventured forth, mingling with the crowd, eyes peeled for their five suspects or any of said suspects' local hosts.

The first they encountered was Mr. Albert Carmichael, squiring Imogen Cranfield through the crowd. Mrs. Cranfield followed a few paces behind, smiling indulgently, fond hope wreathing her round face. Beside her strolled her elder daughter, Mrs. Harriet Netherby.

They stopped and exchanged greetings. Harriet was a contemporary of Penny's; although their acquaintance stretched back over decades, they'd never been friends. Charles engaged Imogen, Albert, and Mrs. Cranfield; after according him a distant nod—she had never approved of Charles and his wild ways—Harriet moved to Penny's side.

"Such a loss to the county." Harriet sighed. "First Frederick, then James. And now we have Charles stepping into the earl's shoes."

Penny arched a brow. "Don't you think he'll cope?"

Harriet cast the subject of their discussion a narrow-eyed glance. "Oh, I daresay he'll manage well enough, but no doubt in his own fashion."

Finding nothing in that with which to disagree, Penny nodded and tried to listen to the conversation Charles was managing.

"Actually, I'm surprised you haven't grasped the opportunity to go up to London—Mama mentioned Elaine and her girls are there."

Barely listening, Penny lightly shrugged. "I was never particularly fond of the giddy whirl." Charles and Albert were discussing the local crops.

"Oh, you shouldn't feel discouraged, my dear." Harriet briefly touched her arm. "You may be getting on in years, but so many ladies die in childbed—there are always widowers looking about for a second wife."

Penny turned her head, met Harriet's pale gaze, and let the calculated spite slide past her. "Indeed. How's Netherby?"

Of average height, with no more than passable looks and frizzy, mouse brown hair, Harriet had always resented her higher birth, her commensurately higher status, and, even more definitely, her more refined features and sleek blond hair. Harriet had snapped up a wealthy landowner from the northern shires in her first Season; that she had succeeded where to her mind Penny had failed had given her reason to gloat ever since.

But Harriet wasn't interested in discussing Netherby; she turned Penny's query aside with a dismissive, "Well enough."

They both gave their attention to the wider conversation, just as it broke up.

Exchanging nods, smiles, and wishes to meet again soon, they parted. As Charles steered her into the crowd, Penny sank her fingertips into his arm. "What did you learn?"

"If Carmichael isn't seriously considering offering for

Imogen's hand, then he's the best actor I've ever come across. Incidentally, although she didn't say so, Mrs. Cranfield was grateful to you for distracting Harriet. I gathered Harriet isn't pleased that Imogen has found such a suitable parti."

"That's Harriet. It's not as if Netherby's anything to sneeze at, not for the Cranfields."

"Indeed. However, I think we can drop Carmichael to the bottom of our list of likely murderers. While it's possible he's using his pursuit of Imogen as a cover for more nefarious activities, Mrs. Cranfield implied he'd been dangling for nearly a year, albeit at a distance."

"Ah . . . that would explain Imogen's distraction. She's been dithering on the edge of happiness for months, certainly since late last year."

Charles nodded and guided her on. A moment later, he said, "There's Swaley, coming out of the Guildhall."

From within the milling crowd they watched as the neat, severely garbed Swaley paused on the steps. His gaze was on the crowd, but he didn't appear to see them. Then, as if making some decision, he went smartly down the rest of the steps and briskly headed down one side of the square.

"I wonder where he's off to?"

A rhetorical question; they followed him at a decent distance. Both tall, they had little difficulty seeing over heads as without haste they weaved their way to the crowd's edge.

Swaley continued down the street toward the river.

Charles lifted Penny's hand and wound her arm more definitely with his. If Swaley glanced back, he would see the pair of them ambling like lovers stealing away to stroll beside the river.

Swaley never looked back. He marched down to Quay Street and turned along it. They reached the corner just in time to see him pause and look up at another imposing building, then enter it.

They halted. "Well, well," Charles murmured. "That explains Swaley, and also his reluctance to discuss his business in our fair neighborhood."

The building Swaley had entered had originally housed the old Stannary courts from where the laws governing tin-mining in the surrounding districts had been administered for centuries.

"All the records are still there, aren't they?" Penny asked.

"Indeed. I heard that some older mines to the west thought worked out had been reopened using new techniques. Swaley's presumably interested in scouting out the nearer claims."

They turned and started back to the market square.

"I wonder if Lord Trescowthick knows of Swaley's interest?"

Charles shrugged. "Swaley went to the Guildhall first, rather than direct to the old courts, which suggests he hasn't inquired of his host."

Regaining the square, they paused to take stock, scanning the heads.

"If Swaley's interest is in reopening tin mines, he seems an unlikely candidate for murdering Gimby."

"True." Charles resettled her hand on his sleeve. "I can see the Essingtons—not her ladyship, thank heaven—and Yarrow is with them."

He steered Penny toward the group clustered before a stall selling embroidered linens.

"Mr. Yarrow's convalesence seems to be progressing well," Penny murmured. "I wonder if he rode over?"

She asked him. Once they'd met and exchanged greetings, she mentioned that she and Charles had ridden over from Wallingham, commented on the lovely ride, and used the moment to inquire if Mr. Yarrow, too, had enjoyed the journey that day.

His hard hazel eyes held hers. "Sadly, no. I fear I'm still less than at full strength. But perhaps, later in my stay, you might consent to show me the beauty spots of the area? I understand you remain here throughout the year?"

Too late, the quality of Yarrow's intent gaze registered; Penny inwardly cursed, but had to answer, "Yes, of course. There are many wonderful places . . . I recall Lady Essington mentioned your home was in Derbyshire. Will Mrs. Yarrow be joining you?"

Yarrow glanced down. "I regret my wife passed on some years ago. I have a young son." He looked up, surveying their surroundings. "After this last bout of ill health, I'm considering relocating to this district. I hear the grammar school is well regarded?"

Penny kept her light smile in place. "So I believe."

Heaven help her! Harriet had spoken of widowers, and here was Yarrow, eyeing her far too measuringly for her liking.

To her relief, Millie turned to her, linking arms. "You're just the person I most hoped we'd meet."

Millie waited, beaming, until Charles, who'd turned to address Yarrow, had him engaged, before tugging Penny more her way and lowering her voice. "I'm expecting again—isn't that *wonderful*?"

Penny looked into Millie's bright brown eyes, aglow with wonder and delight; she smiled warmly in return. "How lovely. David must be thrilled." She glanced at Millie's husband, whose proud presence at her side was now explained; he was chatting to Julia. "Do pass on my best wishes to him, too."

"Oh, I will! I'm so happy . . ."

Fondly, Penny listened as Millie burbled on. This would be her third confinement; her first child had been stillborn, but the second, a sturdy two-year-old girl, was thriving. Although untouched by any maternal streak, Penny was truly pleased for Millie and found no difficulty in sharing her joy.

Eventually, she and Charles parted from the group, she promising to call at Essington Manor in the near future. The words were dying on her lips as her gaze reached Mr. Yarrow. His eyes met hers and he nodded, very correctly, in farewell. Somewhat less enthused, she nodded politely back.

"The others aren't here." Charles steered her toward the King's Arms.

"Well, I don't think Yarrow's our murderer, either."

"Just because he was making cod's eyes at you doesn't mean he doesn't dabble in murder on the side."

"He was *not* making cod's eyes at me—and anyway, I thought it was sheep's eyes."

"Cod's—fishy."

She humphed. "There wasn't anything fishy about him."

"Nothing fishy about inviting you to show him the local sights, then asking your opinion on sending his son to the grammar school?" He snorted back. "Spare me."

That last didn't sound like the Charles she knew at all. She turned to stare at him, but he wasn't looking at her. Lips set, he gripped her elbow and escorted her into the inn's stable yard.

Their mounts were fetched; he lifted her to her saddle, then swung up to his and led the way out. Once they'd cleared the narrow, cobbled streets, he slowed until she came up beside him, then let his big gray stretch his legs; side by side, they cantered up the road to the Abbey.

At that pace, it wasn't easy to converse; she didn't try, but let her mind range over the afternoon, over all she'd heard, seen, learned.

They reached the Abbey; the grooms came running as they clattered into the stable yard, to take their horses and impart the news that a courier had arrived from London at midday.

"Good." Charles closed his hand about hers and set off for the house. He didn't exactly tow her behind him, but she had to lengthen her stride to keep up. She looked at his hand, wrapped about hers, felt the strength in his grip. She was not so much amused as intrigued.

Filchett met them in the front hall, confirming the courier's arrival. "I placed the packet on your desk, my lord."

"Thank you." Charles turned for his study, her hand still in his.

Limpidly innocent, Filchett's eyes met hers as he cleared his throat. "Shall I bring tea, my lord?"

Charles halted, glanced at her.

She met his gaze, then nodded to Filchett. "Please. In the study."

Filchett bowed. "Indeed, my lady."

Charles looked like he was suppressing another snort; turning, he continued to the study.

He released her hand only as they reached his desk.

Subsiding into the chair before it, she watched as he picked up the sealed packet, glanced at the direction, then, dropping into the deep chair behind the desk, reached for the letter knife.

Breaking the seal, he smoothed the three sheets, then started reading.

"Is it from your ex-commander?"

"Yes, Dalziel. This is in answer to the first queries I sent him."

She thought back. "About Nicholas?"

"And Amberly." Charles sat back, scanning the sheets. "Amberly was very high at the F.O., a full secretary responsible for European affairs. He retired late in '08." He set aside the first sheet.

"Nicholas joined the F.O. at the beginning of '06, and rose rapidly through the ranks, courtesy, it seems, of not just his father's name but also his own talents." Charles's brows rose. "It seems those Dalziel consulted consider Nicholas one of their most promising men. He's presently an under-secretary reporting to the principal secretary. Interestingly, he's always worked in European affairs—perhaps not surprising given his father's background." He glanced back at the first sheet. "Amberly's record is impressive—there would have been much to gain by building on that."

"Contacts, friendships, that sort of thing?"

Charles nodded. He'd moved on to the third sheet. Although he hadn't asked for it and time had been limited, Dalziel had investigated Nicholas personally and turned up nothing of note. He'd also added a postscript.

"What?" Penny asked.

He glanced at her, reminded himself that Amberly and

Nicholas were her connections. "Dalziel is going to, very quietly, investigate Amberly. Both Nicholas and Amberly are and were respectively in positions to learn secrets that would have interested the French, but while Nicholas might have continued the trade, it wasn't his creation."

Refolding the sheets, he tapped them on the desk, wondering just how deep Dalziel's desire to bring justice to all spies who had trafficked in secrets to the detriment of English soliders ran. He'd heard whispers, faint but nonetheless there, that gentlemen Dalziel had proved guilty of treason had a habit of dying. Usually by their own hand, admittedly, but dying just the same.

It was a point to ponder, but not aloud.

He stirred, laid aside the packet, and pulled out a fresh sheet of paper. "I'm going to report what we learned today." Including that he didn't think Nicholas was guilty of Gimby's murder, but that he certainly knew the details of whatever scheme had been afoot. "Aside from anything else, the information will give Dalziel some idea which questions will most quickly reveal what those five strangers are doing down here."

Penny nodded and sat back. Filchett came in with the tea tray. She thanked him, and he left; she poured for Charles and herself, then sat sipping, watching while he wrote.

Eventually setting aside the empty cups, she rose and walked to the windows behind the desk, and stood looking out. The view was to the northwest; in the distance, she could see the ruins of Restormel Castle from which the Abbey took its name, and could just make out the silver ribbon of the Fowey sliding past between its lush banks.

It was complicated dealing with Charles and a murderer simultaneously, but she'd always been one to reach for what she wanted, to grasp opportunities as they occurred, to bend situations to her cause. As she had long ago, but long ago was in the past, and the here and now beckoned; she'd always taken advantage of what fate deigned to offer.

For some mystical reason, fate was offering him. Again.

She had to make up her mind what to do, make sure she

wasn't making a huge mistake—again. And it would be wise to do her thinking now, safe and sane, out of his arms, rather than pretend the inevitable wouldn't happen and instead find herself struggling to think when he'd already whipped her wits away.

He was offering physical passion the like of which her stubborn will, her unwavering allegiance to her dreams, had condemned her to live without. When he'd first appeared, she'd been convinced the course of wisdom was to avoid any degree of indulgence with him. To guard her heart at all costs. He, after all, posed the greatest danger to it, and always had.

Now . . . in five days, he'd changed her mind, undermined her resistance. Made her think again. Yet it wasn't just him and his persuasions influencing her. She'd told him the truth—it was her decisions that ruled her life, no one else's. Independence was something fate had granted her from an early age; she'd guarded it zealously and still did.

No one was in any position to dictate to her. That made it much easier to reassess and, when the circumstances warranted, change her mind.

The present circumstances, she firmly believed, suggested a change of direction.

Harriet's gibe over her being suitable marriage fodder for some widower—and Yarrow's clear concurrence—had not so much struck a nerve as reminded her of where she stood, of how others saw her. She was far beyond marriageable age, an acknowledged ape-leader, a confirmed-beyond-doubt spinster; as such, she was no longer subject to the same restrictions that applied to younger ladies. If she wished to take a lover, she could; there might be whispers, but as she wasn't planning on marrying anyone, where was the scandal? She had no desire to return to London, and county folk were prosaic about such matters; where no damage was done, who had the right to cry foul?

Unlike Harriet, she did not feel—never had felt— desperate to marry at any cost. Her identity, her status, had been hers from birth; she didn't need to marry to create it or shore it up. She'd never believed marriage of itself—the ceremony, the institution—had any intrinsic value; its value derived from what it represented—mutual respect and sincere affection at the very least, preferably the far more powerful emotion the poets called love.

The thought brought Millie and David Essington to mind, and their new state. While she could feel pleased for others knowing how much children meant to them, she felt no maternal urges herself; the wish to procreate had never ranked as a reason to marry, as it did for some ladies. Her attitude to children might have changed if she'd ever married, but that was one question to which she accepted she would now never learn the answer.

She glanced back at Charles, still writing, the *scritch-scratch* of his nib across the paper the only definite sound in the room. Half-turning, she leaned against the window frame and studied him; he was concentrating on his report and thus not attuned, as he habitually was, to her.

As usual when they were in the same room, she was aware of him at some level that had nothing to do with conscious thought. Yet with his attention deflected, she could look at him, examine him if not dispassionately, then at least rationally.

His head was bent, silky locks so black they ate the light curling over his collar. He could have been a model for Lucifer, with his rakish, hard-edged, sculpted features, his sensuous mouth, the arrogance of his chin, nose, and heavy-lidded eyes.

Her gaze lingered on his broad shoulders, the wide expanse of his back, acknowledging the power and harnessed strength inherent therein.

She turned back to the window.

On most counts, she'd chosen to let life as other ladies knew it pass her by. She'd held firm to her ideals and even now didn't regret it. Yet Charles had proved to be the only man with whom she could be physically close, share any physical relationship, and here he now was, back again, laying seduction at her feet.

There was no compelling reason to refuse. Whatever he offered—whatever degree of sexual interaction—she would take it. She owed herself that much. She deserved that much. It had been so long since she'd experienced physical hunger, so long since she'd felt its mind-numbing heat.

And this time she knew the score; her heart would be safe. She didn't need to hand it over in exchange; that wasn't, as she'd learned, any part of his contract.

Fate had decreed she couldn't have her heart's desire; her will and her pride had prevented her making do with any other man. She wasn't going to refuse whatever Charles offered to share with her. To her mind, it was rightful consolation.

A sound behind her had her turning to see him affix his seal to the folded packet. He set the seal aside, waved the letter to cool the wax, and swiveled to face her.

"Ready?"

She met his gaze, held it for an instant. "Yes."

Stepping away from the window, she led the way from the room.

IN THE HALL, CHARLES DROPPED THE PACKET ON FILCHETT'S salver, then remembered he needed more clothes.

Penny waved him up the stairs. "Go on. I'll wait."

He went, but she followed. He wasn't surprised when she halted in the open door to his bedchamber and leaned there, arms folded, watching him gather a selection of shirts, cravats, and hose.

"Where have you been keeping them? Your clothes?"

He glanced briefly at her. "In Granville's old room—the one he used before he succeeded your father."

"Why there?"

"So I could search it at leisure, and because, if I were Nicholas, it's the first room I would have searched—it's therefore a room he's unlikely to return to, and the maids don't go in there anymore."

"You didn't find anything?"

"No. A diary would have been too much to hope for."

"From Granville? Indeed." After a moment, she asked, "How did you get back to my room last night? I thought you'd left the house."

He wrapped his selections in a soft hunting jacket. "No. Norris knows I don't leave. I head for the garden door, then go up the back stairs."

So she was never truly alone with Nicholas.

Picking up his bundle, he waved her back, closed the door, and followed her to the stairs and down.

He'd already sent word to the stables; their horses were waiting. Stuffing his clothes into a pair of saddlebags, he tossed them across Domino's neck, then lifted her to her saddle, mounted Domino, and they were away.

This time she led, urging her mare into a gallop as soon as they left the park, streaking up the grassed side of the escarpment, then flying south, riding into the wind. He joined her, thundering along beside her. The wind rose to greet them, shrieked in their faces, dragged at their hair.

They paid it no heed but streamed over the green, checking only to descend to the flat and clatter across the bridge at Lostwithiel before taking to the heights again. The wind followed their progress, whistling like a banshee as they turned east for Wallingham and thundered on.

A sense of *déjà vu* rose and crashed through him. They'd ridden this way, just like this, many times before, but he was so far removed from the youth he'd been, and she from the girl he'd known.

Exhilarating and disconcerting, that sense of sameness only emphasized all that had changed.

And all that hadn't.

They raced, not each other but simply for the sake of it. Late afternoon edged into evening, the sun a ball of fire dousing itself in the ocean ahead of them. In the last of the golden light, they rode wild along the ridge, then down through the fields to clatter into the Wallingham Hall stable yard.

Penny kicked her feet free and slid from her saddle; he met her gaze as, boots touching ground, he hauled the saddlebags free, slung them over his shoulder—and suddenly couldn't breathe.

Awareness, sharp, intense and familiar, flashed between them.

Eyes wide, she stared, then swung on her heel, grabbed up her trailing habit, and headed for the house.

He fell in beside her as she walked past the kitchen garden. She glanced at him; he caught her gaze, held it—sensed the raw energy prickling over his skin, arcing between them, felt its compulsion in his veins.

Knew she felt it, too.

It was he who stepped away, increased the distance between them. He looked ahead. Impossible to whisk her off to her room or anywhere else, not like this, with the elemental hunger their wild gallop had set free riding him. And her. He wasn't going to make that mistake again.

He dragged in a breath, held it. Forced himself to open the garden door and stand back, to let her precede him and walk a safe distance down the corridor to the front hall before he stepped across the threshold.

Pausing just inside the door, he waited.

She realized, stopped, and looked back.

He nodded. "I'll see you at dinner." With that, he turned, walked the other way, swung onto the back stairs, and climbed swiftly upward.

Away from temptation—a temptation that hadn't changed with the years but had simply grown.

By the time she returned to her bedchamber later that evening, Penny's nerves were jangling, taut, tightrope-tense—*waiting*. Not with innocent expectation, but an educated and quite specific anticipation; she knew what she wanted.

Having made her decision, wild impatience had infected her during their ride home and hadn't dissipated in the least, not over their fifteen minutes in the drawing room, where she'd played the dutiful damsel for Nicholas's benefit, nor over dinner, an unusually silent meal.

Charles hadn't been interested in talking any more than she; they'd both had other matters on their minds. As for Nicholas, he'd remained sunk in thoughts that appeared little short of openly distressing. He'd looked wretched, but had shown no signs of confiding in them.

Climbing out of her evening gown, she donned the night-gown Ellie had waiting, then sat at her dressing table to brush out her hair—anything to keep her hands busy, to conceal her rising, nervy impatience.

Charles had been discretion itself, appearing from outside as if he'd just driven over for dinner, then later, after they'd sat through the required hour and the tea trolley had come and gone, formally taking his leave and, apparently, heading out to the stables.

He'd be waiting to see Ellie depart, to hear her go down the back stairs.

"Will that be all, miss?"

"Yes, thank you, Ellie."

Ellie curtsied. Penny nodded in the mirror, watched as Ellie went out.

The instant the door shut, she rose, set down her hairbrush and looked at the bed. Imagined . . . then stiffened her spine.

The candles . . . should she snuff them? The single candle by the bed and the two in the dressing table sconces were all relatively new; they'd burn for hours before guttering.

Years ago, she'd been a prude; she hadn't looked, hadn't wanted him to look. Now . . . drawing in a deep breath, she left the candles burning. She wanted to know *everything*. Wanted to experience all there was, every sight, every sensation, to gather them greedily to her and hoard them.

The latch clicked; by the time she glanced at the door, Charles was inside. He'd seen her; she heard the clunk as he locked the door.

His gaze had locked on her. "Penny . . . ?"

She flew across the room, flung herself into his arms. Knew he'd catch her. She didn't want to talk.

Charles swore, the oath muffled beneath her lips as she framed his face and kissed him. At least he had the answer to the question she hadn't waited for him to ask. He rocked back against the door as he took her weight, without conscious direction his arms wrapping about her and locking her to him.

With a herculean effort, he broke from the kiss. "Pen—"

She caught him again, dragged his mouth down to hers, found his tongue with hers, and breathed fire down his veins.

His next curse was entirely mental; she was racing faster than the wind had blown, and it wasn't wise, wasn't safe—not for her, not with him. He'd been half-aroused before he'd entered the room; now he was rigid, one step from pain, his demons eager and straining, his control seriously weakened.

By her. Again.

He seized her. Tightened his arms, lifted her from her feet, and wrenched control of the kiss from her.

Tried to; to his amazement, it didn't work. She levered herself up in his arms until she leaned over him, her forearms on his shoulders, his head clasped between her palms, and kissed him as if he were the last man on earth and tonight was her only time with him.

Women and their passions were his specialty, but this . . . this devouring, hungry, *ravenous* need—where had it come from? He'd known she wanted him, had known since they'd reached the stable yard; he hadn't anticipated any resistance tonight, but he hadn't expected this.

Hadn't expected to be left gasping, wits reeling, pulse pounding, reduced to elemental need with just a kiss.

She angled her head, pressed the kiss deeper, and he shuddered. She spread her thighs, gripped his hips with her knees, and something inside him quaked. Then his cravat loosened; he felt her hands slide down, working between them, felt his shirt give—felt her hand slide in, fingers spreading, palm gliding over his upper chest.

And down as far as she could reach.

He'd been caressed by courtesans expert in their art; no touch had ever rocked him as hers did. It nearly brought him to his knees.

Never, not ever before, had any woman met him like this. Challenged him like this. Relinquishing any thought of sophisticated play, of hours spent introducing her to all he'd learned in the years he'd been away, he staggered to the bed and fell across it.

Later.

He rolled to pin her beneath him, and succeeded. In position, at least. As for the rest . . . in a blinding flash of insight he realized where they'd gone, where she'd taken him. Straight into blind lust, just like the last time.

He wasn't in control, and neither was she.

Their mouths remained welded, hot and urgent—there was no chance of either of them ending that kiss, not anytime soon, not until they had something else to cling to. Like each other.

Her hands were everywhere, tugging at his clothes; they rolled and tussled as with her help he shed them in a frenzy, one bit here, one flying there. He toed off, then kicked off his boots. At last she broke from the kiss, but only to help him strip off his breeches. Then her hands were on him, sliding up his flanks, along his hips.

It was the innocence in her touch, almost a sense of wonder, that gave him pause, that was just uncertain enough to jerk him back to some semblance of sanity.

He smothered a curse against the silk of her hair, then rolled again and brought her atop him. The sudden change to a position that was new to her momentarily stopped her. He framed her face, pulled her down to him, and covered her lips, dragged her back into their incendiary kiss. He knew what he had to do, knew he had to do it now, before she shattered his control again.

As he knew absolutely beyond doubt she would, and soon.

Just the thought . . .

He had to get his hands on her, now, this minute. Her lawn nightgown had ridden up to her knees, but was inextricably tangled between their legs. The front placket only opened to her breasts; seizing one half in each hand, he yanked—and heard it rip. Frantically, he kept ripping, down and down; through the kiss, through the eager pressure of her lips, the wanton dance of her tongue over his, the almost desperate flexing of her fingers on his chest, she urged him on. Then she shook her arms free and the halves fell away, and were forgotten.

He gripped her waist, felt her skin bare beneath his hands, held her as he plunged deep into her mouth, returning her fire, then he ran his palms up, over her breasts, shuddered as he leaned back and closed his hands.

And kneaded. Not gently but with the same urgency that coursed through their veins. With the same devouring need with which she spread her fingers and desperately clutched.

At last, she broke the kiss, flung her head back, her glorious hair spilling like a living veil down her back, strands sliding over her shoulders, caressing her as he did, as she whimpered and shifted under his hands.

Begging for more.

He rose up on one elbow and gave her what she wanted. Pressed a kiss into the hollow beneath her ear, then traced down. Over the taut line of her throat, over the swell of her breast, full and swollen cupped in his hand, to the furled nipple he was rolling between his fingers.

He took it into his mouth, and she gasped. He suckled, and she moaned.

Penny heard the sound, and could only wonder that he could draw such a confession of surrender from her. Wonder she could manage; thinking was beyond her. Her mind was awash with sensation, her body thrumming with need, every particle of her awareness engaged in this, with him, her very soul bathing in their heat.

She was straddling his lower chest, his ribs solid between her thighs, his naked chest and shoulders displayed before her, a fascination revealed as he suckled strongly at her breast, sending lightning streaking down her veins to condense in pulsing heat deep within her.

His hands roved everywhere. Hard and demanding, caressing, claiming, exploring, urgently learning. He'd always been bold; now hunger added another dimension, a more flagrantly possessive edge to his touch. Heat flared wherever his palms traced, fire danced where his fingers grazed.

Remembered feeling flooded her, an internal sensation of molten emptiness that opened inside her even before he slid a hand between her widespread thighs and touched her swollen flesh. Closing her eyes, she spread her hands over the powerful muscles of his shoulders, slid them over and around, holding tight as he stroked, then caressed, then probed.

His mouth was hot and wet and demanding, leaving flames dancing under the skin of her aching breasts, leaving dampness the air cooled to create a startling contrast, heightening the sensation of fire and burning heat. A heat that was alive, that beat in her veins in a compulsive tattoo, escalating with every heartbeat, spreading beneath her skin and greedily, hungrily, demanding more. More from her. More from him.

She could barely breathe, but oh, she could feel. Every touch, every lick of desire's fiery lash, every knowing touch he pressed on her.

With lips and tongue he tortured the throbbing peak of one breast; the second his hand possessed, kneading, tweaking, blatantly claiming. Between her thighs, his other hand worked, long fingers buried in the slickness he'd drawn forth, forcefully penetrating, pressing deep.

And it wasn't enough; she dropped her head back with a gasp that was half sob, sank her nails into his back in an incoherent plea.

He reacted, rose beneath her and flipped her over, reburied his hand between her thighs as he leaned over her and took her mouth. In a kiss so devastating it stole the last of her breath, so desperate it echoed her own desire, so driven it reassured her as nothing else could—he was with her, wanting her, needing her and all that was to come every bit as much as she.

With him, she'd never felt alone in her need, never vulnerable because of it. It was and always had been something that affected them both—a madness they both endured, and both had to slake.

He pressed her into the bed, his long hard body settling partially over hers. She expected him to spread her thighs with his, expected him to enter her; she was already tensing, memories hovering at the edge of her mind, when he tore his mouth from hers, and she realized he had other plans.

His lips briefly traced her throat, then slid lower to once again torment her breasts. To feed, it seemed, the urgency that racked her, that seemed to well up and spill through her, speeding her heartbeat until the thudding compulsion thundered through her veins, tightening her nerves . . .

She arched beneath him, why she didn't know, her hands desperately clutching his shoulders, sliding into his hair as he left her breasts and moved lower. To press hot, wet, open-mouthed kisses over her midriff, over her waist, down across the taut, quivering skin of her stomach.

He grasped her knee, opened her wide.

The candles were still burning. Lungs starved, breasts rising and falling rapidly, she forced her lids up enough to look, enough to take in the harsh planes of his face, etched with blatant desire as he looked down at her.

He'd slid far enough down the bed that his shoulders were between her thighs. She waited, breath bated, for him to shift back up, to—

He bent his head and set his mouth to her. Pressed his lips to her already throbbing flesh, sucked lightly.

Shock lanced through her. Her heart stood still.

Then she felt his tongue, and she nearly died.

"Charles!" She bucked, but he held her easily. She reached down and tugged at his hair, to no avail. There was no way she could dislodge him, no way she could prevent him . . . from dragging her under.

His mouth moved on her, and a wave of sensation breached her guards, grabbed her, captured her. Pulled her under a roiling, tumultuous tide built of fire and flames and sharp, searing heat, of desperate intimacy and welling need.

She couldn't breathe enough to gasp, moaned instead, and, eyes falling shut, closed her fists in his hair.

The fiery tension mounted, escalated, coiled tight. And still he pressed her, not gently but ruthlessly, relentlessly, as desperate, as driven, as she. As urgently needy. His lips moved on her, evocative, provocative, his tongue traced, caressed, then slowly swirled . . . probed, and entered her.

She fractured, broke apart.

He called it touching heaven; to her it was more like touching the sun. Heat flared, brighter than a starburst; tension locked her heart, her lungs, her nerves, her every awareness, held all immobile for that blessed instant before the heat imploded and shattered, sending shards of glory flying under her skin, then washing in a wave over and through her.

Leaving her at peace.

But not him.

Blindly, she reached for him, and he came to her. Spreading her thighs wide, settling between, his heavy body angled over hers as he reached down between them, opened her, and pressed in.

Her hands clenched on his upper arms in mindless anticipation of pain. She started to tense against his invasion—wanted to, but her lax muscles refused to cooperate.

He didn't go any farther, but settled more fully atop her; she felt his hand smooth back her hair, then cradle her face. "Not this time, *mon ange.*"

Then he kissed her. Filled her mouth, distracted her for the instant in which his spine flexed, and he thrust powerfully into her. Not quick and hard as she'd expected, but slowly, steadily—inexorably. Even as the reality of what he was doing impinged, that he was stretching her, filling her, and wasn't going to stop—that she didn't, even then, want him to stop—she was held captive.

By him. By the sheer sensual pleasure of the feel of him, hard, rigid, hot as forged steel, heavy and foreign yet immeasurably welcome as he slid farther, deeper, pressing so slowly into her despite the muscles that jumped in his arms, despite the cording of the tendons in his neck as he fought against the demons she'd met years before.

She felt her body give and take him in, and gloried in the slick, silken glide. She felt him sink home, filling her impossibly full, felt the engorged head of his staff abut her womb.

Charles inwardly gasped, held still, then felt her, very gently, tentatively, contract around him, and nearly lost what little control he still possessed. Her sheath was scalding hot, tight as the proverbial nun's, and he'd stretched her fully, intentionally seizing the single moment of sanity remaining to him to sink into her to the hilt.

It was a moment he'd promised himself, not consciously but in his wildest dreams, for the past decade. Now it was here, and felt even better than his fervid imagination had painted it.

She was relaxed, heated and open beneath him, the cradle of her sleek body soft and accepting, but with that tempting feminine strength still lurking, investing her spine and the taut muscles of her thighs and the hands that moved lightly on his shoulders.

He wanted, ached, needed to engage with that feminine counter to his own driving need, but he had to hold back, hold still, for just a minute more . . .

With a supreme effort, he pulled back from the kiss and lifted his head enough to look into her face. "Are you all right?"

Her lids lifted just a fraction; her eyes met his.

Then her lips slowly curved, and his control quaked.

"Yes." She raised her head and closed the gap between their lips. Kissed him like the siren she truly was.

Drew back to whisper against his lips. "Now ride me. *Please.*"

"With pleasure." The words were so guttural, it was just as well he'd spoken in English. He caught her eyes. "But only if you ride with me."

Her lids lifted more, her eyes widened.

He didn't wait for her to ask, but kissed her, and showed her.

Showed her how much more there was to experience. To enjoy. Better than any other, he knew what would draw her, entice her, and bind her to him. He deployed every ounce of his expertise to ensure he captured her, that at this level at least, the success of his wooing of her was a foregone conclusion.

In other areas he might have a harder time, but in this, he'd always had her measure, even though he hadn't, long ago, had his own.

Even now, she surprised him; after that initial hesitation, she accepted his invitation wholeheartedly. She followed where he led, met and matched him, too quickly learned the knack of using her body to caress his and drive him wild.

And wilder.

It was a shuddering shock to realize that control had slipped away from both of them. That something stronger, more vibrant and powerful had slid in and filled the void. That it was that instinct, wild and unfathomable, intense and true, that drove them, that fueled the passion with which their bodies slickly joined.

That pushed them both on, through soul-deep kisses and shared gasping breaths, through the repetitive rocking of their joining, to that exquisite peak of sensation beyond which sweet oblivion lay.

They reached the peak, first she, then he, her release sweeping through her and triggering his. Hands locking, fingers linking, they gasped and clutched tight as their senses soared through the flames, then fell away.

Into that landscape where souls communed and hearts beat as one.

On the plane where that wild instinct reigned.

He couldn't think of any words in English or French to adequately describe what he felt in the moment when, rousing, he lifted from her, came down beside her, and, sated and replete, she curled into his arms.

Hardly daring to believe that he'd cleared what had loomed as a major hurdle so easily, he slowly, carefully, closed his arms around her, settled them both in the rumpled sheets, and pulled the covers over them.

Too precious to break, he let the moment lengthen, breathed deeply, and let it, and all it implied, sink to his bones.

No homecoming had ever been so sweet.

So intense, so passionate. So much what he'd needed.

He acknowledged that last, understood what it meant, tried not to dwell on it. Pressing a kiss to the silky veil of her hair just above her temple, he sank into the bed and relaxed.

Penny wasn't sure if she'd fallen asleep, or . . . been elsewhere. Rocketed into another sphere of existence by all she'd felt, all he'd shown her. Rather than awaking in the normal way, her senses returned bit by bit, coalescing and realigning to finally function again.

The first fact they reported, the most overwhelming, was the blissful sense of aftermath that coursed through her veins, through her flesh, to her bones. Every corner of her being, physical and mental, seemed to glow with glorious delight, with a golden satiation, a far more powerful cousin of the sensation she'd touched in passing before.

To use his words, it seemed there was heaven, and *Heaven*.

Lips curving, under cover of her lashes, she glanced at him, at what she could see without shifting. The candles were only half-burned; they shed a warm steady light across the bed. He'd pulled the covers to below her shoulder, halfway up his chest. Beneath the sheet, her arm lay across him, her hand lightly gripping his side; her head rested in the hollow of his shoulder. She felt more comfortable than she could remember ever feeling.

Her body thrummed, the hardness, power, and sheer masculine strength of his imprinted like some elemental memory on her senses. On her very female senses. With him, she knew what she was, could be all she was; she could deal with him confident in herself, and him. He'd always been the same, male to her female in some preordained way neither he nor she had ever questioned. She wasn't about to start questioning now.

Shifting her head, she moved her hand and spread it over his heart. It thudded sure and strong beneath her palm. The crinkly dusting of black hair that laced across his chest, then arrowed to his groin, was a tactile fascination. She played, and knew he watched.

She didn't stop, but pushed the covers down to his waist, baring his chest—and her own, but as to that she no longer cared. His body had always fascinated her, an illicit desire, one she'd denied, then suppressed for years. She didn't need to suppress it now; spreading her hands, she gave it full rein.

And he let her. Remained supine in her bed and let her trace the broad, heavy muscles of his chest, run her palms over the curves of his shoulders and upper arms, then draw her fingers down to outline his ribs.

Then she pushed the covers farther still, down to his hips. Traced the long muscle bands, strong as steel, that bracketed his navel, then reached farther. Ran her palm down along his hip, down to his thigh, down to where the crisp hairs grew thicker again.

He'd tensed, unmistakably; she didn't prolong the torture, more for herself than him. Gliding her hand up, she found him, boldly cupped him, took his scrotum in her hand and let her fingers explore, learning the weight, the texture, even as, with her forearm, she nudged the covers lower still, so that when she stroked upward and closed her hand about his erection, she could see as well as feel. Could use her eyes to guide her fingers as she stroked the ridged length, lingering over the thick, pulsing veins, then with her fingertip traced the circumference of the broad head.

He shuddered, caught her hand.

She looked up; he met her eyes briefly, his nearly black with just a hint of blue remaining. He looked down at her breasts as he laced his fingers with hers, then, pressing her hand and arm back and around, slowly rolled her onto her back.

"My turn."

He lay beside her, one arm beneath her, still cradling her, while with his other hand he traced her body. Lightly. From her jaw, to her shoulders, over her breasts, around their ruched peaks, he drew slow whorls with his fingertips, barely touching.

Long before he sent those trailing fingers questing lower, her breasts had swollen and heated, her body had come alive.

Tantalizing. His touch was a promise, evoking sensual

memories, yet leading her senses to dwell, not on what had been, but on what might be.

His fingers brushed her curls, danced lower, tracing the sensitive inner face of her thighs almost to her knees. Her skin, taut, nerves alive, flickered as he slowly returned up the other thigh, but instead of diverting inward, he took the outward track, following the outer line of her hip up to her waist.

Dragging in a breath, realizing she'd stopped breathing sometime before, she looked up at him.

He was waiting to catch her glance, to smile—devilishly—in complete understanding. "I have a proposition to put to you."

"What?"

He closed his hands about her waist, shifted back and lifted her over him. She ended straddling him, rather lower than before.

"Let's try it this way."

It took an instant for her to realize what he meant, then she felt the head of his erection nudging against her. He gripped her hips, eased her back. Flattening her hands on his chest, she shifted, wriggled, found the right angle, and leaned back, slowly sat. Slowly, inch by inch, took him into her body.

The most amazing sensation, she savored it to the full, eyes half-closed, senses focused. She sat still for a long moment, simply wallowing, then the rigidity that had afflicted him registered; opening her eyes, she looked down into his. Noted the tension in his face, around his lips, evidence of the control she could sense holding back the wildness she knew was in him.

Unsure how his script read, she raised her brows at him.

With one hand, he gestured. "The reins are yours."

Her brows rose higher. Indeed? How satisfying it would be to shatter that smug male control of his—in more ways than one.

She took him at his word and rose upon him. His hands rode lightly about her hips; he gave her little direction but allowed her to experiment, to explore the possibilities as she would. His grip tensed—she suspected involuntarily—when she nearly rose too high.

So that was the limit in that direction. In the other . . .

She settled to her purpose with a will, surprised to learn just how much pleasure she derived from using her body, under her will alone, to pleasure him. His comment about reins proved apt; she was accustomed to riding, and in many ways it was like that, rising up, sinking down in a deliberate rhythm.

But the contol over both rhythm and depth, over, it seemed, the very nature of their joining, was exquisite; she employed it, enjoyed it to the full. Rode him fast, then slow, then at the gallop again. Sensed the different ways she could use her inner muscles, use her hips and bottom to pressure him.

To fray those reins.

Once she was well embarked on her game, his hands rose to her breasts, to fondle, at first gently, then rather more explicitly.

Fingers flexing on his chest, her breath coming in increasingly rushed pants, she looked into his face, saw concentration, and more, possessiveness and something close to devotion. And wondered . . .

There was a glint in his dark eyes that was secretly triumphant. Had he been pleased she'd been with no other man, that he was the only man ever to have her? The thought focused her mind on where they joined; she shuddered, had to close her eyes for a moment, sink her nails into his chest, until the sharp temptation faded and she could pick up her reckless pace again.

She reminded herself of the questions he'd asked. Given his past, strewn with conquests she had not a doubt, had he assumed she would be the same as he? Had he cared in any possessive way about her answer? Or had he asked purely to decide whether to feel guilty or not?

He was watching her closely, pandering, expertly as the tangle of her nerves testified, to her senses, each sweeping touch of his long fingers heightening the delight she received from feeling him, hard, rigid, and hot, sliding into her body. Again, she caught an impression of orchestration; he was focused on her, on ensuring she achieved the maximum pleasure. His pleasure was not incidental, yet secondary and dependent, as least as he saw it.

He was very very good at pleasuring women. She felt the heat rise inside her, felt her nerves tighten. His reins were nowhere near frayed enough.

"You've changed," she gasped, surprised at how thready her voice had become. "You've been with dozens of women—are you always like this, devoting yourself to their pleasure first, rather than your own?"

She'd asked the question to distract him, also because she wanted to know. She was surprised to see a hint of wariness creep into his eyes.

"I've always liked women." His hands slid back to her hips, gripped; he started to undulate beneath her. "You know that."

She did. He had one older sister and three younger; he'd been far more attuned to them than his older brothers had been. The habit of paying attention to women had been his from an early age.

"Yes, but . . ." She was clinging to sanity; their combined movements were driving her harder, faster, toward the sun. "That's not what I meant," she gasped, "as you well know."

She sensed he would have sighed, but he couldn't—their bucking ride was affecting him, too. Those reins, at long last, were unraveling.

Charles dragged his gaze from the junction of her thighs; meeting her eyes, he confirmed that no matter what else was occurring, she was determined to cling to her wits long enough to hear his answer.

He filled his lungs, not easy in the face of all she was doing to him. "With you, it's different. Not the same. It never was." He had to pause, had to wait until she released him again, enough so some blood could reach his brain. He gritted his teeth as she sank slowly down again. "No other woman ever made me feel the way you do."

Her eyes heavy-lidded, she looked down at him, a houri

sleek, sultry, and heated. In the candlelight, her skin glowed rosily. "How do I make you feel?"

"Desperate." He gripped her hips, pulled her fully down on him, and held her there as he thrust into her, once, twice—three times was all it took and the climax that had crept up on her broke and poured through her.

His grip on her hips tightened; every muscle in his body locked as he held back the urge to ravish her. He waited, savoring her contractions, reminding himself to be civilized, or at least not to frighten her, definitely not to hurt her. Finesse, expertise—sanity. All would be useful to deploy . . .

With a long, low moan, her spine gave way, and she slumped forward, but she crossed her arms on his chest, caught herself on them, met his eyes from bare inches away, fleetingly studied them—then she smiled like a very well satisfied cat, leaned closer, and covered his lips with hers.

The kiss shattered, scattered to the four winds, the control he'd fought to retain. His grip on her hips tightened even more, holding her immobile. He started to move within her again, but no longer with any restraint; with deep powerful surging thrusts, he buried himself in her slick softness.

Her hands rose to frame his face; she matched him kiss for kiss, then pulled back enough to gasp against his lips, "The other way."

She tried to shift sideways in his arms. He realized she wanted him to roll, to bring her beneath him.

"Why?" Why was he asking? Every muscle in his body had cinched tight at the prospect.

Penny closed her eyes. *Because I like feeling you above me, surrounding me. Taking me. Because I enjoy the strength of you moving against me, into me, around me.*

Opening her eyes, she met his. "Because I like it that way."

He didn't argue, but rolled, taking her with him; his weight pressed her into the soft mattress. He settled his hips between her thighs, and thrust deeply home again. She wrapped her arms about him, lifted her legs and draped them over his, gripping his flanks with her thighs, angling her hips beneath him.

The reins snapped. All of them.

He groaned, found her lips with his, and plunged into her. Rode her harder, faster, deeper than he ever had—even thirteen years ago.

This time she was with him, urging him on, flagrantly taking as much as he would give. Glorying in his wildness. Meeting it with her own.

She didn't realize how far she'd gone until he sank one hand into her hair, drew her head back, changed the angle of the kiss to one even more plundering, and drove her straight into the fire.

They burned. The dance consumed them, took every last gasp from their bodies, cindered every last sense.

Until they were deaf, blind, far beyond thought.

Until all that was left to them was a holocaust of feeling that burned every vestige of resistance away, that melded and forged them in the fires of passion unrestrained, and at the last gasp left them, wrung out yet replete, sunk, heart to heart, in each other's arms.

PENNY REACHED THE BREAKFAST PARLOR BEFORE CHARLES the next morning, rather surprised to find him so tardy.

In the mornings, Ellie never came until she rang; she had rung eventually, once Charles had left, which had been after he'd demonstrated yet another way of reaching heaven. *Heaven.* For her money, it was still the sun; heaven was too mild and peaceful a concept to describe the reality of where they'd gone. Let alone how.

She felt buoyed, wonderful, on top of her world. She'd never felt so physically glorious in her life. On the emotional front, she'd kept a close guard on her heart; she was managing perfectly well there. As in trusting Charles with her family's secrets, she'd been right in letting him be her lover again; she could go forward without reservations.

Sweeping into the parlor, she exchanged a nod and a good morning with Nicholas, already seated at the table's head. Crossing to the sideboard, she made her selections; returning to the table, she sat, and from beneath her lashes considered Nicholas. He seemed less distressed, more focused today. Had he, perhaps, gone out last night?

No. She and Charles would almost certainly have heard any hoofbeats on the gravel drive. Had someone called on him privately in the night?

She pondered the possibility while attacking her ham and toast.

"Ah—there you are, my dear."

She turned as Charles entered, met his eyes, and wondered what the message in them meant.

Strolling toward her, he cocked his head. "I wondered if you'd care to ride this morning? I have business in Fowey."

He was now close enough for her to see the exasperated expression in his eyes. She realized. "Oh, yes! Good morning. Indeed—a wonderful idea." She glanced at the sideboard. "I daresay you've breakfasted, but would you care for something more?"

Looking back at him, she caught her breath at the unholy light dancing in his eyes; she replayed her words, didn't dare breathe . . . but he merely smiled and inclined his head. "Thank you."

She exhaled and returned to her toast.

Casting a surreptitious glance at Nicholas, she saw him not quite scowling at Charles's back. Nicholas's guarded greetings when Charles came to the table and took the chair beside hers suggested Nicholas had finally realized how consistently Charles was about.

Although Nicholas shot her a disapproving glance, good manners prevailed, and he made no comment.

Charles, apparently blissfully unaware, mentioned meeting Albert Carmichael at Lostwithiel market the day before.

Nicholas professed never to have met Carmichael.

Penny explained the Cranfields' interest, then had to remind Nicholas who the Cranfields were.

"Ah, I see." Nicholas took a long sip of coffee, then shifted his gaze to Charles. "Has there been any advance in your investigation, Lostwithiel? Any suggestion over who is responsible for that luckless young fisherman's death?"

She had to hand it to Charles; he didn't so much as bat an eyelid or pause in cutting his roast beef.

"Yes, and no." His tone was cheery, as if discussing the latest price for fish. "For various reasons, it seems unlikely the killer was anyone normally resident in the area."

Nicholas blinked. "Why is that?"

Charles sat back, reached for his coffee cup. "Gimby wasn't killed—he was interrogated, then executed. It was a professional piece of work."

Nicholas looked like he was going to turn green again. Looking down, he picked up his fork and pushed a small mound of kedgeree across the porcelain. "So . . . no one local . . ."

"No. Which is why I've been assessing all visitors to the area."

"Vagabonds?" Nicholas's brows rose. "Could it be just . . . no, you said professional."

"True, but there's no reason a professional might not have appeared as a vagabond, but if killing Gimby was his only purpose, he'll be long gone by now. Still"—Charles shrugged—"I might draw a bead on him."

Penny kept her head down and her tongue still, for which he was grateful. He didn't want Nicholas distracted.

After a long moment, Nicholas asked, still not meeting his eyes, "Only purpose . . . what other purpose do you imagine this villain might have?"

Gallic shrugs were so useful. "Who knows? But it could, for instance, be someone who didn't want me to be able to question Gimby, not, as one might suppose, to protect whoever Gimby might have betrayed, but because he, this professional, is on the same quest as I am, and he doesn't want me getting to the Holy Grail first."

He was feeling his way, gauging how best to pressure Nicholas. Despite their antipathy, he was starting to get a feel for the man; he wasn't a coward, but was possessed of an extremely cautious nature. Probably a good thing for someone high in the Foreign Office; equally a good thing in a traitor.

Nicholas had blanched at his words, but, this time, had himself well in hand. Lips thinning, he nodded, effectively ending the discussion; Charles got the impression that he'd been fishing for confirmation, having already followed much the same line of thinking.

Penny finished her breakfast; he quickly downed the last pieces of his roast beef, stood, and drew back her chair.

Rising, she glanced at her gown. "I'll have to change." Her back to Nicholas, she looked up and raised her brows. "I'll meet you in the hall."

"In the forecourt—I'll have the horses saddled and brought there. I need to be in Fowey by half past ten."

Her eyes asked *Why?* and *Why didn't you tell me earlier?* but she nodded, threw a quick farewell Nicholas's way, and left.

Nicholas rose as he turned to make his own farewell, joining him as he left the parlor. "Do you conduct a lot of business in the area personally?"

Charles glanced at him, wondering. "No. My steward and agent handle almost everything."

"Ah, I see. I thought the trip to Fowey . . ."

"That's part of the investigation." Halting, he faced Nicholas. "It's Gimby's funeral. There's an old saw that murderers often turn up to watch their victims go into the ground—to witness their final end, so to speak. I'm hoping our professional might not be so professional and turn up."

Nicholas drew a not-quite-steady breath, tightly said, "In that case, I wish it might be so. Anything that removes such a cold-blooded murderer from among the innocent is greatly to be desired."

With a nod, he headed for the library.

Charles watched him go, intrigued; of all the words Nicholas had uttered in his hearing, those last had been unquestionably the most sincere.

He was waiting with their horses in the forecourt when Penny came hurrying out. She came down the front steps; a smile of anticipation lighting her face, she walked quickly to him.

She halted before him, waiting to be lifted to her saddle.

He took a moment to slap down his demons; kissing her witless in the forecourt in full view of the library windows wouldn't be a clever thing to do.

Reaching for her, he lifted her up. He informed her of their reason for hying to Fowey as he held her stirrup for her.

He was mounting Domino when the thud of approaching hooves reached them. They both shortened their reins; holding their horses steady, they watched a dusty rider come galloping in along the drive.

The rider saw them, drew rein, and trotted the last way.

"Mornin', ma'am, sir. I'm looking for Lord Arbry."

Penny waved to the house. "If you'll just ring the bell . . ."

Norris had heard the hoofbeats; he appeared on the porch.

A step behind him came Nicholas. "I'm Arbry. Is that the dispatch from the Foreign Office?"

"Yes, m'lord." The courier dismounted and unbuckled a satchel from his saddle. He handed it to Nicholas, who'd come down the steps to take it.

"Good." Nicholas examined the bag, checking the seals, then nodded at the man. "If you take your horse to the stable, then come up to the house, Norris here will take care of you."

"Thank you, m'lord." With a bow to Nicholas and another to Penny and Charles, the man led his horse away around the house.

Nicholas tucked the bag under his arm.

Leaning on his saddle, Charles said, "I didn't realize you were working down here."

Penny picked up the silky, dangerous note in his voice; she wondered if Nicholas had. He seemed faintly flustered.

"Just a few things they want my opinion on." With a weak smile and a nod, he went indoors.

Charles watched him go, then met her eyes. "Let's go."

They rode out. Not, this time, like a pair of giddy reckless children. Being responsible adults, they cantered down the lane.

And came upon Julian Fothergill. He was climbing over a stile as they turned into the lane to Fowey. Seeing them, he sat on the top of the stile; as they neared, he saluted.

"Good morning!"

Reining in, Penny smiled. "Good morning. Have you been out bird-watching?"

Two spyglasses on cords hung around Fothergill's neck. "Indeed." He gestured across the lane to where the footpath he was on continued toward the estuary. "I'm on my way to have a look around the river mouth to see if there's any good vantage spots there. I heard there's a stretch of marsh—that's always good for spotting."

Charles nodded in greeting. "There's fair cover along the banks—the marsh extends out from them, but is underwater at high tide. Be careful."

Fothergill smiled. "I will."

"Have you had much luck?" Penny asked, wondering what questions might lead Fothergill to reveal more. He was a sunnily personable gentleman; she couldn't see him as a murderer, but they ought to be logical and investigate all five visitors.

"Oh, yes! Just yesterday I spotted a pied gull, and . . ." Fothergill's countenance glowed with a zealot's fire as he recounted numerous species he'd seen.

"You've covered quite a stretch of territory," Charles said. "You must have been down along the cliffs to spot those gulls."

Fothergill nodded. "Until now I've spent most of my days closer to the cliffs. I'm gradually working my way to the estuary and plan to move slowly upriver. Actually," he continued, "I'm glad to have run into you—you both know the area so well. I'm also something of a student of architecture, and I wondered what the best places to visit hereabouts were?"

"Restormel Castle," Penny answered without hesitation. "Its ruins are not to be missed if only for their history, but its structure is informative and there's quite a bit left to see. After that . . ." She glanced at Charles.

"The Abbey—Restormel Abbey, my house—is across the river from the castle. Filchett, my butler, will be happy to show you around. He knows the history as well as I do, and the architecture rather better."

"And you can always stop in at Wallingham Hall," Penny said. "I'm sure Lord Arbry won't mind. There's a very fine Adam fireplace in the drawing room, and the music room is considered notable." She paused, then added, "Looe House is the other house of architectural note, but you'll need to ride to reach it—it's on the road to Polperro, but the owners, the Richardses, are always happy to show people with an interest around."

"Thank you!" Fothergill beamed at them, his expression open, his gaze equally so. "You've been a great help."

Domino sidled. Charles tightened his reins. "I'm afraid we must leave you—we have an appointment in Fowey."

"Yes." Penny sobered. "And we'll have to walk to the chapel by the cemetery—it's the funeral of that poor young fisherman who was murdered."

"Oh?" Fothergill looked blank. "Did you know him, then?"

"No," Charles said, swinging Domino down the lane. "We're attending as representatives of the local families."

"Ah." Fothergill nodded. "Of course."

He saluted them; they both nodded in reply and rode on.

Penny would have liked to discuss Fothergill, but Charles set a pace that precluded conversation. She let her thoughts spin and rode beside him. They went straight to the Pelican, left the horses there, then walked briskly along the High Street. Rather than descend to the quays, then climb up the opposite hill, they followed the High Street along the ridge and out onto the cliff in the lee of which Fowey huddled.

The cemetery was built on the highest and last stretch of land before the cliff fell away to the rocks against which the Channel's waves broke. Today, the waves sent up a murmurous chant, a dirge for a fisherman lost.

They reached the small chapel beside the cemetery; Charles took her elbow and ushered her in. They were just in time. The plain wooden coffin stood on bare trestles before the stone altar. Someone had placed a spray of white lilies on the unpolished wood. There were few there to hear the short service, few who had known Gimby at all, but there were some "mourners." All were known to Charles and Penny; all were inhabitants of Fowey.

Together with the rest, they followed the coffin to the graveside and watched it lowered into the earth. Each person threw a handful of soil upon the lid, then one and all, exchanging nods and glances, turned away and left the gravediggers to their task.

Charles paused to speak to the vicar, then joined Penny where she waited with Mother Gibbs, both hanging on to their hats as the wind, brisker here on the point, tried to whisk them from their heads.

Mother Gibbs bobbed a curtsy as Charles came up.

He took Penny's arm, and the three of them started back to the town. "Have you heard anything?"

"Wish I could say I have, but nay—there's nary a whisper, and you may be sure I've put the word out good and proper."

"Any advance on Arbry or Granville, or any related subjects?"

Pursing her lips, Mother Gibbs shook her head. "All quiet, it's been."

They turned onto the steep path that led down to the harbor; soon they were in the lee of the cliff, out of the wind.

Charles went on, "What about men passing through—gypsies, tinkers, vagabonds, men looking for work?"

"Wrong time of year for most such, but there was a tinker family came through. Near as me and the boys could work out, though, they was camped here, by Fowey town, days before poor Gimby met his end, and though they did head off just before he was found, they said they was heading to St. Austell. Dennis checked with the fishermen thereabouts, and the tinkers did appear there just when you'd expect, so they couldn't've spared time to head the other way and murder Gimby, least not any ways we can see."

"Thank you." Charles fished in his pocket and drew out a sovereign; he offered it, but Mother Gibbs shook her head.

"Nay, not for this." She fluffed her knitted shawl about her old shoulders and looked down at the fleet, bobbing at the quay. "Me and the boys don't hold with this—Gimby might've been a blessed hermit, but he was one of ours. Whatever we can do to help you catch the beggar who killed him, we'll do it and gladly. Dennis said as to tell ye he and the Gallants are at your disposal should you need extra hands."

Charles nodded, returning the sovereign to his pocket. "Warn Dennis and the others to be extracareful all around. It's possible the murderer's already left the area, but something tells me he hasn't."

"Aye." Mother Gibbs nodded. "I'll do that."

They parted from her at the lower end of the steep passageway leading to her door and strolled on along the quay.

Penny glanced at Charles's face, often expressive, presently uninformative. "What are you thinking?"

He glanced at her, almost as if he'd forgotten she was on his arm. She narrowed her eyes on his. "Or should that be what are you planning?"

His swift grin broke across his face; he looked ahead. "Given that Nicholas is receiving dispatches, I was wondering if it was possible to arrange for him to receive the sort of information that would spur him to make contact with the French again. Assuming, of course, that simple treason is what we're dealing with, a fact of which I'm still not convinced."

"You think he might not have been passing secrets, but receiving them?"

"That's one possibility we can't as yet discount, certainly, but . . ." He shook his head. "It's a feeling that the picture isn't properly taking shape. Like a jigsaw with pieces that simply won't fit. No matter what else we learn, at the back of my mind is the nagging fact that despite the assurances we received that there *was* a traitor working out of the Foreign Office, Dalziel never unearthed the slightest evidence that any information from the F.O. had actually turned up on the other side.

"Yes, the other side might have someone smart enough to hide all trace, *however*, Dalziel is terrifyingly good at finding such links, but in this case he turned up empty-handed, and it wasn't for lack of trying."

He stopped; arm in arm, they stood and looked out over the forest of masts lining the quay. "I don't believe Nicholas is Gimby's murderer. I was hoping, still am hoping that he'll see the light and either confess, or at least take me sufficiently into his confidence so we can, regardless of all else, capture whoever killed Gimby. I *am* sure Gimby was the link with the French—the signals prove that. But while Nicholas is involved, just *how* he's involved . . ." He sighed, frustrated.

She squeezed his arm. "I see what you mean about pieces that don't fit."

She sensed a sharpening of his attention, felt the subtle steeling of the muscles under her hand.

"Speaking of such pieces . . ."

She followed his gaze to a tall, thin figure standing on the wharf below in deep and animated discussion with two fishermen.

"The Chevalier." She searched through the others thronging the wharf. "I can't see Mark Trescowthick, or any others of that group."

"No." Charles was watching the exchange between the seamen and the Chevalier. "I have the feeling that while Mark might think he and the Chevalier are close friends, the Chevalier might describe matters differently."

She considered. "The Chevalier's rather older than Mark."

"And far more serious than an overindulged pup like Mark Trescowthick. I'm sure the Chevalier is charming when he needs to be, but I doubt they have much in common."

"If the Chevalier is just using Mark as his excuse to be down here, that rather raises the question of why."

Charles studied the Chevalier for a minute more, then stirred. "With any luck Dalziel will help us with that—he has contacts enough to find out what the Chevalier's real purpose here might be. Meanwhile, I should speak with Dennis, maybe tomorrow, and give him the names of our five visitors. Let's see what he and the Gallants can learn."

Together, they turned and started the climb back to the High Street.

"Perhaps we should ride to the Abbey and see if Dalziel has sent any word."

Charles shook his head. "Not enough time has passed since I sent my report. The reply will come late tonight at the earliest, but most likely sometime tomorrow." He looked at her. "Let's have a quick lunch at the Pelican, and then, given Nicholas had a delivery this morning, I think a stint in the folly might be wise."

They walked on in silence. As they neared the Pelican, she said, "On the way back, I'm going to stop off at Essington Manor. If I'm not seen about, visiting as usual, people will start wondering where I am—"

"And what you're doing." Charles sent her one of his devilish grins. "Good idea. I'll endure the folly on my own. Who knows?" He arched a brow at her as he held the door of the Pelican wide. "I might even catch up on some sleep."

She narrowed her eyes at him, elevated her nose, and swept past.

And hoped, in the dimmer light inside, that he wouldn't see her blush.

That blush hadn't owed its genesis to any prudish start but to her realization of how reluctant she was to forgo an afternoon in the folly with him.

But reason had to prevail.

When she rode into the Wallingham Hall stables at five o'clock—and not a minute earlier, as he'd instructed—he was waiting. Together they walked up to the house.

"Did anything occur this afternoon?"

"No. Nicholas is sitting tight." Charles looked toward the wing that housed the library. "I'm inclining to the notion that he doesn't know who to contact any more than he did when he first came here looking for Granville's friends. If that's so, it'll be pointless to arrange to give him something worth another pillbox to sell. *However*, I think he's very much afraid someone knows to contact *him*, and he doesn't know what to do."

"So he's being extracareful."

"Indeed. I'm going to try to rattle him this evening."

Reaching the garden door they entered, and once again went their separate ways. She repaired to her room, bathed and changed for dinner; given Norris was in Charles's confidence, she expected he was doing the same. Certainly, when she walked into the drawing room fifteen minutes before the dinner hour, he appeared immaculately groomed.

He was standing with Nicholas by the fireplace, dwarfing Nicholas more by vitality than size, and appeared to be in expansive good humor—a fact Nicholas, it seemed, had learned to view with suspicion, as well he might.

She did her best to provide the right foil for Charles's machinations; it didn't truly matter which of them Nicholas decided to trust. If he ever did; despite Charles's best efforts—not overtly intimidating but in a vein any scion of Eton or Harrow would instantly recognize and correctly interpret, such as a largely one-sided discussion of the type of secrets that Gimby might have assisted in ferrying across the Channel—Nicholas remained tight-lipped.

Indeed, his resistance seemed to have hardened. The antipathy between the two that Charles had originally remarked seemed to be resurfacing.

When, hours later, she went into the front hall to farewell Charles, much to Nicholas's transparent relief, she murmured, "He's more . . . *dogged*, don't you think?"

Charles nodded, the line of his lips tending grim. "We're going backward with him. He's come out of his funk and realized we have no evidence whatever. If he just sits tight, he'll escape any net."

"I wonder," she said, walking toward the front door left open to the pleasant night, "if something in those papers he received might account for his change of heart. Perhaps we could look at them later?"

"He's keeping them in his room, but there's nothing there other than what he suggested—memos he needs to approve."

When she turned to stare at him, he smiled. "Norris has missed his calling. He looked, and remembered enough for me to be sure."

She sighed. "In that case . . ." Raising her head, she met his eyes and gave him her hand. "I'll bid you . . . *au revoir*."

His smile deepened. "Indeed." Lifting her hand, he pressed a kiss to her fingertips, paused, his gaze on hers, then turned her hand and pressed a much more intimate kiss—one she felt to her marrow—to her palm, then gracefully bowed, released her, and went out and down the steps.

Leaning against the doorframe, a smile curving her lips, she listened to the scrunch of his boots as he headed around the house toward the stables. Outside, the night was peaceful, serene but dark; the moon had yet to rise. She drank in the silence, let the aura of home wrap her about. And thought of how long it would take Charles to circle the house and slip upstairs.

Her smile deepening, she straightened and turned inside. As she crossed the front hall, Nicholas came out of the drawing room. He halted; a faint frown shadowed his face.

Drawing near, she raised her brows in easy query.

"How does Lostwithiel come and go? I haven't heard wheels on the gravel when he leaves."

She smiled in understanding. "He's most at home in a saddle. Knowing him, he rides over the fields—he never was one to stick to any straight and narrow."

"Indeed?"

Faintly disconcerted, as she'd intended, Nicholas nodded a good night and headed for the library. According to Norris, he'd lost all interest in the local area and was now leafing through her father's books on pillboxes.

Inwardly frowning, she climbed the stairs.

Ellie was waiting. Penny thought about dismissing her, but decided to stick with her usual routine.

Eventually, Ellie left. Rising from her dressing stool, Penny snuffed the candles, then went to the window and opened the curtains. The moon was just rising over the escarpment, sending fingers of silvery light into the room. She remained at the window, looking out as the light strengthened and the familiar landscape was reborn, transfigured by the play of moonlight and shadow.

A minute later, Charles materialized from the shadows behind her. She hadn't heard him enter, but knew he was there before he stepped near.

Reaching past her, he unlatched the window and pushed it open. In the same movement, he stepped close, one large hand sliding across her waist to ease her back against him.

Smiling, she relaxed and crossed her arms over his hand, holding him to her; leaning back into the haven of his strength, she rubbed her temple against his jaw. "Nicholas asked how you traveled back and forth from the Abbey. He noticed the lack of carriage wheels on the drive."

"What did you say?"

"I intimated that, unconventional as you were, you probably rode."

There was a moment's silence. "Unconventional?"

"Hmm."

She could almost hear his mind working.

"You don't like conventional." Statement, not question.

"Conventional is well enough in its place, but there's a time and place for everything, including the other." She turned in his arms, looked into his face. "And the other is certainly more . . . challenging."

His smile would have beguiled an angel. "And," he said, bending his head, "you like to be challenged."

"I do," she whispered, and kissed him.

She'd learned long ago the art of dealing with him, treating with him. It was imperative to stop him from grabbing the bit of their interaction and running with it, leaving her forever trying to catch up. Instead, as before, she boldly seized the reins.

Opened her mouth to him, lured him in, sank into his arms, pressed herself to him, drew him deep, then turned the kiss on him. Let her fire rise and pour through her into him; let her desire—the desire he'd shown her she had—freely rise and take her, and claim him.

She dropped all pretense; she knew what she wanted of him—she let it show. Knew that would provoke him as nothing else could.

Winding her arms about his neck, she held him to the kiss. Pressing into him, she swayed, flagrantly caressing his already rigid erection, deliberately taunting its hardness with the giving tautness of her belly, sliding her thighs against his, sinuously shifting her peaked breasts against his chest.

He stilled, then surrendered, yet even as he gave way, as he let her will dominate and ceded control to her, she knew she hadn't, this time, succeeded in stunning him long enough to seize it; he'd been waiting, ready for her, but had made a deliberate decision to let her lead. To *allow* her to script their play.

That willing subservience was such an un-Charles-like act, at least of the Charles she'd known; with an effort she broke from the kiss that had progressed to beyond voracious, that had already reduced them both to gasps, to, from a distance of an inch, try to read his eyes, his face.

Her wits were her own, but they weren't functioning logically, all but overwhelmed by her senses. Her gaze steadied on his dark eyes, then lowered to his lips. Hers throbbed. "Why?"

She was sure he'd understand, was sure he did, yet he didn't immediately answer.

He hesitated long enough to make her wonder what he was hiding.

She raised her eyes to his.

He held her gaze, thinking for a moment longer, then replied, his voice so low she wasn't sure she heard so much as felt his words.

"Whatever you wish, however you wish. I'm yours. Take me."

Love me. Charles bit back the words—not yet, not now. He might be caught, but he wasn't sure she was. Experience had taught him not to imagine he could read women's minds; heaven knew they were infinitely more complicated than men's.

Her eyes searched his, verifying his meaning, then a slow, sultry smile—one he'd only seen in recent days—curved her lips.

"However I wish . . ." she murmured, and stretched up and kissed him.

CHAPTER
14

INWARDLY SMILING, CHARLES GRIPPED HER WAIST; FOR LONG moments, as her tongue dueled with his, he simply savored the feel of her between his hands, supple, imbued with feminine strength, subtly rather than overtly curvaceous.

Why that last should so attract him he'd never understood; perhaps it was because her body with its svelte charms echoed her elusive and therefore more tantalizing feminine responses.

If she liked challenges, he liked them even more. Especially when they were feminine. Especially when the female was her.

Letting her have her way wasn't easy; his instinct in this arena was always to control, for his partner's pleasure as much as his own. But pleasure was not the only currency he—they—were dealing in; if he wanted that other coin in the mix, he had to give ground, yield as she wished, and accept the risk that whatever was revealed wasn't too frightening. Either for her, or him.

She pressed close again, and he shuddered, then she drew back enough to start on his clothes. Coat, waistcoat, cravat all went while he schooled himself to do no more than return her kisses, to leave his hands riding at her waist. He wasn't sure where her imagination might lead her; he was eager to learn.

Inevitably he responded, not just to her nearness or the touch of her hands, but even more to her intent. From the instant she'd turned into his arms, that had never been in doubt. She wanted to take him inside her, wanted him inside her; that knowledge alone was enough to make him ache.

He tried not to dwell on it, instead reminded himself that courtesy of her relative inexperience combined with her confidence, the moments before they reached any rapturous state were bound to be not just fraught, but full of potential potholes large enough for him to bury himself in. He was feeling his way with her just as much as he was with her relative, but succeeding with her was far more important.

She'd opened his shirt; now she broke from the kiss, spread the halves wide, and visually devoured. "Stand still." She leaned close and set her mouth to his skin.

He closed his eyes, felt his fingers tighten about her, helpless to desist, and reminded himself how vitally important winning her had become. Her mouth felt like flames licking over his already heated skin. Her greedy fingers danced, tangling in the dark hair dusting the muscle bands, finding the flat disc of one nipple and teasing, lightly tweaking.

Her lips and tongue distracted him while her fingers slid down to his waistband. And stilled.

She trailed kisses up the midline of his chest, through the hollow at the base of his throat, then up to his chin. He opened his eyes as she drew back, studying his face. He raised a brow.

"I'm thinking."

That struck him as even more dangerous than usual. "Would you like me to make a suggestion?"

She shook her head, her gaze perfectly steady. "I'm trying to decide which, not what."

It was going to be torture whichever option she chose.

One brow arched; she looked at him consideringly. "I think . . ." She stepped back, out of his hold. "Stay there—don't move."

He watched as she took another step away, then, hands bunching the fabric at her sides, she drew up her nightgown.

He'd been right, much good did it do him; the battle to remain where he was, to not reach for her as she—smoothly, gracefully, and entirely unhurriedly—drew her nightgown up and off over her head, then tossed it to fall across her dressing stool was fraught, as difficult as any he'd faced. Totally naked, she considered his chest, then her gaze drifted down.

"Your boots—take them off."

Leaning back against the edge of her bed, he complied, flicking open his breeches' buckles and stripping off his hose as well, setting all to one side.

As he straightened, he fixed his gaze on her feet, then slowly traced upward, over the curves of her calves, the long, sculpted lines of her thighs, lighting on the thatch of pale blond curls at their apex before idly drifting up over her belly, her waist, her breasts, ultimately to meet her eyes.

Her skin was already faintly tinged; in the moonlight he couldn't tell if his perusal had made it rosier still.

She held his gaze for a moment, then smiled, a cat sighting cream.

"Good," she said, and closed the distance between them.

He'd forgotten his legs were against her bed; she stepped into him, not trapping him but limiting his ability to move—to create any distance between them—without moving her. Her breasts brushed his chest, wickedly evocative, then she lifted her head and set her lips to his—and set her hands and her body willfully to his. To work on his.

That was the option she'd chosen.

She plunged into his mouth, deliberately seized his senses with a scalding kiss, then broke away to take mouth, lips, and tongue on a ride of pleasuring delight over his burning skin, over his tensed muscles, flickering beneath the restraint he'd placed on them.

He hauled in a breath, held it as her fingers dallied once more at his waistband. As her mouth cruised across his chest, then commenced a leisurely descent. Slowly raising his hands, he spread them over her back, holding her lightly, tracing upward to rest on her shoulders as she wended her way down.

Until she flicked the buttons at his waistband free, in one easy stroke slid his breeches down, in the same movement sank to her knees, fitted her mouth over him, and smoothly took him in.

He nearly expired. For one finite instant, his heart stood still, then bolted. Raced as she experimented, hurdled when she bent to her self-appointed task of pleasuring him witless.

His hands had risen, without direction had fisted in her hair. His fingers tightened as she drew him deeper still; he realized he could no longer breathe. Eyes closed, he clung to the only thing she'd left him—sensation—and felt every last scintilla of her devotion as she licked, stroked, sucked, his existence reduced to the hot wetness of her mouth, to the scope of her will as she caressed him.

He'd had no idea she would even think of it, of pandering to his senses, his passions in such an overtly immodest way. In such a blatantly wanton way. Battling to mute the groan she drew from him, he wondered if she'd guessed what her being wanton, so utterly abandoned, did to him.

It was more than torture to stand still and force himself simply to accept all she pressed on him, to look down at her pale head moving against him, her flaxen locks spreading and tangling, catching as she worked, and not respond, not grasp, seize, and demand more.

Simply to receive.

To not have to issue any demands at all, but to have many of the wanton thoughts he'd indulged over the years brought to life. To have caresses he'd dreamed of lavished upon him.

Because she wished to.

The thought very nearly brought him—and her—undone. He endured for ten heartbeats, then, gasping, sensually reeling for the first time in more years than he could count, he guided his hands to her face, slid his thumb into her mouth, and withdrew his erection from that gloriously wet haven. "No more."

The words were so gravelly Penny could barely make them out, but through her hands on his thighs she sensed the tension in him—more than she recalled evoking in him before—and knew enough to heed it. But she'd learned enough for now; the maids she'd overheard whispering hadn't been wrong.

Rocking back on her heels, she rose, trailing her hand up as she did, closing it around his jutting length. With her other hand, she prodded his chest. "Sit on the bed."

His eyes met hers; she glimpsed the predator in him, but he complied. Obligingly, he sat back. She followed, clambering up, setting one knee on either side of his hips, straddling him. Then she locked her eyes with his. One hand on his shoulder for balance, the other wrapped about his erection, she slowly, deliberately, entirely at her own discretion, impaled herself on him.

And he let her.

She felt the effort it cost him, saw how clenched his jaw was, saw his lids drift down in surrender as she sank fully down, her softness sheathing his hardness, her body sliding down his to finally come to rest breasts to chest. Draping her arms over his shoulders, she set her lips to his, slid into his mouth, danced her tongue over his, then started to move upon him.

A dance of a different sort.

It wasn't the same as when he'd lain flat; although she experimented, she couldn't find quite the right angle . . .

Desire had already burgeoned within her; she needed more, soon.

Drawing back from the kiss, dragging in a gasping breath, she clung and pressed closer; her head beside his brought their bodies even tighter against each other, but no . . .

"This"—she had to haul in another breath—"isn't quite right." She whispered the words beside his ear. Dragged in another breath. "Is it?"

She felt rather than heard a chuckle that came out more like a groan.

"You saw this in some book, didn't you?"

She bit his earlobe—hard. "How else?"

"You're too tall—there's a better way for us."

She licked the spot she'd bitten. Purred, "How?"

His hands, until then loose across her back, slid down to grip her bottom. He held her to him as he shifted, swinging his legs up, holding her against him as he came to his knees, then sank back to sit on his ankles.

Resettling her over him, straddling his hips, he resettled himself within her. Brushed back the veil of her hair and met her eyes. "How's that?"

Her hands on his shoulders, she rose up, then slowly sank down. Her knees and thighs now at a different angle, she had much better purchase on the bed. Their bodies entire seemed much better aligned, at least for their present purpose. Sliding her hands up, she framed his face, smiled her answer— and kissed him.

Let go all restraint and gave herself over to the now driving need to love him, to meet him on the physical plane, match him and experience all that together they might know. That together they could share.

And he went with her, but still at her command, following not leading, letting her set the pace and the direction, letting her ride them both hard, furious, and unswerving toward the sun.

She reached it, and burned.

Charles let the conflagration take her, let it consume her. Watched it claim her. He found a strength he didn't know he possessed and held back from the beckoning blaze.

And waited. Until release had swept through her and away.

My turn. He didn't say the words; she wouldn't have heard them if he had. Holding her to him, he fought to free enough of his mind from the heat of her slick sheath to direct his hands and rearrange her limbs.

Her limp arms he draped over his shoulders, her legs he straightened one at a time and wrapped them about his waist, then he took her bottom in both hands, supporting her weight, tipping her hips to him.

And smoothly drove into her. Embedded himself to the hilt, then gripped her bottom and moved her on him. Worked her hips over his. In this position, he only had to thrust a little to fill her, to penetrate her forcefully as deeply as he could. She was fully open to him, totally his, totally helpless to resist. Totally and completely in his power.

Penny awoke to that jolting reality on a rush of intense sensation. Surely he was deeper, farther inside her than he'd ever been?

She gasped, eyes closed, clung tight as she assimilated their new position—assimilated the devastating impact it was having on her already heightened senses. And at some deeper level, on her very being.

The rhythm he set was neither fast nor slow, but perfectly gauged and relentless. Her senses spun. She tried to squirm, to press ahead still faster, to gain even more delicious pressure for her suddenly clamorous nerves, but instead his fingers tightened; he held her immobile, suspended half-off him for a heartbeat, until she sobbed and clutched in desperation, then he filled her, deep and hard and shockingly thoroughly, again.

Oh, yes, her senses sobbed.

Her breasts, riding against his hair-dusted chest, had swollen until they ached, the nipples so tightly ruched and sensitive she longed to feel his mouth soothing them. In desperation, she clutched his shoulders, extended her arms, and leaned back so her breasts were no longer so excruciatingly abraded.

He bent his head and set his lips to one breast, found her nipple, took it into his hot mouth, and suckled.

Lightning streaked through her; she screamed, gasped, and arched in his arms. He held her easily, continued to work her hips, continued to thrust into her body, continued to feast on her breasts . . . until she shattered.

More completely than she ever had.

For long moments, she was floating, out of touch with any world but the sensate, aware only of him, his touch, his . . . worship.

There seemed no other word for it. Even now, he didn't seek his own release, but sought to lengthen and heighten hers. She didn't know the ways, but felt the results, felt the golden pleasure well and swell and buoy her on.

It seemed eons, but could only have been minutes before she drifted back to earth, and found herself wrapped in his arms, secure and safe against his chest, her head on his shoulder. He was still hard and rigid within her.

She shifted her head, found his ear, caressed it with her lips. Murmured, "Lay me down. Take me now."

He drew back to look into her eyes. For a moment, their gazes locked, and she wondered what he saw, what he looked for when he searched her eyes . . . what he wanted from her.

She could sense his heartbeat, feel his tension, yet it wasn't desire that stared at her from his eyes.

But then he shifted, lifted her from him, laid her on the pillows. His touch was assured as he settled her, flicked her hair out, laid it about her, then drew the covers from beneath her and let them fall where they would. She was suddenly aware of the flaring emptiness within her, the emptiness he'd filled, that when he was within her she was whole, in some way complete. His eyes, his hands, never left her; as he spread her thighs and loomed over her, that emptiness swelled to an ache.

Then he filled her.

Relief fell from her in a soft sob. Braced above her, he looked down at her as he moved, and started a slow ride of his own.

Long, slow—how a compulsion so fraught, so driven, could feel so languid in execution was something she couldn't comprehend. He made it seem so, yet it wasn't. He seemed almost relaxed as he rhythmically drove into her, yet he was very far from that.

Reaching up, she ran her hands over his chest, over the locked muscles in his upper arms, over the broad sweep of his shoulders, then she tugged, arched as he drove deeper, harder, then he groaned and obliged.

He lowered his body to hers, and she stopped thinking.

Her existence shrank to just him and her in the soft shadows of her bed, to shared breaths, gasps, to the wonder of swift shared glances in the dark, to their bodies flexing, merging to the dance they performed it seemed instinctively. She didn't need to think to know what to do, but could simply let instinct guide her.

Could be with him in this way without thought or concern, or restraint, could simply give herself up to him. As he gave himself to her.

In the end, wholly, completely, without reserve. The wave reared, then crashed, and swept them both away.

They clung, held tight to the moment, to sensation, to each other.

The wave receded and left them, for a moment adrift on a sea of their own making, then they sank back to earth, to the earthly comfort of her bed.

Wrapped in each other's arms, they slept.

She woke in the deep watches of the night with no idea what had roused her.

She lay still, and listened . . . realized as she registered her breathing and his that she hadn't, not even in that fleeting moment of first awareness, felt surprised to find Charles beside her, to feel his arm lying over her waist.

The moon was now high; silvery light streamed through the open curtains, the bright shaft striking the floor beside the bed, throwing enough light for her night-adjusted eyes to see clearly.

No ripple of the unexpected disturbed the stillness about them.

All seemed peaceful. Comforting. Right.

As it should be.

She shifted just enough to look at him. He was slumped facedown in the bed beside her, deeply asleep. Even so, one arm lay flung over her, long fingers relaxed against her side; she wouldn't give much for her chances of sliding from the bed. Of leaving him.

That odd look she'd seen and even more sensed in his eyes returned to haunt her. Frowning, she tried to fathom what it meant. In that moment, she was perfectly sure neither he nor she could have pretended anything. He'd sworn he was no longer capable of pretense, not in that sphere; she now understood enough of his past to believe him.

Sinking into the soft mattress, she thought back over the night . . . smiled at the success of her strategy.

That strange look floated once again across her mind.

She shook it aside. She knew what they were doing this time; it was a physical engagement, an affair with no emotional strings on either side. That was the mistake she'd made last time, imagining something that hadn't been, not understanding how he saw it. He hadn't felt for her as she'd thought—not as she'd felt for him—and that's how he'd always see her. They were close friends indisputably, lovers in the physical sense, but nothing more.

This time she accepted that that was how it would be; she'd gone into this with her eyes open. They would share and indulge in physical pleasure as they would, until they grew tired of it; she had no doubt that whatever transpired they would remain forever friends. He would go off and do whatever he would do, and she would continue as she had been, but with a wealth of memories to warm her, to reassure her that she was as female, as feminine, as desirable as any of her sex.

She knew, this time, what she wanted from him; this time that matched what she could expect to receive. This time, she hadn't put her heart on the table and expected to receive his in return.

Her gaze drifted to his face, the section she could see. His dark hair lay in heavy locks over his forehead; his beard was starting to shadow his jaw.

Again, that odd, lingering, *wanting* look of his filled her mind . . .

He'd spoken of a jigsaw with pieces that didn't fit; this seemed more like one thread too many for the tapestry she'd thought they'd been weaving. That look was evidence of an extra strand, something she hadn't expected, something that didn't fit with the picture of them she'd assembled in her mind.

But that look had been real, not imagined, not something

concocted for her distraction. It had been raw, undisguised, unshielded.

Which was why it wouldn't leave her mind.

Charles came awake in the instant the tumblers of the lock on Penny's door clunked. He sat up, looked across the room, aware she was awake, too.

The latch lifted, the door swung noiselessly open—all the way open.

The moonlight streaming in was bright; the unlit corridor was pitch-black in contrast. All he could see was the vague outline of a man.

He swore and leapt from the bed.

The man ran.

Grabbing up his breeches, he yanked them on, stomped into his boots. Penny had sat up, covers clutched to her chest, staring at the open door. The sound of running footsteps receding along the corridor reached them.

"Stay there!" He was at the door on the words; he paused only long enough to grab the key from the inside lock, fit it to the outside, then he slammed the door, locked it, and pocketed the key. And raced after the shadowy figure he glimpsed at the head of the stairs.

The man pelted down the stairs, leaping, swinging from the banister. Charles reached the top, and flung himself after him. The man was making for the front door. The bolts would slow him.

Except that the front door stood wide open.

Charles slowed in disbelief as he ran into the wide swath of moonlight pouring into the front hall. Realizing, he swerved to the side, out of the light. He heard the scrunch of booted feet fleeing—then nothing.

Walking out onto the porch, he looked in the direction of the last sound, but as he'd expected, the shrubbery was a mass of dense shadows. The man could be standing there or fleeing through it; it was impossible to tell.

Hands on his hips, he stood waiting for his breathing to

even out, and softly swore. He was far too wise to give further chase. The man had come to Penny's room; if he left the house, the villain might circle around and try for her again. He wasn't leaving her unguarded, not in this lifetime.

But why the hell had the front door been unlocked? Not even the best locksman could get past its heavy double bolts.

He was turning to check the bolts when a shifting shadow made him freeze. Then he stared. Hands in his pockets, Nicholas came walking up along one of the garden paths, one easily reached from the rear of the shrubbery.

Charles waited where he was, in full sight.

Nicholas saw him from some distance away; reaching the steps, he started up. "What are you doing here?"

Charles paused long enough for Nicholas to sense how very wrong things were, then said, "Some man broke into Penny's room."

Nicholas stepped onto the porch. His jaw fell. "*What?*"

It was a convincing performance, yet Charles wasn't sure, and wasn't taking any chances. He waved inside. "The front door was left unbolted."

Nicholas looked at the double doors, both standing wide. "I . . . I left them shut when I went out."

"Shut, but not bolted?"

"Well, no . . . I had to get back inside."

"Where have you been?"

"Out." Apparently stunned, he waved vaguely toward the gardens. "I couldn't sleep—I went for a walk . . ." Suddenly, he focused on Charles's face. "Good God! Is Penny all right?"

Charles almost believed him; his horrified expression appeared very real. "Yes." He paused, then added, "I was with her." He started back into the house. Still apparently in shock, Nicholas trailed after him.

Hauling one huge door shut, Charles added, distinctly grim as he thought things through, "Just as well."

Nicholas closed the other door; he stood back as Charles threw the bolts. "We'd better check the other doors, I suppose."

"Yes." Charles did, confirming that the other doors and

windows on the ground floor were secure. Not that that meant much; any trained operative could find a way in, and he was sure, now, of the caliber of the enemy.

Nicholas trailed behind him, watching but not volunteering, also just as well. Aside from the fact Charles knew the house better than he did, Charles wouldn't have accepted his word for anything, not even that a window was locked.

Finally, Charles climbed the stairs. Nicholas followed. Charles halted in the corridor at the stair head; Nicholas's room was in the other wing, in the opposite direction from Penny's.

Nicholas stepped up to the corridor; his gaze moved over Charles's bare shoulders and chest, slid down to the knee buckles on his breeches, hanging free. Halting, he stared at Charles through the dimness, transparently making the obvious connections.

Charles simply waited.

Nicholas cleared his throat. "Ah . . . you said you were with Penny?"

Crouched behind her bedchamber door, her ear to the keyhole, Penny heard his question and the inference behind it.

"Damn!" She'd already sworn in both English and French at Charles for having locked her in. Panic of an unfamiliar and unprecedented sort had attacked her when she'd heard the thuds as two men—Charles and the mystery man—had gone flying down the stairs. After that, no matter how hard she'd strained her ears, she'd heard nothing. Her window gave onto the courtyard; she'd seen nothing either.

Now she listened with all her might. The door was old, solid, and thick, but so was the lock; the keyhole, with no key in it for Charles had taken it with him, was large. With her ear pressed against it, with night's quiet prevailing through the rest of the house, she could hear their words. She had no idea where Nicholas had come from, but he and Charles were standing along the corridor, she thought near the stairs.

"Indeed." That was Charles at his drawling worst. In the circumstances, pure provocation.

She heard an odd sound—wondered for one instant if Charles was throttling Nicholas—then realized it was Nicholas clearing his throat again.

"Ah . . . you mentioned you and Penny had an understanding. Am I to take it that there'll soon be talk of a wedding?"

Behind her door, she screwed her eyes shut and swore at Nicholas. How *dare* he? She wasn't his responsibility; he had no right to ask such questions, and definitely no right to prod Charles's far-too-active conscience to life. *Damn, damn, damn!*

"Actually . . ." Charles's drawl was getting even more dangerously pronounced. "That's not the sort of understanding Penny and I have. Regardless, as far as I can see, whatever our understanding might be, it's no concern of yours."

Yes—precisely! She held her breath, listened as hard as she could. Given the tone of Charles's last words, Nicholas would have to be witless to do anything other than climb down off his high horse and retreat.

"I see." The words were clipped. After a moment, Nicholas added, "In that case, I'll . . . no doubt see you in the morning."

Charles said nothing; a moment later, she heard his footsteps, soft for such a large man, returning to her room.

Relief swept her; straightening and stepping back from the door, she uttered a heartfelt prayer. The last thing—the *very last thing*—she needed at this point was for Charles to decide that he had to marry her out of some misplaced notion of propriety.

He stopped outside her door; she heard the key slide in, turn, then he opened the door. He saw her, stepped inside, closed the door, and locked it once more. Then he turned to her; his gaze traveled her face. She drew herself up, folded her arms beneath her breasts, thankfully concealed behind the robe she'd hastily donned, and narrowed her eyes at him.

His only response was to raise a faintly resigned brow.

"Why did you lock me in?"

He cocked his head, still watching her face. "I would have

thought that was obvious—so he couldn't easily return to attack you if he slipped past me."

"*And* so I couldn't follow you."

His lips twisted; he looked away and moved past her to the bed. "That, too."

With a swirl of her robe, she followed him. "What if he'd come back and picked the lock—he did the first time, why not again?"

Sitting on the bed and reaching for his boots, he glanced at her. "I credited you with having enough sense to scream. I would have heard you."

Faintly mollified—why she wasn't sure—she humphed. She wasn't going to even attempt to explain the sudden fear for him that had assailed her. He was used to plunging headlong into danger; she'd told herself that. But she'd never before had to stand by and wait while he did it. "Did you see who it was?"

He shook his head. "I didn't get any clear view of him, not even height or build. He was fast. When I got downstairs the front doors were wide-open—he went through like a hare and headed straight for the shrubbery."

"Where was Nicholas?"

He told her. "At least, that's where he said he was."

"Well . . ." She suddenly felt cold. Shrugging out of her robe, she slipped back under the covers, tugging them up to her throat, snuggling back into the lingering warmth. "We do know he hasn't been sleeping well."

"Indeed." Charles had seen her shiver and followed her progress. "What we don't know is whether he's so on edge he decided to do something about you, and left the doors open to create a plausible story of how someone broke into the house and attacked you while you slept. He didn't know until just now that I've been staying every night."

Setting aside his boots, he stood, stripped off his breeches, then crawled over the bed to slump beside her. He looked down at her for a moment, but couldn't read her wide eyes. Reaching for the covers, he tugged them from her grip, lifted them, and joined her beneath.

He drew her into his arms and she came. He settled her head on his shoulder; she draped one arm across his chest, spread her hand over his heart.

They didn't immediately fall asleep, yet despite the appearance of the intruder—something they'd both almost expected and so weren't as surprised as they might have been—there was a sense of peace between them. As if simply being together created a haven of safety and security, a connection of such fundamental rightness no intruder could shatter it.

That rightness closed around them, cocooning them. She fell asleep first. Reassured, he followed suit.

"You can't seriously mean to keep me with you for the entire day!"

Charles turned his head, simply looked at her, then faced forward and walked on, towing her behind him up the bank to the folly. He'd given up even the pretense of leaving; this morning, he'd quit her room only to go and change, then had gone straight down to breakfast—just in case Nicholas had not got his message last night.

From the shuttered but wary look on Nicholas's face when he'd joined him at the table, Nicholas had, indeed, got the salient facts quite clear.

Unlike certain others.

She huffed out an exasperated breath. "And anyway, why here?"

"Because I need to think, and I'd just as soon keep Nicholas under observation while I do." They reached the folly. He didn't pause but towed her up the steps and along to the chaise with the best view, then faced her and released her hand.

Eyes narrowing, she glared at him, then, with a swish of her skirts, sat. He sat beside her.

"Very well," she said. "If you must think, then think about this—why did whoever it was come to my room last night? Are we sure it was the murderer?"

He stared across the lawns to the house, screened by the

intervening trees. "Why would some man come to your room at . . . what was it? Two in the morning?"

"Just before. Hmm . . . but even if he is the murderer, why?"

"That's what I need to think about." He'd left her discussing household matters with Mrs. Figgs and had gone to speak with Canter and the grooms. "I sent a message to Dennis Gibbs this morning, asking him to get the Gallants to keep their ears and eyes open regarding our five 'visitors to the district.' I spoke with Norris, too. Needless to say he was horrified."

"Mmm . . . but I still can't see why this person, whoever he is, would have any interest in me, not to the extent of breaking into the house and coming to attack me in my room. Anyway, how did he know which room was mine? Had he searched all of them?"

A scenario was taking shape in his mind. "I don't think that's how it happened. If we develop our theory of revenge . . . then I think he, whoever 'he' is, was watching the house, possibly with a view to making a move on Nicholas, and he saw Nicholas go out, leaving the front door unbolted. He must have thanked his stars, but then he was faced with two options. He could follow Nicholas and do away with him, or he could enter the house and do away with you—and leave suspicion hanging over Nicholas's head."

"But why *me*?"

"Two reasons. First, you're Granville's sister—he might well see you as Granville's surrogate for revenge. He's punished Gimby—the next on his list would be Granville before Nicholas. On top of that, he'd reason that Nicholas would know your death was, if not directly, then indirectly on his head. As a first attack on Nicholas, attacking you would do nicely."

"You mean this man views me as a *pawn*?"

Her incipient outrage had his lips quirking. He closed one hand over hers. "Strangely, some men would see it that way."

She sniffed, but left her hand under his. After a moment, she asked, "How did he know which room was mine?"

Charles thought back. "The open window. If he'd circled the house, that would have marked that room as the most likely. Once he got to the door and found it locked, he'd have been sure."

She shivered.

He looked at her. "He won't come back—I can take an oath on that. He knows I'll be there, and it's no part of his plans to get caught."

Penny considered, then nodded, feeling rather better, not least because it seemed Charles planned to spend all forseeable nights with her. That was reassuring, and . . . she wasn't sure what the lightening of her heart meant.

They sat for a while, thoughts rambling, then saw an open carriage come rolling up the drive.

"That's Lady Carmody."

They watched as her ladyship was handed out and went inside. Ten minutes later, Nicholas escorted her back to her carriage. He stood watching it roll away, then returned to the house.

"A dinner or, horrors, a musicale?"

She laughed. "Not a musicale—she hates music."

"One point in her favor." Charles stirred, stretched. "I hope she's already called at the Abbey."

"Why?"

"Because I think we should ride over there."

She remembered. "And check if Dalziel has discovered anything and sent word."

Together they rose and headed back to the house.

"I'll speak to Norris—we can leave Nicholas under his eye. I'm sure Nicholas will have understood the significance of last night's intruder—given his behavior to date, he'll most likely remain inside, in safety."

"I'll change into my habit—I won't be long."

"No rush. We can let Filchett and Mrs. Slattery feed us—there's no reason we need return here until dinnertime."

CHAPTER

~~ *15* ~~

CONTRARY TO THEIR HOPES, THEY REACHED THE ABBEY TO find no communication from London awaiting them. Filchett and Mrs. Slattery were delighted to serve them luncheon. Cassius and Brutus were equally ecstatic to have Charles at home again, and even better, with company.

Lady Carmody had indeed called earlier and left an invitation to an afternoon tea party two days hence. Penny bullied Charles into accepting, pointing out that their five visitors could also be expected to attend; in this season with so many in town, those left were starved for entertainment.

In the early afternoon, they returned from walking along the ramparts with the dogs just as a rider clattered up to the front steps. A private courier, he brought the communiqué they'd been expecting. Charles took the packet, dismissed the man into Filchett's care, and headed for his study. Penny followed; she leaned on the back of his chair and read the sheets over his shoulder.

He humphed, but let her. Unfortunately, Dalziel had little to report by way of hard facts. Like Charles, he saw Gimby's death as confirming both the existence of some long-term treasonous conspiracy and its serious nature—people did not kill over a few vague descriptions of troops. The primary thrust of his letter, however, was to disabuse Charles of any notion that the traffic Gimby had facilitated had been incoming rather than outgoing. Dalziel had personally questioned his counterparts in every area; none knew of any source of French intelligence other than via the recognized routes under their purview.

A scribbled postscript acknowledged Charles's subsequent report; Dalziel would see what he could turn up about the five visitors, but none rang any immediate bells.

Charles laid the sheets aside. Penny circled the desk and dropped into an armchair. They tossed comments back and forth, floated possibilities only to shoot them down. Their discussion waned into a companionable silence along with the afternoon. They had tea, then mounted and headed back to Wallingham.

Crossing the river at Lostwithiel, they glimpsed Fothergill striding away from the riverbank some way upstream. Charles held Domino back, studying Fothergill, then flicked his reins and caught up with Penny.

"Could it have been he, do you think?"

Charles shook his head. "I can't say. That's what I was thinking—I didn't see enough to say anything at all."

They returned to Wallingham to learn that nothing had occurred in their absence beyond Dennis Gibbs sending a message that he'd make sure not just the Gallants but their brethren along the coast were alerted. Gimby's murder had clearly left the leader of the Gallants uneasy.

They dined with Nicholas. The knowledge that they were lovers clearly made him uneasy; he didn't know how he should react to their relationship, but as they didn't refer or allude to it in any way, he had no need to, and so the meal passed smoothly enough.

However, as the evening wore on and they sat in the drawing room and Penny exercised her fingers at the pianoforte, it became increasingly obvious that Nicholas's attitude to Charles had undergone another transformation. She couldn't fathom it; later, when Charles joined her in her bedchamber, she asked him what he thought.

He smiled cynically as he sat on the bed to pull off his boots. "Nicholas is not the murderer, *ergo*, it wasn't he who came to your room. Both incidents have shaken him—he's realized that *he* should be, and would be held to be, responsible for your safety." The curve of Charles's lips deepened. "Nicholas finds himself on the horns of a dilemma. He doesn't like me, he doesn't approve of my sharing your bed, but by heaven he's thankful that by being here with you, I've taken one worry—one immediate and very real worry—from his plate."

Lolling on the bed, idly unbuttoning the nightgown she'd recently buttoned up—Charles would have it off her in minutes anyway, a happening she wished to facilitate—she pondered Nicholas. "He is worried, isn't he? I mean, it's concern, anxiety, that type of feeling that's driving him. You thought originally it was fear, but if he was afraid for himself, he'd run away, wouldn't he? But he's staying here, quite deliberately, because he's extremely worried about something. But what?"

"I don't know." Tossing his breeches over her dressing stool, Charles crawled, naked, onto the bed. His gaze had locked on her; he smiled, and reached for her, lifting her to him as he knelt in the center of the bed. "I don't understand Nicholas." He bent his head, kissed her lightly, gently tugged at her lower lip. "But I do understand you."

He settled her straddling his thighs, slid his hands under her gown, and slowly raised it.

What followed proved his point. It was all she'd hoped for, all she'd ever dreamed of, and more. He seemed to know just what she'd like, just what her senses and her prediliction for challenge craved; more, he seemed devoted not just to giving but lavishing such delights on her, until she reeled with giddy pleasure. Until he drew her to him and possessed her, until she gave herself to him and gloried in the giving.

Yet at the height of the giddy whirl there came a point when they stood at the eye of desire's storm, when in that instant's fraught hiatus their eyes met, and something else touched her. A oneness, a sense of communion, of a sharing that went so much deeper than the reality of their skins, their nerves, their bodies. That through that shared glance struck to her core, entwined, and sank deep.

It was a moment of power so great she couldn't breathe; nor could he. Then his lids fell, and his lips found hers; she clung to the kiss, felt desire rise, and let it whirl her away.

She told herself it was just physical, just some linkage she hadn't noticed before. She was indulging, just as he was; there was nothing more.

Yet she remained conscious of that power, aware that it didn't leave them, but flowered, burgeoned; its roots ran deep. It remained with them, within them, yet in the light of day, while she could still detect its shadow, it seemed perfectly normal, as if it were something that had always been there and she'd simply failed to notice.

The following morning began as the one before, with Charles leaving her room as she rang for Ellie—as if he were her husband. She noted the fact, attributed it to his arrogance, his male confidence where she was concerned. She took longer than usual to dress for the morning, but then had to return and change into her riding habit as soon as she'd finished with Figgs. If the morning had been a repeat of the one before, the day looked set to follow suit.

So it proved. They rode to the Abbey and received another communication from Dalziel. In it he confirmed that Mr. Arthur Swaley was known to have considerable business interests in tin mines; rumor had it he was down that way looking to further said interests. Mr. Julian Fothergill was going to be difficult to check up on, there being dozens of branches in that family's tree, but at first glance there was nothing to set him apart. More on him in due course. Carmichael, too, was not a straightforward case; there were hints of debts in the past, but they'd yet to find anyone who knew enough to tell them anything useful. They would pursue Carmichael further. Mr. Yarrow did indeed hail from Derbyshire; there was no one in town who knew much about him. Dalziel had sent a man north to learn more.

Which left Gerond, who, on the face of it, was their most likely suspect. He had military training and was known to be strongly patriotic, however, all links they'd thus far unearthed led to the royalist camp rather than the revolutionary council or any of those bodies that had succeeded it. More information would be forthcoming as and when it was received.

Charles studied the letter for some minutes before folding it and placing it in a drawer.

Penny had been watching him. "What is it?"

He looked at her, then grimaced. "Dalziel's hunting."

"Hunting?"

"His hackles have risen, so to speak. He's mobilizing people, calling in favors. He wouldn't unless he was convinced the situation called for it."

Tilting her head, she studied him. "You don't think it does?"

His gaze had strayed from her; he brought it back and met her eyes. "No. I agree with him. I just wish I didn't."

Well-honed instincts, Charles had often thought, were a blessing; they were also a curse. When alert, as they now were, they rode him, nearly to distraction, more specifically to the point where he was once again toying with plans to get Penny out of the area, preferably to London.

Unfortunately, he couldn't think of a single maneuver that would work. Or rather, kidnapping, transporting, and holding her in his house in London by main force *might* work, but it would irretrievably scupper his plans for the future. He knew her too well to imagine otherwise.

Sometimes, one had to take risks.

So . . . rising, he walked to her, took her hand, drew her to her feet. He called Cassius and Brutus, and they went out to walk the ramparts and enjoy the present, until the next twist in the tale.

Instinct told him that twist was coming, but when and how . . .

As they strolled, they talked, circling the possibility of somehow taking charge of the game—of setting some scheme in train that would allow them to make the running, rather than being, as they had been to date, forever in the position of reacting to the murderer's moves. Nothing useful suggested itself. They still knew too little of what was afoot.

The sun slid behind clouds and they went in to tea. Afterward, they headed for the stables.

This time, with neither a shared word or glance, the instant they passed out of the park, they turned their horses' heads to the northwest. They cantered to the old stone bridge spanning the river not far from the castle ruins. Crossing it, they headed up the long finger of escarpment leading southeast; once atop it, they flew.

The route by the castle bridge was the longest straight ride between the Abbey and Wallingham Hall, but was more difficult, more demanding than the south and east route they normally took; it demanded complete concentration, absolute absorption in the moment, at least at the pace they rode it.

The unrelenting thunder of their horses' hooves rose and engulfed them, sank into them, resonated through them. The compulsive tattoo beat through their blood, surged through their veins.

Instinct, frustation and sheer exhilaration combined into an explosive mix. Rampant desire provided the spark; all it took was one shared glance as they slowed to descend to the Hall to light their fuse and propel them into a state of mindless need.

Charles changed course, knew she would follow. Instead of heading down to the flat and around to the stables, they angled down to the bank on which the folly stood.

They pulled up in a welter by the folly. Their feet hit the ground, he seized both sets of reins, tied them to the balustrade, then grabbed her hand, dragged her up the folly steps and through the door into the inner room.

If she hadn't been equally as urgent as he, Penny would have protested, but his strides were longer, being dragged was faster, and . . . she couldn't wait.

She couldn't breathe as he strode past the chaise, then whirled her, twirled her so her back was to the rear wall of the folly, then he lifted his hands, clamped them about her face, and kissed her.

To within an inch of her life.

Her back hit the rear wall; she felt grateful for the support. She slid her arms up, twining them about his neck, stretching against him, frantically pressing to him as he moved deliberately into her; she returned every pressure, suggestively undulating against him in blatant invitation.

His hands left her face and raced, flagrantly possessive, over her velvet-clad body, over her breasts, her waist, her hips. He gripped her bottom, kneaded briefly, then released her and dragged up the front of her habit. She couldn't get her arms down to help; instead, she encouraged him in every other way, taunting him through their kiss, nipping his lower lip, gasping, her head falling back against the wall as he lifted her, his large hands now gripping bare skin as he braced her against the wall—and pressed in.

Suddenly, she was teetering on a sensual brink. Then he thrust, hard, deep, and she shattered. Convulsed around him, sobbed her pleasure.

He covered her mouth with his, and drove her further.

Into the most glorious mind-numbing pleasure she'd yet experienced. Into the hottest, tightest, most fiery furnace they'd yet to explore. She wrapped her arms about his shoulders, her legs about his hips and clung. Between them, through every deep thrust, through every hungry, greedy grasping, ran an urgency, a thread that was close to desperation, yet colored by conviction, by the absolute assurance of ultimate satiation.

A satiation that ultimately enraptured them both. Caught them, took them, and poured through them. Soothed them.

When, panting, chests heaving, they finally regained sufficient control to lift their heads and meet the other's eyes, they searched, then their lips started to curve. By the time he'd withdrawn from her and tumbled them both onto the chaise, they were laughing like children.

For long minutes, they simply lay there, exhausted yet pleasantly, even euphorically, so. Time passed, and neither felt any compulsion to move. She lay slumped on his chest, listening to his heart slow. With the fingers of one hand, he played with her hair, with the long strands that had come loose from her chignon either during the ride or later; his other hand lay possessively beneath her skirts, curved over her naked hip.

She was aware to her bones of that intimate yet, she was sure, absentminded touch. His fingers drifted a little now and then, but she didn't think he was thinking of anything. Any more than she was.

The moment itself was enough.

Eventually he sighed, and stirred. "I suppose we'd better go down. It must be time to dress for dinner." With a reluctance that showed, he drew down her skirts, sat her up, then rearranged his clothes.

She tweaked her blouse and jacket back into place, decided the wild ride would excuse her hair. She stood, and her knees gave way.

He'd been watching; he grasped her hips, steadied her, then stood and offered his arm. Met her gaze as she took it. "You obviously need more practice."

Another laugh bubbled up. "I'll think about it."

She thought she'd had the last word, but as he handed her down the steps, he murmured, "Do."

Wicked promise and arrogant warning combined.

They remounted and ambled down and around into the stable yard. Canter came himself, reporting that there'd been no action through the day.

Much *he* knew. She refused to meet Charles's eyes as he lifted her down. Taking his arm, they strolled, not as quickly as usual, into the house.

He saw her to her room, then continued down the corridor to his.

Still pleasantly aglow, she sighed, and rang for Ellie. Sitting on her dressing stool, she unpinned her hair, brushed it, then slowly, wits drifting, re-coiled it.

Only then did she realize Ellie hadn't appeared.

That was such a strange occurrence, she rose and went to the door. Opening it, she headed for the back stairs. Reaching the landing, she heard voices; peering over the balustrade, she saw Figgs patting Ellie's shoulder firmly, but the look on Figgs's face was distracted.

"I know, ma'am." Ellie hiccupped. "I'll go right up."

Ellie had obviously been crying.

"What's the matter?" Penny went quickly down the stairs. "Is something wrong?"

Figgs and Ellie straightened; they exchanged glances, then Figgs faced Penny as she stepped onto the tiled floor. "It's Mary, my lady. The parlor tweeny. She went out last evening—I thought it was for a walk to meet Tom Biggs down by the stable, but Tom didn't see her, and Ellie thinks Mary went to meet some other new fellow."

"And?" Penny prompted when Figgs fell silent.

"Mary didn't come home last night. We've been expecting her any hour, but then we thought maybe one of her brothers had come and met her while she was out and called her urgently home, or something of the sort." Figgs sighed, and met Penny's eyes. "We sent a lad and he's just got back—Mary's family hasn't seen her either, not since her last day off."

A cold, black vise closed about Penny's stomach. "No one's seen her since she left last night?"

"No, my lady. And she's not the sort to do such a thing— not at all. And her things are still here—she didn't take anything with her."

Penny looked at Ellie, woebegone and clearly imagining the worst. "Did Mary say anything about this man she went to meet?"

"Not particular, m'lady. Just that he was tall and 'andsome, and not in the usual way of things."

Figgs drew in a breath. "We was wondering, my lady, Norris and me, whether we should tell his lordship?"

Nicholas wouldn't have the first idea what to do, but it was now his house, or at least his father's. Penny nodded. "Yes, tell Lord Arbry." Lips firming, she turned back to the stairs. "And I'll tell Lord Charles."

"Indeed, my lady." Figgs's relief rang clearly. "Do you want Ellie to attend you now, ma'am?"

Penny glanced back at the wilting Ellie. "Just bring my washing water and lay out a plain gown. I'll change after I've spoken with Lord Charles."

Figgs and Ellie bobbed, and turned back to the kitchens.

Reaching the top of the stairs, Penny stopped at the first door and knocked lightly. "Charles?"

The door opened an instant later. "What?" He looked at her, looked past her. He'd just shrugged on a fresh shirt; the halves framed his chest.

She fixed her gaze on his face. "We have a problem."

He waved her inside. She sat in a chair and told him all she knew while he buttoned the shirt, tucked it in, and quickly tied his cravat.

"And no one knows who this man is?" He shrugged on his coat.

"Apparently not." She met his gaze. "It doesn't sound good, does it? Why would Mary suddenly go missing just now?"

"Don't extrapolate too far, too fast." Charles glanced at the window, checking the light. "The first thing we need do is confer with Nicholas and set up a search. If someone's seen her about with a man, maybe there's some other, less dire explanation."

They found Nicholas in the library with Norris; he looked stunned. "Have you heard?" he asked.

Penny nodded. She sat and let Charles take charge; he'd always been good at that sort of thing.

Nicholas, a civil servant to his toes, responded to the voice of command; within minutes, Charles had him writing to Lord Culver, informing him of the missing maid and that they were instituting a search immediately.

Charles turned to Norris. "Send to the stables, the home farm, and the workers' cottages—round up as many men as you can, but we'll need to leave yourself and a handful of others here to hold the fort."

Norris nodded, glanced at Nicholas, saw him absorbed in composition, bowed to her, and hurried out.

Charles reached over Nicholas and tugged a fresh sheet of

paper free. Pulling a chair to the desk, he sat and picked up Nicholas's other pen and checked the nib. When Nicholas looked at him, he said, "I'm going to send to Essington Manor for more men. The Abbey's too far, at least for tonight—it'll be dark soon. We need to do all we can while there's still light enough to see."

Penny hesitated, then said, "What about the estuary?"

Charles looked at her, then nodded. "I'll get the Gallants and the others out, too. They can search the shallows."

She sat for a moment, listening to the scratch of nibs on paper, then rose. "I'll go and change."

She returned downstairs just as the Essingtons and the males of their household arrived. Both David and his brother Hubert had come, mounted and ready to search; they'd always been good neighbors and had understood the need—they'd come with all speed.

Millie and Julia had driven themselves over in the gig to keep her company. "So horrible to have to sit and wait alone," Millie said.

Charles greeted the Essington ladies with heartfelt approval; Penny had changed out of her riding habit, but from the look on her face, she'd been planning to drive herself about in the gig, supposedly assisting the search, but not assisting him in the slightest.

He didn't want her in any way involved. He had a very bad feeling over what they were going to find. In this part of the country, maids did not walk out and not come back. Not unless they couldn't come back.

While Millie and Julia claimed Penny's attention, he conferred with the Essington brothers; they quickly agreed on the area they'd each scour. He and the Wallingham staff would search the north hemisphere, David the southwest quadrant, and Hubert the southeast, including the estuary banks. "I've sent word to the Gallants—they'll take the estuary."

"Right." David pulled on his gloves, exchanged a glance with his brother. "We'll be off, then."

While they farewelled their ladies, Charles murmured to Penny, "I'll have a word to Nicholas before I go."

She looked at him. "Isn't he going with you?"

He met her gaze. "I'd rather he remained here."

Penny read his eyes, then nodded and rose. "He's in the library—I'll come with you."

Excusing herself to Millie and Julia, she accompanied him to the library. Nicholas was looking out of the window and pulling on his gloves; he patently intended riding out, too.

He turned as Charles shut the door. "Are we ready to go?"

Stepping past her, Charles halted in the middle of the room. "I am, but you need to remain here."

"Oh?" All the antagonism between them resurfaced; Nicholas eyed him with incipient dislike. "Why?"

Holding Nicholas's gaze, Charles evenly stated, "Because we must have someone with authority here to direct the search. If any information comes in, there has to be someone here who can analyze it and act on it—by that I mean give orders. *You* are the most appropriate in that role—this is your house or as near as makes no difference. On top of that, I grew up here, and so did the others. We know this ground like the backs of our hands. And time is limited. Night's not far off—we need to be quick and certain of the ground we're covering."

He paused, then added, his gaze locked with Nicholas's, "And I'm sure I don't need to remind you that two nights ago someone tried to attack Penny."

Nicholas stared at Charles for a long moment, then his gaze switched to her. Another moment passed, then he glanced back at Charles, a faint, puzzled frown in his eyes. "Very well. I'll remain."

Charles nodded and turned for the door. "We'll search until it's full dark."

Pausing beside her, he searched her eyes. Instead of taking her hand, he bent and swiftly kissed her. "We'll be back within an hour of that."

She nodded and watched him go. He left the door ajar; his boot steps died away down the hall, then she heard him call to the men as he joined them. An instant later, the thud of many hooves and the scrunch of many feet declared the searchers were away.

Looking at Nicholas, she watched as he, frowning more definitely, came toward her.

"Are the Essington ladies staying?"

"Yes. They're in the drawing room. I'll order dinner to be served in an hour."

"Dinner?" He looked revolted.

She grimaced. "We still have to eat."

He paused, then said, "I don't understand Lostwithiel." The words came out in a frustrated undertone. Nicholas briefly met her eyes, then looked away. "He doesn't like me—he distrusts me, suspects me, and yet . . ."

He brought his gaze back to her face. "Someone tried to attack you the other night, and yes, I realize that for all you or he know, it could have been me. Despite that, he blithely leaves me here with you."

Penny met his gaze. "Yes, exactly. And figuring out why might be the best thing you could do."

With that tart comment, she led the way back to the drawing room.

The news, when it came, wasn't good. Darkness had fallen when they heard the searchers returning. Penny knew what was coming when she heard the horses not riding in crisply, but walking very slowly.

She briefly closed her eyes, then, opening them, met Millie's and Julia's equally apprehensive gazes.

"Oh, dear," Millie whispered, one hand rising to her throat.

Penny exchanged a glance with Julia, then rose. "I think you both should stay here—there's no need for you to see . . ."

Turning, she headed for the door. Nicholas had risen when she did; he joined her. When they reached the door, he closed his hand on the knob, and looked at her. "You don't have to see, either."

She met his gaze levelly. "I've been *de facto* mistress here for the last umpteen years. I hired Mary. Of course I need to see."

Neither Charles nor David were happy with her decision, but when she joined them in the cool store where they'd laid the limp body, neither attempted to gainsay her.

Someone had lit a lamp, but left it by the door; only faint light reached the table where Mary's body lay. Even so, it wasn't hard to see the purple marks circling her white neck, nor the protruding eyes and tongue. Penny stood just inside the door and looked, then Figgs pressed her arm and moved past, going to the table and straightening the rumpled skirts. She cleared her throat, addressed her question to the air, "Was she . . . do you know . . . ?"

"No." It was Charles who answered. "She was strangled, nothing else."

Figgs nodded. "Thank you, my lord. Now, if you'll leave us, Em and I will take care of her."

"Thank you, Figgs," Penny murmured. Figgs and Em, who helped Cook, were the oldest women in the household; to them rightly fell such tasks.

Charles moved to her side; she felt his hand close about her arm, sensed his strength close, and was grateful. He steered her out into the kitchen yard; David and Nicholas followed.

They stopped in the middle of the yard; all drew in deep breaths.

"Where did you find her?" Penny asked.

"In the woods this side of Connell's farm." David shook his head. "Not far at all—we'd met up and were on our way back, searching as we came." He shivered. "The blackguard had stuffed her body under a fallen tree. If Charles hadn't thought to poke there . . ."

David looked white as a sheet. Penny gripped his arm. "Come inside—you should all have something to warm you."

They went in. She detoured via the kitchens to give orders that all the men in the search party should be served ale and cold meats, then swept into the house to supervise the same for their masters.

A dark and brooding atmosphere enveloped the house. Even though most hadn't known Mary well, all had met her at one time or another, and this was the country—servants were people with families one knew. There was grief and confusion, shared by all; that sense of sharing, of adversity faced together, drew them closer, even Nicholas.

Hubert, having sent his men straight home, appeared alone to report no sighting. He was told the news; he insisted on going out to the cool store. He returned shortly, greatly cast down. The Essingtons took their leave. Charles, Nicholas, and Penny saw them off with thanks, then returned to the library.

Nicholas complied with Charles's suggestion—more a direction—to write a note to Lord Culver informing him of their discovery.

Charles, meanwhile, openly wrote a brief report for London.

Ensconced in a chair, with no wish to spend time in her room by herself, Penny saw Nicholas glance at the sheet Charles was covering, but could read nothing beyond the deepening concern etched in his face.

Completed, both notes were dispatched by a rider.

Seeing no reason to abrade Nicholas's sensibilities unnecessarily, Penny bade both him and Charles a good night in the front hall and climbed the stairs. She'd sent a message earlier excusing Ellie from waiting on her. Ellie and Mary had been friends; Ellie would be grieving.

As for herself . . . in her bedroom, she walked to the window, unlatched it, and pushed it wide. Looking out on the peaceful courtyard, she drew a deep breath and held it.

She thought of the man who'd come looking for her one night, thought of Mary, who that same man, it seemed, had now taken.

Why Mary? Why her?

Regardless, alongside her grief for Mary, she was immensely glad to be alive.

Charles came in. She sensed rather than heard him; he always moved so silently. He joined her before the window; his hands about her waist, he stood looking out over her shoulder, then he turned her to him.

She lifted her arms, draped them over his shoulders, and went into his arms. Felt them close around her, tight, felt the primal shudder that rippled through him as he pulled her against him. He bent his head, and their lips met, and nothing else mattered but that they were there, now, together and alive.

Together they'd been before, but never had it been quite like this. Never before had they both, he and she, simply dropped every shield, released every inhibition, and celebrated the simple primitive fact.

That they could be together like this. At this level, on this plane.

Their clothes littered the floor between the window and the bed; their hands roved, not so much urgently as openly, flagrantly, blatantly possessively—neither doubted the other would be theirs tonight.

The moon had yet to rise when he lifted her, when she wrapped her long legs about his hips and, head back, gasped as he impaled her.

Gasped again as he moved within her.

Then she raised her head, wrapped her arms about his neck, found his lips with hers, and they settled to the dance.

No desperation this time but a soul-deep communion, a wanting, a need they both shared.

Charles held her, thrust into her, following no script but that of deepest instinct. Tonight he didn't need consciously to pander to her needs; tonight her needs and his were the same.

No rush, no hurry; inevitable tension, yes, but no mindless urgency.

So he felt every slick slide of his body into hers, savored the heat, the giving pressure, the incredible pleasure as she willingly took him in. Willingly enclosed him, held him, released him, only to welcome him in once more.

Pleasure and more engulfed them, wrapped them about, lifted them from the world. They traveled on beyond the earth, to the moon, the stars and the sun, and never once lost their connection.

They were together when they toppled from the last fiery peak, together when at last they collapsed on her bed. Together when they brushed hair from each other's eyes so their gazes could meet and they could look, and know.

And wonder.

Neither said a word; they were both too afraid, and they knew that, too.

They took refuge in the physical, in that reflection of their togetherness, in the warmth between them. Lids falling, they exchanged sleepy kisses, drew up the covers, sank into the bed, and slept.

BY MORNING THE NEWS OF MARY MAGGS'S MURDER HAD spread throughout the county. Gimby had been known to few; his murder had attracted little notice. Mary was another matter. The searchers had taken the ill tidings home with them; from there the news had spread far and wide.

The Wallingham Hall household was, if not precisely in mourning, then somber and subdued. After breakfasting on tea and toast, Penny went to speak with and comfort Figgs. Together they planned the household chores, keeping all to a minimum, doing only what was needed to keep the house running. Penny decreed that the meals should be simple for the next several days.

"Aye, well," Figgs said on a sigh. "Mrs. Slattery at the Abbey sent two game pies and a lemon curd pudding this morning. She said as she suspected I had an extra mouth about, and as it was rightly one that was hers to fill, she hoped I'd accept the help." Figgs sniffed. "Nice of her, I thought."

"Indeed." Aware there were proprieties to be observed between households that were every bit as rigid as within the ton itself, Penny could only applaud Mrs. Slattery's tact.

Leaving Figgs, she returned to the front hall just as Lord Culver arrived. Charles had left her bed early; he'd ridden out to look around the site where they'd found Mary's body, deliberately leaving Nicholas to deal with Culver. Charles was doing all he could to force the consequences of his silence on Nicholas, without compunction using any lever that came to hand to pressure Nicholas into telling him what he knew, or at least enough to capture the murderer.

Nicholas had been expecting Culver; he came out of the library to greet him. She went forward as they shook hands, but merely exchanged greetings with Lord Culver, who murmured, "Distressing business, my dear." She glided on into the drawing room. Being reclusive, Lord Culver was very definitely one of the "old school"; discussing anything so horrendous as murder within a lady's hearing would render him acutely uncomfortable.

Besides, she, too, was determined to convince Nicholas to confide his secrets; he could deal with Culver alone.

From just inside the drawing room, she listened to him doing so. When the pair walked away down the hall, she turned and followed; it wouldn't matter if they saw her, just as long as she remained apart from their discussion. Hanging back in the shadows of the kitchen courtyard, she watched as they entered the cool store. Their voices echoed in the stone building; Culver asked the expected questions, and Nicholas answered.

Last night, Nicholas had looked stunned—horrified and unable to take in a second murder. This morning, when she'd met him briefly over the breakfast table, he'd looked ghastly—appalled, deeply disturbed, yet oddly resolute. It was almost as if the increasing pressure, instead of making him break, was increasing his resistance.

Even though she thought him culpable for trafficking in secrets, and grossly misguided in not confessing now Charles was so blatantly there, camped on his doorstep, she was nevertheless starting to view Nicholas with a certain grudging respect. Even more telling, so was Charles.

Nicholas and Culver came out of the cool store; Nicholas closed the door and faced his lordship.

"A dreadful business." Culver looked shaken. He was a slight man no taller than Penny, and lived for his books. "Not the sort of thing that generally happens hereabouts."

The sound of a familiar footstep had Penny glancing to the right; Charles strode up from the stables. He saw her, nodded, but went directly to Culver.

Both Culver and Nicholas looked relieved. Culver asked, and Charles confirmed that he believed Mary's murder was connected to Gimby's, although he omitted to say why. However, as such, it fell within his brief to investigate. Culver declared that that being the case, he would merely record the murder and await further direction from Charles.

The formalities concluded, Charles and Culver shook hands. Nicholas offered to walk Culver to the stables. The three men parted; watching, she saw Charles wait . . . as if it were an afterthought, he commented to Culver, "I bumped into a young relative of yours—Fothergill."

"Oh?" Culver halted, nodded. "Indeed, a connection of my late wife's. Visited with us as a child and was taken with the area—interested in birds, it seems. He's a likable enough chap, easy to have about—well, he's not in much, really, so there's no fuss in having him. I daresay he was out looking at pigeons through those spyglasses of his."

"Indeed."

Culver and Nicholas headed on to the stables. Charles watched them go, then turned and joined her.

"At least that's Fothergill vouched for." He waved her into the house. "If he's connected to Culver, that makes it unlikely he's here for any nefarious purpose. An amazing coincidence to have a relative one had visited as a child living in precisely the district in which one wished to commit murder."

"Still"—she glanced at him as they walked down the corridor—"I would have thought you'd ask if he was at Culver House on the night before last."

"I would have if I could place any reliance on Culver's word. Fothergill might have been sitting in an armchair within three yards of Culver all night, but I wouldn't trust Culver's word for it. Once absorbed in his books, a cannonade outside his windows would probably pass unnoticed."

She grimaced; he was right.

Norris came to meet them. "Shall I serve luncheon, my lady?"

"As soon as Lord Arbry returns from the stables. Lord Charles and I will wait in the parlor."

"Indeed, my lady."

Nicholas joined them in the dining parlor as they took their seats. He went to the head of the table, his face even more graven with care than before.

She glanced at Charles, but he gave no sign. Norris and the footman brought in the cold collation she'd ordered; Charles fixed his attention on the cold meats, cheese, and fruit, and spared Nicholas not a glance.

However, when Mrs. Slattery's lemon curd pudding appeared and Charles consumed half of it, Penny wasn't sure he even noticed. He might not be looking at Nicholas, but she was quite sure he was thinking about Nicholas. And about the murderer.

It was Nicholas who broke first.

"Why did you ask about Fothergill?"

Charles glanced up the table, past her, meeting Nicholas's eyes. He paused for one instant, then said, "Because it seems likely the murderer is one of our five visitors, and at present, all of them are in the running."

Calmly peeling an apple with a paring knife, he recounted for Nicholas without concealment or evasion not just their hypotheses about the murderer, but all they'd learned from London thus far about the five men in question.

She watched Nicholas. Saw again his puzzlement that Charles should be so forthcoming, sensed beneath it a growing confusion; that, she hoped, would be to the good.

Charles held nothing back. Returning from where he'd found Mary's body mangled like a rag doll's and discarded with less care, he'd decided to pull out all stops to convince Nicholas to tell him what he needed to know.

Gimby's death had been serious enough; Mary's murder increased the stakes. The game would escalate; he knew it would.

They were running out of time, and the murderer was

moving closer. If dropping his guard with Nicholas was what it took to learn what he needed to capture the murderer and bring him to justice, so be it.

His duty was one thing, his allegiance to justice another, yet at the back of his mind he was very aware of an even more pressing, more fundamental need. He had to keep Penny safe. He was grimly aware that that compulsion no longer sprang from a simple, uncomplicated wish to protect her purely for her own sake. Protecting her was now vital to him; she was the foundation of his future—the one thing he couldn't lose.

So he broke with the tenets of a lifetime and told Nicholas all.

He eventually fell silent. Glancing at Nicholas, he saw him frowning at his plate, clearly deeply troubled.

Beside him, Penny reached across and lifted a slice from the apple he was quartering. He followed the fruit to her mouth. The crunch as she bit into the apple's crisp flesh seemed to break some spell.

"Lady Carmody's afternoon tea," she said. She looked up the table at Nicholas. "It's this afternoon—we should attend."

Nicholas blanched. "Oh, surely not. No one will expect—"

"On the contrary," Penny calmly stated, "everyone will expect us to be there, not least to tell everyone what's going on. Rumors will be rife, and some will be quite extraordinary, so the truth needs to be told. Aside from all else, our five visitors should be there. In this district, in this season, there's not so many entertainments that one can pick and choose. And with the news of Mary's murder widely circulating, avoiding the only gathering in the area would be far more a cause for comment than attending it would."

Nicholas stared at her; he really did look ill. After a moment, he said, "Perhaps if you and Lostwithiel go . . ."

It was a question, indeed, a plea, the closest Nicholas had yet come to it. She didn't respond, wondered.

"No." Charles spoke quietly but decisively from beside her. His gaze was fixed on Nicholas. "Just think. Mary Maggs was a maid in your household. She went to meet a man she didn't name but described as handsome and 'not in the usual way.' Then she's found strangled. If you avoid a gathering like Lady Carmody's, no matter what we say or do, some degree of suspicion is guaranteed to fix on you."

Nicholas's pallor was once again faintly green. "That's . . ."

"Human nature." Charles regarded him, not without sympathy. "I take it you haven't spent much of your life in the country."

"No." Nicholas frowned. "I went from Oxford to London—I've lived there ever since."

"Where's your father's seat?"

"Berkshire. But he's been in residence for years—there's rarely any need for me to be there . . ."

Watching the expressions flit across Nicholas's face, Charles wondered what the last—was it regret?—meant. There was clearly some sensitivity between Nicholas and his father—something to do with their treason, perhaps.

He tucked away the notion for later examination. "Regardless, you do need to attend Lady Carmody's event." He glanced at Penny. "But there's no reason we can't all go together."

She nodded. Beneath the table, she touched his thigh. "Indeed not. Granville's pair needs exercising—you can drive me in the curricle, and Nicholas can ride one of the hacks."

So they went to Lady Carmody's tea party, and if it was every bit as bad as Nicholas had feared, at least he survived.

"Indeed," Penny murmured, her gaze fixed on Nicholas as he satisfied Mrs. Cranfield's and Imogen's appalled curiosity, "he seems to be one of those people who appear to have no backbone, until one leans on him."

Charles looked down at her. "A shrewd and insightful observation—with which, incidentally, I agree—but unfortunately that very quality is the one most holding us back. Or rather, holding him back from telling us what he knows."

"Mmm." They were standing sipping tea at one side of Lady Carmody's sunken garden. The pool in the center formed a focus for the gathering, the high hedges surrounding the garden providing useful shade. They'd been required to tell their tale numerous times, but then Charles had insisted they needed their tea and moved them out of the ruck; no one had yet had the nerve to follow.

Penny set her cup on her saucer. "The more I see of Nicholas, the more difficulty I have in casting him as a villain of any sort. I know you agree that he's not the murderer." She glanced up and met Charles's eyes, darkest sapphire blue in the sunlight. "But can you truly see him as a traitor, someone who knowingly passed military secrets to the French?"

He held her gaze for a moment, then looked at Nicholas. "Sometimes, people get caught up in affairs without realizing, not until it's too late. I've been wondering if perhaps Nicholas, unaware of the illicit trade his father and yours had undertaken, blithely followed his sire into the Foreign Office, then found himself expected to, as it were, continue the family business."

She followed his gaze to Nicholas. "That would explain why he won't speak."

Charles nodded. "He knows we have no real evidence, yet it's not just him and his career, but his father's reputation and the rest of the family's at stake. As you pointed out, this matter's a blot that once known would stain all the family, including innocents like Elaine and her girls."

After a moment, he added, "I can understand why he's holding against us, but understanding doesn't make it any easier to break him."

Indeed, understanding made it that much harder, because they both had a great deal of sympathy for Nicholas's stand.

As Penny had predicted, all five of their "suspects" were present, all, when discussing the tragedy, had evinced the right degree of revulsion, made the right comments, the expected expostulations.

"Not one," Charles commented acerbically, "put a foot wrong."

But only one of them would have been tested, and whoever he was, he was a professional; that Charles already knew and thoroughly appreciated.

He and Penny moved through the crowd, chatting here, exchanging news of their families there. He kept a surreptitious watch on Nicholas, but although Nicholas watched the five "visitors," he made no move to engage any of them. Even more telling, he didn't favor one over the other in his observations. Or his peregrinations; he passed each of the five with a nod, a look, and smoothly moved on.

Given he was now convinced he had Nicholas's measure, that last puzzled Charles. Did Nicholas truly have no idea which of the five was the most likely? If so . . .

"Damn!"

Startled, Penny glanced up at him. Mercifully, there were no matrons within hearing range. He tightened his hold on her elbow. "You're feeling faint."

"I am?"

"You are—we need an excuse to leave *now*. With Nicholas."

She didn't argue, but obligingly wilted against him. He took her weight, solicitously guided her to where Lady Carmody sat. They made their excuses; while her ladyship fussed, Charles collected Nicholas with a look.

He came, puzzled, then concerned when he heard of Penny's indisposition. He readily agreed they should leave at once; of course he would accompany them.

Lady Carmody was gracious, understanding, and content enough that they'd appeared and thus ensured her tea party was a huge success. She patted Penny's hand. *"Quite* understandable, my dear. You are looking rather wan."

Mrs. Cranfield tut-tutted. "You need a good night's rest, my dear. Make sure you get it, and leave the worrying to others."

Lady Trescowthick looked uncertain, but kissed Penny's cheek and glanced at Charles. "Do take care, dear."

They made their exit as fast as they dared. Penny held to her pose of an incipient faint until they'd turned out of the drive and were heading along the lane, out of sight.

She exhaled and straightened. Looking at Charles, she noted the rather grim set of his lips. "Why did we have to leave?"

"I'll tell you when we get back to Wallingham."

She would have argued and insisted he tell her now, but his tone reminded her there was another with them—Nicholas, to wit. Folding her hands in her lap, she composed herself in patience, and waited.

Her mind ranged back over their departure; thinking of Lady Trescowthick's puzzled look, she couldn't help but smile.

"What?" Charles asked.

She glanced at him, but he was looking at his horses. She looked ahead. "I was just wondering when it will occur to them that I've never fainted in my life."

Charles heard the amusement in her voice and bit his tongue. Hard. No need to point out that while those three ladies, who had known them both since birth, might indeed note the oddity of her faint, instead of supposing the faint a sham, they might come up with quite a different reason to account for it.

A reason that, already or at some point in the not overly distant future, might indeed be real. Would be real.

Would she feel faint? Penny? Would she enjoy carrying his children?

He hadn't even asked her to marry him yet. He told himself he was foolish to imagine he knew any woman's mind, let alone hers, well enough to predict her answer, yet after last night he felt unreasonably confident. And ridiculously buoyed by the mere thought of her carrying his child.

Almost distracted enough to forget the revelation he'd had in Lady Carmody's sunken garden. But not quite.

He pulled up in the stable yard, gave the reins to a groom, and handed Penny down. They waited for Nicholas to join them, then walked together to the house.

"That wasn't as bad as I'd feared," Nicholas said. "At least their curiosity wasn't morbid—more that they simply wanted to know, to be reassured they had the facts correct and weren't falling prey to mere rumor."

"Indeed." Penny glanced at Charles as they entered the house. "Now—why did we have to leave just then?"

He met her gaze, then looked at Nicholas. "Could we have a word with you in the library?"

Nicholas blinked. "Yes, of course."

He led the way. She followed with Charles, wondering; once she'd focused on him, she'd realized he was tense. Annoyed, but not at her.

What had Nicholas done?

Nicholas led them into the library. Charles stood back and let her precede him, then followed and closed the door. Nicholas had gone to the large desk; he sat in the chair behind it.

Charles steered her to one of the chairs before the fireplace. "Sit down," he murmured.

She did.

He didn't. He paced to the hearth, turned, and looked at Nicholas.

Nicholas looked back at him, his diplomat's mask very much in place. The conviction Nicholas had done something she hadn't noticed grew.

When the silence had stretched as far as it could, Charles said, his tone hard and harsh, "Just tell me this. You aren't, by any chance, setting yourself up as a target here, are you?"

Nicholas's expression didn't change, but his pallor was so pronounced that the slight flush that rose to mantle his cheekbones might as well have been red flags. "I have no idea what you're suggesting."

Charles looked at him, then shook his head. "I hope you lie better when negotiating trade treaties."

Stung, Nicholas replied, "When negotiating trade treaties I deal with diplomats."

"Indeed, but I'm not a diplomat, and it's me you have to deal with here."

Nicholas sighed and closed his eyes. "What I do is none of your concern."

"If what you do has any connection whatever to the murderer of Gimby Smollet and Mary Maggs, it's very much my concern."

"I have no more notion than you which of those five is the murderer, or even if it *is* one of those five."

The words were weary, but definite.

Penny broke in, "Just what did he do?"

Charles glanced at her, exasperation in his eyes. "He waltzed back and forth before their noses as if daring the murderer to come after him."

Penny looked at Nicholas. "That wasn't wise."

"None of this was ever wise," Nicholas returned.

She and Charles both picked up the allusion to something beyond the immediate subject.

"I know the caliber of this man," Charles said. "Believe me, you don't want to tangle with him."

"No, you're quite right. I don't." Nicholas drew in a breath. Opening his eyes, he looked at Charles. "But I don't know who he is, and I can't tell you anything. I'm glad enough that you're here—at least that means Penny's safe. But . . . there's nothing more you—or I—can do."

Charles's eyes, fixed on Nicholas's face, narrowed. "You mean," he said, in his silkily dangerous voice, "that we'll just have to wait for him to show his hand."

Nicholas inclined his head.

She waited to see which way Charles would go, whether he would push, or . . .

Eventually, he nodded. "Very well, we'll play the next scene by your script." He caught Nicholas's gaze. "But I'll find out the truth in the end."

For a long moment, Nicholas held his gaze, then quietly replied, "Perhaps. Perhaps not."

An uneasy truce prevailed for the rest of the day. Charles was concerned, and on more than one front. He left her with

Nicholas in the drawing room and spoke with Norris. Nicholas smiled faintly when Charles returned, but said nothing.

By early evening, the entire household was as weary and wan as she'd earlier pretended to be; by unspoken consent, they retired early.

She and Charles found pleasure and, even more, comfort in each other's arms. The revelation of the previous night—that moment in which it had been shatteringly obvious that what lay between them was definitely not purely physical—was still there, waiting to be acknowledged, examined, and dealt with. She couldn't deal with it now, not with so much other tension surrounding them. Although the connection remained, a deep and very real link between them, Charles didn't allude to it, and for that she was grateful. Sated, as much at peace as they could be, they fell asleep.

About them, the old house settled, and slept, too.

Penny woke, and felt the mattress shift. Instantly alert, she lifted her head and saw Charles padding around the bed. He stopped by her dressing stool, picked up his breeches, and proceeded to climb into them.

"Where are you going?"

He glanced at her. "I woke up, and thought I may as well check the doors and windows downstairs."

She listened, but could hear nothing. He wasn't hurrying as he pulled on his boots.

"Stay there." He headed for the door, glanced back. "I'm going to lock the door—I won't be long."

She sat up as he opened the door, started to whisper, "Be careful."

Crash!

Downstairs, glass shattered, wood splintered.

Charles swore and shot out of the door. Penny bounced from the bed, grabbed up her robe, struggling into it as she raced after him. The ruckus continued. Reaching the stairs, she saw Charles ahead of her, leaping down. She reached the landing as he gained the hall and swung around, heading for the library.

She followed as fast as she could.

Charles slowed as he neared the open library doors. Thuds and grunts came from within. Noiselessly, he glided into the doorway.

Poised to react, every nerve tensed, he swiftly scanned the shadowy room. The curtains had been left open, but there was little illumination from outside; it took an instant to separate the destruction on the floor from the figures wrestling amid the wreckage most of the way down the long room.

Then one man gained the ascendancy, reared above the other, raised his arm, and struck down. Immediately, he raised his arm again—faint light glinted along a blade.

"Hold!" Charles shouted, muscles tensing to race in.

The man looked up, and changed his hold on the knife.

Penny moved behind Charles, peering past his shoulder.

Charles swore, and flung himself back.

The man threw the knife.

Pushing Penny out of the double doorway, Charles flattened her against the hall wall beside the door. Her "*Ooof!*" coincided with the thud of the knife as it hit the paneling on the opposite side of the hall, then clattered to the tiles.

He was back through the doorway as the tinkling died.

The room was a mass of shadows. He searched, then saw the man frantically climbing through the long window at the end of the room. His face was black—a scarf or mask; a hat was pulled low over his forehead.

The knife from Charles's boot was in his hand before he'd even thought. It was a long throw; he took an instant to gauge it, then sent the knife streaking down the room.

It thudded into the window frame where the man had been standing a bare second before, pinning his coat. Charles raced forward. He heard a curse, then material ripped and the man, already outside, was gone.

Glass crunched beneath Charles's boots; he called back, "There's broken glass—be careful!" He hurdled the slumped figure and finally reached the window; wrenching aside the billowing curtains, he looked out.

The man was briefly visible, a denser shadow pelting toward the dark mass of the shrubbery. Charles watched, itching to pursue but restrained by experience. The man would reach the shrubbery long before he could catch him; once amid the high hedges, the man could wait for him to venture in, then slip past him and return to the house to finish what he'd started.

Swallowing an oath, Charles turned and headed back to where Penny had picked her way to the slumped form and was now crouched by its side.

She glanced up as he neared. "Nicholas."

No surprise there.

"He's been stabbed, I think twice."

A curse slipped out. "The *idiot!*" Scuffing away the broken glass from around Penny, Charles hunkered down. "Light the lamp on the desk."

Penny rose and went to do as he'd asked. Nicholas was unconscious; grasping his shoulders, Charles rolled him fully onto his back. As the wick flared, then steadied, he saw two wounds, one in each shoulder.

The pattern spoke volumes. The next strike would have gone just above the heart, fully incapacitating, potentially fatal. The last strike would have been a quick jab between the ribs, directly into the heart. Always fatal.

If they'd been a few seconds slower, Nicholas would have died.

Both shoulder wounds were bleeding, but not as much as the next wound would have. Loosening, then dragging free Nicholas's cravat, Charles ripped the muslin in two, folded each piece, and firmly pressed one to each wound.

He looked up at Penny. She was as white as a sheet, but a long way from fainting. "He's not going to die." Her gaze lifted from Nicholas's deathly pale face to his. He nodded to the bellpull. "Wake the household. We'll need help with him, and we need to set a guard."

The next hour went in organized chaos. Already on edge, every member of the staff turned out in response to the jangling bell. Explanations had to be given; reassurances made. Maids had to be calmed, then some were sent to boil water while Figgs ordered the younger ones back to bed.

Figgs herself took charge of Nicholas. Working with Charles, she packed the wounds, then organized two footmen to carry Nicholas upstairs, back to his bed.

"Not even slept in!" Bustling ahead of the laboring footmen, Figgs hurried to turn down the covers. "Lay him there, gently now."

Charles sank into the armchair by the bed. Penny sat on its arm and leaned against his shoulder. Together, they watched as Figgs sent maids for water, clean linen for bandages, and ointment from the stillroom. While they scurried to obey, with brisk efficiency Figgs stripped Nicholas's ruined coat and shirt away. Once they'd delivered all she'd requested, Figgs shooed the maids off to bed; carrying the bowl to the bedside, she carefully lifted their improvised bandages and washed away the blood.

Patting the wounds dry, Figgs glanced at Charles. "Can't say I've much experience of stab wounds, but these don't look all that bad."

"They're not." Charles leaned forward and looked more closely. "At least they're clean—one benefit of being attacked by a professional." The last comment was uttered *sotto voce*, for Penny's ears alone as he sat back again.

She leaned more firmly against his shoulder. "Has he lost a lot of blood?"

"Not that much—his faint is most likely due to shock."

"Aye." Figgs looked decidedly grim.

"My lord?"

Charles looked up to see Norris in the doorway. He was carrying a lit candelabra; he glanced at the figure on the bed, then looked at Charles. "A guard, do you think, my lord?"

"Indeed." Charles rose, lightly squeezed Penny's shoulder. "Wait here—I'll be back. I need to speak to him when he comes around."

Penny nodded. She'd belted her robe tightly about her and was glad of its warmth, especially now Charles had moved away. She'd stopped by her room and put on her slippers, but even warm toes didn't alleviate her chill.

When Figgs started to smear on the ointment and lay gauze over the raw wounds, she shook herself, rose, and went to help. Working together, they secured bandages around Nicholas. Figgs had used warm water to wash away the blood, but Nicholas's skin felt icy.

Figgs noticed her concern. "It's the shock, like Lord Charles said. There." Pulling up the covers, she patted them down around Nicholas. "He's as comfortable as can be."

Piling her cloths in the basin, she hefted it. She glanced again at Nicholas. "I'll send up a footman with some hot bricks. That'll warm up the bed and bring him to himself."

"Thank you, Figgs." Penny sank into the armchair, her gaze fixed on Nicholas's effigy-like face.

Figgs humphed. "Em brews a tisane as calms the nerves something wonderful. I'll have some sent up for you all. After all this fuss, you'll be needing it, no doubt."

Penny smiled. "Thank you."

Figgs bobbed and left.

Charles walked back in as Figgs neared the door. He held it, then closed it behind her and crossed the room to Penny.

She raised her brows at him.

"Shutting the door after the horse has bolted, but . . ." With a light shrug, he sat on the arm of the chair. "If it was me, I'd come straight back in. Better safe than sorry."

"What have you organized?"

He told her of the orders he'd given, two men in each patrol, with two patrols circling the corridors, passing in sequence from one wing to the next. "One man alone, this villain will kill him, but he won't use a pistol—too much noise—and unless he's a wizard, he won't try to take on two men at once."

Penny nodded. Everything seemed so unreal. This was her home, yet patrols of footmen were now required to keep a murderous intruder at bay.

"I'd send you to bed, only I'd rather you remained in the same room as me."

She blinked, looked up at Charles. "I've no intention of returning to my bed. I want to be here when Nicholas awakes—I want to hear what he says."

He smiled, wry, resigned, and said no more.

Em's tisane arrived, and they each drank a cup; a pot under a knitted warmer sat waiting for Nicholas. Footmen came with the bricks wrapped in felt; Charles oversaw their disposition. Another footman stoked the fire into a roaring blaze. Penny thanked him and dismissed him. Then she and Charles settled to wait.

The clock on the mantelpiece ticked on.

Another hour passed before Nicholas stirred.

"You're in your own bed," Charles said. "He's gone."

Nicholas frowned. It took effort to open his eyes; he blinked at them, went to move, and winced. His eyes widened. "He stabbed me."

"Twice." Charles's tone was caustic. "What possessed you to tackle him alone?"

Nicholas grimaced. "I didn't think it through—there wasn't time."

Charles sighed. "What happened?"

"I was sitting in a chair in the hall, waiting—"

"Why there?" Charles asked, perplexed.

"Because I reasoned he'd go to the library, and I could see the library door from there. I didn't think he'd come through the window. The first I knew of him was a great crash—he'd smashed one of the display cases."

"Hmm." Charles's eyes narrowed. "What happened next? How much do you recall?"

"I rushed in—he saw me and swore, but I was on him in a flash. We tussled, fell." Nicholas's gaze grew distant. "It was so dark. It was more guesswork than science, grappling, rolling—then he flung me back, and stabbed me." He paused, then continued, "Then he stabbed me again. It felt so cold . . ." After a moment, Nicholas looked at Charles. "I heard a shout, but it seemed to come from a long way away."

"That was me—I was in the doorway."

"I must have fainted. What happened next?"

"He threw the knife at me"—Charles glanced severely at Penny—"at *us*, instead of plunging it into your heart. Then he fled."

"He got away?"

"The shrubbery is too damned close to the house—it's the perfect escape route." Charles studied Nicholas's face. "I need you to tell me all you can remember about your attacker."

Nicholas nodded; gingerly, he eased up in the bed.

Charles rose and went to help him, stacking the pillows behind his back. "You've lost a fair amount of blood—you'll be weak for a day or so, and those wounds will pull like the devil as they heal, but you were lucky—he didn't have time to be as professionally vicious as he'd have liked."

Penny rose and poured the tisane; when Nicholas was settled again, she handed him the cup. "It's Em's special recipe. It'll help."

Nicholas accepted the cup, sipped gratefully. Slipped back into his thoughts.

"So?" Charles prompted, returning to sit on the arm of Penny's chair.

Nicholas grimaced. "I couldn't see anything of his face—he had a scarf tied over his nose and mouth. In the dark, I couldn't get any idea of his eyes, and he wore a hat jammed low—it didn't come off."

"Don't think of features—you wrestled with him. How did he feel to you—old, young, supple, strong?"

Nicholas blinked; his expression grew distant. "Youngish, but not that much younger than I. Quite strong—leanish."

"How tall?"

Nicholas looked at Charles. "Not as tall as you. More my height, maybe an inch or so taller." He paused, then asked, "Did you see anything—anything to identify him?"

"Not specifically, but I believe we can cross Yarrow and Swaley off our lists. From what we both observed, Swaley's too short, and there's no way a man of Yarrow's weight could have moved as your attacker did. I agree with your youngish—younger than you or me—and leanish, too, although on that I'm less clear." Charles leveled his gaze on Nicholas's face. "Now think back—you said he swore when you entered the library. What did he sound like?"

"He was swearing even before he saw me—he seemed enraged about the pillboxes."

"Well, then?"

Nicholas's grimace was self-deprecatory. "It was all in French—fluent, and . . . well, if you work with people who speak multiple languages, you realize they sound different in one tongue versus another." He shook his head. "I couldn't even hazard a guess as to how he would sound in English."

Charles humphed, but nodded. "Carmichael, Fothergill, or Gerond, then."

"But from what you said before, Fothergill and Carmichael are unlikely." Nicholas handed his empty cup back to Penny. "And it was very fluent French."

Charles shook his head. "Don't build too much on that. I swear in very fluent French, too. As for the rest, 'unlikely' isn't definite. Those three are all still suspects."

Nicholas fell silent.

Penny studied him, then looked at Charles. He was thinking, furiously, not about what they'd learned, but about how to learn more. He was weighing his options; she knew the look.

After a long moment, he refocused on Nicholas, who met his gaze.

"When are you going to tell me—us—what's going on?"

When Nicholas's lips merely tightened, Charles went on, "If I hadn't decided to come down and check the doors and windows, I would never have been in time to stop his next blow, one that would very likely have ended your life. And no, I'm not telling you that so you'll feel grateful. I want you to understand how serious this is. This man has killed, not once but twice that we know of, and he will kill again. He has no compunction whatever. Who knows who it might be next time? Figgs, perhaps—she tended your wounds. Or Em, who made the tisane. Or Norris. Or Penny."

His voice had grown progessively colder. When he said her name, even though she'd guessed it was coming, Penny had to fight to quell a shiver.

When Nicholas glanced down at his hands, lying atop the covers, and said nothing, Charles continued in the same, coldly judgmental tone, "You said you'd reasoned he'd make for the library, and that he was swearing over the pillboxes. Am I right in guessing that you believed the pillboxes would be part of his target?" He stopped, waited.

"Yes," Nicholas eventually said. Closing his eyes, he rested his head back on the piled pillows.

"I assume you thought that because he'd gone after Mary—she was the downstairs tweeny, so she was responsible for dusting in the library."

Eyes still closed, Nicholas nodded.

Charles studied him, then looked at Penny. Mouthed what he wanted her to say. She nodded and sat forward.

"Nicholas, we know of the pillboxes in the priest hole."

His eyes jerked open; he stared at her. "You know . . . ?"

He looked at Charles, who nodded.

"Not easy to explain, not at all."

Nicholas sighed, and dropped his head back once more. He stared at the canopy over the bed.

"The thing I can't fathom," Charles went on, "is how the pillboxes fit with our theory of revenge. No one could have known . . ."

He paused. He'd been speaking his thoughts as they occurred, as he followed the train, yet hearing it aloud . . . suddenly he saw the light. "Not quite true, of course. The one group who most definitely would have known about the pillboxes is those who handed them over—the French."

Fixing his gaze on Nicholas, he felt the jigsaw shift, saw the difficult pieces slide smoothly into place. But he was still missing one major piece.

Nicholas had a stubborn look on his face—one Charles

actually recognized; it was very like Penny's intransigent mask.

"Very well." Settling back, he watched Nicholas. "This is what I know so far. Your father and Penny's set up some scheme decades ago passing secrets to the French. The French paid in pillboxes. The secrets were delivered mostly verbally to a contact from a French lugger who met one of the Selbornes out in the Channel. The Smolletts arranged the meetings using their yacht and the appropriate signal flags, then Penny's father and later Granville would go out with one of the smuggling gangs, meet the French, effect the transfer, and come away with a pillbox."

"A very neat exchange for everyone concerned, except the soliders who died in the wars." He was unable to keep the icy contempt from his voice.

Nicholas heard it; he paled, but otherwise didn't react. He continued to stare at the canopy. But he was listening.

"Now, however," Charles continued, reining in his feelings, "for some reason we have a French agent sent to recover some or all of the exchanged pillboxes, and"—watching Nicholas's face he guessed—"to punish the Selbornes, indeed, to kill any of those involved, or even their relatives."

Nicholas didn't react. Charles's blood ran cold as Nicholas's lack of shock or surprise confirmed he'd guessed right. He glanced at Penny; the stunned look on her face as she stared at Nicholas showed she'd followed the exchange and read it as he had.

Drawing a deep breath, he looked again at Nicholas. "Nicholas, you have to tell me what you know. This man is a killer—he'll continue until he succeeds in what he's been sent here to do, or he's stopped. He can be stopped."

He paused, then added, "Regardless of the past, the current situation is that you have a French agent about who wants to kill you. That puts you and me on the same side."

Nicholas's lips curved fractionally. "An enemy of my enemy must be my friend?"

"War makes strange bedfellows all the time." Charles

waited, then quietly said, "You have to tell me. If you don't, and he kills again, that death will be on your head."

His final card, but he suspected, from all he'd seen of Nicholas, perhaps a telling one. He certainly hoped so.

"Nicholas." Penny leaned forward and laid her hand on Nicholas's. "Please, tell us what's going on. I know the family's reputation weighs with you." Nicholas lifted his head enough to meet her eyes; she grimaced. "No matter how bad the past has been, the family might not have a future at all if you don't speak now. You must see that."

Nicholas held Penny's gaze.

Charles held his breath.

A long moment passed, then Nicholas sighed and let his head fall back. He stared at the canopy unseeing. "I have to think."

Charles fought to keep impatience from his voice. "This killer's on the doorstep. We don't have much time."

Nicholas lifted his head and met his gaze squarely. "It's not my story. I can't just"—he gestured—"make you free of it. I have to think what I can reveal, should reveal, and what isn't mine to tell at all."

"You just have to tell me enough."

Nicholas searched his eyes. "Twenty-four hours. You can give me until after dinner tomorrow"—he glanced at the clock—"no, that's now today." He drew in a shaky breath, and met Charles's eyes. "Give me until then, and I promise I'll tell you all I can."

CHARLES HAD TO BE CONTENT WITH THAT. ASIDE FROM ANY-
thing else, Nicholas was exhausted and needed to rest.

Returning with Penny to her room, he checked that no villain was lurking, then locked her in and went to check on his
patrols. All was quiet, yet the silence was rife with anxiety.
After chatting to the four men presently on watch, he slipped
back into Penny's room, stripped, and slid under the covers.

She turned to him and tugged him close. He went, found
her lips with his, kissed. Grumbled, "What is the matter with
your family? It's never *your* story, and you all want twenty-
four damned hours. . . ."

Penny looked into his dark eyes, softly smiled. "It's not
us—it's *you*. It's obvious that once we tell you, all control
will be out of our hands."

He humphed, and kissed her again.

She let him, met him, then encouraged him. Not just invited but dared him to take her, to give himself, let her give
back to him and so reassure them both. To touch again and
share the comfort they now found in each other, through the
physical to reach further once again, onto that other plane.

Responding, accepting, he rose over her, pressed her
thighs wide, sank between, and with one powerful stroke
sheathed himself in her softness, joined them, and set them
careening on their now familiar wild ride. She gasped,

clung, and rode with him, absorbed, drawn wholly into the moment, yet dimly aware of the contradiction between his nature and his behavior with her.

He never pushed, cajoled, pressured; he never had. In this arena, he'd always been the supplicant, and she his . . . not mistress, but perhaps empress, dispensing her favors as she chose. As she decided and deemed him worthy.

And he'd never once argued with that. Never once sought to change their status quo, to demand or simply seize control and take.

A wall of flames rose before them, a surging, greedy conflagration; they plunged into it, rode through it, fell into it. Wrapped in each other's arms, they let the fire have them, consume them, weld them, leaving them at the last clinging to the edge of the world. Gasping, shuddering, gazes meeting, locking, holding . . .

Then that too-brief instant of absolute communion faded; lids falling, all tension released, they tumbled headlong into the void.

They settled to sleep, him sprawled beside her, one arm slung possessively over her waist. Her thoughts circled, spiraling down, yet despite her languid state, they didn't stop.

His breathing deepened and slid into the cadence of sleep.

Her mind continued to drift.

His willingness to cede the reins to her, to allow her to dictate their play, continued to nag, to register as, if not suspicious, then certainly significant, but in what way she couldn't tell. She'd already asked him why. He'd replied with words she'd interpreted as a challenge: *Whatever you wish, however you wish. I'm yours. Take me.*

She mentally paused, through half-closed eyes stared unseeing into the darkness as she replayed those words in her mind. What if they hadn't been a challenge, but instead an honest reply?

Her instinctive reaction was to scoff, but she could hear his voice in her head; he hadn't spoken lightly. What *if* . . . ?

The possibility shook her, tightened her nerves, sharpened her wits. Her mind whirled and drew another puzzle piece into her mental picture.

The link that had opened between them, that emotional communion that had somehow become an integral part of their joining, was still there, consistently there, and very real. She'd been stunned initially, shocked that he of all men would reveal so much of himself in such a way. That first moment, so intense, had taken her aback, left her momentarily uncertain. Now, however . . . she needed and wanted to learn more, to explore that connection and see where it led, learn what it meant.

He wanted her, not just physically but on some deeper, more emotion-laden level. That was what that connection, by its very existence, conveyed; she'd seen the yearning, the longing, woven through it.

She accepted he couldn't pretend to such emotions; she couldn't recall that he ever had, not with her. But he could conceal; he was a past master at hiding what he felt, one of his most spyworthy talents. While she could sense and be sure of his wanting her, of the sincerity of his belief that he needed her, she couldn't see what was driving it, what lay behind it. What, indeed, had given rise to it.

One thing she knew beyond question. At twenty, he'd neither wanted nor needed her, not as he did now. She'd been right in defining how the years had changed him—at twenty, the superficial, the obvious, had been all there was; now he was a complex, complicated man, one with hidden depths, still ruled by intense and powerful emotions, but those emotions were now harnessed, controlled, often screened.

The man behind the superficial mask had grown in many ways, had developed depths he hadn't previously possessed. What drove him to want her was new, one of those facets the years had wrought in him. But what was it?

Her thoughts continued to circle, examining that question from every possible angle . . . until sleep crept up on her and dragged her down.

* * * *

The next morning, Nicholas remained confined to his bed awaiting a visit from Dr. Kenton, who Penny had summoned over Nicholas's protests to check his wounds. When Nicholas appealed to Charles, wordlessly man-to-man, Charles met his gaze stoically and refused to countermand Penny. If it made her feel better to have the doctor call, so be it.

They left Nicholas still weak, but now sulking. Charles hoped he'd grow restless and consent to speak sooner; he was very conscious of wasting the day. He filled the morning writing reports; the first, to Dalziel, he dispatched by rider, the second, a succinct note to Culver informing him of the attack on Nicholas, he left on Norris's salver.

Culver would be shocked. He would sit in his library and tut-tut, then retreat into his books. He was one person whose reactions Charles could predict with confidence. Not so others in this game.

Once both reports were gone, there was little else for him to do. Dr. Kenton came and went, gravely noting how lucky Nicholas was that neither knife thrust had nicked anything vital. After commending Em's ointment and Figgs's bandaging, Kenton advised Nicholas that rest was all he required for a complete recovery.

After seeing Kenton off, Charles prowled around the house. Penny was still in conference with Figgs. He wandered through the library, now cleared of the debris from the smashed display cases, then circled the ground floor, growing ever more restless and edgy. The combination was familiar, the prelude to battle; patience had never been his strong suit.

Yet the battle to come would not come today. Everyone at the house was alert, watchful, careful, very much on guard. While he might have thought to surprise them by returning last night, the French agent—Charles felt confident in dubbing him that—would not call today. Soon, yes, but not yet; he'd wait, hoping they'd relax at least a little of their vigilance.

To pass the time, he walked through the shrubbery, confirming his memories of the villain's favorite escape route. He'd been right in not following the man into its shadows in the black of night. The shrubbery was old, its trees and shrubs thick and dense; it would be child's play for anyone fleeing into it to circle any pursuer and return to the house, leaving said pursuer chasing shadows, unaware.

He walked out of the shrubbery and saw Penny on the terrace. She saw him and waved, then descended the steps and headed his way.

They met in the middle of the lawn; smiling, she linked her arm in his and strolled by his side. He listened while she told him of the household's reactions, of the staff's determination to hold firm against the unknown attacker who had taken one of their own, then dared to violate their domain.

Lifting his head, Charles looked at the house. With the staff so resolute and guards in place, Nicholas was safe; he could have so many hours to think. For himself, he wanted to keep Penny with him, which meant keeping her occupied. Nothing from London would reach the Abbey before the afternoon . . . "If I don't get out of here, I'll start badgering Nicholas." He caught her eye. "Why don't we take a picnic and ride to the castle? I haven't been there in years."

She blinked, then her eyes lit and she nodded. "You get the horses. I'll order a picnic, then change. I'll meet you in the stables."

He let her draw away. Smiling, she headed for the house, clearly eager despite her tiredness. They'd got precious little sleep last night, but more, battling an unidentified assailant was inherently draining. He was accustomed to it, she wasn't, yet she was holding up well.

Better than most females would, but then he'd always known there was a spine of tempered steel concealed within her slender form.

He watched that slender form cross the lawns and reenter the house, then he stirred and strode for the stables.

Distraction was what they both needed.

* * *

It was noon when they reached the ruins of Restormel Castle, dramatically perched above the Fowey valley with sylvan views over field and estuary to the distant cliffs and the sea beyond. A favorite picnic spot for the surrounding families in summer, today it was theirs alone.

Built by the Normans from local gray stone, the castle was a rarity—perfectly circular. Disused for centuries, the curtain wall and outer bailey were long gone; they rode across the dry ditch and into the courtyard of the inner keep, a place preserved out of time.

Dismounting, they exchanged glances. Every child from both their families had run wild here; it was a special place, a well for the imagination to draw on. As he tied Domino's reins to an ancient ring in the wall, Charles recalled battles he and his brothers had staged there, in the courtyard, their boots scuffing on the stones as they fought with wooden swords, high-pitched voices echoing from the walls. Their parents and sisters had looked down from the battlements, and laughed and smiled.

Penny, too, had her own hoard of memories, in similar vein, happy moments bright with the magic bestowed by childhood's eyes. She handed her reins to Charles, looked around while he tethered her mare. "Leave the picnic for now." It was stored in their saddlebags. "Let's walk the battlements first."

He nodded. Taking her hand, he led her to the flight of steps that gave access to the now empty hall; from there they took another flight up to the crenellated outer wall.

She stepped onto the stone walkway and paused to look around, to confirm that the building below them, the inner keep, was still as she remembered it, then she turned and let her eyes drink in the sweeping views.

The wind was cool yet soft with the promise of summer, the air fresh and clean, the sun warm but not hot. White wisps of clouds streaked across a cerulean sky. It was an idyllic place, soothing to the soul.

"I don't know why," she said, tucking back wisps of hair the breeze had teased free, "but I feel as if the villain, whoever he is, can't penetrate here. Simply can't exist here."

Charles squeezed her hand gently; they started to stroll. "I used to think this was one of those faerie places our nurses used to whisper about. A place that was of this world, but also of the other—a spot where the real and the faerie worlds met, and time didn't behave as it does elsewhere."

She shivered delicately, but it was a delicious shiver. "An enchanted place—yes, you're right. But it never felt haunted to me."

"No. I decided that was because no bad battles, or betrayals, happened here. It's as you said. This place has always simply been, and bad things aren't allowed to happen here."

Glancing at him, she saw the self-deprecatory smile playing about his lips. She smiled, too, and looked ahead.

Noting the various landmarks, they unhurriedly circled the keep. Nearing the hall once again, Penny paused to glance out one last time. To the left across the river and a little way southeast lay the Abbey; Wallingham Hall lay to the right, farther away and concealed behind a spur of the escarpment.

"Where will we eat?" Charles asked.

Hiding a smile, she turned and followed him down the steep stairs.

They spread a rug under a tree that had sprung up by the side of the dry ditch. The spot still gave them views, albeit more restricted, but also protection from the stiffening breeze. In their oasis of comfort, they munched their way through the delicacies Em had packed into the bags. There was a bottle of wine, but no glasses; Penny laughed and accepted the bottle when Charles opened it and, with a flourish, offered it. They passed the bottle back and forth while commenting on this and that, all matters of local life.

Nothing to break the spell.

When Charles had demolished Mrs. Slattery's game pie, and between them they'd finished Cook's almond tart, they drained the bottle, then packed everything away. Hand in hand, they walked back to the courtyard.

Charles attached the empty bags to their saddles. Penny

handed him the folded rug; he tucked that away, too. "It's too early for any courier, isn't it? They won't have reached the Abbey yet."

Charles glanced at her. "Unlikely."

"In that case"—she looked up at the rooms giving onto the courtyard—"let's explore."

Anything to prolong their time in this place, this haven from the world; Charles fell in with her wish without quibble, inwardly acknowledging his own inclination. Outside a murderer might stalk their families' lands, but while here, time and place were theirs, sacrosanct, inviolable.

He caught up with her in the hall and took her hand. Together, they ambled through the rooms, recalling incidents from earlier times, laughing, smiling at their younger selves. Restormel was a shell keep, the various rooms built around the courtyard. They were traversing the armory beneath the south battlements when Penny glanced out of an arrow slit— and stopped. "Charles?"

He was beside her in an instant.

She pointed. "Isn't that Gerond?"

A tiny figure on horseback was trotting along the road to Lostwithiel; it was, indeed, Gerond. He was wearing a caped riding cloak.

"He's alone," Penny murmured.

"Hmm . . . I wonder where he's been."

"That cloak . . ." Penny glanced up at him. "You kept that scrap your knife caught last night. Couldn't we check to see which of them has a torn greatcoat?"

"We don't need to check—the answer is none."

She frowned. "Because he would have got rid of it?"

He nodded. "And in this season, it's perfectly reasonable for a gentleman to go visiting without a greatcoat."

Staring at the dwindling figure was pointless; it reminded him of their lack of success in identifying the villain thus far. He nudged Penny. "Come on—let's go on."

They did, passing through the rest of the chambers, some still roofed, others open to the elements, eventually reaching the ladies' solar. A small chamber built on a mezzanine level above the main hall, it faced southwest and was bathed in sunshine for most of the day. Its roof was intact. A stone platform worn smooth over the years filled the space beneath a series of thin vertical windows, each narrow enough not to be out of place in a keep, yet the mullions had been cunningly shaped so that, from inside, the series appeared as one large divided window spilling golden light into the room.

As usual, the chamber was invitingly pleasant. Penny stepped onto the stone platform and felt the warmth seep through her boots' soles. For her purpose, this was the perfect setting. Walking to one window, she looked out; long, thin, and open, the windows stretched from above her head to a foot above the platform. "I used to sit here and stare out, and imagine I was the lady of Restormel Keep, waiting for my husband to return from some typical male military endeavor, like chasing off a band of outlaws."

Charles came up behind her. He stepped close, then his hands slid around her waist, and he eased her back against him. It felt wonderful to stand there, supported and surrounded by his strength in the sunshine; she leaned back, relaxed, closed her eyes, let her senses unfurl.

And sensed a sudden sharpening of his attention. Opening her eyes, she immediately saw what had caused it. Another of their three suspects, Fothergill this time, was striding across a field, heading west. "He must have been out looking at birds."

"Hmm." Charles's response came as a low growl. "At least he's heading away from here."

So he wouldn't disturb them in their enchanted place. Penny smiled. She had no difficulty following Charles's thoughts; leaning back against him as she was, it was apparent in which direction they'd gone.

Fothergill marched steadily on, then disappeared over a rise. They'd seen no one else; no one else was likely to stop by. They were as alone and as safe as they could be.

Memories and questions hung suspended in her mind. Possibilities beckoned.

She swayed, just a little, against Charles, then turned sinuously in his arms. He met her gaze, arched a brow as she draped her arms over his shoulders. His hands firmed and he drew her close, her hips flush to his thighs. "So what else did you think of when you sat here, all those years ago?"

His voice had lowered to a tone she thought of as distilled seduction. Her lips curved, but she kept her eyes on his. Wondered for one second if she truly dared . . . decided she did. Would. "I thought about us."

"Us?" One brow arrogantly arched. "You and me?"

She nodded. "Yes, even then. I used to think about you being half-Norman, and the other half French, very much like your ancestor who came over with the Conqueror."

Eyes locked on his, she knew when he picked up her train of thought. He started to follow it, not quite sure . . .

"And, of course," she continued, "I'm Norman with a healthy dash of Viking, enough to make me interesting, more of a challenge to a French-Norman lord." She opened her eyes wide, stared into the midnight depths of his. "Don't you agree?"

His hold on her firmed. "As a French-Norman lord, I definitely agree."

He bent his head; before she could stop him he covered her lips with his and demonstrated, amply, just how interesting he found her. For an instant, the rising tide of desire threatened to sweep her before it—the gloriously familiar heat of his mouth, the flaming brand of his tongue, the silkily slow, sensuous claiming of her senses—then she remembered her goal.

He was holding her too tightly, too close to break away. Reaching up, she grabbed a handful of his thick locks and tugged.

Lifting his head just enough to meet her eyes, he looked his question.

She managed to find enough breath to ask, "Don't you want to know the rest of what I thought about?"

He stilled. Not a freezing type of stillness but one even more absolute, a predator holding perfectly steady so as not to frighten its prey. Not a cold-blooded stillness but an elementally hot-blooded one, one that set their pulses pounding.

His eyes, dark and intense, bored into hers; he searched, confirmed—went to answer . . . and hesitated.

She felt that hesitation like a rein snapping taut, holding him back. Tilting her head, she studied his face, then returned her eyes to his. "What?"

He held her gaze for a moment, then pressed his lips tight, closed his eyes, and murmured, "I . . . don't know if I dare."

Charles not accept a dare? She could barely believe her ears.

As if expecting that, he opened his eyes and looked at her—wordlessly warning her not to say what she was thinking.

It was her turn to look inquiringly at him.

He heaved a deep sigh and rested his forehead against hers. "I don't want to hurt you. I don't know what you might be about to say, but . . ." After a moment, he raised his head and met her eyes. "You do know that I'm not entirely sane when it comes to you, don't you?"

It took a minute of searching his face, his eyes, for her to be sure she'd correctly interpreted what he was not very clearly trying to tell her. The look she bent on him was chiding. "Charles, you won't hurt me—you never have." He opened his mouth; she cut him off. "Yes, all right, except for that once, but that was inevitable, as you should by now realize—I don't hold that against you. I do wish you'd forget it!"

Especially if that sensitivity was going to interfere with what she had in mind. Before he could respond, she sank against him, let her fingers trail across his cheek to his lips, followed her fingers with her eyes.

His hold on her firmed again.

"Please . . . ?" She infused just the right amount of coercion into the word.

He sighed, then drew breath. "So what else did you imagine?"

"Well, if I was the lady of Restormel Keep, then obviously"—she lifted her gaze once more to his eyes—"you were my lord."

He swore softly in French. "Do you really want to venture there"—bending his head, he nipped her lower lip—"lady?"

She laughed softly and drew him back to her. "Oh, yes." She breathed the affirmation over his lips, then kissed him voraciously, then drew back. He let her, just.

"So," she said, moistening her lower lip, her gaze lowering to his lips, "you're my lord, and you've just returned from chasing brigands, and I've been waiting for you here." She swayed in his arms, swishing her hips side to side against him. "You've just ridden in and come up, ordered my ladies from the chamber, and here I am, in your arms." She lifted her gaze to his. "What would you do next?"

His eyes had darkened, their expression more intense; the planes of his face seemed harder—more, indeed, like the lord of legend she'd painted him.

"What I do next . . . would depend on a number of things. Such as . . ." One hand slid down and around; cupping her bottom, he jerked her up and to him, so the vee at the junction of her thighs cradled his rigid erection. His eyes held hers, watching her reaction as he evocatively rocked. "Have you been obedient? Or not?"

Her nerves were already unraveling with anticipation; it was an effort to cling to enough wits to respond appropriately. Holding his gaze, she arched one brow haughtily. "Me? Obedient? I'm part Viking, remember?"

"Ah. I see." His gaze, hard and ruthless, raced over her face. "So you haven't yet been tamed?"

"Oh, no," she affirmed. "Not yet."

She pretended to push him away, to wriggle from his hold; he didn't budge. Relentlessly he held her close, pressed her to him; on a gasp, she turned her head as if spurning him. Locking her to him with one arm, he raised a hand to frame her face, not gently yet as he forced her face to his, there was neither violence nor the threat of it in his touch.

He looked down at her, deep into her eyes.

She glimpsed him behind the ruthless mask, sensed his hesitation. "*Don't stop.*"

A whispered plea, it sent a faint shudder through him.

His lids flickered, then he locked his eyes, intent and burning, on hers. Slowly bent his head. "I'm not even sure I can."

His lips covered hers. Firmed, then forced hers apart. He surged into her mouth, claiming, branding, devastatingly commanding, and passion, unleashed, swept them away. Within seconds she was reeling, unsure if the turbulent tumultuous tide came from him or herself. Or them both. It was her imagination that had scripted the scene, but her words, her fantasy, had struck a chord in him.

Struck a deeply buried vein of ruthless possessiveness and sent it raging.

His hands raced over her, impressing even through the plush velvet of her habit, in some strange way even more erotic than if he'd stripped her naked. She shivered, a reaction that came from her bones. His tongue whipped fire down her veins; his hands roamed, claiming, kneading, flagrantly possessing, and she wondered what she'd invited, what degree of surrender he'd demand.

Realized she didn't care. She'd asked for this, wanted it, needed to know of it, of him and what, once stripped of the restraint of civilization, lurked within him when it came to her.

So she played her part, simultaneously acquiescent, for no lady could deny her lord his rights to her body, yet also holding back, denying him the ultimate surrender, making him work for that, demanding he conquer her before she would yield that, too.

A dangerous game; the last remnant of sanity remaining to her knew it, yet equally knew that with him, despite him being the very source of the danger, or perhaps because of that, she was safe.

She had nothing to fear and everything to gain. And a great deal to learn.

Such as how desperate he could make her, that simply through the combination of his heavily shielded if blatantly explicit caresses and the voracious demands of his lips and tongue, he could reduce her to a state of sobbing need. To where her blood thundered in her veins, to where her skin burned and her flesh throbbed, and a telltale empty ache blossomed inside her.

Their kiss turned savage, primitive and demanding, then he broke from it and growled, "Do you want me inside you?"

"Yes," she gasped, breathless, the word faint. "Now."

His hands closed about her bottom and he moved provocatively against her. "As my lady desires."

The words rang with maleness, arrogant and sure, dominant and demanding.

He'd been holding her high on her toes; he eased her down so her feet touched the stone slab. Relief flashed through her; she reached up to twine her arms about his neck—he released her, caught her hands and spun her around, then locked her against him, her bottom to his hips, her back to his chest.

"First things first."

The gravelly words brushed her ear; releasing her hands, he reached for the buttons of her short jacket. He opened it and pressed the halves wide; she used the moment to catch her breath—lost it again when his hands closed over her breasts and kneaded possessively, then he set deft fingers to the buttons of her blouse. The change in protection from velvet to fine linen had made her senses spin, but then he spread her blouse wide, with two tugs stripped down her chemise. A breeze threaded through the window slit before her, caressing her flesh with cool fingers, then his palms cruised over the swollen mounds; his hands closed, hot and hard, taking possession. They kneaded, then his fingers found her nipples and she gasped.

Arched as he knowingly played. She was suddenly brutally conscious of the flaring need to have him inside her, to take him into her body, already ripe and waiting. Wanting.

As if he knew, he released her breasts, caught her hands, drew them forward until her arms were straight, then pressed her hands palms down against the beveled edge of the window slit before them, where the carving in the stone formed a small ledge at hip height.

"Your hands stay there."

An absolute order. Reflexively, she gripped, wondering;

the stone was at least solid beneath her hands. She was half-bent forward; before she could think, she felt him gathering the back of her skirts, felt the rush of cool air across her heated skin as he lifted them. He pushed them to her waist as his hand boldly roved, making free with her body as a lord might with his lady's. His hand caressed, blatantly claiming; his fingers probed, tracing her softness, opening the swollen folds, then sliding into her, pressing in, then explicitly stroking until she sobbed with frustrated need.

"How disobedient have you been, lady?"

She tried to catch her breath, tried to think—couldn't, not with his fingers playing so evocatively. "Ah . . ."

"Never mind."

She felt him shift behind her.

"You still need to be tamed."

He thrust into her. In one smooth, powerful, relentless invasion he filled her to the limit, until she could feel him beneath her heart, in her throat, throughout her body.

Then he rode her that way.

Hands locked about her hips, he held her immobile and repetitively filled her, the fabric of his breeches against her bare bottom an added stimulation, emphasizing that to him she was exposed, vulnerable—his for the taking.

And he took.

He'd entered her from behind before, but only in their bed; she'd had no idea it could be this . . . primitive. This powerful, this erotic. Far beyond breathless, she clung to the stone, arms braced, her body riding his thrusts as he filled her again and again. Lids falling, she gave herself up to the moment, to the experience, to the building excitement as he expertly pushed her sensually further, then further still.

Until she gasped, "Why here? Like this?"

Instinct told her that was important to understand.

"So when you scream my people in the bailey will hear and know of your surrender."

It took a moment for her reeling mind to digest the implications, to assess the intensity of the sensations buffeting her. "I don't scream."

"You will."

Charles volunteered nothing more, his mind totally engrossed in ensuring she did. Her fantasy, the fact she'd so long ago had the thought of him as her lord . . . any chance of him retaining even a semblance of control had flown the moment she'd told him. The role she'd created for him was so close to the one he wanted, to the one he needed to claim; had any other lady made the suggestion he'd have thought she was insane to tempt him so, yet with her . . . it was one of the reasons he had to make her his.

Her breathing had fractured into sobbing gasps; arms braced, she rode his thrusts instinctively, her scalding sheath closing about him, clasping, clinging, drawing every ounce of sensation from each strong stroke, from each powerful penetration. She was close to the edge, the tension inside her coiling ever tighter. He pressed even deeper, freed one hand and reached for her breasts.

Swollen and firm, the heated flesh filled his palm. He played briefly, his thumb roughly circling her aureola, then he caught her nipple between his fingers and squeezed. Hard. Then he synchronized the squeezes with the movement of his hips.

And she shattered.

Screamed.

The sound, purely feminine, intensely evocative, sank into him like a spur and shattered what little control he had left. He thrust harder, deeper, then held still as she convulsed around him; eyes closed, head back, he savored her release.

But it wasn't enough.

The instant the last of her tension left her, he withdrew from her, letting her skirts fall as he swung her into his arms, then went to his knees. He laid her back on the warm stone before him, arranging her as he wished.

From beneath heavy lids, she watched him, her eyes storm-wracked gray glittering in the aftermath of the tumult she'd just weathered, her lips swollen and parted, her bared breasts rising and falling dramatically. The pulse at the base of her throat throbbed wildly.

Her voluminous riding skirts had spread across the slab, the old gold velvet sheening in the sunshine, the back trapped beneath her, protecting her from any abrasion from the stone. Raising the front hem, he tossed the heavy skirt back, exposing her long legs, the damp triangle of fair curls at the apex of her thighs, the white curves of her hips.

He could hear the blood pounding in his head, could feel it pounding throughout his body, echoing the compulsion that drove through his veins. Grasping her thighs, he spread them wide and knelt between. His phallus rose rigid and urgent from the open placket of his breeches. Running his hands up the backs of her thighs, he gripped her lower hips, and lifted her to him.

Slid slowly into the scalding haven of her body. Watched her as he did, sensed her body rise to meet his, welcoming him in, her softness easing about his hardness, accepting, wanting him as much as he did her. When he'd fully impaled her, he withdrew halfway, then thrust deeply in.

Her breath tangled in her throat. Her eyes locked with his, for one long moment she was with him as he rocked deeply into her, then on a shuddering sigh, her lids fell and she wrapped her long legs about his hips and let him have his way. Let him use her body as he wished for his pleasure, ultimately for hers, too. The time came when she could no longer remain passive, when desire rose again and whipped her back into the dance.

And then she matched him. Strove with him as the dance whirled ever faster, as they joined ever more deeply, ever more completely. As they started up the last rise to the pinnacle, she sobbed and reached for him.

He spread his hands beneath her back and lifted her, let her clutch his arms, then bent his head and feasted on her breasts.

The tempo escalated, then whirled out of control.

She screamed again, clutched his head to her breast, arching wildly. Eyes closed, he clung to her, clung until her contractions faded, then eased her back, gripped her hips in an unforgiving grasp and with a series of short, deep thrusts, joined her. Pumped himself into her.

Untold moments passed; his head spun. Eventually, he withdrew from her, slumped beside her, and let oblivion close over him, overwhelming and complete.

Penny wasn't sure why she woke; her senses stretched, but there was no one else there, just the two of them slumped on their sides on the stone slab, the sunshine pouring over them in gentle benediction.

Peace and stillness enveloped her. Her body felt limp, gloriously so; the passion Charles had wrung from her had left her deliciously weak. Lips curving, she closed her eyes and let her mind range over their recent engagement. It had been far *far* better than even her wildest dreams.

Gradually other thoughts spun into her mind. Thoughts of him, her unresolved questions, possible answers. In the bliss of aftermath with her mind clear, relaxed, open, it was impossible not to see what the last hour had proved.

Charles lay behind her, deeply asleep, his arm heavy across her waist. She hesitated, then slowly, supplely pushed up from the floor, drawing her legs up and swiveling so she was sitting, her skirts twisted but not yet pulling, still within the circle of his arm, which slid down to cradle her hip.

She looked down at him. For long moments, she studied his face, the features she'd known since childhood, the lines the last decade had etched. It was still a very strong face. She let her gaze roam downward. Still a very strong body, one her own responded to in a flagrantly wanton way. Still.

Slowly, she brought her gaze back to his face, then, drawing in a deep breath, she clasped her arms about her calves, rested her chin on her knees, and looked out over the fields.

How foolish she'd been to imagine she could somehow *suspend* loving him, could somehow keep her heart from him. Her heart had been his all those years ago; it had never changed, never vacillated no matter what her intellect had dictated. Yet she *had* changed.

At sixteen, she'd loved him; she could remember what it had felt like—a mere wraith of emotion compared to what she felt now. In the last hour . . . connecting past with present had revealed how much her love had matured, into something stronger, more vibrant, impossible to suppress, let alone deny. It might have been born long ago, but it was of the here and now, not the past; it was very much a woman's love, confident and demanding, not a young girl's fantasy.

She was no longer afraid that he might break her heart—if he hadn't destroyed it years ago, then he couldn't now. The years had changed him, but they'd changed her, too; she was now much stronger.

She refused to regret or in any way step back from what had, this time, grown between them. Last time, she had in effect run away, drawn back from loving him because he hadn't loved her. Not this time. This time, she'd learned what not just love but *loving* was, how deeply satisfying it could be; she wasn't going to give up the glory of loving him of her own accord. This time, if anyone was to step back, it would be he.

But would he?

Eyes narrowing, she looked again at his sleeping face, shuttered and closed. She'd assumed that in seducing her he was looking for an affair, a lover for the weeks he was here investigating. She'd stepped into his arms believing that, built her vision of what he was about on that basis.

But her vision was wrong.

He grew suspicious when facts didn't fit; so did she. The emotional link that had grown between them, that he'd allowed and encouraged to grow between them, didn't fit with a fleeting affair. Nor did the way he'd dealt with her, until today.

With her eyes, she traced the lines of his face, the sensuous lips, the squared chin. In the last hour, she'd deliberately set out to shake him free of his self-imposed restraint, to see what lay behind it. She'd succeeded well enough to learn what she'd needed to know; the wolf hadn't changed his pelt for a curly fleece. Regardless of what he allowed to show, underneath he was a conquering French-Norman lord, dominant and domineering, and blatantly, ruthlessly possessive, at least with respect to her.

So why, so consistently over their recent enounters, had he taken the supplicant's role?

There was only one answer; he wanted something from her. Specifically, he wanted *her*.

The damned man was *wooing* her.

That explanation was the only one that fitted; reviewing his behavior, she could see nothing that argued against it. Indeed, he'd even told her she was his perfect bride. He'd been fixed on marrying her from then, but with her mind flatly disavowing any such likelihood, she hadn't caught the admission in his words.

At some point, he was going to ask her to marry him. She knew him; he would ask in such a way that she wouldn't be able to avoid giving him an answer. So how was she going to reply?

Inwardly she swore, relieved her feelings by scowling at him, thankfully still sleeping, then looked away across the fields.

Why did he want to marry her? A critical question to which the answer might be a host of partial reasons. He'd mentioned some in declaring her his perfect bride; none was a reason she would accept.

She loved him, but she didn't know what he felt for her. If it was some mild, impermanent emotion, affection laced with lust and desire, even now she would rather live the rest of her life an old maid than see affection fade and die, know her love was no longer wanted, and have them both grow bitter.

If they weren't married, then if and when her love was no longer enough for him, they could part; if they were married, they'd be doomed. She could easily see herself as his long-time lover, but tied to him in marriage? Not without love on both sides.

But did he love her? Thirteen years ago, she'd been sure of the answer. Now . . . her uncertainty felt very strange, but it was real. Worse, not knowing—not knowing what gave rise to his emotional need of her—left her trapped, unable to accept him yet equally unable to refuse him, not until she learned the truth—was *love* one of the mature emotions he kept hidden behind his mask?

Not for anything this side of hell could she let that question lie unanswered. She'd put away her dream of loving him and having him love her, and all the rest her youthful heart had assumed would follow, thirteen long years ago. She'd never found another dream with which to replace it. Until now, she hadn't had to face what that meant, that being his wife, lover, and friend was still the only future she truly wanted.

Now . . . eyes fixed unseeing on the distant sea, she felt that reality to her bones.

Eventually, he stirred; the hand lax about her hip tensed, gripped. Turning to him, she put her thoughts away. She had a week or more, until they caught the murderer, before he would ask, and she would have to answer.

His eyes opened; deepest sapphire blue in the afternoon sunlight, they looked into hers, then he smiled. He reached for her and drew her back down, into his arms, into a succession of increasingly intimate kisses—until she drew him over her, parted her thighs, and wordlessly welcomed him into her body.

Into a slow, heated dance, with his weight moving over her, against her, into her, with her clasping him and holding him close, of her fractured cries as she climaxed, of his low groans as he sought his pleasure in her, of the warmth that flooded her when he found it, of the shattering sensations that sped down her veins, then dissipated in pulsing glory.

The glory slowly faded, leaving, as she was learning it was wont to do, her emotions exposed, at least to herself. She'd never had any choice but to accept them; they were immutable, unswerving. Holding him close, idly stroking his hair, she reminded herself she had time to learn his secrets, to find some way of reading, not just his mind, but his heart—before he demanded hers.

CHAPTER

18

THEY REACHED THE ABBEY IN MIDAFTERNOON. FILCHETT met them in the front hall and informed them nothing had arrived from London, but that Fothergill had called that morning.

"Very interested in architecture. I took him on the usual tour."

"Did he ask many questions?" Charles asked.

"Indeed. Quite a knowledgable young man."

Charles pulled a face at Penny. "Tea in the study?"

Penny nodded.

Charles glanced at Filchett. "Some cakes wouldn't go amiss." He returned his dark gaze to her. "We've been riding in the fresh air—it's left me with an appetite."

Her expression limpidly innocent, she absolutely refused to react.

Cassius and Brutus had come to greet them; they danced around, then circled them, herding them into the study, Charles's lair. Charles spent five minutes petting the dogs, running his fingers through their shaggy coats and reducing them to ecstasy. When Filchett arrived with the tray, Charles left the hounds stretched at her feet and headed for his desk to sort through the letters and notes piled there while she poured.

Returning to fetch his cup, he filched the plate of cakes.

Nibbling the one she'd already selected, she watched as he went back to the desk and settled to deal with all he'd left to pile up while he'd been guarding her.

He steadily demolished the cakes.

Eventually he glanced up, and noticed her smile. "What?"

"It wasn't that appetite I thought I evoked."

He held her gaze, took another bite of cake. Swallowed, then said, "It isn't. This appetite is the consequence of adequately slaking the other."

"Adequately?"

Looking back at his accounts, he shrugged. "Thoroughly might be more accurate."

She grinned and left him to his work, content to relax in the chair and let the peace envelop her. The Abbey had always been a contentment-filled house; even his brothers' unexpected deaths hadn't changed that. Closing her eyes, she let the quiet claim her; idly stroking the hounds with her boot, she turned her mind to devising some way of learning what the emotion driving Charles to want her was . . . and found herself dozing.

Sometime later, the hounds got quickly to their feet and shook themselves; she opened her eyes to see Charles push away from the desk. "Done?" she asked.

He nodded. Rounding the desk, he looked at the dogs, amber eyes shining as they patently willed him to take them for a run. He raised his brows at them, hesitated, then looked at her. "Shall we? We've time enough for a walk on the ramparts before we ride back."

She acquiesced with a smile, held out her hands, and let him pull her to her feet. Into his arms. He bent his head and stole a swift kiss, then, closing his hand about one of hers, headed for the door.

The hounds followed, eager and excited. They bolted the instant Charles opened the side door, but returned within a minute to gambol about them before rushing off to follow some scent.

Hand in hand, they walked down the lawns and climbed the steps up to the broad curve of the ramparts. The breeze had turned brisk, plucking at her hair, sending errant wisps curling about her face. Catching them, vainly trying to tuck them back, she glanced at Charles; no matter how strong the wind, his curls merely ruffled, then fell back into place.

She stifled a humph; they strolled on.

They'd reached the middle of the long curve when Charles stopped. He turned to her, looked into her eyes, his face set, his expression serious.

She looked back at him, was about to raise her brows in query when his grip on her hand tightened.

"Marry me."

Her eyes flew wide; her jaw dropped. "*W-what?*"

His gaze hardened, the line of his lips thinned; the dominant and domineering Norman lord looked down at her. "You heard me."

She managed to catch her breath. "That's not the *point*!" She tugged and he released her; she put both hands to her head, as if she could hold her whirling wits down.

He was the only person who could throw her so off-balance; it took her a moment to steady her thoughts. She stared at him. "I only realized this afternoon what you were about, what you've been leading up to—that you were going to ask—but I thought you'd wait at least until after your investigation is ended and this horrible murderer was caught!"

"So I thought, so I intended, until you favored me with your recent revelations."

His accents were clipped, his words uninflected. She eyed him, increasingly wary. "What have my recent revelations to say to anything?"

Dark blue eyes bored into hers; he wasn't amused. "You cannot expect to tell me you've fantasized for years about being my lady—*and* in such an explicit way—and *not* expect me to suggest that, in the circumstances, marrying me would be a good idea."

In this mood, focused and intent on gaining victory, he could be quite devastating; the scent of leashed aggression—leashed at his whim—was strong. Feeling very like his prey, she blinked at him. "I haven't had time to think—"

"You don't need to think, just answer." He stepped toward her.

"No!" She held up a hand, pressed her palm to his chest. "Wait, just *wait*!" He stopped; she caught a quick breath and stepped back—put enough distance between them so her wits could function—and shifted her gaze from his face. "I have to think."

His response to that, muttered beneath his breath, wasn't complimentary. She ignored it, but had to fight to ignore him, to dim the effect of him at close quarters in his present mood. Her senses flickered, acutely alert; she was supremely conscious of the steely purpose in him, and that it was directed, fully, at her.

He was much more forceful, more potent, than he'd been years ago, battle-hardened, but also battle-scarred; to her, the latter only made him more interesting, more compelling, not less. Their attraction now operated on multiple levels, direct and indirect, physical and emotional; refusing to meet his eyes, she drew in a deeper breath and tried to reach past it.

His need of her was real; she didn't question that. For it, he'd been willing to play the supplicant to seduce and persuade her; he'd asked rather than demanded or, worse, commanded—which, she knew, he could have done. But he'd wanted her to give herself, and been willing to give himself to gain that . . . was his need for her a symptom of love?

She glanced at him, but could see nothing beyond hard-edged impatience in his face, and an intensity of emotion in his dark eyes that took her breath away . . . she hurriedly unfocused. Even so, she could feel that emotion focused on her; whatever drove him, whatever compelled him with respect to her, was strong and immensely powerful.

Was it love? If he loved her . . . did he know? Even if he did, and she asked, would he acknowledge it?

All she had were unanswerable questions, but she needed an answer, now. What was it to be? No?

The instant the word formed in her mind, her inner self

rose up and dug in its heels. After all these years, to have all she'd ever desired, the future she'd always wanted and still so desperately yearned for, dangling before her . . . how *could* she refuse without knowing if the prospect was real? She wasn't such a coward; *no* wasn't an option, not yet.

Regardless, she wasn't about to settle for anything less than love; on that, her conviction had never wavered. So she couldn't say *yes* either, not unless she was sure . . .

Drawing in a tight breath, she refocused on his eyes, felt his instant attention, the honing of his senses. "*If* you give me what I want, then yes, I'll marry you." She held his gaze steadily, lifted her chin. "As soon as you like."

Something leapt in his eyes at her "yes," but he quickly concealed it, screened it. He didn't immediately respond, but searched her eyes, then flatly asked, "What you want. Am I to take it that's the same thing your other suitors didn't know to give you?"

"Didn't know, didn't know how to give, or couldn't or wouldn't give." She nodded. "Precisely."

Exasperation flared in his eyes as he considered her; she could see him assessing his options. Then he nodded—once, determinedly—and caught her hand. "Agreed."

She blinked.

Charles raised her hand to his lips, kissed, and searched her eyes again; she hadn't yet seen the truth, hadn't yet identified his motive. "Until I discover what this thing you want is, and give it to you, we continue as we are—as lovers."

His tone made it clear there was no question, not one he would countenance; after a moment, she nodded. "I never was one to slice off my nose to spite my face."

His lips twitched; he hurriedly straightened them, but the fraught tension that had enveloped them nevertheless eased.

She studied him, puzzled, suspicion dawning in her silver-gray eyes.

"Come." He closed his hand about hers, whistled for the dogs. "We can leave the dogs in the stables. We'd better head back."

Frowning, she let him turn her; hand in hand, at his direction, they walked briskly back along the ramparts—too briskly to talk.

He'd got what he wanted; his impulse was to crow and dance, but he reined in all expressions of triumph—time enough for that when this was all over and the murderer caught.

She'd been right about that; it would have been wiser to wait and ask her then, but as usual between her and him, wisdom hadn't featured—it had flown the instant she'd told him she'd indulged in erotic fantasies about them all those years ago. Even now, with victory assured, although he accepted the impulse, and on one level—a purely male, highly possessive level—understood it, he wasn't thrilled that it had been strong enough to *compel* him to seize the moment and ask her to marry him, outright, without any preparation.

He was also not thrilled over the way she'd replied—*yes* would have been much neater—but at least she hadn't said "No." "No" hadn't been an option; he was mildly relieved not to have been forced to point that out.

But he'd achieved what his conqueror's soul, that part of him she'd so efficiently stirred to action, had demanded— her agreement to marry him. To be his countess, to be always by his side, his anchor in this world, the mother of his children; his list of the facets of her role was extensive. He'd already decided he'd give whatever it took to make her his— she already had his soul, even if she didn't know it—and he had a very good notion of what the "thing" she wanted was.

If he'd wished, he could have given her the words there and then, and convinced her of their truth, but they did still have a murderer to catch, and until they did, he'd keep the news of his surrender secret.

Too much knowledge could be a bad thing. He didn't know how the game would play out, what the next days would bring, but if she knew he loved her with all his heart and would give her anything, he could foresee scenarios where doing what he knew to be right and necessary to protect her would only be more difficult. Even more nightmarish were those imagined scenarios where the murderer realized just how much she meant to him and thought to use her as a hostage.

A mental shudder racked him. For one instant, the vulnerability of loving her shone bright as crystal and pierced him to the heart. Yet he couldn't stop; all he could do was grit his teeth and bear the consequences.

He'd involuntarily tightened his grip; he felt her hand, delicate bones, feminine warmth and softness, enclosed in his, let his senses reach farther and registered her supple, svelte form beside him, her long legs keeping pace, and felt the momentary apprehension fade.

He smiled, nearly laughed, then remembered and abruptly sobered. He glanced at her, and caught her now openly suspicious scowl. He met it with blank innocence and looked ahead.

They reached the stable. Their horses were waiting; he lifted her up and held her stirrup, then crossed to where Domino stood and threw himself into the saddle. The triumph buoying him was almost too great to hide. Across the stable yard, he met her eyes, and waved to the entrance. "Let's ride."

Side by side, they thundered up to the escarpment. Then they flew.

Nicholas, exceedingly pale, wan yet transparently determined, joined them in the dining room for dinner. By unspoken accord no mention was made during the meal of the revelations he'd promised to make, but when they were finished, they all rose and repaired to the library.

Penny led the way to the armchairs grouped before the fireplace. She sank into one; Nicholas went to the other. Charles picked up a straight-backed chair, set it beside her armchair, and subsided in his usual graceful sprawl.

He looked at Nicholas, and raised one black brow. "So— where do you propose to start?"

Nicholas met his gaze, hesitated, then said, "At the beginning. But before I say anything, you need to know that no real secrets were ever sold, traded or in any other way given to the French, at least not by any Selbornes."

Charles studied him for an instant, then quietly said, "You aren't going to tell me that this whole business—my involvement, my ex-commander's, even the murderer's—is, for want of a better phrase, wide of the mark?"

"Oh, no." Nicholas's lips twisted. "The murderer certainly knows the right score. Even you and your ex-commander—everything you've been investigating is perfectly real, not any conjuror's trick. But you and he have throughout been ignorant of one vital element."

Charles grunted. "That much I'd guessed."

Nicholas nodded. "So . . ." He leaned back in the chair, rested his head against the padded back and fixed his gaze on them both. "It started in the 1770s. My father was a junior aide at our embassy in Paris. Paris in those days was the city of civilization; everyone who was anyone lived there much of the time. Howard, your father"—he looked at Penny—"like mine, was as yet unmarried. He came to visit my father and stayed for some years. During that time, my father was approached, oh, at a very friendly level, to, I believe they termed it *advise* the French on a minor matter of English-French diplomacy.

"At first our fathers were shocked, but that was soon overtaken by excitement." Nicholas looked at Charles, wearily said, "To understand what happened next, you have to understand the Selborne wild streak."

Charles raised his brows, fought not to glance at Penny. "Wild streak?"

Nicholas nodded. "I don't have it, thank God. My father does. You haven't met him, but he's . . . I think the most apt adjective is 'incorrigible.' You knew Granville—suffice to say he and my father were kindred spirits. If anything, my sire was—still is—the more outrageous. Howard, Penny's father, had the streak, too, but a milder version. He wasn't so likely to instigate outrageous schemes, but he responded to the lure nonetheless."

Nicholas sighed. "So there my father was, a young, titled, wealthy nobleman with connections to everyone, in Paris, then the shining capital of the world, with his closest friend and stalwart supporter by his side—with an opportunity to play a grand game with the French being laid before him."

"A game?" Charles said.

"That's how they saw it, the three of them—my father, Howard, then Granville. It was always a game, a great, glorious, outrageous game, with them always the victors."

Charles exchanged a quick glance with Penny, then asked, "What were the elements of this game?"

"My father more or less drew up the rules. He agreed to advise the French, but because of his position within the embassy, they needed an intermediary they could trust, namely Howard and later Granville. Payment was to be a pillbox for Howard for successfully passing on the advice, and a snuffbox for my father for the advice itself. They'd both been toying with starting collections; this seemed to them god-sent. At that time in France, all things aristocratic were already being devalued, so those dealing with our benighted parents were ready enough to promise them items of a certain value, drawn from various private, often royal, estates, in exchange for said advice.

"*That* was the basis of the agreement. What the French didn't know was that my father was truly brilliant—still is— at anything to do with Eurpoean diplomacy and foreign affairs. He sees into things, picks up nuances"—Nicholas shook his head—"I still go in awe of him, as does everyone in his section at the F.O."

After a moment, Nicholas met Charles's gaze. "The critical thing the French didn't know was that my father fashioned his 'advice' from whole cloth."

Charles blinked. "He made it up?"

Nicholas smiled wryly. "Therein lay the challenge of the game."

Charles stared at him, then slumped back in the chair and looked at the ceiling. A full minute passed, then he looked at Nicholas. "I've seen the pillbox collection. We're talking of one or two pieces of concocted advice passed every year for fortysomething years."

Nicholas nodded.

"And the French never found out?"

"Not until after Waterloo. I told you my father's brilliant, but not about military affairs. Initially, he avoided anything military in his 'advice.' The French didn't care—back in the seventies they were more interested in politics, treaties, and bureaucratic secrets. They were so impressed by my father's 'advice,' which always seemed so accurate, over the years they came to regard him as an unimpeachable source."

"How," Penny asked, "could his advice have appeared accurate if it was made up?"

"The French were asking about real situations—there was always a framework of real events." Nicholas shifted, easing his bandaged shoulders. "In politics and diplomacy, when you're studying events in another country, what you see is essentially puppets on a stage. You see what's played out on the stage—but you can't see what's going on behind the curtain, what's being done, what strings pulled and by whom, to cause the actions on the stage. With his insight, my father created alternate behind-the-curtain scenarios to the real ones, scenarios that nevertheless accounted for the actions the French could see."

Charles nodded. "I've come across that sort of thing— misinformation of the highest caliber, almost certain to be believed."

"Exactly."

Charles shook his head, not in disbelief but in amazement. "I still can't believe he managed it for so long."

"Part of that was due to his success within the F.O. The higher he went, the more he knew, the more he understood, the more his 'advice' fitted the observed outcomes—and the more the French believed him."

"What brought the game undone?"

"In a way, it was Napoleon. When the Peninsula Wars started, the French unsurprisingly wanted information on military matters. Initially, that wasn't hard to refuse on the grounds it wasn't something my father would be privy to, but then came Corunna, and the early losses, and, of course, Selbornes have always been patriotic to our toes.

"M'father knew whatever he told the French stood a good chance of being believed. He considered telling the appropriate authorities of his 'game,' but decided they would probably not approve, and quite possibly not understand. So, essentially on his own, he decided to embark on military misinformation by including in his otherwise diplomatic advice snippets about military affairs. To do so, he cultivated a friend in the War Office. Given his high status, that was easy enough. He didn't need to know much, just enough to, with a minor comment, steer the French in the wrong direction, or misadvise them of the timing of events—that sort of thing. Nothing the French actually wanted to know about, just low-level events, very hard to check, very much open to change at the last minute."

"And they continued to be taken in?"

"Yes. At that time, he'd been their 'advisor' for decades and had, as far as they knew, never let them down. He'd also encouraged them to think he was addicted to his collecting." Nicholas shrugged. "I'm not sure that he's attached to the snuffboxes themselves so much as that they represent each 'triumph' he's had in misleading the French."

"I take it," Charles said, jumping ahead, "that the murderer has been sent here to, in effect, render punishment?"

Nicholas's expression turned grim. "That seems to be the case."

"You said they found out after Waterloo." Penny's head was reeling. "How? What happened?"

"Remember what it was like then," Nicholas said, "just a year ago? The near frenzy, tales of the 'Corsican Monster,' and so on. My father was tired of it—he wanted an end. Especially when Granville insisted on enlisting."

Penny straightened in her chair. "Your father came here, just before Granville left. He tried to talk Granville out of going—I heard him."

Nicholas nodded. "He didn't want Granville to go. He

tried to convince him by sending a last message to the French, tried to get Granville to believe that that was enough for him to do. Granville ran the message, of course, but he wasn't about to stop there. He still rode off the next day."

"What was that last message?" Charles asked.

Nicholas met Charles's eyes. He was patently exhausted, but gamely went on, "My father knew very little of Wellington's plans. No one did. But through the years of the Peninsula campaigns, my father had, through misdirecting the French, learned a great deal of Wellington's strategies. When it comes to predicting how people will react when faced with given situations, my sire possesses an innate flair. So he tried to predict Wellington.

"He had access to excellent maps. He studied the terrain, and accurately picked the battlefield. He wanted a snippet, something to divert French attention, just a tiny push in the wrong direction. And this time he didn't care if they found him out, because he knew this time the dice were being rolled for the last time."

"What did he tell them?" Charles was leaning forward, elbows on his knees.

Nicholas smiled. "He told them precious little, but he dropped one place name."

Charles stared at him, simply stared. "Don't tell me. It begins with an 'H.'"

Penny glanced at Charles, surprised by the sheer awe in his voice. She looked back at Nicholas.

Who nodded. "He told them Hougoumont."

Charles swore softly, at length, in French.

"Indeed." Nicholas shook his head. "For all that I think he's a madman—" He broke off, gestured. "What can you say?"

Charles swore again and surged to his feet. He paced back and forth, then halted and looked at Nicholas. "I was on the field, not near Hougoumont, but none of us could understand why Reille was so obsessed with taking what was simply a protective outpost."

"Precisely. He thought it was more than an outpost, because he'd been led to think so. My father is a past master at planting ideas without ever actually stating them."

"*Hell!*" Charles raked a hand through his hair. "The French will *never* forgive him for that."

"No. And I don't think it's only that, either."

Charles looked at Nicholas; after a moment, he nodded. "Once they had reason to suspect, they looked back, and realized . . ."

"With the passage of years there would now be enough information available—diplomats have a terrible tendency to write memoirs—to expose at least some of his early 'advice' as completely bogus."

"And once they started looking . . . good God! Talk about rubbing salt into an open wound." Charles slumped back in his chair; his expression grew distant and progressively stony. "That's why," he said softly, "they've sent an executioner."

Nicholas studied his face, then asked, "Are you using that term figuratively, or literally?"

Charles met his gaze. "Literally." He glanced at Penny, verified that although she was pale, she was her usual composed self. "In the world of informers and 'advisors,' there are such people."

After a moment, he frowned at Nicholas. "Why didn't you tell me this as soon as I informed you why I was here?"

Nicholas looked back at him. "Would you have believed it?"

When Charles didn't immediately answer, Nicholas continued, "Think back to what you said last night. You had most of the information, and from it you deduced we, the Selbornes, had been passing secrets for decades. The evidence is the boxes—the pillboxes here and the snuffboxes my father has. Who would believe they'd all been paid for essentially by one man's imagination? You know more than most about the business, yet you admitted you found it difficult to believe."

Nicholas paused, then said, "There is no evidence my father passed concoctions and not the truth. It's much easier to believe, given the boxes and their value, that he passed real information for decades, and for some reason has now fallen out with his ex-masters."

Charles held his gaze, then straightened in his chair. "You're right except for one piece of information, and that you don't know."

"What?"

"There's evidence by default that whatever your father passed, it wasn't real. My ex-commander, Dalziel, is very good as his job, and he never could find evidence of any F.O. secrets actually turning up on the other side." Charles stood, and stretched; at long last, the whole jigsaw was in place, barring only the executioner's identity. He looked at Nicholas. "If it comes to it, and I don't believe it ever will, not now, I'm sure Dalziel will be able to trace, and prove, instances of your father's misdirection."

"Oh." Nicholas blinked up at him, then asked, "So what do we do next?" He grimaced. "I hope you're reading your ex-commander correctly because you haven't seen the snuffboxes."

"Knowing Dalziel, he'll be more interested in talking with your father."

"In that, I wish him joy. The old man drives me insane."

Charles grinned. "He'll probably take to Dalziel." He studied Nicholas's careworn face, and sobered. "When did you learn of"—he gestured—"your father's wild game?"

Nicholas snorted and closed his eyes. "He never told me. He, Howard, and Granville all knew I wouldn't approve, that I'd force them to stop, so they kept it their secret."

"They didn't tell me, or anyone else, either," Penny said.

Nicholas nodded. "I found out last December when by chance I came upon him in the priest hole here. He was examining the pillboxes. Once I'd seen them, they had to be explained. That was the first I'd heard of it."

Charles hesitated, then said, "Your father retired from the F.O. in '08."

Without opening his eyes, Nicholas nodded again. "But I was there by then, and senior enough to have dispatch boxes frequently with me at home, preparing them for the secretary or the minister, or analyzing the latest developments." He sighed. "My father was always a night owl. He knew how to handle the boxes. It was easy to take a peek when everyone else was abed. I never guessed . . ."

"Why would you?" Charles paced. "When the murderer killed Gimby, you must have suspected what he was after. Why didn't you leave?"

Eyes still closed, Nicholas's lips twisted. "Granville was gone, and so was Howard. The French didn't know me specifically, but I assumed whoever they'd sent would believe that, as my father's son, I'd been a player in the game. Then when Mary was killed, I realized he must have been sent to get some of the boxes, too . . ." He shrugged, winced, and caught his breath as his wounds pulled. "It seemed wiser to stay, and give him a target here . . . and you were here, too."

"Better here than at Amberly, or in London?"

Nicholas's lips quirked, but he didn't reply.

Charles looked at Penny, read her concern; Nicholas was wilting fast. "The next thing we need do is to lay the whole before Dalziel—we can work on that tomorrow. There's nothing more to do tonight—we may as well retire."

Nicholas nodded, opened his eyes, and struggled to sit up.

Sliding a hand beneath Nicholas's arm, Charles helped him to his feet. Nicholas stood, almost swaying, then he gathered himself. "Thank you."

Penny rose. She and Charles walked with Nicholas, one on either side, up the stairs. When they reached the top, Nicholas smiled, tired but faintly amused, and saluted them. "I can manage by myself from here."

Impulsively, Penny put a hand on his arm, stretched up, and kissed his cheek. "Take care. Ring if you need help. Charles has guards doing the rounds all night, so don't be surprised at the footsteps. We'll see you at breakfast."

Nicholas nodded and turned away. They watched him walk slowly to his room, open the door, and go inside.

Together, they turned. She slipped her hand in Charles's arm, and they headed for her room.

Ten minutes later, she slipped under the covers, and snuggled up against Charles. He was lying on his back, hands behind his head, staring up at the ceiling. One hand on his chest, she pushed back enough to look into his face. "What are you thinking?"

His gaze flicked down to meet hers. "That strange though it seems, having disliked him and having him dislike me on first sight, I now have a certain sympathy for old Nicholas." His lips curved. Drawing his hands from under his head, he closed his arms about her and lifted her so she lay atop him. "He's had to deal with the Selborne wild streak, and he's really not up to it."

She arched a brow. "And you are, I suppose."

He smiled, devilishly, and shifted beneath her. "Oh, yes."

CHAPTER

19

THEY RECONVENED OVER THE BREAKFAST TABLE THE NEXT morning and decided on their way forward. Nicholas and Charles would work on a detailed report for Dalziel. Penny, meanwhile, would make a detailed inventory of the pillboxes.

Charles insisted on instituting formal guard patrols around the house as well as maintaining those inside. "We want to leave him in no doubt that we've taken his measure. Later, we can appear to be less vigilant and invite him in—when we're ready, and on our own terms."

Nicholas was hesitant over potentially exposing the staff to further danger. Penny argued that that wasn't how they, the staff, would see things; in the end, she summoned Norris and Figgs, whose patently genuine reactions to Charles's suggestion reassured Nicholas.

They left the breakfast parlor together. Penny went with Nicholas to the library, ostensibly to get papers and pencil to make her inventory, in reality in response to Charles's silent direction to keep an eye on Nicholas, who was still very weak, while Charles went to organize his patrols.

She busied herself making a list of the pillboxes in the library. With both display cases smashed, Figgs and the maids had arranged the boxes on two side tables, leaving the cards scribed in her father's hand in a neat pile. Matching each card with the correct box took time. She'd just completed the task when Charles returned.

He nodded to her and went to join Nicholas at the desk, pulling up a chair to one side. Quickly listing the boxes and their descriptions, Penny listened as he and Nicholas discussed how best to structure their report. Detecting no difficulties between them, she collected a magnifying glass and headed for the door—and the sixty-four boxes concealed in the priest hole.

When she came downstairs more than two hours later, her wrist was sore. Entering the library, she saw Charles writing at the end of the desk; she knew he was aware of her, but he didn't look up. Nicholas was sitting in his chair, his head back, eyes closed.

As she neared, his eyes opened; he went to smile, but the gesture turned into a pained grimace. "I think we've got the salient points covered."

"Nearly finished," Charles said. "I'll send one of your grooms to carry it to the Abbey. One of my lads will take it to London."

Presumably Charles's grooms knew where to deliver such missives. Penny murmured, "Luncheon will be ready as soon as you've finished."

Charles nodded and kept writing.

Fifteen minutes later, with the final draft completed, reread, and signed by Nicholas, then countersigned by Charles and dispatched with not one but two grooms to the Abbey, they headed for the dining parlor.

They dallied over the meal. According to Charles, there was little they could do but wait.

"We know who he is—a French agent. We know his mission—to execute the Selbornes, Amberly at the very least, for crimes against the French state, and to recover all or some of the pillboxes and snuffboxes. What we don't know is what disguise he's wearing. So we wait until either he shows his hand, or we learn something to the point from Dalziel."

"Dalziel . . ." Nicholas sipped the red wine Em had insisted he drink. "He seems to wield considerable power."

Charles nodded. "I have no idea whether that power derives from his position, secret as it is, or from his real self—his personal standing, his real title, his real name—all of which are even more secret than his position."

Nicholas studied his glass. "I've heard . . . whispers, never anything more. He seems a conundrum, at least within the bounds of Whitehall. He behaves as if he has no personal ambition whatever."

Penny watched Charles roll the comment around in his head, fitting it with his own observations.

He shook his head. "That's not quite accurate. I seriously doubt Dalziel has any personal ambition toward political or public life—I suspect it wouldn't be an option for him. That must make him an oddity in Whitehall; with no civil service future at stake, the mandarins would have no leverage over him. *However*, when it comes to ambition of a different sort, relentless determination . . ." He drained his glass. "I think he could give us all lessons."

Nicholas raised his brows, intrigued; Penny kept her own counsel.

The conversation drifted to other things, but they were merely passing the time. Charles had sent instructions to Filchett to redirect any communication from London to the Hall, so they no longer needed to ride to the Abbey but could remain with Nicholas—keeping a watch on Nicholas.

Penny, Figgs, Em, and Norris had discussed the advisability of Nicholas's resting; he was still pale and drawn. Penny held herself ready to distract him with some comment every time Norris, with the unobtrusive deftness of the best of his kind, refilled Nicholas's wineglass.

At two, Nicholas could no longer stifle his yawns. "I think," he said, blinking dramatically, "that perhaps I should lie down for a while."

"An excellent idea." Laying aside her napkin, she pushed back her chair. "While you're upstairs, I'll use your desk to make a proper list of the boxes."

They rose and went into the hall; she and Charles watched as Nicholas climbed the stairs. Once he'd disappeared, Charles turned to Norris.

Who forestalled him. "Two of the footmen are already upstairs, my lord."

"Good." Taking her hand, he started for the door. "Your list can wait. Let's get some air."

She'd had enough of describing boxes and makers and marks; she let him tow her out onto the porch. "We could walk through the shrubbery."

He glanced at the high green hedges, shook his head. "I've developed a dislike of your shrubbery."

She looked at him in surprise.

"It's too closed in, and this madman seems to like it." He drew her arm through his and set off across the lawns, away from the shrubbery.

She thought, then glanced around at the wide lawns, the occasional trees, and nearby fields. "What if he uses a pistol?"

"He'd need to be reasonably close, within good range, and pistols have only one shot, have to come from somewhere, go somewhere, and are not all that easy to hide." He paced beside her, looking down yet, she was quite sure, not seeing. "Besides, we've seen two of his kills. He likes to be close, for the act to be personal. He wants to kill Nicholas, and probably you, too, and certainly Amberly, but he'll use a knife or his bare hands."

She shivered.

He glanced at her, squeezed her hand reassuringly. "It's actually his weakness. As long as we can keep him at a distance from you three, make sure he can't get close, he'll be stymied. Eventually, he'll try something reckless, then we'll have him."

Looking up into his face, into his dark eyes, she saw nothing but supreme confidence. "You're very sure of all this."

Charles shrugged, looked down as they walked on.

"I suppose you're used to it."

For a moment, he didn't reply, then he said, "That's true in a way, but . . . I was usually in his position."

Drawing breath, he looked up, met her eyes—and saw not the faintest vestige of shock or consternation. Rather, her expression was a mirror for his own arrogant resolution; she'd guessed the truth and didn't care.

His lips quirked self-deprecatingly; looking ahead, he conceded, "You're right. In this instance, it helps."

They circled the house, then returned to the library, refreshed. Penny sat at the desk and composed a neat list. Halfway through, she put down her pen and wiggled her cramped fingers. "Remind me—why is this necessary?"

"Because once you've completed it, Norris and I will verify it as accurate, after which we'll both sign and date it. Then even if anything subsequently goes missing, we'll still have proof it was here."

She considered the reasons why that might be useful, sighed, picked up the pen, and continued transcribing.

When she'd completed the list, Charles took it and, leaving her to enjoy her cup of tea alone, retreated with Norris to the priest hole. She mentally wished them joy. Then Nicholas joined her, looking better than he had; she poured him a cup, and they sat in silence—a more companionable silence than she'd shared with him to date. One benefit of adversity shared.

Half an hour later, Charles returned. He handed the list to Nicholas. "I'd put that somewhere safe."

Nicholas glanced at it, then nodded. "Thank you." His gaze shifted to Penny. "Both of you." He drew in a deep breath, opened his mouth.

Charles dropped a hand on his shoulder. "Don't bother. We're all in this together, and aside from anything else, after learning the whole story, I'm dying to meet your father."

The comment surprised a bark of laughter from Nicholas. He swiveled to face Charles, but Charles, frowning, was moving to the windows that looked out along the drive.

"Visitors?" Penny wouldn't have been surprised; news of the attack on Nicholas would have percolated through the local grapevine.

Charles didn't immediately respond. Both she and Nicholas could now hear what he had; horses trotting up to the front steps. Charles started to smile, a smile that grew to unholy proportions as he turned back to them.

"Not visitors—Dalziel's sent reinforcements."

Two of them. Charles strode out to the front porch to greet them. Penny and Nicholas followed more slowly.

Charles went down the steps as the pair handed their horses to the grooms who'd come running. The men turned eagerly to meet him; there followed much shaking of hands and slapping of backs, and a few pointed, distinctly jocular remarks Penny suspected she wasn't supposed to hear.

The newcomers saw her and Nicholas; the trio turned and came up the steps.

"Your man at the Abbey told us you'd left instructions for all communications from London to be forwarded here—we decided, in the circumstances, we qualified." The taller of the two, a few inches shorter than Charles, smiled winningly at Penny as the three men stepped onto the porch. With fairish, wavy brown hair and hazel eyes, his clear-cut features set in an amiable expression, he was startlingly handsome in a quintessentially English way; he bowed gracefully to her. "Jack Warnefleet." His eyes twinkled as he straightened. "Lady Penelope Selborne, I presume?"

"Indeed." She smiled and shook his hand.

"Lord Warnefleet of Minchinbury," Charles clarified, halting beside him. "And this—"

The second gentleman smiled and reached for her hand. "Gervase Tregarth."

"Earl of Crowhurst," Charles added.

Surrendering her hand, Penny instantly placed Tregarth as a fellow Cornishman; he had the typical long planes to his face, the long limbs, and the short, curly hair often found on denizens of the region close to Land's End. His hair was a soft mousy brown, his eyes an amber shade of hazel, paler in color than Jack Warnefleet's, also sharper.

Smiling in return, she shook his hand. "It's a pleasure to welcome you both to Wallingham Hall."

They turned to Nicholas; Charles performed the introductions. Standing back, Penny seized the moment to examine Dalziel's reinforcements.

They were an interesting pair, tall, well proportioned, attractive; presumably, like Charles, they possessed other talents, too. Physically Charles was the most flamboyant of the trio, the one who caught the eye. Jack Warnefleet wasn't far behind him in that, albeit in very different style, yet watching him greet Nicholas with genial bonhomie, she wondered how much of his lazy, laughing amiability was a mask. Like Charles, she would swear his cheeriness was a facade and, behind it, he was a man with secrets.

As for Gervase Tregarth, his was a quieter, more austere handsomeness. He was altogether quieter; a quality of stillness hung about him that even the fluid grace with which he moved did not disturb. It occurred to her that like the others, he possessed a reserve, a distance he preserved from the world, but in his case, it was part of the cloak he habitually wore.

They were different, yet in many ways alike.

The introductions and exchanges complete, she moved forward to lead them into the house. "I'll have rooms prepared for you." She glanced back, met their eyes. "Your luggage?"

Jack looked at Charles. "We weren't sure of your dispositions—we left our things at the Abbey."

"I'll have them brought here." Charles waved them on.

Penny led them into the library. Crossing to the bellpull, she tugged, then moved to sink down on the chaise. The men gathered chairs about the fireplace, leaving the chaise to her and Charles. When they sat, she asked, "Tea and crumpets, or bread, cheese, and ale?"

They all opted for the cheese and ale. Guessing Jack and Gervase hadn't eaten since morning, when Norris appeared, she ordered a substantial tray. Charles asked for the luggage left at the Abbey to be fetched.

"So," Jack said as Norris departed, "what's been going on down here?"

"All Dalziel told us," Gervase said, "was that you'd fallen feetfirst into murder and mayhem, and could probably use a little support."

"Murder certainly," Charles said. "As for mayhem, that might yet come." He proceeded to outline events as they'd unfolded, digressing to describe the Selbornes' wild game. Like Charles, Jack and Gervase were intrigued; they, too, expressed ardent interest in meeting Nicholas's incorrigible sire.

By the time Charles brought them up to date, the bread, cheese, and ale Norris had quietly supplied had been devoured. Even Nicholas had partaken. Penny thought he looked considerably better.

"The one thing I really don't like is that business of him smashing the display cases." Gervase looked at Nicholas. "You said he sounded enraged?"

Nicholas nodded. "He was swearing, and that was before he saw me."

"Not the usual coolness one associates with a professional." Jack looked at Charles.

Tight-lipped, Charles nodded; Penny was instantly certain the point had occurred to him previously, but he hadn't deigned to mention it. "It fits with him being younger than we are, less experienced. Killing the maid, for instance, was an unnecessary act that called attention to his presence and alarmed and alerted the staff of the very house he needed to enter. He didn't need to do it, but he did."

"He's vain," Jack concluded. "He's also a bully, thinking to frighten people, and sure he'll get away with anything."

"That sounds right," Gervase said. "Which is where we step in to teach him otherwise."

Charles and Jack murmured agreement.

After a moment, Gervase looked up; he raised his ale mug to Charles, Penny, and Nicholas. His smile dawning, he drawled, "We haven't said so, but we're deeply grateful to you for giving us a chance to quit London."

Jack wholeheartedly agreed, and drank.

Eyes wide, Charles regarded them in mock-surprise. "I thought you both had plans?"

Jack and Gervase exchanged glances, then Gervase nodded. "We did."

"Unfortunately," Jack said, "the matchmaking mamas had even bigger plans." He shuddered eloquently. "In reality we're refugees seeking asylum."

The day had flown; it was soon time to change for dinner. Penny had Norris show Jack and Gervase to their rooms, then headed for her chamber. Half an hour later, they foregathered in the drawing room, then went into the dining room. Taking the chair at one end of the table, she sat Gervase and Jack to either side of her and had them recount all they knew of the latest London events.

They proved excellent sources of information; like Charles, their powers of observation and recall were acute, even though it quickly became apparent they had little real interest in the entertainments of the ton. They'd expected to take an interest, or have such interest develop; instead, they'd been disappointed. The ton, even at its frenetic best, was not, she suspected, exciting enough—not at base real enough—to satisfy such men, not after their recent experiences.

She listened, encouraged them; Charles sat back, a smile playing about his lips, adding the occasional taunt or leading question. Nicholas watched, quietly amused; to Penny's eyes, he was improving with every hour, although his wounds still clearly caused him pain.

Once the covers were removed, she remained while they passed the decanters, then at her suggestion they took their glasses and repaired to the drawing room to sit in comfort and talk. Inevitably, the discussion returned to the man they now referred to as "the French agent."

"I agree it's unwise to guess his identity when any day Dalziel will likely find enough to point an unerring finger at him." Jack drained his glass, glanced at Gervase, then looked at Charles. "But can't we work out some trap? One that will work regardless of which of the three he is?"

Charles leaned forward, his glass cradled between his hands. "Now you're both here, that would be my choice. He doesn't know you, or of you; there's no reason he'll know you're here. Quite aside from any Selbornes, he's after the pillboxes, but now knows they aren't easily accessible."

He sipped, then went on, "Tomorrow I'll show you the priest hole—it's the perfect hiding place, obvious once you know of its existence. Our first hurdle will be getting details of the priest hole to him in a way he'll believe."

"There are ways and means." Gervase grinned. "He'd believe a priest, wouldn't he? I do quite a good impersonation— how about as a clerical scholar come to study the priest holes of the district? Give a minor social event, get the suspects together, and let me expound on my fascinating studies."

Charles stared at him, then smiled and saluted him with his glass. "That would work."

The clock chimed eleven. Penny glanced at Nicholas. He was wilting again. She caught Charles's eyes.

He nodded almost imperceptibly, stood, and stretched. "We can develop our approach tomorrow, after you've viewed the hiding place itself."

They all got to their feet. Penny led the way upstairs, paused at the stair head to bid them all good night, then sailed—alone—down the corridor to her room.

Charles joined her ten minutes later, entering the room a mere minute after Ellie had left. Seated at her dressing table brushing out her hair, Penny glanced at him in the mirror, a warning on her lips, simultaneously realized how silly any such warning would be. Given the state of her bed every morning for the past week, Ellie would long ago have realized she was no longer spending her nights alone.

The thought sent a small, self-seductive shiver through her. She studied Charles's face as he walked farther into the room, shrugging off his coat, then starting to unknot his cravat; from his expression, he was already formulating, rejecting, and developing elements of a possible plan.

Refocusing on her reflection, she fell to more vigorously

brushing her hair while she considered, absorbed, how *re-lieved* she felt now Jack and Gervase were there. She knew beyond question that Charles would stand between her, Nicholas, and everyone else who was innocent, and the murderer, like a human shield protecting them. It wasn't that she'd thought, not even entertained the thought, that he'd fail.

But he was no longer facing the murderer alone.

Gervase had said he and Jack were grateful for the opportunity to leave London. She in turn was grateful they'd come.

Rising, she snuffed the candles in the dressing table sconces, leaving the candle on the table beside the bed to cast a soft glow. She'd donned a long white nightgown, purely on Ellie's account. Charles, in shirtsleeves and breeches, sat on the bed to ease off his boots. Drifting to the open window, she leaned against the frame and looked out at the courtyard, a sea of moon-washed shadows. "Jack and Gervase are members of your club, aren't they?"

When Charles didn't immediately reply, she glanced back to see him standing, barefoot, stripping off his shirt. She sensed his hesitation, and softly laughed. "You needn't think you're giving anything away. It's rather obvious—you're all very much alike."

"Alike?" He tossed the shirt over a chair, slowly walked toward her. "How?"

She watched him draw near, considered the excitement that licked down her nerves, that slowly tightened them. "There's a scent of danger about each of you. Beneath your glossy veneer, you're all dangerous men."

He halted before her, studied her face. "I'm not dangerous to you."

She reserved judgment on that; she let her lips curve, her brows quirk teasingly. "It's rather . . . fascinating."

He stepped closer, backing her against the window frame. "I'm not sure I approve of your being fascinated by them."

Latent jealousy roughened his drawl. She laughed, relaxing against the wood at her back, sliding her arms around his neck. She looked into his dark eyes, black as the midnight sky. "I'm hardly likely to exchange your attentions for theirs."

He looked down at her; in a flash of insight, she realized he was sure of her, that he knew he no longer needed to ask, but could be his true self, that he could demand and be certain of her response. His gaze lowered to her lips; one palm cruised the side of her waist and made her shiver.

His dangerousness hung in the air, shimmered, alive, around them. "Perhaps," he murmured, his voice deep and low, "I ought to convince you."

She licked her lips, felt her pulse accelerate, her body respond. "Perhaps," she replied, locking her gaze on his lips, "you should."

He didn't wait for further encouragement; his hands gripped her waist, his lips covered hers, and the danger closed in.

She gave herself up to it, caught her breath when he ravaged her mouth, then stepped into her, trapping her against the wall beside the window. Excitement flared and raced down her veins. The hard wall was cool, her skin screened only by the fine fabric of her nightgown, no real protection. Not from the elements, not from his hands. They roughly searched as if learning her anew, as if he'd never had her naked beneath him before.

His lips and tongue commanded, held her senses captive, riveted on the dizzyingly potent threat he represented. Even though she knew it wasn't real, that it was perception, not reality, her senses remained mesmerized, tensing, reacting, as if it were. As if she truly were his prey, and he was dangerous, as unrestrained and sexually powerful as she knew he had it in him to be.

Shivers of anticipation coursed her spine. She was dimly aware he'd pushed a hand between them, unfastening her nightgown, then he raised that hand and pushed the gown off her left shoulder, baring her breast.

He broke from the kiss and looked down, with deliberation cupped the lightly swollen mound, smiled as her flesh firmed. He closed his hand, then with his fingers caressed, slowly drawing sensation to the peak before closing his fingertips about it.

Head back against the wall, she sucked in a tight breath, tried to steady her whirling head. Watched his face as he possessed, for it was definitely that, a claiming. "Did you ever imagine . . . make up stories . . . ?" Her voice was a breathless thread, but he heard.

After a moment, he consented to reply, "My youthful fantasies ran more to pirates and the sirens they captured. Who then captured them."

His gaze flicked briefly to her face, then returned to her breast, now aching and tight. He shifted, pressing down the other side of her gown, transferring his attentions to her other breast. His face, chiseled and hard, looked unbearably male, unbearably beautiful in the moonlight.

She licked her lips. "Those sirens . . . what were they like?"

He glanced again at her face, then reached up and caught her wrist, lifted her limp hand from his shoulder, drew it down, and pressed her palm, closed her hand, about his erection.

She heard the sharp intake of his breath, sensed the sudden leaping tension as she boldly obeyed and caressed him.

From beneath heavy lids, eyes gleaming, he watched her, shifting his hips, thrusting languidly into her hand. "Strange to tell, those sirens were like you."

He bent his head and found her lips, teased, taunted, while his hands ministered to her breasts, fracturing her senses.

She drew back, gasped weakly, "Like me?"

Beneath her hand, his erection felt like iron—heavy, hard, and rigid.

"They looked like you." Releasing her breasts, he framed her face, tipped it up, searched her face, her eyes, then bent his head and took her mouth in a searing kiss that abruptly plunged them back into dangerous waters. Into the dark, swirling promise of what might be.

Into the realm where fantasy and reality wove one into the other and back again.

His hands drifted from her face, gripped her hips; he

shifted into her, pressing her to the wall, impressing his hard, flagrantly masculine body on hers. Insinuating one hard thigh between hers, he lifted her until she rode the steely muscle, potent threat and promise combined.

Brusquely, he pulled back from the kiss, murmured against her lips, "Like you, they were always wild."

His lips returned to hers, dominant and commanding, rapaciously plundering; she met him, matched him, and refused to yield. Boldly challenged him instead, then shuddered under the onslaught, the undisguised, unrestrained, elemental passion he unleashed.

Abruptly her wits were spinning beyond her control, her senses dragged down, immersed in the greedy heat pouring from him, in the furious clash of desire and need. Her limbs weakened, her flesh softened, waiting, wanting, yet still daring to hold against him; with every passing second, the empty ache burgeoned and grew, and drove her to surrender.

Then she felt her nightgown shift, realized he was raising it. Without conscious thought she eased her grip on him, drew her palm slowly, tauntingly, up his length, then searched for the buttons at his waist. She found them, flicked them free, pushed aside the folds of his clothing, and found him.

Closed her hand and slid it down his length, hot, hard, burning. Clasped, lightly scored. Deliberately incited him.

He dragged his lips from hers, dragged in a labored breath. Muscles bunched; he yanked her gown to her waist.

"Like you"—his words were almost too deep to make out, gravelly, grating, dark with forceful menace—"they were always in need of claiming."

He reached down, gripped her naked thighs, and lifted her.

Excitement, flaring anticipation and relief rushed through her; giddy, she closed her eyes, sucked in a breath, grabbed his shoulders for balance. Head back, braced against the wall, she felt him nudge into her softness, ease in just a fraction—then he stopped.

Held them both on the brink, nerves coiled, clenched, waiting . . .

She raised her lids, through the dimness found the dark glint of his eyes. Held them for a pregnant second, then provocatively murmured, "And did you claim them?"

He thrust into her, and filled her, not slowly, not fast, but powerfully, forging in, the latent strength in his body, so much greater than hers, blatantly evident. She couldn't have prevented him, denied him her body, held him out had she wanted to, not by any physical means.

He thrust deep, impaled her fully, then leaned close, and whispered against her lips, "I tried."

Her lips curved in response.

Physically, she was his. Emotionally, he was hers.

As if in acknowledgment of that truth, his gaze lowered to her lips. "I was never sure I succeeded."

He kissed her rapaciously, and their ride began. More forceful, less civilized, more real than before. The sense of being a figment of the other's fantasy released what little inhibitions they possessed, unlocked and let fall the last restraints.

Let them both be as they dreamed of being, a revelation deeper, more intimate, more telling.

He held her against the wall, supporting her weight, and thrust heavily into her. She gasped, clung to his shoulders, gripped his hips with her knees, and rode every deep penetration.

When she broke from the kiss on a sob, he bent his head and feasted on her breasts. Took all he wished without quarter.

Ravished her, body, mind, and soul.

Even while her body shuddered, racked by a superbly gauged intimate assault wholly focused on bringing about her surrender, the elements of desire their roles revealed spun around her, through her.

Slowly coalesced even while he drove her to the brink, and over.

Until she screamed his name on a breathless cry, and shattered.

He withdrew from her and carried her to the bed, tossed her across it, stripped her nightgown away, stripped off his breeches, and joined her. Trapped her beneath him, with his thighs spread hers wide, settled between, caught her hands one in each of his, raised them level with her head, then pressed them to the coverlet as he braced his arms and rose over her, held her down as with one powerful surge he joined with her.

And took more. Demanded more, every last gasp, every last sob of helpless desire she had it in her to give.

Heat poured from him, turned their skins slick, burned through their veins, and still she met him, matched him, stayed with him. Gave all he asked, took all he gave in return. Exulted as from under weighted lids she watched him above her.

Hot, relentless, unforgivingly hard—and hers.

He drove her ruthlessly up and over the peak; her awareness fractured into slivers of glowing gold. She felt him follow hard on her heels into physical oblivion; he slumped atop her and she freed her hands, slid her arms around him and held him close—and that power that had grown immeasurably in the last weeks rose up and engulfed them.

In that moment of blessed peace, a sense of certainty bloomed and burgeoned within her.

Long moments passed before they eventually moved, just enough to find the pillows and slip under the covers, not enough to disturb the heavy pleasure that lay upon them, that had sunk to their bones, and deeper.

Curled within his arms, her head on his shoulder, she felt her lips curve as, borne on the cusp of sated slumber, the truth gleamed, clear, in her mind. Her fantasy had been an extension of their real lives—lord and lady—that was who they were. His fantasy, however . . . in it was embedded the real truth of what they were, what they meant to each other.

He was the pirate who had captured her.

She was the siren who, his captive, had captured him.

CHAPTER

❧ *20* ❧

THE NEXT MORNING, WHEN THEY GATHERED FOR BREAK-
fast, Nicholas was much improved, yet to his irritation was
straitly informed by Charles, Jack, and Gervase that he could
not stir a foot without a guard.

As their clear message was that they wouldn't permit him
to stir that foot, he had no option but to acquiesce.

"The patrols I set in place—in light of your arrival"—
Charles looked at Jack and Gervase—"I'm calling them
off. Normal enough seeing we've gone two days without
incident. If he's scouting about, he'll doubtless wait another day or so for all alarm to subside before making his
move."

"Regardless," Jack declared, working his way through a
plate of sausages, "we'll be here."

"I need to go into Fowey and check what my sources
there have unearthed," Charles said. "It might not be anything, but we can't afford to miss whatever scraps fate
deigns to throw us."

Gervase and Jack nodded. Nicholas looked resigned.
"Perhaps I should show these two the priest hole?"

Jack brightened. "Good idea."

Penny set down her teacup and pushed back her chair.
"I'll come with you, Charles—I want to speak with Mother
Gibbs." She rose with a smile for the others, but didn't catch

Charles's eye. Turning to the door, she spoke over her shoulder, "I'll change into my habit and meet you in the stables."

She could feel his gaze narrowing, arrowing on her back; blithely ignoring it, she glided out of the dining room.

He was waiting when she reached the stables; from the look in his eyes, he was less than impressed. She held up a hand before he could speak. "If I stay here, I'll be forced to go for a walk—I'll be safer with you."

The comment gave him pause, then, with a grimace, he surrendered and lifted her to her saddle.

Neither they nor their mounts had been out for two days; they took to the fields and galloped, eager for the exercise. When the outskirts of Fowey lay ahead, they reined in to a sensible pace.

In perfect empathy, they trotted toward the town. That empathy was deeper than before; from the moment she'd agreed to marry him, regardless of her qualification, she'd sensed the change in him. The absolute, unshakable confidence that she would be his come what may. Initially, she'd been suspicious, but there was no denying he knew her and her stubbornness well; after last night, his rock-solid confidence in their ultimate outcome had infected her. It could only mean that he was sure he could meet her condition, was committed to meeting it, confident he would. Which meant . . .

A *frisson* of expectation, of shining hope, surged through her; she glanced his way, let her gaze slide over him, then looked ahead. Perhaps, at last, their time had come . . . but first they had to catch the murderer.

They left their horses at the Pelican, took the downhill lanes to the quay, then wended up the familiar alleys to Mother Gibbs's door.

Even though it was midmorning, Charles had to knock three times before a towheaded lad opened it. Recognizing the youngest Gibbs, Charles asked for his mother, only to be informed in an uncertain tone, "Ma's in the kitchen givin' the others merry 'ell."

Charles blinked; sounds of a shrill altercation drifted up from the depths of the house. "Dennis and your brothers?"

The boy had recognized him; he nodded.

"We'll go in." Charles grasped Penny's hand and towed her past the lad, who blinked in surprise.

"Close the door," Charles reminded him.

Shaking free of his stunned stupor, the boy jumped to obey.

The kitchen lay at the end of the corridor that ran the length of the house. Penny ignored the closed doors they passed; the nearer they got, the louder and shriller the argument became. Charles ducked his head and they stepped down into the kitchen.

Mother Gibbs stood before the stove, in full flight, punctuating her statements with a heavy ladle that she banged on a chopping board on the table before her. Ranged on the other side of the table were her three eldest sons, all hulking, brawny sailors who towered over her, yet all three appeared to be trying to make themselves small, an impossible feat.

Glimpsing movement behind the wall of her sons, Mother Gibbs shifted, saw Charles, and broke off in midharangue.

The three brothers followed her gaze to Charles and Penny; Penny could almost hear their sighs of relief fall into the sudden silence.

Charles took in the situation in one glance; he held up a placating hand. "My apologies for interrupting, but I need to speak with you all, and time is short." When no one responded, just stared at him, he shifted his gaze from Mother Gibbs's florid countenance to Dennis's studiously blank face. Charles paused, tasting the silence. "Has anything happened?"

"*I'll* tell you what's happened!" Mother Gibbs thumped the ladle down. "These numbskulls sent my sister's boy off to keep watch somewhere and he's not been home and his mother's been here whining all morning."

She brandished the ladle at Dennis. "You know what I've told you 'bout getting your cousins involved—they're younger'n you lot. And now here we've had spies this and spies that for the last week 'til Sid's up and told Bertha he was out to keep watch last night, and he's not been back since."

Leveling the ladle at Dennis, she narrowed her eyes. "So you just get on out there to wherever you've sent him and tell him to get along home sharpish, or I'll have Bertha here whining over our teatime, and that I won't have, do y'hear?"

"Yes, Ma." The words were uttered in unison by all three brothers.

Dennis slid a harrassed look at Charles, then looked, somewhat sheepishly, at his mother. "Did Aunt Bertha say where he'd gone?"

"'*Course* not!" Lowering the ladle, Mother Gibbs opened her mouth—then registered the import of the question. She stared at her eldest son. "You know, don't you? You sent 'im—"

She broke off because Dennis was shaking his head, as were his brothers beside him.

"We didn't send him—or anyone—anywhere. Didn't need to." Dennis glanced at Charles. "His lordship here asked could we learn anything about those three gents he had his eye on—easy enough to get the stable lads as run with us to keep their eyes open and report anything odd they see."

Dennis looked at his mother. "We didn't send Sid anywhere—honest, Ma."

"But . . ." Mother Gibbs blinked, then looked at Charles. "Sid went out yesterday evening while it was still light. Told Bertha he was going to keep watch on some spy. She thought . . ." Mother Gibbs stepped to the side and sat heavily on a stool as the color drained from her face. "Oh, dear."

Charles agreed with her. He caught Dennis's eye. "Any idea who Sid took it into his head to watch?"

Grim, Dennis shook his head. "He didn't speak to me." He glanced at his brothers; both shook their heads.

Dennis sighed. "Sid's been itching to go out with us for months, but"—with his head, he indicated his mother—

"we've always put him off. Might be he heard what's been going on and thought to try his hand."

Charles held Dennis's gaze for a moment. "We need to search."

"Aye." Dennis looked at his brothers. "So I'm thinking."

There was a quality in their voices that both Penny and Mother Gibbs recognized; they exchanged glances, then Penny eased past Charles and went to crouch beside Mother Gibbs as the four men discussed organizing a search.

Mother Gibbs's hands clasped and unclasped in her lap; she looked more stunned than if one of her boys had struck her. Penny laid a hand over the old woman's fingers. "We can't do anything but wait—they'll find him."

Mother Gibbs blinked. "Bertha's Sam was lost at sea—that's why she's been so set against Sid going with the others. If something's happened to him because he *wasn't* running in Dennis's harness like all the others do . . ." She exhaled gustily; her gaze grew distant. "She'll be beside herself, our Bertha."

Penny wished she could offer some heartening platitudes, but when it came to this man—the murderer who'd walked among them for the past weeks—she couldn't believe enough to even hope.

She looked up to hear Charles commit the stable hands from both the Hall and the Abbey to the search, then he glanced at her.

"We need to get back."

She nodded and rose, her hand still resting over Mother Gibbs's. As before, the three Gibbs brothers had behaved throughout as if she wasn't there. She looked down at the old woman, met her old eyes, squeezed her hand, then went to join Charles.

He ushered her out of the house. They strode back to the Pelican Inn in record time. Charles paused only to speak with the grooms, spreading the word, then they were galloping back to the Hall even faster than they'd left it.

* * *

The news sobered everyone. Only Nicholas was game to suggest, "It *could* just be a coincidence."

The others all looked at him; although no one argued, none of them agreed. Penny knew what she hoped, but the sinking feeling in the pit of her stomach doused her usual confidence.

As Charles had called off the patrols, the Hall's grooms and stable lads joined in the search, spreading out to scout through the Hall's acres. Immediately after luncheon, one of the Abbey's grooms arrived bearing a missive from Dalziel. Charles took it and sent the groom back with orders for the Abbey staff to search the riverbanks from river mouth to the castle ruins.

He watched the groom ride off, then, hefting Dalziel's packet, walked inside.

Penny was waiting in the front hall; he waved her to the library and followed. The other three were there. All watched as he walked to the desk, picked up the letter knife, and slit the packet open.

Without bothering to sit, he spread out the sheets and read. Reaching the end of the second sheet, he glanced at their expectant faces. "Carmichael has no links with anyone suspicious, and he lost a brother and two cousins in the wars. Three friends have confirmed he's been dallying with a view to getting leg-shackled to Imogen Cranfield for more than six months. Altogether, I think that puts him lowest on our list of three."

Looking again at the second sheet, he came around the desk and sat. "Fothergill . . . they're still checking but have turned up nothing suggestive yet. The family's large—they're having trouble tracking down the right branch. As for Gerond, Dalziel reports that some of his inquiries have started to meet with Gallic shrugs . . . interesting. They're pressing as hard as they can but have nothing definite yet."

Jack nodded, jaw firming. "So Gerond goes to the top of our list, Fothergill is an outside chance, and Carmichael is unlikely."

"That," Charles said, refolding the letter, "sums it up."

"Tell me again," Gervase said, "what we know about Gerond."

Charles obliged. Jack asked, and Nicholas confirmed that his attacker had sworn in fluent French.

"Dalziel confirmed that Gerond has strong links with rabidly patriotic groups among the French." Gervase's lips thinned. "Those boxes—the pill- and snuffboxes. They might not rate all that highly to us, but if some ranked as French national treasures, that might account for someone like Gerond throwing in his hand with the new regime, even if to avenge old crimes."

Jack leaned forward, clasped hands between his knees. "He's of the right age, and he's seen some action, hasn't he?"

Charles nodded. "Some, but all on our side."

"Whoever this is, he's definitely had training, and some experience."

Penny sat on the chaise and listened as they discussed the characteristics and traits they felt the killer possessed; from there, they progressed to formulating plans to draw him into the open, into their grasp. It was clear Jack and Gervase, and even more Nicholas, had focused on Gerond as their man; to them, the evidence pointed that way. Charles, however . . . he was usually quick to act on instinct, yet in this he hung back, refraining from distinguishing between Gerond and Fothergill.

Consulting her own feelings, she had to admit that, to her, all fingers pointed to Gerond. It was Charles's quiet resistance to focusing solely on Gerond that emphasized the point she and the others were missing, but that Charles was not. Would not.

Charles had been a successful spy in France for years because he was, superficially, French; the French had always seen him as one of their own. What if their man was, in essence, a Charles-in-reverse?

The notion was chilling, but as she watched Charles steer their plans in such a way that they didn't preclude the enemy's being Fothergill, she realized just how real the possibility was.

They were still in the throes of tossing around possible

plans when the clatter of an approaching rider silenced them. They all listened, then Charles rose and went to the window overlooking the forecourt.

"A fisherman, presumably with a message from Dennis. This doesn't look good."

He headed for the door. Jack rose and followed him; the others remained in the library.

Charles went down the front steps as the fisherman slid to the ground. The man was plainly relieved to see him.

"M'lord." The man ducked his head, nodded to Jack behind him, then faced him. "Dennis Gibbs sent me. His cousin Sid . . ." The man swallowed, then went on, "They found him on the cliffs by Tywardreath. Throat slit. A bad business—the lad weren't no more'n eighteen. There were things—a knife, cloak, and other stuff—scattered about. Dennis said as you'd want to take a look."

Grim-faced, Charles nodded. He clapped the man on the shoulder. "Go around to the kitchen. I'll send for you once I'm ready."

The man ducked his head and went, following the groom who'd appeared to take his horse.

Jack stepped down beside Charles; they both watched the man walk away, head and shoulders bowed. "A bad business, right enough." Jack glanced at Charles. "You're going?"

Charles turned back into the house. "Yes, but you're staying."

Jack followed him back to the library. He told the others the news. Penny paled, but said nothing. Nicholas blanched; some of his recovered strength seemed to drain from him.

"You shouldn't go alone—there might be more we can do when we see the site." Gervase stood, joining Jack and Charles. "I know the area well enough, and the locals will accept me."

Jack hesitated, then nodded curtly. "Agreed. You two go—I'll hold the fort here."

Charles looked across the room, met Penny's eyes. "We'll be back before dusk or send word—if there's any scent to follow, that'll be our priority."

Penny nodded, watched him turn and stride out, Gervase at his heels. Jack watched them, too, then sighed, and came back to his chair. He smiled, resigned yet charming. "Just think of me as your watchdog."

They were still in the library, Nicholas at the desk dealing with estate matters, Jack sprawled in an armchair with a book, Penny frowning at the household accounts she'd fetched, Jack having declared he'd be much happier if both she and Nicholas remained in the same room, when the knocker sounded on the front door.

All three of them looked up. A second later, Norris's stately footsteps trod over the tiles; they heard the door open.

A rumble of male voices reached them—one Norris's, the other lighter. Straining her ears, Penny couldn't place the speaker. They hadn't heard any horse on the drive; whoever it was had walked to the door.

She turned as the door opened and Norris stepped in. Closing the door, he looked at her, then Nicholas. "Mr. Fothergill has called, my lord. He wishes to inquire whether it would be convenient to look around the house. I understand he's spoken with Lady Penelope on the subject. I would, of course, be happy to conduct him through the rooms we usually show."

Penny looked at Jack. "He's a student of architecture—he asked Charles and me what houses to view in the area. He called at the Abbey a few days ago, and Charles's butler showed him around."

Everyone looked at Jack.

Gaze distant, he frowned, then swiveled to look at Norris. "Send him in. Let's see how he shapes up."

Norris withdrew; Jack met Penny's, then Nicholas's eyes. "It's suggestive he's turned up just when Charles has been called away, but on the other hand, that could just be coincidence. Regardless, we should turn the opportunity to our advantage and see how much we can discover—if we can exclude him from our list, we could move more definitely against Gerond."

Penny nodded; she rose as the door opened, and Norris ushered Julian Fothergill in. He came to greet her, enthusiasm and eagerness in his face.

He shook hands with her, then Nicholas, thanking them with disarming candor for seeing him. "I would be quite happy to be shown around by your butler if you're busy."

"I'll take you around the house later," Penny said, "but first, won't you sit and tell us how your stay in Cornwall has gone?" Smoothly, she asked Norris for tea to be brought, then introduced Fothergill to Jack, giving no reason for the latter's presence.

Jack supplied one as the two shook hands. "I, too, opted for the allure of country life rather than endure London during the Season."

Fothergill grinned. "Just so. As my primary interest lies in things feathered and winged, London has little to offer by way of attraction."

They resumed their seats, Jack moving to sit beside Penny on the chaise while Nicholas took the armchair he'd vacated. At Penny's wave, Fothergill sat in the armchair opposite her.

"I take it," Jack drawled, "that you're lucky enough not to have to dance attendance at some office in town?"

"Indeed. I have enough to allow me to wander at will, and the family, thank heaven, are plentiful."

"So you're not from around here?" Jack asked. Fothergill's accent was unremarkable, unplaceable.

"Northamptonshire, near Kettering."

"Good hunting country," Jack returned.

"Indeed—we had some very good sport earlier this year."

Penny exchanged a glance with Nicholas; Jack and Fothergill embarked on a lengthy and detailed discussion of hunting, one which, to her ears, painted Fothergill as one who knew. Used to reading Charles, she picked up the little signs—the easing of tensed muscles—that stated Jack thought so, too.

Norris appeared with the tea tray; while she poured and dispensed the cups, then handed around the platter of cakes, the conversation turned to places visited in England, especially those known for bird life. Nicholas joined in, mentioning the Broads; Fothergill had wandered there. He seemed in his element, recounting tales and exploits during various trips.

At one point, they all paused to sip. Penny noticed Fothergill eyeing the books along the shelves behind the chaise. His eyes flicked to her face; he noticed her noticing. Smiling, he set down his cup. "I was just admiring your books." He glanced at Nicholas. "It's quite a collection. Are there any books on birds, do you know?"

Nicholas looked at Penny.

"I imagine there are, but I'm not sure where . . ." She glanced over her shoulder at the nearest shelves.

"Actually"—Fothergill set down his cup and pointed to a shelf behind the chaise—"I think that's a Reynard's *Guide*."

Rising, he crossed to the shelves and bent to look. "No." He sent them a smile. "Like it, but not." Straightening, he walked along the shelves, scanning the volumes. Penny faced forward as he passed behind the chaise.

Beside her, Jack leaned forward and placed his cup on the low table before them. Straightening, he started to turn to keep Fothergill in view—

Violence exploded from behind the chaise.

A heavy cosh cracked against Jack's skull. He collapsed, insensible.

Half-rising, Penny opened her mouth to scream—

A hand locked about her chin, forced it high, yanked her against the back of the chaise.

"Silence!"

The word hissed past her ear. Eyes wide, staring upward, she felt the blade of a knife caress her throat.

"One sound from you, Selborne, and she dies."

Penny squinted, saw Nicholas on his feet, pale as death, hands opening and closing helplessly as he fought to rein in the urge to react. His gaze was locked on the man behind her—Fothergill, or whoever he was.

"Stay exactly where you are, do exactly what I tell you, and I might let her live." He spoke in a low voice, one that held not the faintest thread of panic; he was master of the situation, and he knew it.

Nicholas didn't move.

"The pillboxes—where are they? Not the rubbish that was on display in here, but the real ones."

"You mean the ones my father appropriated from the French?"

Contempt laced Nicholas's tone.

She felt a tremor pass through the hard fingers locked about her chin, but all Fothergill said was, "You understand me perfectly."

His tone had turned to ice. He lifted Penny's chin higher until she whimpered; the knife pricked. "Where are they?"

Nicholas met Penny's eyes, then looked at Fothergill. "In the priest hole that opens from the master bedchamber."

"Priest hole? Describe it."

Nicholas did. For a long moment, Fothergill said nothing, then he quietly stated, "This is what I want you to do."

He told them, making it abundantly plain that he would feel not the slightest compunction over taking Penny's life should either of them disobey in the smallest way. He made no bones of his intention to kill Nicholas; it was Penny's life only with which he was prepared to bargain.

When Nicholas challenged him, asking why they should trust him, Fothergill's answer was simple; they could accept his offer, show him the pillboxes, and Penny might live, or they could resist, and they both would die.

"The only choice you have to make," he informed Nicholas, "is whether Lady Penelope's life is worth a few pillboxes. Your life is already irredeemably forfeit."

"Why should we believe you?" Penny managed to mumble; he'd eased his hold on her chin enough for her to talk. "You killed Gimby, and Mary, and now another young fisherman. I've seen you—you won't let me live."

She prayed Nicholas could read the message in her eyes; the longer everything took, the more time they could make Fothergill spend down there . . . it was the only way they could influence anything.

Briefly, Nicholas met her eyes, then looked at Fothergill, clearly waiting for his response.

Fothergill hissed a curse beneath his breath, a French one. "After today, my identity here will no longer be in question—why should I care if you've seen me or not?"

He paused. A moment passed, then he softly, menacingly drawled, "I'm not interested in wasting further time convincing you—I want to be finished and away before Lostwithiel and his friend return. So . . ."

Again he lifted Penny's chin, drawing her throat taut. Again the blade of his knife caressed. "What's it to be? Here and now? Or does she live?"

Nicholas's face was white, his lips a tight line. He nodded once. "We'll do as you ask."

"Excellent!" Fothergill wasn't above sneering.

Turning, Nicholas walked to the door. Reaching it, he halted and looked back, waiting.

At Fothergill's direction, Penny rose slowly from the chaise, then, chin still held painfully high, the knife riding against her throat, she walked before Fothergill to the door.

Her neck ached.

Halting her a yard from Nicholas, Fothergill spoke softly by her ear. "Please don't think of acting the heroine, Lady Penelope. Remember that I'm removing the knife from your throat only to place it closer to your heart."

He did so, so swiftly Penny barely had time to blink; she lowered her chin and simultaneously felt the prick of the blade through her gown, had an instant to regret she'd never taken to wearing corsets.

Fothergill clamped his left hand over her left arm, holding her to him, also hiding the knife he held pressed to her ribs between them.

He studied her face, then looked at Nicholas, and nodded.

Nicholas opened the door, scanned the front hall, then glanced back. "No one there."

Fothergill nodded curtly. "Lead the way."

Nicholas did, walking slowly but steadily across the front

hall and up the main stairs. Locked together, Penny and Fothergill followed.

In slow procession they approached the master bedchamber. Once inside, Fothergill told Nicholas to lock the door. Nicholas did.

Penny gasped as Fothergill seized the moment to release her arm and lock his arm about her shoulders, once again placing the knife at her throat.

Nicholas swung around at the sound, but froze when he saw Fothergill's new position.

Fothergill backed, dragging her with him to the side of the room opposite the fireplace. With the knife, he indicated the mantelpiece. "Open the priest hole."

Nicholas studied him, then slowly walked to the heavily carved mantelpiece. He took as long as he dared, but eventually twisted the right apple. Farther along the wall, the concealed panel popped open.

Fothergill stared at it. "I'm impressed." He motioned to Nicholas. "Prop the panel wide with that footstool."

Still moving slowly, Nicholas obeyed.

"Now walk around the bed, and sit on the side, facing the windows."

Feet dragging, Nicholas did.

"Keep your gaze fixed on the sky. Don't move your head."

Once assured Nicholas was going to obey, Fothergill urged her forward. He steered her to the corner of the bed, closer to the priest hole. When they reached it, he turned her so her back was to the bedpost; the tip of his knife beneath her chin held her there while, with a violent tug, he ripped loose the cord tying the bed-curtain back.

He lifted the cord, gripped it in his teeth, then grabbed first one of Penny's hands, then the other, securing both in one of his on the other side of the bedpost, stretching her arms back so she couldn't move. Only then did he take his knife from her throat, deftly placing it between his teeth as he removed the cord and quickly used it to lash her wrists together, effectively tying her to the post.

She mentally swore, searched desperately for something to slow things down, to delay or distract.

Fothergill tied the last knot, took his knife from his mouth, and moved around her; silent as a ghost, he glided toward Nicholas.

Who was still staring, unknowing, at the windows.

Penny kicked out as far as she could—and managed to tangle her feet and skirts in Fothergill's boots. Fothergill staggered, tried to free himself, tripped, fell. His knife went skittering across the floor.

"Nicholas—run! *Go!*"

Penny fought to keep Fothergill trapped, but he rolled away, wrenching free of her skirts.

Nicholas sprang to his feet, took in the scene, saw the knife lying free. His features contorted. Instead of obeying Penny, he flung himself on Fothergill.

"*No!*" Penny screamed, but too late.

Rolling on the floor, Nicholas grappled with Fothergill. Even had he been hale and whole, it would have been an uneven match. But Nicholas was injured and Fothergill knew where. Penny saw the punch aimed directly for Nicholas's injured right shoulder, saw it land, heard Nicholas's shocked, pained gasp. Fothergill's next blow plowed into Nicholas's jaw and it was over. Nicholas slumped unconscious; Fothergill clambered to his feet.

Swearing softly, continuously, in French.

From beneath lowered brows, his gaze locked on Penny.

She screwed her eyes shut and screamed—

He struck her savagely with the back of his hand.

Her head cracked against the bedpost, pain sliced through her brain. She sagged against the post, momentarily nauseated, dizzy, her wits reeling.

Fothergill swore viciously in her ear; she understood enough to know what he was promising. Then he moved away.

She dragged in a breath, forced her lids up enough to see. Through her lashes she watched as he swiped up his knife.

Hefting it, he turned to her, then his gaze went past her—to the priest hole.

The glittering boxes distracted him. She didn't move, sagging as if unconscious. He walked past her without a glance, paused on the threshold of the priest hole, then stepped inside.

Should she scream again? She had no idea whether there had been or would be anyone in the front of the house to hear. Her head was ringing; just thinking was painful. If she screamed again, now he had the knife once more in his hand . . .

Before she could decide if it was worth the risk, she heard a faint scraping sound. She thought it was Fothergill in the priest hole, but then it came again—she looked at the main door.

Nicholas had locked it, yet now it slowly, very slowly inched open.

She knew who stood in the shadows beyond even though, with the sun slanting in through the windows, with her eyes still watering with pain, she could only make him out as a vague shape.

Hope leapt and flooded through her. Her brain started to race. Opening her eyes wide, she frantically signaled to the open priest hole beside her. Not knowing where Fothergill was, she didn't dare move her head, but he couldn't see her eyes.

Slowly, clearly, Charles nodded, then silently closed the door.

Penny stared at the panel. What was he up to? Her head throbbed. She heard Fothergill's footsteps on the priest hole's stone floor; he was no longer slinking silently as he returned. Lowering her lids, she stayed slumped against the post, feigning unconsciousness.

Fothergill strode out of the hole; he marched straight past her to the side of the bed. She heard the tinkle of metal, then other, softer sounds . . . after a moment, she understood. He'd made his selection from her father's collection and was stripping off a pillowcase to use to carry them.

He was loading the pillboxes into the case when the knob of the main door rattled.

"My lady?" Norris's voice floated through the door. "Are you in there, my lady?"

Fothergill froze. Penny knew the door was unlocked; Fothergill didn't.

In the next breath he was at her side, his knife in his hand, his gaze on the door. Then his eyes cut sideways—and caught the glint of her eyes before she shut them.

He moved so fast she had no chance to make a sound; he whipped a kerchief from his pocket, forced her jaw down, and poked the material deep into her mouth. She choked. It took a few seconds of wheezing before she could even breathe—screaming was out of the question. She couldn't get enough breath even to make loud noises.

Satisfied he'd gagged her, Fothergill left her; silently crossing the room, eyes on the door, he went to the double windows, looked out, all around, then unlatched the windows and set them wide.

His escape route?

Turning, he looked at Nicholas, still slumped unmoving on the floor. Silently, he walked over, then hunkered down at Nicholas's side. After a moment, Fothergill lifted his head and looked at her. Then he reached for Nicholas, hauling his unconscious form around so he half sat, slumped before Fothergill. Facing Penny.

Balancing Nicholas against his knees, Fothergill looked again at Penny. His knife flashed in his right hand as he raised it. A smile of inestimable cruelty curved his lips.

He was going to slit Nicholas's throat while she watched.

Her mouth went dry. She stared.

And felt a cool draft drift across her ankles.

It could only come from the priest hole.

She screamed against the gag, flung herself against her bonds, stamped her feet—made as much noise as she could to cover any sound Charles might make.

Fothergill only grinned more evilly. He reached for Nicholas's chin, drew it up.

His gaze deflected, going past her. His smile froze.

Charles appeared—was simply suddenly there—beside her.

"I think she means don't do it." He moved farther into the room, away from her. "Wise advice."

He held a dagger, a much more wicked-looking weapon than the one Fothergill had; he turned it in his fingers, his dexterity screaming long and intimate acquaintance with the blade.

Fothergill saw. Understood. They each had a knife. If he threw his and missed killing Charles . . .

Quick as a flash, Fothergill threw his knife at Charles.

Charles dived, rolling back toward Penny. Fothergill's knife hit the wall and bounced off, spun away, landing closer to Charles. Charles surged to his feet between Penny and Fothergill. He'd expected Fothergill to go after Penny, the best hostage, or if not that, the door, behind which half the household staff waited.

He'd forgotten the old rapier that hung on the wall above the mantelpiece. Fothergill flung himself at it, yanked it from the fixed scabbard. It came free with a deadly hiss.

His lips curled as he swung to face Charles.

With one quick, swirling turn, Charles grabbed up Fothergill's dagger, crossed it with his, and met Fothergill's first rush. Catching the rapier between the crossed blades, he steadied, then flung Fothergill back.

Fothergill staggered, but immediately reengaged.

Much good did it do him. Charles let his lips slowly curve. Despite the furious clashing of the blades, the sparks that flew as dagger countered flexing steel, within a minute it was clear that Fothergill wasn't up to his weight, at least not in experience of the less-civilized forms of hand-to-hand combat.

The rapier was longer than Charles's blades, giving Fothergill the advantage of reach, but Fothergill had never been trained to use the weapon—he wielded it like a saber, something Charles quickly saw. Trained to the use of every blade imaginable, he could easily predict and counter.

While he did, he planned and plotted how best to disarm Fothergill; he would really rather not kill the man in front of Penny. The others were gathered outside the door, waiting for his word, but he had no intention of inviting anyone in; in his increasingly panicked state, Fothergill would undoubtedly run someone through. Enough innocents had already died.

The thud of their feet on the rug covering the floorboards was a form of music to his ears. Through the fractional changes in tone, he could judge where Fothergill was shifting his weight and predict his next attack. Combined with the flash of the blades, the almost choreographed movements, he had all the information he needed; his instincts settled into the dance.

Fothergill pressed, and pressed, trying to force him to yield his position before Penny, defending her—and failed. Desperate, Fothergill closed; again with relative ease, Charles threw him back.

Fothergill stumbled, almost falling. Charles stepped forward—realized and leapt back as Fothergill dropped the rapier, grabbed the rug with both hands and yanked.

On the far edge, Charles staggered back, almost into Penny.

Fothergill grasped the instant to fling himself out of the open window.

Charles swore, rushed across and looked out, but Fothergill was already on the ground, racing away, hugging the house so Charles had no good target. Charles thought of his direction, extrapolated, then swore again and turned inside. "He's heading for the shrubbery—one will get you ten he has a horse waiting there."

Penny blinked as he neared. He gently removed the gag and she gasped, "Send the others after him."

Tugging at the knot in the cords binding her, Charles shook his head. "He's a trained assassin—I don't want anyone else cornering him but me, or someone equally well trained."

He jerked her bonds loose, caught her as she sagged.

Eased her back to sit on the bed. Only then saw the bruise discoloring the skin over her cheekbone.

His fingers tightened involuntarily on her chin, then eased.

Penny didn't understand the words he said under his breath, but she knew their meaning.

"He hit you."

She'd never heard colder, deader words from him. Words devoid of all human emotion, something she would have said was impossible with Charles. His fingers gently soothed, then drifted away; turning her head, she looked into his face. Saw resolution settle over the harsh planes.

"What?" she asked, and waited for him to tell her.

Eventually, he drew his gaze from her cheek, met her eyes. "I should have killed him." Flatly, he added, "I will when next we meet."

Penny looked into his eyes, saw the violence surging. Slowly, she rose; he didn't step back, so she was close, face-to-face, breast to chest.

Arguing would be pointless. Instead, she held his gaze, and quietly said, "If you must. But remember that this"—briefly she gestured to her cheek—"is hardly going to harm me irreparably. Losing you would."

He blinked. The roiling violence behind his eyes subsided; he refocused on her eyes, searched them.

She held his gaze, let him see that she'd meant exactly what she'd said, then she patted his arm. "Nicholas has been unconscious for some time."

He blinked again, then glanced at Nicholas's slumped form, and sighed. He stepped away from her. "Norris! Get in here."

The door flew open; pandemonium flooded in.

CHAPTER

21

NICHOLAS STIRRED AS SOON AS THEY LIFTED HIM. NOT SO
Jack. By the time he opened his eyes, then groaned, Dr. Kenton had arrived. The dapper little doctor lifted Jack's lids, moved a candle before his eyes, then gently probed the huge contusion above his right temple.

"You were lucky—very lucky." Kenton glanced at the cosh Charles had retrieved from behind the chaise. "If your skull wasn't so thick, I doubt you'd be with us enough to groan."

Jack grimaced; he bore with the doctor's fussing, but signaled to Charles the instant Kenton's back was turned.

If Jack was up to making such faces, he was at least in possession of his wits; Charles eased the doctor from his patient's side and bore him away.

Fifteen minutes later, Gervase returned, grim-faced. They gathered again in the library as they had hours earlier; this time, both Jack and Nicholas looked the worse for wear, pale and drawn, both in pain, Jack from his head, Nicholas from the shoulder wound Fothergill's blow had reopened.

They took it in turns to relate their story. Penny described how Fothergill had arrived, how he'd seemed so innocent to begin with, and how that had changed—how he'd incapacitated Jack, then used her to force Nicholas to do his bidding. She stopped at the point where Charles had appeared at the bedchamber door. She looked at him, sprawled beside her on the chaise. "How did you know to return?"

"I shouldn't have left." He looked grim. "We were galloping toward Fowey when the penny dropped. Dennis's cousin couldn't have had any direct connection with our nemesis; the knife and cloak were stage dressing to ensure I connected the death with the intruder here and raced off to investigate, presumably so something could then happen here. I turned back. Gervase went on to see if there was anything we could learn from Sid Garnut's death."

Gervase shifted restlessly. "Other than being proof beyond doubt that our man—Fothergill as we now know—is cold-bloodedly callous, there wasn't anything more to be learned." He paused, then added, "The boy had been dispatched with almost contemptuous efficiency. Fothergill, or whoever he really is, feels nothing for those he kills."

Penny quelled a shiver. Charles took up the tale of what had transpired in the master bedchamber. He abbreviated the proceedings, stating only the necessary facts. He'd just reached the point at which Fothergill went out of the window when the crunch of approaching hooves reached them.

Charles rose and looked out. "One of my grooms. Looks like Dalziel has unearthed something."

He strode out, reappearing two minutes later, one of the now familiar plain packets in his hand. He went to the desk and slit it open; unfolding the sheets, he returned to the chaise.

Swiftly scanning, he grimaced. "Dalziel writes that while they still haven't cleared Gerond, the Julian Fothergill who's a connection of Culver's wife is a twenty-year-old with pale blond hair who, according to his mother, is presently on a walking tour of the Lake District with friends. He is, however, a budding ornithologist."

Charles glanced at Gervase, then Jack.

Who humphed. "Other than the hair color and a few years, he had all the rest right."

"Not only that, he used it to best advantage," Charles said.

"No one's surprised to find an avid bird-watcher marching over their land."

"How was it that Culver didn't realize?" Gervase asked. "If our man's been staying there pretending to be one of the family, surely the usual questions about Aunt Ermintrude or whoever would have tripped him up."

"Not necessarily." Charles glanced at Penny. "If the family's as large as Dalziel suggests, then it's always possible he truly is a member, just not *that* member, not of an English branch."

"And Culver would never notice," Penny said. "Aside from all else, the Fothergills are his wife's connections, and with the best will in the world I doubt his lordship remembers his own connections. If this man hadn't remembered Aunt Ermintrude, Culver would have thought he himself had got things wrong—he's awfully disconnected."

"He's a true recluse," Charles said, "but a terribly correct one."

"What's more," Penny added, "his reclusiveness is well-known."

Looking up at the ceiling, Jack sighed. "I just can't get over how glibly he took me in. I was on guard when he walked in, but by the time he got behind me, I'd started to relax, to believe he was as harmless as he appeared." He grimaced. "He was so damned *English*."

Charles regarded him wryly. "Now you understand how I survived so long in France. No matter how alert and on guard one is, the eyes see what they see, and we react accordingly."

Penny remembered her earlier thought; Fothergill was indeed a Charles-in-reverse.

"Regardless," Charles said, "we can't afford to sit back and reflect. He had a horse waiting. If he wasn't worried about being identified, then he was ready to leave this area. If his mission is to punish the Selbornes and retrieve some of the pill- and snuffboxes, having failed here, where will he head next?"

Already pale, Nicholas turned a ghastly hue. "He'll go after my father."

"Where is he?" Gervase asked.

"London—Amberly House in Mayfair." Nicholas struggled to get up.

Charles waved him back. "If we're right, he can't kill your father, not out of hand. He'll know by now that he has no chance of laying his hands on the pillboxes—we're not going to leave them here unguarded, and besides, he didn't get you to show him how to open the panel."

"Overconfident." Gervase nodded. "But it does mean he won't bother coming back here."

"It also means," Charles said, looking at Nicholas, "that he'll feel compelled to get to thesnuffboxes. You said they're at Amberly Grange, in Berkshire, in a priest hole much like the one here. Fothergill might not know of the priest hole, but he'll now suspect something of the sort—some well-hidden chamber that only your father or you can open."

"That's why he won't kill your pater outright." Jack narrowed his eyes consideringly. "If I were he, I'd go to Amberly Grange, to where the snuffboxes are, and wait—use the time until Amberly returns there to learn the lay of the land, even ingratiate my way into the household, or at least into a position of being able to gain access to the house." He glanced around at them all. "There's no time limit applying for him, and the only pressure he knows of is that Charles now knows who he is and presumably will be searching for him."

"Given his actions to date, I don't think that'll deter him," Charles said.

"More, he seems young enough, arrogant enough, to see it as a challenge." Gervase's gaze was hard. "That should work to our advantage." He looked at Charles. "So how do you want to play this?"

Charles rose. Seated beside him, sensing his impatience, Penny had wondered how much longer he'd stay still. He strode to the hearth, then faced them. "I need one of you to stay here—Jack, for obvious reasons. Gervase—you can get the word out along the coast as well as I. We need to shut the stable door so he can't bolt."

Gervase nodded.

Glancing at her, Charles continued, "I'll go to London."

"As will I." Nicholas again struggled forward in the chair.

"No."

Nicholas looked up, but the edict was unequivocal.

"I'm leaving now—tonight," Charles said. "I'll travel straight through and be in London by midday, possibly even before Fothergill. I'll speak with your father, and Dalziel, and determine our best way forward." He paused, his gaze on Nicholas's determined but drawn face, then more quietly added, "I understand your wish to aid your father, but you're in no condition to do so. A long, jolting journey will land you in a sickbed for days if not longer."

"He's my father—"

"Indeed, but I was sent here to deal with this matter." Charles paused, then added, "You may safely leave it to me. Fothergill won't succeed—and he *will* pay."

"And you needn't worry about your father, Nicholas, for I'm going to London, too."

Her voice, so much lighter than theirs, rang like a bell. They all looked at her, but it was Charles's gaze she met. She held it for a pregnant instant, then softly said, "Either with you, or independently—and, of course, I'll be calling on Amberly." She glanced at Nicholas. "Whatever else, he'll have family beside him through this."

Nicholas blinked; his dilemma showed plainly in his face—he was too tired to hide it. Should he be grateful to Penny and support her, or side with Charles as instinct prompted and keep her safely at home?

Gervase shifted; Jack frowned. Both were aware of the undercurrents; neither was in a position to say anything, a fact they were forced to accept. They had no authority here.

When, unable to make up his mind, Nicholas said nothing, Penny looked back at Charles. And raised a brow. *With him, or by herself . . .*

No real choice for him, either.

His jaw set; the planes of his face hardened, but, stiffly, he inclined his head. "Very well."

He was too far away for her to read his eyes, but in this, she didn't need to. She was perfectly aware of the various trains of thought—the swift and decisive plans—running through his head. Those she would deal with later; one step at a time.

She rose, waving the others back as they started to their feet. "If you'll excuse me, gentlemen, I'll go and pack." She glanced at Charles. "My carriage or yours?"

He considered, then replied, "Yours will do."

She nodded and turned for the door. "I'll give orders to have it prepared. Half an hour, shall we say?"

Glancing back from the door, she saw his lips thin; he nodded curtly. Suppressing a grimly satisfied smile, she opened the door and went on her willful way.

She next saw Charles when she decended the front steps, attired in a comfortable carriage dress and prepared for a long, uncomfortable drive. He was standing with the coachman and groom, confirming his orders. When her boots crunched on the gravel, he turned, flicked a comprehensive glance over her, noting the warm shawl draped over her shoulders, then looked back to the coachman and groom, and gave the word. They scurried to climb up to their perches as he joined her.

He took the door the footman had opened, held it and held out his hand. She put her fingers in his, felt him grip. Hard.

"I am not happy about this." The words were a growl as he helped her up the carriage steps.

She glanced at him, met his eyes. "I know. But we can't always have what we want."

Moving into the carriage, she sat. He looked up at the coachman, nodded, then leapt into the coach, slammed the door, and flung himself on the seat beside her.

Head back against the squabs, he looked up at the coach's ceiling. "As it happens, I usually do manage to get what I want from women. With you, however . . ."

She took a moment to subdue her smile, then, lifting a hand, she gently patted one of his where it rested half-clenched on his thigh. "Never mind."

His response was a growl of elemental male frustration.

But he opened his hand and closed it about hers.

The drive was as grueling as she'd expected; the coachman had his orders—he drove like one possessed. The crest on the carriage door gave them a certain license. The carriage was relatively new and well sprung, and Charles and his commanding presence ensured that the teams they were provided with at every halt were the very best to be had.

They made excellent time, racing on into the night. Other than easing the pace a fraction to allow for the fading light, the coachman made no other concession. As night closed in, they met fewer and fewer carriages; when full darkness fell, it seemed as if they were the only occupants of the road, streaking ever onward, the carriage lights faintly bobbing, throwing faint gleams that the darkness swallowed as they rocketed along.

The regular thud of the horses' heavy hooves, the repetitive rattle of the wheels became a soporific lullaby. Drawing her shawl about her, she leaned against Charles; he raised his arm and gathered her in. She smiled, turned to him, lifted her lips for a kiss . . . which was truncated by the next jolt.

His arm tightened, holding her against him. She patted his chest, then settled her cheek on the warm, resilient muscle, and closed her eyes.

She awoke at their next stop, when he left her to see to the horses. When he returned, and their rattling trip resumed, he drew her back to him and rested his cheek against the top of her head.

A fitful rest at best, yet despite the rigors, the journey was restful in other ways. They spoke little; there was no point in arguing yet.

When dawn broke and Charles took a turn on the box, spelling the coachman who'd driven through the night, her gaze fixed unseeing on the landscape flashing past, Penny grasped the chance to consider the landscape forming between them.

Within it, she felt comfortable; the farther they traveled

together along their road, the more the position at his side felt right, increasingly hers. Increasingly meant to be hers. His confidence in that, that that's what would be, remained unwavering, feeding her confidence that this time . . .

Once they'd dealt with Fothergill, they would see.

Charles rejoined her in the carriage at Hammersmith, leaving the coachman to tool the coach through the outskirts and into Mayfair. They came to a rocking halt before Lost-withiel House in Bedford Square.

A mansion of gray stone, it was old enough to have developed its own charm. Penny had visited there frequently in years gone by; when Charles's butler, Crewther, opened the door, she smiled and greeted him by name.

Crewther's face lit; he was about to bow, then his gaze went past her to Charles, giving her coachman directions to the mews. Crewther's eyes widened. As Charles turned and strode up the steps, Crewther stepped back and bowed them in. "My lord, Lady Penelope. Welcome back."

Charles nodded. "Thank you, Crewther. Lady Penelope and I will most likely be here for a few days." He fixed Crewther with a direct look. "Are my mother and sisters in?"

"I believe the countess, your sisters, Mrs. Frederick and Mrs. James, are attending a luncheon at Osterley Park, my lord."

Charles's relief showed. "In that case . . ." He looked at Penny. "Lady Penelope and I have business to attend to—our movements are uncertain."

"Indeed, my lord."

Knowing Charles would leave it at that, she turned to Crewther. "Please inform the countess that she shouldn't delay dinner or her evening's entertainment on our account—we'll speak with her when we return."

Lips thinning, Charles nodded. "We should call on Amberly without delay."

She glanced down at her crushed gown. "Just give me time to wash and change into something more appropriate."

Crewther stepped in, sending a footman for the housekeeper, directing the two who'd fetched their bags to take them upstairs.

Charles gave orders for his town carriage to be brought around, then took her arm; they started up the main stairs in the footmen's wake. The housekeeper, Mrs. Millikens, came bustling up to meet them at the stair head. She greeted Charles, then bore Penny off to a bedchamber.

"Twenty minutes in the front hall," Charles called after her.

Mrs. Millikens looked scandalized. "Twenty minutes?" She huffed. "He's not in the army now—what is he thinking? Twenty minutes? I've sent Flora to unpack your things—" Millikens paused and opened a door. "Ah, yes, here she is." She ushered Penny in. "Now, let's see . . ."

With Millikens, who'd known her from childhood, and Flora assisting, Penny was ready, gowned in a walking dress of blue silk twill, in just over twenty minutes. Descending the stairs, she saw Charles pacing in the front hall below. Hearing her footsteps, he glanced up; the set of his features, the frown that lurked, told her he'd been debating ways and means of detaching her from their pursuit of Fothergill— and he didn't care that she knew.

He walked to meet her, taking her hand, tucking it in his arm as they turned to the front door. "I sent a message to Elaine that you were here—it wouldn't do for someone to see you about town and mention it. She's staying with Constance, isn't she?"

"Yes." Penny shot him a glance as they went down the steps. "What did you tell her?"

He met her eyes briefly, then handed her into the carriage. "That you and I both had business to deal with, so I'd brought you up to town, that you'd be staying here, that our movements were uncertain, but that you'd explain when next you saw her."

He followed her in and shut the door, then sat beside her. She studied his face. "Nothing else?"

Turning his head, he met her gaze. "Having you involved in this is bad enough—I'm hardly likely to say anything to bring both our chattering families down on my head . . ." He looked forward. "No matter the aggravation you cause me."

She smiled and looked ahead. "Better the devil you know . . . ?"

After a moment, he murmured, "Actually, I'm not that well acquainted with this particular devil."

She pondered that comment as the carriage traversed the few streets to Amberly House. To their relief, the marquess was at home, but he wasn't alone.

Charles had sent a rider ahead of them with a message for Dalziel; as they were shown into the library, Penny glanced briefly at her relative as he struggled up from the chaise, then transferred her attention to the gentleman who rose from the armchair opposite.

He was tall, well built; although neither as tall nor as heavy as Charles, he was every bit as physically impressive. His hair was dark brown, almost black, his face pale with the austere planes and strong features that marked him as an aristocrat. Deep brown eyes of that shade most often referred to as soulful took her in; as his gaze, outwardly lazy yet intelligent and acute, met hers, she had little doubt of the caliber of mind behind those bedroom eyes.

If anything, she would have labeled him even more dangerous than Charles. No matter that his manners were polished and urbane, the unmistakable aura of a predator hung about him.

She curtsied to Amberly, then less deeply as she offered her hand to—

"Dalziel." He bowed over her hand with the same effortless grace Charles possessed. "Lady Penelope Selborne, I presume."

His gaze flicked to Charles. There was the faintest trace of a question in his eyes.

When Charles didn't respond, Dalziel looked at her, his lips lightly lifting as he released her.

She moved on to join Amberly. Behind her, Dalziel turned to Charles. "After receiving your missive this morning, I decided my presence here might be wise."

Charles nodded and stepped forward to greet Amberly and shake his hand. "Nicholas is well—he sends his regards."

Amberly was over eighty years old, white-haired, his blue gaze faded. He blinked, frowned. "He's not here?"

Charles exchanged a glance with Penny. Gently, she eased Amberly back to the chaise, then sat beside him. "Nicholas would have come with us, but he's a trifle under the weather at the moment."

"Perhaps," Dalziel said, glancing at Charles as he resumed his seat, "you could bring us up to date with recent events?"

Charles drew up another chair, using the moment to marshal his thoughts. Amberly was attentive, watching and waiting, yet while his mind might still be acute, he didn't look strong; there was no need to shock him unnecessarily. However glibly he couched his report, Dalziel would read between the lines.

Dalziel mumured, "I've already explained to the marquess all that happened up to the point of Arbry's grappling with the intruder one night, the intruder's subsequent escape and Arbry's recovery from his injuries. Perhaps if you recount all that's happened since."

Charles did, relating only the bare facts in the most unemotional language. Dalziel picked up his omissions, but said nothing, just met his gaze and nodded for him to continue.

Despite his efforts, the tale left Amberly distressed. Fretfully plucking at his coat buttons, he looked at Charles, then Dalziel; finally, he turned to Penny. "It was never meant to be like this. No one was supposed to die."

Penny patted his arm, murmuring that they understood; he didn't seem to hear. He looked at Charles. "I thought it was all over—finished. All's fair in war, and it was war, but the war's ended." Tears in his old eyes, he waved weakly. "If they want the boxes—the snuffboxes and pillboxes—they can have them. They're not worth anyone's life."

Gaze distant, Amberly drew a short breath. "That poor boy Gimby, and a little maid, and now a fisherboy . . ." After a moment, he refocused; he looked at Charles and Dalziel. Confusion clouded his eyes. "Why? They weren't part of the game."

"No, they weren't." Dalziel sat forward, capturing Amberly's gaze, steadying him by the contact. "This assassin's not playing by the recognized rules, which is why, with your help, my lord, we need to bring his assignment to a swift end."

Amberly looked into Dalziel's eyes, then spread his hands. "Whatever I can do, my boy—whatever I can do."

They spent the next hour discussing the possibilities. Charles was relieved to have his reading of Amberly's abilities confirmed; although physically doddery, and sometimes vague when he became distracted, there was nothing wrong with his grasp on reality, his memory, or his courage.

Dalziel's reading of the events to date, his prediction of what Fothergill was most likely to do next, tallied with Charles's. The plan they agreed on was simple; give Fothergill what he wanted—the marquess at Amberly Grange.

"There's no value in pretending you haven't been warned," Dalziel told Amberly. "A man of your age and standing, when threatened, would most likely retreat to his own estate, to be kept safe by his loyal staff. Given the snuffboxes are there, too, and he'll imagine you're obsessed with them and will know he means to take them, such a move makes even more sense."

Dalziel's gaze shifted to Penny, then he looked at Charles. "He won't be surprised to see you there, acting as protector."

Charles noted Dalziel didn't clarify whom he would be protecting, Amberly alone, or Penny, too. That, he understood, was left to him to define.

"What Fothergill won't know is that I'll be there as well." Dalziel met Amberly's eyes. "I'll remain with you for the rest of today, just in case—no sense taking any unnecessary risks. We'll leave tomorrow morning—I'll travel down in your carriage. Easy enough to slip into the house after we arrive."

Dalziel's gaze grew harder, colder. "Fothergill knows

Charles—he'll be expecting to have a guard he needs to distract to get to you, and Charles will obviously be that person. Once Charles is decoyed away, Fothergill will come in—from all we've seen of him to date, he'll be overconfident. The last thing he'll expect is to walk into me."

Dalziel's lips lifted in a faint, cold smile. Penny quelled a shiver.

"That," Dalziel said, glancing at them all, "is how we'll catch him."

"And stop him," Charles said.

There'd been a degree of finality in Charles's tone, echoed in Dalziel's murmured affirmation, that seemed to set the seal on Fothergill's fate.

Once again in Charles's town carriage rocking steadily back to Bedford Square, Penny thought of Gimby, Mary Maggs, and Sid Garnut—remembered Fothergill's expression when he'd been about to slit Nicholas's throat—and couldn't find any sorrow for Fothergill in her.

One point puzzled her. She stirred and glanced at Charles. "Dalziel—I'm surprised someone in his position would . . . how do you phrase it? Go into the field?"

Charles glanced at her. After a moment, he said, "I would have been more surprised if he'd left it in my hands alone." He considered, then went on, "We've always spoken of Dalziel as if he simply sits behind his desk in Whitehall and directs people hither and yon. Recently, we've known that isn't the case—in fact, it's probably never been the case. Our view of him reflected what we knew, and that wasn't the whole picture. Still isn't the whole picture. We've always recognized him as one of us—he couldn't be that without similar background, similar training, similar experience. In this instance . . ."

Charles paused, then glanced at her. "I told you whoever corners Fothergill has to be one of us."

Penny nodded. "You or someone equally well trained." She slipped her hand into his. "Like Dalziel."

"Indeed." Grasping her hand, Charles leaned his head

back against the squabs. Of all those he knew who were "like him," prepared to kill when their country demanded it, there was none other more "like him" than Dalziel.

They reached Lostwithiel House to discover Charles's mother, sisters, and sisters-in-law all waiting to pounce. Not that his mother pounced; directed by Crewther to the drawing room, Charles ushered Penny in—his mother immediately saw them and held out her hand, compelling him to cross the room to her side. Clasping her hand, he bent and kissed her cheek.

Her gaze lingered on Penny, who had stopped to talk with Jacqueline and Lydia, who had squealed and pounced on her—the reason he'd made sure she preceded him into the room. Seated nearby, Annabelle and Helen were eagerly listening to Jacqueline's inquisition and Penny's replies.

Smiling, his mother looked up at him. "Business?"

Dragging his eyes from the scene, his mind from wondering how Penny was coping, he nodded. "We've just come from Amberly House."

His mother's eyes widened—the marquess was the titular head of Penny's family. He rapidly clarified, "It's the same business that took me away." Pulling up a chair, he sat beside her. "Arbry was at Wallingham."

He hesitated, then lowered his voice. "I haven't yet told Elaine—we need to keep the whole quiet, at least for the moment, but . . ." Briefly he explained how the Selbornes had been involved in a long-running scheme providing incorrect information to the French, and how some French agent was now intent on exacting revenge.

"Good God!" His mother's gaze went to Penny. "Penny will remain here, of course."

His frustrated sigh had her glancing back at him. He felt her eyes searching his face, but kept his gaze on Penny. "I would, quite obviously, prefer she remain here, with you or with Elaine, but I doubt she'll agree."

A moment passed, then his mother merely said, "Hmm . . . I see."

When he looked at her, she was studying Penny.

"Still," she mused, "at your relative ages, it's to be hoped you both know what you're doing."

He did. It didn't make the doing—the adjusting—any easier.

"So." His mother turned to him. "How long will you be in town?"

"Just tonight—and no, we won't be attending any events. We'll be leaving for Amberly Grange in the morning."

He stood, intending to go back down the room and greet his sisters and sisters-in-law. The twinkle in his mother's eye made him pause. "What?"

At his suspicious tone, she smiled—gloriously smug. "I'm afraid you won't be able to hide away here, not tonight."

A hideous thought bloomed. "Why?"

"Because I'm hosting a dinner, followed by a ball."

When he only just succeeded in biting back an oath, she raised her brows at him, not the least bit sympathetic. "Without the distraction of organizing your life, your sisters fell back on theirs. As it happens"—she gave him her hand and let him help her to her feet—"there's a captain in some regiment who's been casting himself at Lydia's feet, and a rakehell if ever I saw one sniffing at Jacqueline's skirts—not that either Lydia or Jacqueline is likely to succumb, but it's just as well that you're here."

She patted his arm, ignored his groan. "Now come, I must warn Penny."

It was two o'clock in the morning before, with the captain and the rakehell routed and most of the guests long gone, Charles finally succeeded in seizing Penny's hand and dragging her upstairs. To his room.

She protested; her hand locked in his, he kept walking down the corridor to the earl's apartments, now his private domain. He didn't release her until they were in his bedroom and he'd locked the door.

Exasperated, she sighed and met his eyes. "This is hardly the right example to set for your sisters."

He shrugged out of his evening coat, then looked down as

he unlaced his cuffs. "I'm not sure this isn't exactly the right example to set them."

Placing her earrings on a side table, she looked at him, puzzled, but he made no move to explain. Insisting she spend the night in his room, in his bed, with absolutely no concern over who in his household knew of it, was, to his mind, a clear declaration of his commitment to their goal—to her being his wife. Nothing else could explain such a blatant act; he was certain his mother, sisters, and even more his sisters-in-law, would see it for the admission it was.

They'd probably coo. Thank God he wouldn't be about to hear them.

Penny pulled pins from her hair, then unraveled the intricate braid Jacqueline's maid had set her long tresses in. She assumed she was in his room rather than him being in hers because her room was near his sisters', and thus far since returning from Amberly House they hadn't had a chance to talk—he hadn't had a chance to persuade her to remain in London. She knew the argument was coming, had known it from the moment she'd jockeyed him into bringing her to town. In London with his mother, or Elaine, was where he would deem her safest, where he would prefer her to be.

That was not, however, where she needed to be.

But she couldn't explain until he broached the subject. Combing out her long hair with her fingers, she shook it free, then started undoing the buttons on her gown.

Still in his trousers, he stopped behind her and undid her laces. She murmured her thanks, then drew the long silk sheath off over her head; she felt his hands slide around her as she shook the gown out. Tossing it aside, clad only in her fine chemise, she let him draw her back against him. Let him wrap his arms around her and surround her with his strength.

Bending his head, he pressed his lips to her throat, lingered there. She could almost hear him thinking how best to open the debate, then he raised his head, steadied her, and stepped back. "Before I forget . . ."

Crossing to his tallboy, he lifted a letter from the top.

"This was waiting for me." He handed it to her. "It's really for you."

Puzzled anew, she took it, unfolded the sheets, smoothed them, and read. It was an account of an engagement at Waterloo, written by a corporal who'd been in the same troop as Granville.

She read the opening paragraph, slowly moved to the bed and sank down as the action unfolded, told in the young corporal's unpolished phrases. She read on, aware that Charles sat beside her; blindly, she reached for him. He took her hand, wrapped his around it, held it while through the corporal's eyes she saw and learned of the circumstances of Granville's death.

When she reached the end, she let the letter refold, sat for a moment, then glanced at Charles. "Where . . . how did you get this?"

"I knew Devil Cynster led a troop of cavalry in the relief of Hougoumont. It was likely he or some of his men would know various survivors, so I asked. One of his cousins had assisted Granville's troop afterward; he remembered the corporal and searched him out." He nodded at the letter. "The corporal remembered Granville."

Mistily, she smiled at him. "Thank you." She glanced at the sheets in her hand. "It means a lot *knowing* he died a hero. In some way it makes it, not easier, but less of a waste."

After a moment, she looked at him. "Can I give this to Elaine?"

"Of course."

She rose, crossed to the side table, and left the letter with her jewelry. Turning back, she paused, studied him waiting for her, broad chest bare, his dark mane framing his dramatically beautiful face, his midnight eyes steady on her. He held out one hand. She walked to him, gave him her fingers, and let him clasp them as she sat again on the bed, angling to face him as he shifted to face her.

He searched her eyes, then simply said, "Please stay here and let me and Dalziel handle whatever happens at Amberly Grange."

She studied his eyes, equally simply replied, "No."

The planes of his face hardened. He opened his lips—she stayed him with a raised hand. "No—wait. I need to think."

His eyes widened incredulously, then he flopped back on the bed, gave vent to a pungent curse, followed by a muttered diatribe on the quality of her thought processes and her familial failing regarding same.

She fought to straighten her lips, aware of the tension riding him—aware of its source. "I know why you want me to stay here."

His dark gaze flicked down to fix on her face. "If you know what violence it does to my feelings to have you exposed to any danger, let alone a madman who'd be quite happy to slit your throat"—he came up on one elbow, patently unable to keep still—"then you shouldn't have to think too hard."

She met his blatantly intimidating gaze. "Except that there's more at stake here, something more important than just catering to your protective instincts."

For a moment, he stared into her eyes, then he sighed tensely and looked away. And *sotto voce* in idiomatic French reminded himself of the futility of arguing with her.

She tightened her fingers, squeezing his hand. "I understood that."

He glanced at her, and humphed.

They were both trying to lighten a fraught moment—fraught with emotion rather than threats. Dealing with emotions had never come easily to either of them; what they now had to face, to manage, accommodate and ease, was daunting.

He was descended from warrior lords; one of his strongest instincts was to protect, especially those he cared about, especially the females in his life. Especially her. She'd accepted that in drawing close to him again, his protective instinct would flare again, and it had, even more fiercely than before. But she was neither weak nor helpless, and he'd always acknowledged that and tried to rein in his impulses so they didn't unnecessarily abrade her pride. However, this time the danger was immediate and very real; he wouldn't easily be persuaded to let her face it with him.

She searched his dark eyes, saw, understood, and felt certain, this time, that it was important she be with him; why, however, wasn't easy to explain.

Slipping her fingers from his, she slid from the bed and stood; clasping her elbows, she walked a few paces, then turned and slowly paced back.

Charles watched her, saw the concentration in her face as she assembled her thoughts. As she neared the bed, he sat up. She lowered her arms; he reached for her hands and drew her to stand between his knees.

She looked into his eyes, her gaze steady; her fingers locked with his. "There are two reasons I need to go with you. The minor one is that this 'game' was a Selborne enterprise—concocted, instituted, and executed for years by Amberly and my father. Amberly represents his side of it, I represent my father and Granville, who are no longer here. It's right that Amberly should have one of us beside him to the end."

She paused, then went on, "I could point out how old and frail he is, but it's more a question of family loyalties, and that's something I know you understand."

He arched a resigned brow. "No point arguing?"

"In my shoes, you'd do the same."

He couldn't contradict her. "What's the other, more important reason?"

You. Sliding her fingers from his, Penny raised her hands and framed his face, looked into his midnight eyes. She watched his expression harden as he read the resolution in hers. "It's important to me to see this through *with you*, by your side. We've been apart for a long time; I've been out of your life for more than a decade, and you've been out of mine. *If* we're to marry, if I'm to be your wife, then I'll expect to share your life—*all* of it. I won't be cut out, shielded, tucked away even for my own safety. *If* we're to marry, then I'll be by your side not just figuratively but literally."

She now understood how important that was—for him no

longer to be alone, for her to be with him. She'd decided to accompany him to London more than anything because instinct had insisted she should.

Instinct hadn't lied. Alerted by it, she'd watched him since they'd left Wallingham; she could now see beyond his mask most of the time. She'd observed how he'd behaved and reacted during the grueling journey, through their arrival here, their interview with Amberly and Dalziel, and even more tellingly, in dealing with his womenfolk. She'd seen how he'd coped with her beside him, and contrasted that with how he would have managed if she hadn't been.

If she'd harbored any doubt of the difference her presence made, his behavior over the evening would have slain it. When they'd greeted the first guests, she'd seen how inwardly tense he'd been, although not a hint showed, even to his sisters; his mask of devil-may-care bonhomie was exceptionally good, exceptionally distracting. At first, knowing his background and experience in ballrooms, she'd been at a loss to understand his difficulty, then she'd caught him swiftly scanning the room, and realized—he held everyone at a distance. He was used to being completely alone, even in a crowd, guarding against everyone, trusting no one . . . except *her*.

As the evening wore on, and he realized she didn't mind being used, that she was amenable to being his link, his connection with the glittering throng, his interactions with others subtly changed, shifted. By the end of the night, much of his defensive tension had left him. When he laughed, it was more genuine, from his soul.

She was the only person he trusted unreservedly, without thought. She could be his anchor, his trusted link with others, one he now, after all his years of being alone, desperately needed. His mother understood, possibly the only other who saw clearly; from across the ballroom, she'd smiled her approval. A few other matrons who knew them both well probably suspected.

He needed her. He'd told her so, in multiple ways, but she hadn't truly appreciated how real that need was. She was still getting used to the situation; she had yet to learn how, between them, they needed to deal with it.

Lost in his eyes, in all she could now see, she drew in a deep breath; releasing his face she lowered her hands, found his and let their fingers twine and grip. "We've missed a lot of each other's lives, but there's no reason for that to continue. If we're to face the future together, it has to be *all* the future, side by side."

His eyes had narrowed, gaze sharp as he searched hers, reading her message. She wasn't agreeing to marry him; she was establishing parameters. After a moment he confirmed, "That's the sort of marriage you want—the sort of marriage you'll agree to?"

"Yes." She held his gaze. "If you want all of my future, then I want all of yours, not just the parts you think safe for me to share."

Not the wisest ultimatum to put to a man like him. She'd tried to avoid it, but cloaking his need and her determination to fulfill it in her usual willful stubbornness seemed the simplest way forward.

His expression impassive, he stared at her for ten heartbeats, then he carefully set her back from him, stood, and paced away. His back to her, he stopped. Hands rising to his hips, he looked up at the ceiling, then swung around and impaled her with a gaze that held all the turbulent power of a storm-racked night. He'd spoken of violence and it was there; she knew it wasn't feigned.

"What you ask isn't—" He sliced off his next word with an abrupt gesture.

"Easy?" Propping her hip against the bed, she folded her arms and lifted her chin. "I know—I know you."

He held her gaze, then exhaled through clenched teeth. "If you know me so well, you know that asking me to let you go into danger—"

"That's not what I asked."

He frowned.

"I said I wanted to be *with you*. If I am, by definition I'm not in danger." Pushing away from the bed, she walked to him. "If there's danger, I'll be perfectly content to stand behind you. I don't even need to help with what you have to do." Halting, she laid a hand on his chest, over his heart. "I simply need to be *with* you."

A certain wariness filled his eyes. Raising a hand, he closed it over hers, held her palm to his chest. "You don't have to be with me physically—"

"Yes, I do. Now, I do. Years ago, perhaps not." She held his gaze. "The youth you used to be is not the man you are. The man you are learned to be alone—very alone, very apart. You can keep the rest of the world at bay, but if we marry, you can't and won't keep me at a distance." After a moment, she softly added, "I won't let you—I won't accept that."

She wouldn't accept leaving him to deal with life alone.

He understood what she was demanding; she saw comprehension in his eyes, a center of calm coalescing in the darkness.

A long moment passed, then he exhaled. He briefly closed his eyes, then opened them. "Very well." His eyes were still stormy when they met hers. "*We'll* go to Amberly Grange tomorrow, and . . . we'll see."

HE'D KNOWN WINNING HER WOULDN'T BE EASY, BUT HE hadn't expected it to be this hard. It had been bad enough when she'd returned to Wallingham; given all that had evolved between them since, taking her with him to Amberly Grange was a hundred times worse.

As the carriage rocked and swayed, four horses swiftly drawing them into Berkshire, Charles sat beside Penny and contemplated fate's ironies.

Beside him, calmly expectant, sat the lady he wanted for his wife—the one and only lady who would do, who could fill the position as he needed it filled. A fortnight ago, he'd been staring at the fire in the library at the Abbey, impatient for her to appear—and she had. She'd marched into his house, reclaimed him, and nothing had been the same since—nothing had gone quite as he'd planned.

Last night, in the ballroom, without a word she'd stepped in and eased his way, acted precisely as he'd needed her to, been what he'd needed her to be. For the first time since returning to England, he'd been able to relax in a crowd. Later still, after forcing him to accede to her view of how things should be . . . he hadn't been in any mood for gentle loving—she not only hadn't cared, she'd taken wanton delight in encouraging him to be as demanding as he'd wished, so she could match him and meet him, drive him wild, and in her own inimitable way soothe his soul.

She'd proved she was the only lady for him—then blithely extrapolated his need for her to encompass his entire life, and made his agreement to her constant presence by his side a condition of their future union.

He'd got precisely what he'd wanted, but not as he'd expected. Looking back, looking forward, he strongly suspected that would be the story of their lives.

It was midafternoon when the carriage swept into the graveled drive of Amberly Grange. Dalziel and Amberly had been half an hour ahead of them in Amberly's carriage.

They were welcomed as expected guests. Shown into the drawing room, they found Amberly awaiting them. He looked tired, but his gaze was shrewd. He greeted Penny, shook hands with Charles, then waved them to chairs. "Let's have tea, then we can commence."

The first step proved easy enough; his butler and housekeeper hadn't hired anyone in recent weeks. All the staff in the large house had been there for years.

Charles went out to the stables to convey the news to Dalziel, who'd spent the hour since they'd arrived dozing in the carriage. Charles returned to the house alone; when darkness fell, Dalziel joined them.

Over dinner, they put the final touches to their plan.

The next morning, after breakfast, Penny and Charles went for a short ride. On returning, they joined Amberly on the terrace for morning tea. Afterward, all three went for a stroll in the gardens, keeping to the wide lawns circling the house. When the luncheon gong rang, they repaired to the dining parlor; later, Penny and Amberly strolled about the conservatory while Charles read the news sheets on the terrace outside. In the late afternoon, the marquess retreated to the pianoforte in the music room. Penny and Charles saw him launched on a sonata, then, arm in arm, they left the room, strolled along the terrace, then descended to the lawns.

After a lengthy stroll, never out of sight or hearing of the music room and the delicate airs wafting forth on the breeze, they returned and, shortly after, all three withdrew to their rooms to dress for dinner.

Dinner, and the evening spent in the drawing room, followed the predictable pattern, then they retired to their bedchambers, to their beds, and slept.

The next day, they repeated the performance. Exactly. The program was precisely what one might expect of a nobleman of Amberly's age being attended by a female relative and watched over by someone like Charles.

All believable, and all very regular. They adhered to their schedule like clockwork. Dalziel was never visible to any outside the house. They'd agreed their best route was to exploit Fothergill's arrogance and overconfidence, so they set the stage for him, and waited for him to make his entrance.

They'd accepted it might take a week and had resigned themselves to playing their roles for at least that long.

On the afternoon of the first day, while sorting through music sheets with the marquess, Penny overheard a muted discussion between Charles and Dalziel. It was clearly a continuing argument between them. In typical fashion, neither said what they meant outright, but the crux revolved about who would deliver the *coup de grâce* once they had Fothergill trapped between them.

Charles had a strong case; ruthlessly, with a few quiet phrases, Dalziel demolished it. Penny gave no indication she heard his words, nor felt their glances as they rested on her. Charles wavered; Dalziel subtly pushed, and he gave in. The final act in the drama would fall to Dalziel.

Days passed, and they religiously played their parts, their assigned roles. Amberly, accepting that he could do no more than that, cocooned himself in the regimen; through the hours they spent together strolling the conservatory and lawns, Penny learned more of him, leaving her with a degree of respect and burgeoning affection for the, as Nicholas had correctly termed him, incorrigible old man.

For herself, she was conscious of a heightened awareness, of her senses being alert, alive, and always awake in a way they never had been before. Waiting, watching, ready. Confident that she, Amberly, and his staff were safe under Charles and Dalziel's protection, she found the tension more exciting than frightening.

That alertness, however, made the changes in Charles and Dalziel very apparent. The tension that invested them was of a different caliber, possessed a far more steely, battle-ready quality. And day by day, hour by hour, that tension escalated, subtle notch by notch.

By the third day, Amberly's staff were walking very carefully around them. Neither had raised their voices, neither had done anything to frighten anyone; the staff were reacting to the portent of barely leashed danger that emanated from them.

Every night, when Charles joined her in her room and her bed, she opened her arms to him and met that dangerous tension. Welcomed it, not for one instant turned aside from it, but challenged it with her own confidence, channeled it into the wildness of passion.

On the third night, when he collapsed in the bed beside her, he reached out and drew her into his arms, cradled her against him, gently smoothing back her tangled hair. "Do you still want to be with me, even now—even through this?"

She shifted to look into his face, into his darkly shadowed eyes. "Yes—even now. Especially now." Freeing a hand, she brushed back a black lock from his forehead, drinking in the hard planes of his face. "I need to be here, with you. I need to know all of you—even this. There's no reason to hide any part of what you are, not from me. There's nothing, no part of you, I won't love."

He studied her face as their hearts slowed, then he tightened his arms about her, murmured against her hair, "I'm not sure I deserve you."

He was too tense, too brittle at present for this; she drew back to smile at him. "I'll remember you said that when next you complain about my wild Selborne streak."

He smiled back, accepting her easing of the moment; he

settled his arm over her waist, she snuggled her head on his shoulder, and they slept.

The following day they were returning from their afternoon stroll about the lawns while the marquess spent his customary hour at the pianoforte, when Penny noticed a gardener kneeling before the flower beds a few yards from the steps leading up to the terrace.

Why her senses focused on him she had no idea; she was used to seeing staff constantly about—there was nothing about him to alarm her. He was weeding the beds, an understandable enough enterprise.

As she and Charles approached, idly discussing the Abbey and the missive that had arrived from London that morning, matters about the estate Charles needed to decide, she watched the gardener pull three weeds and toss them into the trug beside him. He had streaky, fairish brown hair and wore the usual drab clothes the gardeners favored; he also wore a battered hat jammed down to shade his face and a tattered woolen scarf loose about his neck.

She and Charles reached the steps, passing the man; as they climbed to the terrace, she suddenly knew—was absolutely certain—but didn't know why. She didn't dare look back; forcing her mind to retread the last minutes, she reviewed all she'd seen.

Charles noticed her absorption. He looked at her, caught her eyes, a question in his.

They reached the music room and stepped over the threshold; she exhaled and sank her fingers into his arm. "He's here." Across the room, she met Dalziel's eyes as he rose from a chair against the wall. "He's the gardener weeding the beds by the steps."

"You're sure?" Charles kept his voice low.

She nodded. "He doesn't look the same—he's dyed his hair—but his hands—no gardener has hands like that."

Charles looked at Dalziel, who nodded. "Your move."

Charles returned his nod, looked at Penny, lifted her hand to his lips. "Remember your part."

"I will." She squeezed his hand and let him go.

Turning, she watched as he strode back onto the terrace. She followed as far as the open French doors and reported for Dalziel and Amberly in the room behind her. "Fothergill's gathered his things and is walking off across the lawns toward the back of the house. Charles has just reached the lawn."

"Here—you! Wait!"

Charles's voice reached them. Penny watched as Fothergill glanced back, realized Charles wasn't far behind. He dropped his tools and ran.

"He's off. Charles is following."

Inwardly, she started to pray. They'd assumed Fothergill wouldn't try to face Charles, but would lead him well away from the house. The grounds were extensive, with large areas devoted to gardens and stands of trees and shrubs—lots of places to hide and lose a pursuer.

If they'd assumed wrong, Charles would face Fothergill alone. Waiting, not knowing, not doing, was harder than she'd thought, but she'd accepted they had to script their play that way to leave Fothergill believing he was still in control.

So she waited and watched, and prayed.

Charles raced after Fothergill, keeping him in sight, simultaneously keeping mental track of their progress through the grounds. As they'd guessed, Fothergill was leading him away from the house; he didn't stick to the gardens, but plunged into a wooded stretch. Charles saw him leaping down a winding path; following, he forged up the rise beyond, followed the path over the crest—and saw no one ahead of him.

Bushes closed in a little way along; Fothergill might have made their shelter in time. Charles felt certain he hadn't. There was a minor path to the left that would lead back to the house; catching his breath, he plunged on, keeping to the major path heading away from the house. He didn't glance back; senses on a knife-edge, he strained to hear any movement behind him—anything to suggest Fothergill was intent on becoming his pursuer and killing him.

He heard nothing. Not a rustle, not a snap. Beyond the thick bushes he moved off the path, halted and listened.

Nothing near. Closing his eyes, he concentrated, senses searching.

Faint, at some distance, he detected a large animal moving stealthily back toward the house.

Fothergill had swallowed the bait.

Lips curving in a cold smile, Charles turned and headed across the grounds; he needed to get into position for his next appearance in their play.

Once Charles had disappeared, Penny quit the doorway and went to sit beside Amberly at the pianoforte. As agreed, the marquess continued to tinkle out a melody—the lure to draw Fothergill back, to assure him his target was still there.

Dalziel had summoned reinforcements; two burly footmen and the butler, a stalwart individual, stood by the wall nearby, ready to provide additional protection if needed. By the window, Dalziel kept a silent watch over the lawns, waiting to see if Fothergill would behave as they'd predicted.

"He's coming."

The words were uninflected, curiously dead. Amberly dragged in a labored breath and kept his fingers moving unfalteringly over the keys; Penny briefly touched his shoulder reassuring, supporting. She looked at Dalziel. He gave no sign of being aware of anything or anyone beyond the man he was watching. Tension thrummed through him; he was a powerful, lethal animal, leashed but knowing the leash was about to be released. Poised to act.

Without sound or warning, he moved, walking to the doorway and stepping out onto the terrace.

Penny left her seat and equally silently followed; halting in the doorway, she saw Fothergill coming quickly up the steps, scanning the lawns behind him—back in the direction he'd led Charles.

Relief flooded her; Charles was still out there—Fothergill hadn't attacked him.

Detecting no pursuit, Fothergill stepped onto the terrace, lips lifting coldly as he turned to the music room—and came face-to-face with Dalziel.

Three yards separated them.

Fothergill's mouth opened; incomprehension filled his face. Then his eyes met Dalziel's.

Fothergill whirled, flung himself down the steps and fled across the lawn. Toward the maze. Dalziel paused for an instant, then went after him.

Penny watched the pair race away, then Fothergill ducked through the arched gap in the high green hedges; a few seconds later, Dalziel followed.

Turning indoors to reassure the marquess, Penny wondered if Fothergill had yet realized that he was no longer running to his plan, but theirs.

At the center of the maze, Charles stood at the end of the long narrow pool farthest from the house, and waited. The maze was a symmetrical one in which it was possible to enter from one side and exit from the other. He could hear Fothergill approaching; his lips curved, not humorously. He'd predicted that in the absence of Fothergill's favorite escape route—a shrubbery—he would instead use the maze, and he had. Whoever he was, Fothergill would shortly reach the end of his road; he and Dalziel intended to make sure of it. Cornering a man on an open lawn wasn't easy; capturing him in a room of green twenty feet by eight feet was a great deal more certain. The yew hedges were high and densely grown; the only routes out of the rectangular court were the gap in the hedge at Charles's back, and the other gap Fothergill was fast approaching, Dalziel on his heels.

Fothergill burst into the court—and skidded to a halt. Wide-eyed, he stared at Charles, then his gaze fell to the throwing knife Charles held in his hands.

Turning the knife lightly end over end, Charles demanded in rapid-fire French who had sent him.

Off-balance, his gaze locked on the knife, Fothergill swallowed and replied, confirming it was elements of the French bureaucracy attempting to conceal past follies.

"Attempting to cover their arses so that no one would know how gullible they'd been—how they'd been taken in, not once but countless times over the years by an English lord . . . is that right?"

White-lipped, Fothergill nodded.

Charles watched him like a hawk, ready to use the knife. Fothergill hadn't yet reached for his own knife, but his fingers were flexing, tensing.

Behind him, Dalziel glided soundlessly from the shadows of the opening.

Straightening the knife in his hands, Charles waited until Fothergill glanced up; he caught his eye. "What's your real name?"

Fothergill frowned, then answered, "Jules Fothergill." He hesitated, then asked, "Why do you want to know?"

Charles felt all animation drain from his face. "So we know what name to put on your gravestone."

It was done quickly, neatly, with barely a sound. Fothergill heard nothing, suspected nothing, not until the dagger passed between his ribs; Dalziel was that quiet, that efficient. That effective. Realization flashed through Fothergill's eyes as he stared at Charles, astonished that retribution had caught up with him, then all life leached away, his eyes glazed, and his body crumpled at Dalziel's feet.

Jaw set, Charles rounded the long pool and joined Dalziel; they stood looking down at the body. "That was a faster, cleaner death than he deserved."

After a moment, Dalziel murmured, "Think of it more as the type of death we deserve to deal in. No need for us to descend to his level."

Charles drew breath, nodded. "There is that."

Dalziel stepped back, absently lifting his dagger, taking

out a cloth to clean it. "I'll take care of this." With his head, he indicated Fothergill's body. "I'd appreciate it if you kept Lady Penelope and Amberly at bay."

Charles grunted. He lingered a moment longer, looking down at the crumpled form, then he looked at Dalziel. "He isn't the one you seek, is he?"

Dalziel looked up, met his eyes, his dark gaze cold, saber-sharp and incisive. After a moment, he shook his head. "No. But he was, in his fashion, efficient—he was dangerous, and he was young. I'm grateful we had the chance to remove him—who knows what the future holds?"

Charles murmured an agreement, then turned away, and walked out of the central court, back toward the house.

He was halfway across the lawn when Penny came out of the music room. She paused on the terrace, her gaze racing over him, then, somewhat to his surprise, she picked up her skirts, rushed down the steps, and flew across the lawn to him.

She flung herself at him; he caught her, staggered back a step before he got his balance. Arms around him, she hugged him ferociously. "Thank God you're all right!"

For a frozen moment, he simply stood as the world about him tilted and swung, then he closed his arms more definitely around her, tightened them. Laying his cheek against her hair, he closed his eyes and breathed in, let the subtle fragrance of her slide through him. Let the feel of her in his arms claim him. With all his other missions, he'd never had anyone waiting for him, anyone eager to see him, to anchor him and welcome him back into the normal world—to reassure him that he still belonged.

They stood locked tight, then, releasing him, she pushed back, reached up and framed his face, looked deep into his eyes, then stretched up and kissed him. Hard. Lips to lips, then she parted hers and drew him in; for uncounted heart-beats, they drowned—then she pulled back, and simply looked at him, her gaze devouring his face.

Penny sighed, reassured, relieved and so much more. Stepping back, she looked toward the maze. "He's dead, isn't he?"

Charles nodded. He took her hand and drew her on, back toward the house. "He's been stopped."

She glanced at him. "So no one else will die."

He met her gaze, then nodded. He tightened his hold on her hand, she tightened her hold on his; looking ahead, they walked on.

Amberly was relieved; so were the staff. Dalziel disappeared, but was back in time for dinner; he was talking quietly to Amberly when Penny and Charles joined them in the drawing room.

Later, after a meal that, courtesy of Amberly and Penny, verged on the celebratory, Amberly invited them to view his secret collection. They'd earlier refused so if things had gone wrong, he would be protected by virtue of being the only one who knew how to open the priest hole.

It was similar to the one at Wallingham Hall, just a few feet larger. And filled with snuffboxes the like of which the three of them had never seen. Sitting in a chair while they admired the craftsmanship of the various styles represented, Amberly related how their "game" had started, how he and Penny's father had worked out the mechanism of the scheme that had run for so long.

"But now he's gone, and so is Granville." As they left the priest hole, he nodded toward the contents. "I've been thinking, now it's all over, that those should be put in a museum somewhere, perhaps with the pillboxes."

He looked inquiringly at Penny.

She nodded. "I don't think they should remain in the priest holes, either here or at Wallingham."

Amberly smiled wryly. "I know Nicholas will agree with you—poor boy, this has all been such a worry to him." He looked at Dalziel. "Do you think it might be possible to create a story to account for them that people would believe?"

Dalziel smiled. "I'm sure, if we put our minds to it, we'll be able to come up with something. And"—he glanced at the snuffboxes—"I doubt any curator you offer the 'Selborne collection' to is going to ask too many questions."

"Do you think so?"

Charles tugged Penny's arm. They left Dalziel and Amberly discussing potential tales with which to allay any public concern.

"Without having to explain the whole unlikely past." Charles shook his head. "He must have been a formidable adversary on the diplomatic front."

Penny smiled and led the way down the corridor. They reached her room and went in. On arriving at the Grange, she'd puzzled the housekeeper by insisting she did not wish the maid assigned to her to wait on her at night; as Charles had yet to sleep in the bed in the room he'd been given, she assumed the housekeeper would by now have guessed why.

Undressing in the same room, being physically close, had come very easily to them both. Standing before the dressing table unpinning, then brushing out her long hair, she watched Charles in the mirror, watched him strip off his coat, then unknot and unwind his cravat. Unbuttoning his shirt, unlacing the cuffs, he drew it off over his head; clad only in trousers, he prowled absentmindedly to come up behind her—he looked up, and met her gaze. She felt the tug as he undid her laces.

She held his gaze as he did; her senses still alert, very much alive, she considered all she saw. He was taller than she by half a head—his hair was dark, black as the night, while in the faint candlelight hers held the silver of moonlight.

His shoulders and chest were broader than hers; she could see his body on either side of hers, a visual promise of his strength, of his ability to surround her with it.

Raising his hands, he pushed her loosened gown off her shoulders; she withdrew her arms and let it fall to the floor with a soft *swoosh*. The sound focused her mind, her eyes, on the contrasts revealed, on the steely muscles that flexed in his arms as he ran his palms down her arms—over the delicate skin, the subtle feminine curves.

She was slender, delicate, where he was broad, heavily muscled; she was pale to his dark, weak to his strong, yet she didn't, never had, feared his strength; instead, she reveled in it.

Complementary, well matched. Equals, but not the same. A pair, perfect foils each for the other.

Reaching out, she placed her brush on the table, quelled a shiver of anticipation as he shifted closer, as his hands slid around her and she felt his strength slowly, carefully engulf her. Easing back in his arms, she watched as he lowered his head, as he nuzzled her throat, then nudged her head aside so he could fasten his lips over the point where her pulse raced.

A smile curved her lips. She knew beyond question that she was the only woman who had ever interacted with him as she did, as she always had—close with no barriers, inside his mask, dealing with the real man rather than the persona he showed to the world. Seeing his vulnerabilities as well as his strengths, being allowed to know of them and ease them.

There was no other man she had ever wanted, ever needed to be with. Only him.

She could feel the tension still thrumming through him, not so much the aftermath of the day's events as a sense the episode had yet to be laid to rest.

Her smile deepening, she turned into his arms.

Charles had no idea what she meant to do when she insisted on taking the reins. But he yielded, let her do as she wished with his body, with his heart, with his soul. He'd given her all three long ago; it was a relief to be able to consign them so simply into her keeping. Into her care.

Hours later, lying on his back, sated, exhausted, and at peace beside her in the rumpled bed, he acknowledged how different this was to the end of any previous mission. This time, thanks to her, he'd reached a completion that had never before been his; he'd traveled full circle from initiating protectiveness to final conclusion, and she'd welcomed him back, guided him back—absolved him. She'd acted as his anchor, his guardian and mentor in the personal sense; he'd never before had that connection, had someone not just acknowledging but personifying the link between his mission and those he sought to protect.

He glanced down at her, slumped, boneless, beside him.

Accepted wisdom held that a lady's life revolved about her lord's; with them, he knew beyond doubt that his life would always and forever revolve about her. His place would be wherever she was, his bed would always be hers, not the other way around, no matter what society thought.

She stirred; after a moment, she lifted her head, glanced at his face, then shifted over him, leaning her forearms on his chest so she could study his eyes.

He studied hers, but could read little beyond a certain satisfaction, a certain decisiveness. "What?"

Her lips lifted. "Can we go directly back to Lostwithiel rather than going via London?"

He blinked. "Yes. Why?"

She held his gaze. "If we're going to get married, then there's a lot we need to organize, and if we announce our engagement in London, you know what will happen—we'll be expected to make a social event of it, attend all the right balls and allow the major hostesses to dictate to us. We'll be placing ourselves in your and my sisters' and our mamas' hands, and much as we love them, it'll be so much easier if we keep the reins in our hands—"

He shut her up in the only way he could—he kissed her. Kept kissing her until she was floundering as much as he was. She was racing impulsively ahead again. Raising his hands, he cradled her face, aware to his bones of the simple honesty behind the kiss, of the unalloyed sweetness of what they now shared.

Drawing back, he looked at her, with his thumbs brushed wisps of her hair aside, met her bright eyes. Took a moment to wallow in the light that lit them, in the warmth he could feel even through the shadows.

His mind was still reeling. "I don't understand. I haven't yet given you what you want, or at least you don't know I have—I haven't yet told you I love you, or sworn undying love forever more."

A wise man would have hidden his surprise, seized her acceptance, and kept his mouth shut, but . . . he frowned. "I thought, being you, that you'd at least demand a red rose and me on my knees." He'd been anticipating doing something rather more flamboyant when the time came; strangely, he now felt cheated of his moment.

She blinked at him. "A red rose . . . on your knees?" She looked faintly stunned, as if he'd told her something new.

He frowned more definitely. "I haven't yet shouted it from the steeple—that can be rectified—but you *know* I love you, that I always have."

She frowned back. "You haven't always loved me—you didn't years ago."

He stared at her. Felt his muscles harden, tried to keep them relaxed. "I've loved you for forever."

At his flat tones, her frown grew more direful; she pushed up from his chest. "You *didn't*. Not before."

Jaw setting, he came up on his elbows. "I've loved you—only you—since I was sixteen! What the devil did you imagine that episode in the barn was about? How did you think it came about? Just because you decided?"

"That was lust!" Face-to-face, eye to eye, she dared him to deny it.

"Of course it was lust!" He heard his roar and fought to lower his voice. "Good God—I was twenty and you were sixteen. Of *course* it was lust, but it wasn't *only* lust. I never would have accepted your invitation if I hadn't been in love with you!"

He glared at her. How *could* she not have known, not have seen that? "Dammit, woman, you're my mother's goddaughter, my godmother's stepdaughter! What the hell do you think—"

Penny flung herself at him, covered his lips with hers, and let all the emotion that had suddenly welled and was now sweeping her away pour through her, let it flow unrestrained through her into him. Let him see, taste—know.

His hands closed on her sides; the kiss deepened, ignited their fire, fanned it until passion rose full and deep and swirled around and through them.

He gripped and tried halfheartedly, as if he thought he should, to ease her back. She dragged her lips half an inch from his, dragged in enough breath to say, "Shut up—just love me."

Twitching the sheet from between them, she straddled him. Set her lips to his, met him when he surged and claimed her mouth, sighed through the kiss when his hands closed around her hips and he eased her back and down, then thrust up, in, and filled her. Her nerves slowly unraveled as she took him into her body, sheathed him to the hilt; her senses exulted.

She couldn't think, and neither could he. Good; he could wonder why she'd agreed to marry him without the assurance she'd always insisted she had to have later. He didn't need to hear that she couldn't now imagine a future apart from him, that the thought of not being with him, there to meet his need, was a fate she couldn't bear even to contemplate.

To be needed that much, that deeply, that exclusively— what woman wouldn't give her heart for that? But he would work out her feelings for himself soon enough; he didn't need to have her spell them out for him.

Closing her eyes, she rose above him, and he filled her, savored her, went with her.

The world closed in, and there was just her and him and the dance that held them, empowered them, enthralled them. And the emotion that rose, higher and more powerful than ever before, and at the last engulfed them, fused them and left them, two halves of a sundered coin at last together and whole.

Dawn broke over a world that had altered, at least for them. Charles lay on his back idly playing with strands of her hair, in some dislocated part of his mind aware that that was something he'd done years ago.

He knew she was awake, like him savoring the changes, the subtle shifts in their landscape.

Eventually, he drew a deep breath, and softly said, "I didn't know what love was all those years ago—I knew what I felt, that you were special in ways no other was, but at twenty, I knew very little of love." He hesitated, then went on; he'd always imagined the words would be hard to find, yet they came readily enough to his tongue. "What I feel for you now is immeasurably more than what I was even capable of feeling then. Back then, I wasn't even sure what it was I felt for you, so when it seemed you'd had enough—that you didn't want me and whatever it was anymore—I let it go. I told myself that if that's what you wanted, then it was probably for the best."

Penny heard the distant note in his voice, knew he was remembering what was essentially a past hurt she, unwittingly, had inflicted on him.

"I didn't know," she murmured, then sighed. "I suppose I didn't understand well enough either, certainly wasn't sure enough, although I told myself I was." She listened to his heart beating steadily beneath her cheek. "Perhaps, in truth, it was for the best. If we'd attempted to cling to what we had then . . ."

Lifting her head, she looked into his face, into the dark gaze that, as always, seemed to embrace her. "If we'd done something about it then, got engaged before you left or some such thing, then you wouldn't have become a spy, wouldn't now be who you are." She paused, then added, "You wouldn't have become the man I love now."

"And you wouldn't have been who you are now, either. You're stronger, more independent, more certain of what you want." His lips twisted wryly. "More challenging than you would have been if we'd married years ago."

She arched her brows haughtily, but replied, "Very likely. Perhaps those years were the price for what we have now."

"And for what we'll have in the future." He held her gaze. "We've paid fate's price."

"Indeed. And now we have the prize." Her smile dawned, glorious and sure; she settled back down in his arms. "From now on, we get to enjoy the fruit borne on the tree of our past."

He chuckled, closed his arms about her, and sank deeper into the pillows. The fruit of the tree of their past. Love evolved and grown and acknowledged between them, the pleasure of having the other in their arms, the anticipation of an unclouded future—it might have taken thirteen years, but few were as lucky as they.

Penny would have been perfectly happy with a small ceremony with a select group of guests. Instead, Charles insisted on a huge wedding with a cast of hundreds and a guest list that in reality had no end.

Everyone in the district was invited, and everyone came. She'd known she commanded a certain level of acquaintance, of loyalty throughout the surrounding area, and that, of course, Charles did, too; what neither had appreciated until they came out of the church and saw the gathered multitude, was that combined, their acquaintance covered most of those within riding distance and droves from farther afield, too.

It was bedlam, but wonderful. Once she'd realized and dragged enough from him to confirm just why he'd wanted such a public affair, she'd acquiesced with good grace, indeed, had thrown herself into making his vision come true. What lady wouldn't have, given he'd wanted their wedding to be a very public declaration of not just their union, but of what he felt for her—his version of shouting his love from the steeple?

She could only love him all the more, until her heart felt literally like it was overflowing, for making such a grand, dramatic, so-very-Charles-like gesture, yet it wasn't the organization, the numbers, the sheer scope of the performance that carried the banner of his feelings, but the light that shone in his midnight blue eyes, the way his awareness so rarely strayed from her, the quality implied in the way he touched her, held her hand, kept her close. By his decree, they were now closer than they'd ever been.

Happier than she sometimes felt they'd any right to be.

She'd learned simply to accept it, that this, between them, was meant to be.

From the early-morning rush, through the ceremony at the church, through the wedding breakfast and on through the extended celebrations, the day was perfect.

"Can you imagine anything daring to be otherwise with my mother and Elaine, your sisters and mine, my sisters-in-law and Amberly and Nicholas all supervising?" Charles arched a brow at her. "Even I'm cowed."

As he chose that moment to whirl her into a waltz—a very *fast* waltz—she could only laugh, and let him entertain her, and at the end of their moment, lead him back to their guests.

One group she was especially keen to meet were the other members of the Bastion Club. Having met Jack and Gervase, both of whom were present, she wasn't surprised to find that the others were of similar ilk. She shook hands and had to laugh at the numerous comments they made about Charles, the warnings, the *sotto voce* confidences, all of which he deflected with his usual glib charm.

She was especially pleased to meet Leonora, Countess of Trentham, and Alicia, Viscountess Torrington, the wives of the other two club members thus far married. The instant the introductions were complete and they'd touched fingers, their gazes met, switched one to the other, then the three of them laughed. Their husbands, naturally, inquired over what had struck them. They met each other's eyes again, then each said they'd explain later.

None of the club members were impressed by that, but had to, in this company, accept it.

"Have you met Dalziel?" Leonora asked.

The inquiry seemed innocent, but it immediately diverted the men's attention.

"We invited him, of course," Charles told the others, "but as usual he hasn't appeared."

"He never appears anywhere in public," Alicia told Penny. "At least, not that any of us have discovered."

"While we were staying with Amberly, along with Dalziel, I got the impression as we were leaving that Amberly knew who Dalziel really was. I asked him this afternoon."

"And?" Jack prompted.

"Amberly lapsed into vagueness as if he had absolutely no idea who I was referring to." Charles sighed. "Amberly's memory's like a vise—he was clearly told to conveniently forget."

"Dalziel's true identity can't be scandalous," Gervase pointed out.

"No." Christian Allardyce raised his brows. "But it could be highly sensitive in certain quarters."

"One day," Charles vowed, "we are going to learn the truth."

The others all echoed the sentiment.

Later, while ambling through the guests, they stopped to talk with Amberly and Nicholas. As her nearest male relative, Amberly had given her away; he'd been thrilled and so patently pleased she'd asked, Penny had felt touched.

"We'll be at Wallingham for a few days—ride over if you get the chance." Nicholas shook hands with Charles. "I've decided to spend more time down here—now you've taken Penny away, someone will need to keep watch on the place."

"Good for you to get away from those damn dispatch boxes," Charles returned.

Nicholas grinned. "You're probably right."

They parted, Nicholas helping his father toward the forecourt, where their carriage was waiting. Other guests sought them out to make their farewells; gradually, the day wound to a close.

Night was falling when they finally slipped away from the family parlor where the females of their combined families, slumped in exhaustion, were indulging in the customary postmortem.

The earl's suite was separated from all others, distant and very private. Passing through the door Charles held open, Penny glanced around. Until then, she'd only seen the room from the doorway, yet with her brushes on the dressing table, her robe on a chair, it already seemed familiar. As if she belonged.

Crossing to the dressing table, she lifted the tiara from her hair, then removed the jeweled pins and let the long tresses hang free. She shook her head to untangle them, in the mirror met Charles's midnight eyes.

She turned, faced him, saw in his eyes the same awareness she felt. They'd been lovers for weeks, yet this, now, was different—a declarative step acknowledging a deeper commitment.

The end of one road, the first step on another.

A moment passed in which they searched each other's eyes, then he stepped toward her and held out his hands.

She met him, put her hands in his, felt him clasp them and gripped in return.

His lips lifted, his eyes held hers. "I love you."

She returned his smile and walked into his arms. "I love you, too."

The World of Stephanie Laurens

Enter the unforgettable world of Stephanie Laurens, a world of sizzling romance, page-turning intrigue and astonishing passion. As you turn the pages of *any* Stephanie Laurens novel, you will enter a place where the rules of society and courtship—and the rules of desire—are often at odds. For the lady who puts a foot wrong can face ruin; a man who acts too rashly faces trouble.

But oh, those men! First, meet the Cynster males—strong and powerful, each with only one weakness: the woman he loves. Next, walk through the gates of the Bastion Club to meet the heroes of war who plan to remain single. But plans, as we all know, can change.

However, there is one unchangeable fact: every Stephanie Laurens book can be savored (again and again!) on its own. Dip into any story at any time! Don't hold back. You'll quickly discover that, while the world of Stephanie Laurens is a very easy one to enter, it's almost impossible to leave.

Now open the door, and enter the world . . .

Devil's Bride

When Devil Cynster, the Duke of St. Ives and leader of the Cynster males, is caught in a compromising position with governess Honoria Wetherby, some scandalous behavior follows . . .

A Rake's Vow

Vane Cynster vowed he'd never marry, until he encountered irresistible Patience Debbington, a young woman who tempts him as no other. Soon he has seduction—and more—on his mind!

Scandal's Bride

Catriona Hennessy, honorable Scottish Lady of the Vale, receives the prediction that Richard "Scandal" Cynster will father her children. So she forms a daring plan to avoid this fate . . . but she can't resist him!

A Rogue's Proposal

Demon Cynster has seen love bring his fellow Cynsters to their knees. He decides not to share that fate—until he spies Felicity Pargeter riding one of his horses!

A Secret Love

Gabriel Cynster cannot resist a lady in distress, and when Lady Alathea Morwellan appears before him—her face hidden by a veil, begging for his help—he cannot refuse her!

All About Love

Lucifer Cynster is still unclaimed—so he escapes to the country, believing he can keep himself unattached. Instead he meets his destiny in Phyllida Tallent…

All About Passion

Fate has deemed Gyles, the Earl of Chillingworth, be welcomed into the Cynster clan, an honorary member of that tribe. He is determined to control his own destiny; then he discovers a daring wedding-day deception!

The Promise in a Kiss

Sebastian Cynster, head of the Cynster family, literally falls at the feet of Helena de Stansion. He believes that this gently bred miss could be no match for his wicked ways . . . and he would be wrong!

On a Wild Night

Where, oh where, are the exciting London men? Amanda Cynster wonders. So she takes matters into her own hands, goes where no woman dares, and is unexpectedly rescued by the Earl of Dexter.

On a Wicked Dawn

Amelia Cynster risks scandal with Lucien Ashford by appearing at his doorstep, unchaperoned, at dawn. Yet even she is shocked when he accepts her marriage proposal—before falling in a dead faint at her feet!

The Perfect Lover

Sometimes the perfect lover and the perfect wife are one and the same. Simon Frederick Cynster is determined to find a woman who could be both! He is astonished that his youthful nemesis Portia Ashford is the lady he seeks...

The Ideal Bride

Those "honorary Cynsters," such as Michael Anstruther-Wetherby, cannot help but follow their ways. Michael's future in Parliament seems assured, however he requires a biddable wife. But Caroline Sutcliffe is far from what he thinks he needs!

The Truth About Love

Cynster protégé Gerrard Debbinton is one of the most eligible gentlemen of the *ton*. Besieged by offers to paint one of his amazing creations, he is tantalized by the idea of re-creating the famous, but never seen, gardens of Hellbore Hall, but can do so only if he also paints Jacqueline Tregonning, the daughter of the manor. But secrets haunt the hall, and Jacqueline is the key to discovering the truth about many of them . . .

What Price Love?

Just how much will you risk for love? Dillon Caxton, only son of General Caxton and cousin-by-marriage to Demon Cynster, finds himself asking this question. Priscilla Dalloway asks for his help in rescuing her twin brother from a swindle she fears he is involved in, and Dillon soon finds himself becoming involved in a risky affair of the heart . . .

Now, before you enter **the Bastion Club**, take a peek at the book that started it all:

Captain Jack's Woman

Captain Jack is Kit Cranmer's dream lover come surprisingly, tantalizingly alive . . .

Then, London's most eligible bachelors band together to form **the Bastion Club**, an elite society dedicated to allowing these heroes of the Crown the freedom to determine their own fate where marriage is concerned.

In *The Lady Chosen* meet Tristan, the Earl of Trentham, who chooses to wed the independent lady next door—Leonora Carling.

In *A Gentleman's Honor* the next member of **the Bastion Club**, Anthony Blake, Viscount Torrington, discovers Alicia standing over a dead body in his godmother's garden. He knows she is innocent of the crime . . . and innocent of love.

In *A Lady of His Own* Charles St. Austell returns to Cornwall to uncover a band of smugglers. And the first unusual thing he discovers is his former love, Lady Penelope Selborne, marching through his house after midnight. What is she after?

In *A Fine Passion* Jack, Baron Warnefleet, the last of his line, rescues Lady Clarice Altwood, a startlingly beautiful woman, from a menacing, unmanageable horse. However, while he begins by taking command, the lady continues by taking it back. Clarice is delectably attractive, beyond eligible, undeniably capable, and completely unforgettable. Why on earth is this woman, so clearly full of passion, rusticating in the country?